D1172739

WISE WORDS
FROM ACROSS
SPACE AND TIME

BBC *The Official Quotable*
DOCTOR WHO

Cavan Scott and Mark Wright

HARPER
DESIGN
An Imprint of HarperCollins Publishers

HarperCollins books may be purchased for educational, business, or sales promotional use.
For information please e-mail the Special Markets Department at SPsales@harpercollins.com.

First published in 2014 by:
Harper Design
An Imprint of HarperCollins*Publishers*
195 Broadway
New York, NY 10007
Tel: (212) 207-7000
Fax: (212) 207-7654

Distributed throughout the world by:
HarperCollins*Publishers*
195 Broadway
New York, NY 10007

Library of Congress Number: 2014935024
ISBN 978-0-06-233614-9

Commissioning editor: Albert DePetrillo
Editorial manager: Lizzy Gaisford
Series consultant: Justin Richards
Project editor: Steve Tribe
Illustrations: Ben Morris Illustration
Design: Seagull Design
Production: Alex Goddard

Printed and bound in the United States.

First printing, May 2014

CONTENTS

INTRODUCTION

'I'm a Time Lord. I've been around, you know. Two hearts, respiratory bypass system. I haven't lived seven hundred and fifty years without learning something…'

THE DOCTOR, *THE ROBOTS OF DEATH*

Have you ever wondered what it would be like to travel with the Doctor, have you? To be wanderers in the fourth dimension?

All that running. All those corridors. All those monsters.

They say that travel broadens the mind, in which case the Doctor's mind must be the broadest of them all. Over a thousand years of rattling around the universe in his big blue box… Imagine all the wisdom he's gathered in his meanderings, all the lessons he's learnt.

Perhaps that would be the best part of jumping on board the TARDIS – having the greatest tour guide in all of history. He shows you the big stuff, the galaxies and planets and constellations, but the small things too. The simple things. A pretty painting. A stupid joke. A cup of tea and a jammy dodger. Real life in all its wonder and whimsy.

The good news is that we can travel with the Doctor, and his friends and enemies too. We have been since 23 November

1963. He's taken us from a junkyard at the end of a lane to the end of time – and back again.

And there are lessons to be found in his adventures too. Some serious. Some silly. Some profound. Some potty. And more fezzes than you'd expect.

In many ways, this has been a nightmarish task. Cherry-picking the Doctor's best quotes, quips and sayings from over fifty years of adventures? The man never shuts up – and nor do his friends. Long may that continue.

For all this we must thank and pay homage to a select group, because first came the word. We would like to dedicate this compendium to the scriptwriters of *Doctor Who*; those wits and wise men and women who have toiled late into the night over typewriters and word processors. Across half a century they have put words in the mouths of the Doctor, his companions, friends and enemies. Their desire to tell a rattling good adventure yarn, their quick humour, their outlook on life, the universe and everything, have all given life and sparkle to the words we hear on screen – then taken the rest of the way by those brilliant actors. And let's not forget the script editors who kept them on the straight and narrow, provided guidance and contributed their own words of wonder. The quality and sheer inventiveness of their work has always set *Doctor Who* apart from other TV shows, and that is what we are celebrating in the pages of this book.

And the stories keep coming.

Brigadier Alistair Gordon Lethbridge-Stewart once told his daughter that science leads. He said he learnt it from an old friend.

What will the same old friend teach you today? Or tomorrow? Or maybe even yesterday? It's all a bit timey-wimey, to be honest.

Happy Times and Places!

Chapter One: The Doctor

I.M.MAN
Servant
LANE
76,

'I suppose you might say that I am a citizen of the universe, and a gentleman to boot.'

THE DOCTOR, *THE DALEKS' MASTER PLAN*

FAMOUS
FIRST WORDS

'What are you doing here?'

THE FIRST DOCTOR, *AN UNEARTHLY CHILD*

'Slower… Slower… Concentrate on one thing. One thing!'

THE SECOND DOCTOR, *THE POWER OF THE DALEKS*

'Shoes… Must find my shoes.'

THE THIRD DOCTOR, *SPEARHEAD FROM SPACE*

'… typical Sontaran attitude… stop Linx… perverting the course of human history… I tell you, Brigadier, there's nothing to worry about. The brontosaurus is large and placid… and stupid! If the square on the hypotenuse equals the sum of the squares on the other two sides, why is a mouse when it spins? Never did know the answer to that one.'

THE FOURTH DOCTOR, *ROBOT*

'I… oh.'

THE FIFTH DOCTOR, *CASTROVALVA*

'You were expecting someone else?'

THE SIXTH DOCTOR, T*HE CAVES OF ANDROZANI*

'Oh no, Mel. Ah, that was a nice nap. Now, down to business.'

THE SEVENTH DOCTOR, *TIME AND THE RANI*

'Who am I? Who am I?'

THE EIGHTH DOCTOR, *DOCTOR WHO* (TV MOVIE)

'Doctor no more.'

THE WAR DOCTOR, *THE NIGHT OF THE DOCTOR*

'Run!'

THE NINTH DOCTOR, *ROSE*

'Hello. OK – oh. New teeth. That's weird. So, where was I? Oh, that's right. Barcelona.'

THE TENTH DOCTOR, *THE PARTING OF THE WAYS*

'Legs. Still got legs, good!! Arms. Hands. Ooh, fingers. Lots of fingers. Ears, yes. Eyes, two. Nose, I've had worse. Chin, blimey. Hair. I'm a girl! No. No, I'm not a girl. And still not ginger. And something else. Something important. I'm, I'm, I'm… Crashing! Geronimo!'

THE ELEVENTH DOCTOR, *THE END OF TIME*

'Kidneys! I've got new kidneys. I don't like the colour.'

THE TWELFTH DOCTOR, *THE TIME OF THE DOCTOR*

THE NAME OF THE DOCTOR

'Eh? Doctor who? What's he talking about?'

THE DOCTOR, *AN UNEARTHLY CHILD*

'I'm the Doctor. Well, they call me the Doctor. I don't know why. I call me the Doctor, too. Still don't know why.'

THE DOCTOR, *THE LODGER*

'You may be *a* doctor, but I'm *the* Doctor. The definite article, you might say.'

THE DOCTOR, *ROBOT*

CLARA: Doctor who?

THE DOCTOR: Oh, dangerous question.

CLARA: What's wrong with dangerous?

THE SNOWMEN

THE DOCTOR: I help where I can. I will not fight.

OHILA: Because you are 'the good man' as you call yourself?

THE DOCTOR: I call myself the Doctor.

OHILA: It's the same thing in your mind.

THE DOCTOR: I'd like to think so.

THE NIGHT OF THE DOCTOR

ADELAIDE BROOKE: State your name, rank and intention.

THE DOCTOR: The Doctor. Doctor. Fun.

THE WATERS OF MARS

TYRUM: We are grateful to you, human, for saving Voga.

THE DOCTOR: Oh, please, don't call me human. Just Doctor will do very nicely, thank you.

REVENGE OF THE CYBERMEN

THE DOCTOR: Doctor von Wer, at your service.

SERGEANT: Doctor who?

THE DOCTOR: That's what I said.

THE HIGHLANDERS

THE DOCTOR: I'm just Lord President of the Supreme Council of Time Lords on Gallifrey.

STOR: Your description fits that of one called Doctor.

THE DOCTOR: Well, that's not my fault. I'm Lord President, and I'm called 'sir'.

THE INVASION OF TIME

MADGE: Are you the new caretaker?

THE DOCTOR: Usually called the Doctor. Or the Caretaker or Get Off This Planet. Though, strictly speaking, that probably isn't a name.

THE DOCTOR, THE WIDOW AND THE WARDROBE

'Look, three options. One, I let the Star Whale continue in unendurable agony for hundreds more years. Two, I kill everyone on this ship. Three, I murder a beautiful, innocent creature as painlessly as I can. And then I find a new name, because I won't be the Doctor any more.'

THE DOCTOR, *THE BEAST BELOW*

'The name I chose is the Doctor. The name you choose, it's like a promise you make. He's the one who broke the promise.'

THE DOCTOR, ON THE WAR DOCTOR, *THE NAME OF THE DOCTOR*

'You haven't seen the last of me. Bad Penny is my middle name. Seriously, the looks I get when I fill in a form…'

THE DOCTOR, *THE GOD COMPLEX*

'Great men are forged in fire. It is the privilege of lesser men to light the flame, whatever the cost.'

THE WAR DOCTOR, *THE DAY OF THE DOCTOR*

'You've been asking a question, and it's time someone told you you've been getting it wrong. His name, his name is the Doctor. All the name he needs. Everything you need to know about him.'

CLARA, *THE TIME OF THE DOCTOR*

THE TRUTH OF THE MATTER

'I never lie. Well, hardly ever.'

THE DOCTOR, *THE TIME WARRIOR*

'Rule one. The Doctor lies.'

THE DOCTOR, *LET'S KILL HITLER*

WHO IS THE DOCTOR?

'I'm the Doctor. I'm a Time Lord. I'm from the planet Gallifrey in the constellation of Kasterborous. I'm nine hundred and three years old. And I'm the man that's going to save your lives and all six billion people on the planet below. You got a problem with that?'

THE DOCTOR, *VOYAGE OF THE DAMNED*

LUX: Who is the Doctor?

RIVER: The only story you'll ever tell, if you survive him.

FOREST OF THE DEAD

'They call me the Doctor. I am a scientist, an engineer. I'm a builder of things.'

THE DOCTOR, *THE AZTECS*

'I'm just a traveller, wandering past. Believe it or not, all I'm after is a quiet life.'

THE DOCTOR, *BAD WOLF*

'He saves planets, rescues civilisations, defeats terrible creatures. And runs a lot. Seriously, there's an outrageous amount of running involved.'

DONNA, *THE DOCTOR'S DAUGHTER*

EARL: You're a nice guy, Doctor, but a little weird.

THE DOCTOR: Enough of the little.

THE HAPPINESS PATROL

'Do you know like we were saying about the Earth revolving? It's like when you were a kid. The first time they tell you the world's turning and you just can't quite believe it because everything looks like it's standing still. I can feel it. The turn of the Earth. The ground beneath our feet is spinning at a thousand miles an hour, and the entire planet is hurtling round the sun at 67,000 miles an hour, and I can feel it. We're falling through space, you and me, clinging to the skin of this tiny little world, and if we let go… That's who I am.'

THE DOCTOR, *ROSE*

THE BRIGADIER: Sir, this is the Doctor, our scientific adviser.

GENERAL FINCH: Oh. We've been waiting for you, you know. May I ask where you've been?

THE DOCTOR: Certainly.

GENERAL FINCH: Well?

THE DOCTOR: You can ask but I don't guarantee that you'll get a reply.

INVASION OF THE DINOSAURS

'He's like fire and ice and rage. He's like the night and the storm in the heart of the sun… He's ancient and forever. He burns at the centre of time and he can see the turn of the universe… And he's wonderful.'

TIM LATIMER, *THE FAMILY OF BLOOD*

THE DOCTOR: I'm a Time Lord. A man of science, temperament and passion!

PERI: And a very loud voice.

ATTACK OF THE CYBERMEN

'I have lived a long life and I have seen a few things. I walked away from the Last Great Time War. I marked the passing of the Time Lords. I saw the birth of the universe and I watched as time ran out, moment by moment, until nothing remained. No time. No space. Just me. I walked in universes where the laws of physics were devised by the mind of a mad man. I've watched universes freeze and creations burn. I've seen things you wouldn't believe. I have lost things you will never understand. And I know things. Secrets that must never be told. Knowledge that must never be spoken.'

THE DOCTOR, *THE RINGS OF AKHATEN*

'Oh, he's like a rubber ball. He'll come bouncing out of there soon, full of ideas.'

BARBARA, *MARCO POLO*

ADELAIDE BROOKE: You the doctor or the janitor?

THE DOCTOR: I don't know. Sounds like me. The maintenance man of the universe.

THE WATERS OF MARS

'I've got a friend who specialises in trouble. He dives in and usually finds a way.'

IAN, *THE ROMANS*

'Some fifty years ago, I knew a man who solved the insoluble by the strangest means. He sees the threads that join the universe together and mends them when they break.'

ZASTOR, *MEGLOS*

ROSE: I can see everything. All that is, all that was, all that ever could be.

THE DOCTOR: That's what I see. All the time. And doesn't it drive you mad?

THE PARTING OF THE WAYS

'I'm not a human being. I walk in eternity.'

THE DOCTOR, *PYRAMIDS OF MARS*

'Whatever you've got planned, forget it. I'm the Doctor. I'm nine hundred and four years old. I'm from the planet Gallifrey in the constellation of Kasterborous. I am the Oncoming Storm, the Bringer of Darkness, and… you are basically just a rabbit, aren't you? OK, carry on. Just a general warning.'

THE DOCTOR, *THE DAY OF THE DOCTOR*

THE DOCTOR'S NATURE

'There is so much, so much to see, Amy. Because it goes so fast. I'm not running away from things, I am running to them before they flare and fade for ever.'

THE DOCTOR, *THE POWER OF THREE*

SARAH: Whatever's in that Tower, it's got enormous powers and, well, what can we do against it?

THE DOCTOR: What I've always done, Sarah Jane. Improvise.

THE FIVE DOCTORS

'I never take life. Only when my own is immediately threatened.'

THE DOCTOR, *THE DALEK INVASION OF EARTH*

KLIEG: But, how did you know in the first place?

THE DOCTOR: Oh, I use my own special technique.

KLIEG: Oh really, Doctor? And may we know what that is?

THE DOCTOR: Keeping my eyes open and my mouth shut.

THE TOMB OF THE CYBERMEN

'He is not a man to side with chaos.'

NEFRED, *FULL CIRCLE*

'I am and always will be the optimist. The hoper of far-flung hopes and dreamer of improbable dreams.'

THE DOCTOR, *THE ALMOST PEOPLE*

PALMERDALE: Are you in charge here?

THE DOCTOR: No, but I'm full of ideas.

HORROR OF FANG ROCK

'Oh, I always like to do the unexpected. Takes people by surprise.'

THE DOCTOR, *THE TRIAL OF A TIME LORD: THE MYSTERIOUS PLANET*

'So is this how it works, Doctor? You never interfere in the affairs of other peoples or planets, unless there's children crying?'

AMY, *THE BEAST BELOW*

VINCENT: You're not armed.

THE DOCTOR: I am.

VINCENT: What with?

THE DOCTOR: Overconfidence…and a small screwdriver. I'm absolutely sorted.

VINCENT AND THE DOCTOR

'I'd better get going. Things to do, worlds to save, swings to swing on.'

THE DOCTOR, *THE POWER OF THREE*

'He was the most alive person I ever met.'

SARAH, *THE MONSTER OF PELADON*

THE DOCTOR: You're going to fire me at a planet? That's your plan? I get fired at a planet and expected to fix it.

RORY: In fairness, that is slightly your MO.

ASYLUM OF THE DALEKS

'I hate being patient. Patience is for wimps. I can't live like this. Don't make me. I need to be busy.'

THE DOCTOR, *THE POWER OF THREE*

'The Eye of Orion's restful, if you like restful. I can never really get the hang of restful.'

THE DOCTOR, *THE DOCTOR'S WIFE*

'What's the point in two hearts, if you can't be a bit forgiving, now and then?'

THE DOCTOR, *DAY OF THE MOON*

'I've got one of those faces. People never stop blurting out their plans while I'm around.'

THE DOCTOR, *THE LODGER*

'Don't worship me – I'd make a very bad god. You wouldn't get a day off, for starters.'

THE DOCTOR, *BOOM TOWN*

THE DOCTOR: I'll be back for you soon as I can, I promise.

AMY: You always say that.

THE DOCTOR: I always come back.

FLESH AND STONE

'Something's interfering with time, Mr Scarman, and time is *my* business.'

THE DOCTOR, *PYRAMIDS OF MARS*

CAPTAIN COOK: I wonder you manage to explore anything. Everything seems to alarm you so.

THE DOCTOR: Not everything. I trust my instincts, and you may recall they're not always wrong.

THE GREATEST SHOW IN THE GALAXY

'But Doctor, listen to me. Don't get emotional because that's when you make mistakes.'

AMY, *THE DOCTOR'S WIFE*

CRAIG: Has anyone ever told you that you're a bit weird?

THE DOCTOR: They never really stop.

THE LODGER

'Doctor, the more you try to convince me that you're a fool, the more I'm likely to think otherwise.'

THE COUNTESS, *CITY OF DEATH*

'Why do I always let my curiosity get the better of me?'

THE DOCTOR, *BLACK ORCHID*

'I'm always serious. With days off.'

THE DOCTOR, *COLD WAR*

THE COUNTESS: My dear, I don't think he's as stupid as he seems.

SCARLIONI: My dear, nobody could be as stupid as *he* seems.

CITY OF DEATH

'Interfere? Of course we should interfere. Always do what you're best at, that's what I say.'

THE DOCTOR, *NIGHTMARE OF EDEN*

BARBARA: Doctor, I thought we were never going to see you again.

THE DOCTOR: You should know by now, young lady, that you can't get rid of the old Doctor as easily as that.

THE REIGN OF TERROR

QUALIFICATIONS

'The Doctor is not weaponless. He has the greatest weapon of all. Knowledge.'

CAMILLA, *STATE OF DECAY*

'The Doctor's qualified to do almost everything.'

THE BRIGADIER, *DOCTOR WHO AND THE SILURIANS*

THE DOCTOR: I am the Doctor.

ENLIGHTENMENT: A doctor? Of what?

THE DOCTOR: Of everything.

FOUR TO DOOMSDAY

'My colleague is a doctor of medicine and I'm a doctor of many things.'

THE DOCTOR, *REVENGE OF THE CYBERMEN*

'I'm every kind of scientist.'

THE DOCTOR, *COLONY IN SPACE*

BORUSA: You make me regret teaching you anything at all.

THE DOCTOR: You taught me nothing. Nothing that instinct couldn't provide better.

THE INVASION OF TIME

'I am not a student of human nature. I am a professor of a far wider academy, of which human nature is merely a part.'

THE DOCTOR, *THE EVIL OF THE DALEKS*

ZONDAL: You do not look like a scientist.

THE DOCTOR: Well, looks aren't everything, you know.

THE ICE WARRIORS

NEFRED: You understand a great deal, Doctor.

THE DOCTOR: True.

NEFRED: But not everything.

THE DOCTOR: That's certainly true.

FULL CIRCLE

MODESTY

OVERSEER: I suppose you think you're very clever.

THE DOCTOR: Well, without any undue modesty, yes!

THE REIGN OF TERROR

'Your leader will be angry if you kill me. I'm a genius.'

THE DOCTOR, *THE SEEDS OF DEATH*

IAN: You're a genius.

THE DOCTOR: Yes, there are very few of us left.

THE DALEK INVASION OF EARTH

THE DOCTOR: Jamie, some of the most brilliant scientists in the universe have assembled here to work together in pure research. I don't want them to know that I've arrived.

JAMIE: Why not?

THE DOCTOR: Think of the commotion! They'll all be scrambling around wanting my autograph.

THE TWO DOCTORS

CANTON: You, sir, are a genius.

THE DOCTOR: It's a hobby.

THE IMPOSSIBLE ASTRONAUT

SERGEANT: I'm sorry, sir, you're not allowed in there.

THE DOCTOR: Not allowed? Me? I'm allowed everywhere.

THE FIVE DOCTORS

THE DOCTOR: So you're just about an expert in everything except the things in your museum. Anything you don't understand, you lock up.

VAN STATTEN: And you claim greater knowledge?

THE DOCTOR: I don't need to make claims, I know how good I am.

DALEK

'I can feel my hair curling, and that means either it's going to rain or else I'm on to something.'

THE DOCTOR, *THE DEADLY ASSASSIN*

'This is magnificent. And I don't often say that because… well, because of me.'

THE DOCTOR, *UTOPIA*

ROSE: You think you're so impressive.

THE DOCTOR: I am so impressive.

ROSE: You wish.

THE END OF THE WORLD

'Oh, you know, K-9, sometimes I think I'm wasted just rushing around the universe saving planets from destruction. With a talent like mine, I might have been a great slow bowler.'

THE DOCTOR, *THE HORNS OF NIMON*

'Well, to be fair, I did have a couple of gadgets which he probably didn't, like a teaspoon and an open mind.'

THE DOCTOR, *THE CREATURE FROM THE PIT*

THE DOCTOR: Well, you'd better introduce me.

ROMANA: As what?

THE DOCTOR: Oh, I don't know, a sort of wise and wonderful person who wants to help. Don't exaggerate.

THE POWER OF KROLL

THE DOCTOR: I think my idea's better.

LESTER: What is your idea?

THE DOCTOR: I don't know yet. That's the trouble with ideas. They only come a bit at a time.

REVENGE OF THE CYBERMEN

'This is a situation that requires tact and finesse. Fortunately, I am blessed with both.'

THE DOCTOR, *THE TRIAL OF A TIME LORD: TERROR OF THE VERVOIDS*

'Look, it's perfectly understandable. I go zooming around space and time, saving planets, fighting monsters and being well, let's be honest, pretty sort of marvellous, so naturally now and then people notice me.'

THE DOCTOR, *TIME CRASH*

IAN: You know, Doctor, sometimes you astound me.

THE DOCTOR: Only sometimes, dear boy?

THE DALEK INVASION OF EARTH

'I have the directional instincts of a homing pigeon.'

THE DOCTOR, *THE CHASE*

CHASE: What do you do for an encore, Doctor?

THE DOCTOR: I win.

THE SEEDS OF DOOM

'Well, you can't expect perfection, you know. Not even from me.'

THE DOCTOR, *THE FACE OF EVIL*

ROMANA: You are incredible.

THE DOCTOR: Yes, I suppose I am, really. I've never given it much thought.

STATE OF DECAY

THE AGE OF THE DOCTOR

'Back when I first started at the very beginning, I was always trying to be old and grumpy and important, like you do when you're young.'

THE DOCTOR, *TIME CRASH*

'There is something new in you, yet something older than the sky itself.'

JOANNA, *THE CRUSADE*

SHAKESPEARE: How can a man so young have eyes so old?

THE DOCTOR: I do a lot of reading.

THE SHAKESPEARE CODE

THE DOCTOR: I've lived for something like seven hundred and fifty years.

SARAH: Oh, you'll soon be middle aged.

THE DOCTOR: Yes!

PYRAMIDS OF MARS

'I'm called the Doctor. Date of birth difficult to remember. Sometime quite soon, I think.'

THE DOCTOR, *NIGHTMARE OF EDEN*

'I'm afraid I'm much too old to be a pioneer. Although I was once amongst my own people.'

THE DOCTOR, *THE DALEKS*

'Oi! Listen, mush. Old eyes, remember? I've been around the block a few times. More than a few. They've knocked down the blocks I've been round and rebuilt them as bigger blocks. Super blocks. And I've been round them as well.'

THE DOCTOR, *NIGHT TERRORS*

'Can't remember if I'm lying about my age, that's how old I am.'

THE DOCTOR, *THE DAY OF THE DOCTOR*

LIFE WITH THE DOCTOR

MICKEY: Is this like normal for you? Is this an average day?

ROSE: Life with the Doctor, Mickey? No more average days.

THE GIRL IN THE FIREPLACE

'When I say run, run.'

THE DOCTOR, *THE EVIL OF THE DALEKS*

'It's the way it's always been. The monsters and the Doctor. It seems you cannot have one without the other.'

REINETTE, *THE GIRL IN THE FIREPLACE*

ROMANA: You nearly got us killed.

THE DOCTOR: If you call that being nearly killed, you haven't lived yet. Just stay with me and you'll get a lot nearer.

THE RIBOS OPERATION

'Trouble seems to follow you, doesn't it, Doctor?'

THE BRIGADIER, *INFERNO*

'I don't work for anybody. I'm just having fun.'

THE DOCTOR, *NIGHTMARE OF EDEN*

'This is my life, Jackie. It's not fun, it's not smart. It's just standing up and making a decision because nobody else will.'

THE DOCTOR, *WORLD WAR THREE*

THE DOCTOR: The situation's worse than you imagine.

PERI: It always is.

THE TRIAL OF A TIME LORD: THE MYSTERIOUS PLANET

CLARA: Doctor, what are you going to do?

THE DOCTOR: Oh, I don't know. Talk very fast, hope something good happens, take the credit. That's generally how it works.

THE TIME OF THE DOCTOR

'If I knew everything that was going to happen, where would the fun be?'

THE DOCTOR, *THE KEEPER OF TRAKEN*

'I mean, this is what he does, Jacks, that Doctor bloke. Every where he goes, death and destruction, and he's got Rose in the middle of it.'

MICKEY, *WORLD WAR THREE*

'Oh, I must be mad. I'm sick of being cold and wet, and hypnotised left right and centre. I'm sick of being shot at, savaged by bug-eyed monsters, never knowing if I'm coming or going or been.'

SARAH, *THE HAND OF FEAR*

'As long as he does the job, he can wear what face he likes.'

THE BRIGADIER, *THE THREE DOCTORS*

'Wish I'd never met you, Doctor. I was much better off as a coward.'

CAPTAIN JACK HARKNESS, *THE PARTING OF THE WAYS*

'Flying the TARDIS was always easy. It was flying the Doctor I never quite mastered.'

TASHA LEM, *THE TIME OF THE DOCTOR*

'When you run with the Doctor, it feels like it will never end. But however hard you try, you can't run for ever. Everybody knows that everybody dies, and nobody knows it like the Doctor. But I do think that all the skies of all the worlds might just turn dark, if he ever, for one moment, accepts it.'

RIVER SONG, *FOREST OF THE DEAD*

'I'd hate to have to live my life by some boring old rulebook like you do.'

THE DOCTOR, *PARADISE TOWERS*

ROSE: He thought you were brilliant.

DONNA: Don't be stupid.

ROSE: But you are. It just took the Doctor to show you that, simply by being with him. He did the same to me. To everyone he touches.

TURN LEFT

BRIAN: Go save every world you can find. Who else has that chance? Life will still be here.

THE DOCTOR: You could come, Brian.

BRIAN: Somebody's got to water the plants.

THE POWER OF THREE

LIFE WITHOUT THE DOCTOR

'You were my life. You know what the most difficult thing was? Coping with what happens next, or with what doesn't happen next. You took me to the furthest reaches of the galaxy, you showed me supernovas, intergalactic battles, and then you just dropped me back on Earth. How could anything compare to that? … We get a taste of that splendour and then we have to go back.'

SARAH, *SCHOOL REUNION*

'It's life. Just life. That thing that goes on when you're not there.'

AMY, *ASYLUM OF THE DALEKS*

AMY: After everything we've been through, Doctor. Everything. You can't just drop me off at my house and say goodbye like we've shared a cab.

THE DOCTOR: And what's the alternative? Me standing over your grave?

THE GOD COMPLEX

'Our lives won't run the same. They can't. One day, soon maybe, you'll stop. I've known for a while.'

THE DOCTOR TO AMY, *THE POWER OF THREE*

CRITICISING THE DOCTOR

'Don't trust him. There's a sliver of ice in his heart.'

EMMA, *HIDE*

CLARA: I trust the Doctor.

CAPTAIN: You think he knows what he's doing?

CLARA: I'm not sure I'd go that far.

NIGHTMARE IN SILVER

'Oh yes. I'm only his assistant. He's the one you should be talking to. Or rather, listening to, if you have the stamina.'

ROMANA, *THE PIRATE PLANET*

HARRIET: Excuse me, people are dead! This is not the time for making jokes.

ROSE: Sorry. You get used to this stuff when you're friends with him.

HARRIET: Well, that's a strange friendship.

WORLD WAR THREE

COMMODORE TRAVERS: If I seem to lack gratitude, young woman … it is because on the previous occasion that the Doctor's path crossed mine I found myself involved in a web of mayhem and intrigue.

THE DOCTOR: Ah, saved your ship though, Commodore.

COMMODORE TRAVERS: Yes, you did, though whether it would have been at risk without your intervention is another matter.

THE TRIAL OF A TIME LORD: TERROR OF THE VERVOIDS

'Don't listen to me. I never do.'

THE DOCTOR, *THE KEEPER OF TRAKEN*

VIVIEN: I'm sure the Doctor's perfectly capable of looking after himself.

ROMANA: I'm not sure I'd entirely agree with that remark.

THE STONES OF BLOOD

'The Doctor. The man who keeps running, never looking back because he dare not, out of shame. This is my final victory, Doctor. I have shown you yourself.'

DAVROS, *JOURNEY'S END*

'You know what's going on … You always know. You just can't be bothered to tell anyone. It's like it's some kind of a game, and only you know the rules.'

ACE, *THE CURSE OF FENRIC*

'How like a man to have fun while there's disaster all around him.'

AGATHA CHRISTIE, *THE UNICORN AND THE WASP*

'It's funny, you know, but before I met you, I was even willing to be impressed … Of course, now I realise that your behaviour simply derives from a sub-transitory, experiential hypertoid-induced condition, aggravated, I expect, by multi-encephalogical tensions … to put it very simply, Doctor, you're suffering from a massive compensation syndrome.'

ROMANA, *THE RIBOS OPERATION*

'The Doctor has no idea of time. For someone who's travelled about in time as much as he has, that's rather funny.'

DODO, *THE SAVAGES*

'Call yourself a Time Lord? A broken clock keeps better time than you do. At least it's accurate twice a day, which is more than you ever are.'

TEGAN, *THE VISITATION*

ROMANA: I told you you'd got the time wrong, Doctor.

THE DOCTOR: Yes, but you're always saying that.

ROMANA: You're always getting the time wrong.

SHADA

ROMANA: Is that why you always win?

THE DOCTOR: Yes. What?

ROMANA: Because you always make mistakes.

THE DOCTOR: Mistakes? Me? Well, perhaps once a century or so.

DESTINY OF THE DALEKS

JOSIAH: You're so smug and self-satisfied, Doctor.

THE DOCTOR: I try.

GHOST LIGHT

THE DARK SIDE OF THE DOCTOR

'I'm so old now. I used to have so much mercy. You get one warning. That was it.'

THE DOCTOR, *SCHOOL REUNION*

'The Doctor is a legend woven throughout history. When disaster comes, he's there. He brings the storm in his wake and he has one constant companion … Death.'

CLIVE, *ROSE*

'You look deep enough on the internet or in the history books, and there's his name, followed by a list of the dead.'

MICKEY, *ALIENS OF LONDON*

'Every time the Doctor gets pally with someone, I have this overwhelming urge to notify their next of kin.'

RORY, *THE GOD COMPLEX*

'Answer me this. Just one question, that's all. If the Doctor had never visited us, if he'd never chosen this place on a whim, would anybody here have died?'

JOAN, *THE FAMILY OF BLOOD*

'No, you've noticed something. You've got your noticing face on. I have nightmares about that face.'

CRAIG, *CLOSING TIME*

'The man who abhors violence, never carrying a gun. But this is the truth, Doctor. You take ordinary people, and you fashion them into weapons. Behold your Children of Time. Transformed into murderers. I made the Daleks, Doctor. You made this.'

DAVROS, *JOURNEY'S END*

'Good men don't need rules. Today is not the day to find out why I have so many.'

THE DOCTOR, *A GOOD MAN GOES TO WAR*

'You know what's dangerous about you? It's not that you make people take risks, it's that you make them want to impress you. You make it so they don't want to let you down. You have no idea how dangerous you make people to themselves when you're around.'

RORY, *VAMPIRES OF VENICE*

'I don't know what you are, the two of you, or where you're from, but I know that you consort with stars and magic and think it fun. But your world is steeped in terror and blasphemy and death, and I will not allow it. You will leave these shores and you will reflect, I hope, on how you came to stray so far from all that is good, and how much longer you may survive this terrible life. Now leave my world, and never return.'

QUEEN VICTORIA, *TOOTH AND CLAW*

'You gave me hope, and then you took it away. That's enough to make anyone dangerous. God knows what it will do to me. Basically, run!'

THE DOCTOR, *THE DOCTOR'S WIFE*

JOHN SMITH: You're this Doctor's companion. Can't you help? What exactly do you do for him? Why does he need you?

MARTHA: Because he's lonely.

THE FAMILY OF BLOOD

'You've got an unconscious death wish.'

ROMANA, *THE RIBOS OPERATION*

'You know, Stephen King said once, he said, salvation and damnation are the same thing. And I never knew what he meant. But I do now, because the Doctor might be wonderful, but thinking back, I was having such a special time. Just for a bit. I had this nice little gang, and they were destroyed. It's not his fault, but maybe that's what happens if you touch the Doctor. Even for a second. I keep thinking of Rose and Jackie. And how much longer before they pay the price.'

ELTON, *LOVE & MONSTERS*

'Falling in love? That didn't even occur to him? ... Then what sort of man is that?'

JOHN SMITH, *THE FAMILY OF BLOOD*

THE DOCTOR: You've seen it out there. It's beautiful.

DONNA: And it's terrible. That place was flooding and burning and they were dying, and you were stood there like, I don't know, a stranger. And then you made it snow. I mean, you scare me to death.

THE RUNAWAY BRIDE

'Just promise me one thing. Find someone ... Because sometimes, I think you need someone to stop you.'

DONNA, *THE RUNAWAY BRIDE*

'I choose my friends with great care. Otherwise, I'm stuck with my own company, and you know how that works out.'

THE DOCTOR, *AMY'S CHOICE*

'People have died. The Daleks are all over the place, fit to murder the lot of us, and all you can say is you've had a good night's work.'

JAMIE, *THE EVIL OF THE DALEKS*

'I'm the Doctor. And if you don't like it, if you want to take it to a higher authority, then there isn't one. It stops with me.'

THE DOCTOR, *NEW EARTH*

'He never raised his voice. That was the worst thing. The fury of the Time Lord. And then we discovered why. Why this Doctor, who had fought with gods and demons, why he'd run away from us and hidden. He was being kind.'

SON OF MINE, *THE FAMILY OF BLOOD*

'When you began, all those years ago, sailing off to see the universe, did you ever think you'd become this? The man who can turn an army around at the mention of his name. Doctor. The word for healer and wise man throughout the universe. We get that word from you, you know. But if you carry on the way you are, what might that word come to mean? To the people of the Gamma Forests, the word Doctor means mighty warrior. How far you've come. And now they've taken a child, the child of your best friends, and they're going to turn her into a weapon just to bring you down. And all this, my love, in fear of you.'

RIVER SONG, *A GOOD MAN GOES TO WAR*

'If he's singled you out, if the Doctor's making house calls, then God help you.'

CLIVE, *ROSE*

'From what I've seen, your funny little happy-go-lucky life leaves devastation in its wake. Always moving on because you dare not look back. Playing with so many people's lives, you might as well be a god.'

MARGARET BLAINE, *BOOM TOWN*

THE ONCOMING STORM

'Do you know what they call me in the ancient legends of the Dalek Homeworld? The Oncoming Storm. You might've removed all your emotions but I reckon right down deep in your DNA, there's one little spark left, and that's fear. Doesn't it just burn when you face me?'

THE DOCTOR, *THE PARTING OF THE WAYS*

'I'm a dead man. I knew that as soon as I came through that door, so you'd better watch out. You see, I've nothing to lose, have I?'

THE DOCTOR, *THE DAEMONS*

'You have the mouth of a prattling jackanapes, but your eyes – they tell a different story.'

SHARAZ JEK, *THE CAVES OF ANDROZANI*

THE DOCTOR: Even monsters from under the bed have nightmares, don't you, monster?

YOUNG REINETTE: What do monsters have nightmares about?

THE DOCTOR: Me!

THE GIRL IN THE FIREPLACE

'His entire history is one of opposition to conquest. While he lives, he is a threat.'

CHEDAKI, *THE ANDROID INVASION*

'The Doctor is never more dangerous than when the odds are against him.'

THE MASTER, *THE DEADLY ASSASSIN*

'Didn't anyone ever tell you there's one thing you never put in a trap? If you're smart, if you value your continued existence, if you have any plans about seeing tomorrow, there is one thing you never, ever put in a trap: Me.'

THE DOCTOR, *THE TIME OF ANGELS*

VASTRA: The Doctor has been many things, but never blood-soaked.

DR SIMEON: Tell that to the leader of the Sycorax, or Solomon the trader, or the Cybermen, or the Daleks. The Doctor lives his life in darker hues, day upon day, and he will have other names before the end. The Storm, the Beast, the Valeyard.

THE NAME OF THE DOCTOR

'Just remember who's standing in your way. Remember every black day I ever stopped you, and then, and then, do the smart thing. Let somebody else try first.'

THE DOCTOR, *THE PANDORICA OPENS*

Chapter Two: The Light

'The way I see it, every life is a pile of good things and bad things. Hey. The good things don't always soften the bad things, but vice versa, the bad things don't necessarily spoil the good things or make them unimportant.'

THE DOCTOR AND HIS COMPANIONS

'I only take the best.'

THE DOCTOR, *THE LONG GAME*

'How do you do? Have you met Miss Smith? She's my best friend.'

THE DOCTOR, *THE SEEDS OF DOOM*

'The Doctor sort of travels through time and space and picks people up. God, I make us sound like stray dogs. Maybe we are.'

MARTHA, *UTOPIA*

'I've seen a lot of this universe. I've seen fake gods and bad gods and demi-gods and would-be gods, and out of all that, out of that whole pantheon, if I believe in one thing, just one thing, I believe in her.'

THE DOCTOR ON ROSE, *THE SATAN PIT*

BARBARA: We worked upwards from the three Rs ... Reading, writing, 'rithmetic.

VICKI: Oh, it was a nursery school.

BARBARA: It was not!

THE WEB PLANET

'I'm being extremely clever up here, and there's no one to stand around looking impressed! What's the point in having you all?'

THE DOCTOR, *THE IMPOSSIBLE ASTRONAUT*

THE VALEYARD: I have calculated on a random Matrix sample that the Doctor's companions have been placed in danger twice as often as the Doctor.

THE DOCTOR: Well, there have been many companions, but only one me.

THE TRIAL OF A TIME LORD: MINDWARP

'Anything you have to say to me, you can say in front of Clara. Well, quite a lot of it. Probably about half. Maybe a smidge under. Actually, Clara, would you mind waiting out here, please?'

THE DOCTOR, *THE TIME OF THE DOCTOR*

SARAH: What you're trying to say is that you're busy and you'd like us to push off.

THE DOCTOR: I'd phrase it more elegantly myself, of course. But yes.

THE SONTARAN EXPERIMENT

ROSE: You're not keeping the horse.

THE DOCTOR: I let you keep Mickey.

THE GIRL IN THE FIREPLACE

'Exotic alien swords are easy to come by. Aces are rare.'

THE DOCTOR, *BATTLEFIELD*

'What you need, Doctor, as Miss Shaw herself so often remarked, is someone to pass you your test tubes and to tell you how brilliant you are. Miss Grant will fulfil that function admirably.'

THE BRIGADIER, *TERROR OF THE AUTONS*

THE DOCTOR: Sarah. What are you doing here?

SARAH: Rescuing you, actually. For a change.

THE ANDROID INVASION

'Well, look round. Ask questions. People like it when you're with a baby. Babies are sweet. People talk to you. That's why I usually take a human with me.'

THE DOCTOR, *CLOSING TIME*

DONNA: I'm sorry. I'm going home.

THE DOCTOR: Really? ... I had so many places I wanted to take you. The fifteenth broken moon of the Medusa Cascade. The lightning skies of Cotter Palluni's World. Diamond coral reefs of Kataa Flo Ko. Thank you. Thank you, Donna Noble. It's been brilliant. You've... you've saved my life in so many ways. You're... you're just popping home for a visit, that's what you mean.

DONNA: You dumbo.

THE SONTARAN STRATAGEM

ROMANA: My name is Romanadvoratrelundar.

THE DOCTOR: I'm so sorry about that. Is there anything we can do?

THE RIBOS OPERATION

'Is that why you travel round with a human at your side? It's not so you can show them the wonders of the universe, it's so you can take cheap shots?'

DONNA, *PLANET OF THE OOD*

ROMANA: I don't like 'Romana'.

THE DOCTOR: It's either 'Romana' or 'Fred'.

ROMANA: All right, call me 'Fred'.

THE DOCTOR: Good. Come on, Romana.

THE RIBOS OPERATION

'Your mind is beginning to work. It's entirely due to my influence, of course. You mustn't take any credit.'

THE DOCTOR TO HARRY, *THE ARK IN SPACE*

'Do you think that for once in your life you could manage to arrive before the nick of time?'

THE DOCTOR TO THE BRIGADIER, *THE MIND OF EVIL*

STEVEN: You know, I'm beginning to like the idea of being a crewmember on a time machine.

VICKI: A crewmember? You'll be lucky. He's the crew. We're just the passengers.

THE TIME MEDDLER

THE DOCTOR: I wanted to see how you were. You know me, I don't just abandon people when they leave the TARDIS. This Time Lord's for life. You don't get rid of your old pal, the Doctor, so easily.

AMY: Hmm. You came here by mistake, didn't you?

THE DOCTOR: Yeah, bit of a mistake.

AMY'S CHOICE

THE DOCTOR: How do you feel now?

TEGAN: Groggy, sore and bad-tempered.

THE DOCTOR: Oh, almost your old self.

THE VISITATION

THE DOCTOR: Well, come on, old girl. There's quite a few millennia left in you yet.

ROMANA: Thank you, Doctor.

THE DOCTOR: Not you, the TARDIS.

THE HORNS OF NIMON

'Sometimes I do worry about you, though. I think once we're gone, you won't be coming back here for a while, and you might be alone, which you should never be. Don't be alone, Doctor.'

AMY, *THE ANGELS TAKE MANHATTAN*

FAMILY

ROSE: He's your dad.

TOMMY: He's an idiot.

ROSE: Of course he is. Like I said, he's your dad.

THE IDIOT'S LANTERN

'Weak and strong. It's a translation. Translated from the base code of nature itself. You and I, Cyril, we're weak. But she's female. More than female, she's Mum. How else does life ever travel? The Mother ship.'

THE DOCTOR, *THE DOCTOR, THE WIDOW AND THE WARDROBE*

'There isn't a little boy born who wouldn't tear the world apart to save his mummy. And this little boy can.'

THE DOCTOR, *THE DOCTOR DANCES*

'Your dad's trying his best, you know. Yes, I know it's not his fault he doesn't have mammary glands. No, neither do I.'

THE DOCTOR, *CLOSING TIME*

'Nine hundred years of time and space, and I've never been slapped by someone's mother.'

THE DOCTOR, *ALIENS OF LONDON*

'Oh, who needs family? I've got the whole world on my shoulders.'

THE DOCTOR, *THE AGE OF STEEL*

ROSE: This is my fault.

PETE: No, love. I'm your dad. It's my job for it to be my fault.

FATHER'S DAY

THE DOCTOR: My dear girl, the one purpose in growing old is to accumulate knowledge and wisdom, and to help other people.

SUSAN: So I'm to be treated like a silly little child.

THE DOCTOR: If you behave like one, yes.

THE SENSORITES

'You're a mother, aren't you … There's kindness in your eyes. And sadness, but a ferocity too.'

KAHLER-JEX TO AMY, *A TOWN CALLED MERCY*

DROXIL: There's nothing you could say that would convince me you'd ever use that gun.

MADGE: Oh really? Well, I'm looking for my children.

THE DOCTOR, THE WIDOW AND THE WARDROBE

THE DOCTOR: I just want you to know there are worlds out there, safe in the sky because of her. That there are people living in the light, and singing songs of Donna Noble, a thousand million light years away. They will never forget her, while she can never remember. And for one moment, one shining moment, she was the most important woman in the whole wide universe.

SYLVIA: She still is. She's my daughter.

THE DOCTOR: Then maybe you should tell her that once in a while.

JOURNEY'S END

CRAIG: Yes, I meant on my own with the baby. Yes. Because no one thinks I can cope on my own. Which is so unfair, because I can't cope on my own with him. I can't. He just cries all the time. I mean, do they have off switches?

THE DOCTOR: Human beings? No. Believe me, I've checked.

CLOSING TIME

VICTORIA: You probably can't remember your family.

THE DOCTOR: Oh yes, I can when I want to. And that's the point, really. I have to really want to, to bring them back in front of my eyes. The rest of the time they sleep in my mind, and I forget.

THE TOMB OF THE CYBERMEN

HAPPINESS

'Build high for happiness.'

THE KANGS, *PARADISE TOWERS*

'I think it does us good to be reminded the universe isn't entirely peopled with nasty creatures out for themselves.'

THE DOCTOR, *CASTROVALVA*

'Happiness will prevail.'

HELEN A, *THE HAPPINESS PATROL*

'You want moves, Rose? I'll give you moves. Everybody lives, Rose. Just this once, everybody lives!'

THE DOCTOR, *THE DOCTOR DANCES*

PEACE AND UNDERSTANDING

'As we learn about each other, so we learn about ourselves.'

THE DOCTOR, *THE EDGE OF DESTRUCTION*

'Mankind doesn't need warfare and bloodshed to prove itself. Everyday life can provide honour and valour, and let's hope that from now on this, this country can find its heroes in smaller places.'

JOHN SMITH, *HUMAN NATURE*

THE DOCTOR: I could rule the universe with this, Chancellor.

BORUSA: Is that what you want? Destroy that gun. Destroy all knowledge of it. It'll throw us back to the darkest age!

SONTARAN: No, Chancellor, forward.

THE INVASION OF TIME

WATSON: They're the most powerful missiles we have.

THE DOCTOR: On your standards, perhaps. I think we should try much older weapons… Speech. Diplomacy … Conversation.

THE HAND OF FEAR

MARSHAL: We must have the weapon that will wipe the Zeons clear of our skies once and for all. Can you provide it?

THE DOCTOR: Yes, I think so.

MARSHAL: What is it?

THE DOCTOR: Peace.

THE ARMAGEDDON FACTOR

'Some days are special. Some days are so, so blessed. Some days, nobody dies at all. Now and then, every once in a very long while, every day in a million days, when the wind stands fair, and the Doctor comes to call, everybody lives.'

RIVER SONG, *FOREST OF THE DEAD*

BRAVERY

'Brave heart, Tegan.'

THE DOCTOR, *EARTHSHOCK*

DESTROYER: Pitiful. Can this world do no better than you as their champion?

THE BRIGADIER: Probably. I just do the best I can.

BATTLEFIELD

'Unless we are prepared to sacrifice our lives for the good of all, then evil and anarchy will spread like the plague.'

THE DOCTOR, *THE TRIAL OF A TIME LORD: THE ULTIMATE FOE*

'It was a better life. And I don't mean all the travelling and seeing aliens and spaceships and things. That don't matter. The Doctor showed me a better way of living your life. You know, he showed you too. That you don't just give up. You don't just let things happen. You make a stand. You say no. You have the guts to do what's right when everyone else just runs away, and I just can't.'

ROSE, *THE PARTING OF THE WAYS*

OCTAVIAN: I will die in the knowledge that my courage did not desert me at the end. For that I thank God, and bless the path that takes you to safety.

THE DOCTOR: I wish I'd known you better.

OCTAVIAN: I think, sir, you know me at my best.

FLESH AND STONE

'I've a young friend on the Beacon. Sarah Jane, the girl who was here. She risked her life to save mine. The least I can do is accept the same risk for her.'

THE DOCTOR, *REVENGE OF THE CYBERMEN*

'Courage isn't just a matter of not being frightened, you know… It's being afraid and doing what you have to do anyway.'

THE DOCTOR, *PLANET OF THE DALEKS*

THE DOCTOR: I'm going to save Rose Tyler from the middle of the Dalek fleet. And then I'm going to save the Earth, and then, just to finish off, I'm going to wipe every last stinking Dalek out of the sky!

DALEK: But you have no weapons, no defences, no plan.

THE DOCTOR: Yeah. And doesn't that scare you to death.

BAD WOLF

TRUTH

JENNY: Madame Vastra will ask you questions. You will confine yourself to single-word responses. One word only, do you understand?

CLARA: Why?

VASTRA: Truth is singular. Lies are words, words, words.

THE SNOWMEN

'For a lie to work, madam, it must be shrouded in truth.'

THE MASTER, *THE TRIAL OF A TIME LORD: THE ULTIMATE FOE*

'I have the two qualities you require to see absolute truth. I am brilliant, and unloved.'

MISS EVANGELISTA, *FOREST OF THE DEAD*

'The very powerful and the very stupid have one thing in common. They don't alter their views to fit the facts. They alter the facts to fit their views. Which can be uncomfortable if you happen to be one of the facts that needs altering.'

THE DOCTOR, *THE FACE OF EVIL*

'Only in mathematics will we find truth.'

THE DOCTOR, QUOTING BORUSA, *THE DEADLY ASSASSIN*

FRIENDSHIP

'If it's time to go, remember what you're leaving. Remember the best. My friends have always been the best of me.'

THE DOCTOR, *THE WEDDING OF RIVER SONG*

THE DOCTOR: I imagine you'd prefer to be alone.

MADGE: I don't believe anyone would prefer that.

THE DOCTOR, THE WIDOW AND THE WARDROBE

DONNA: That Martha must've done you good.

THE DOCTOR: She did, yeah. Yeah. She did. She fancied me.

DONNA: Mad Martha, that one. Blind Martha. Charity Martha.

PARTNERS IN CRIME

'People fall out of the world sometimes, but they always leave traces. Little things we can't quite account for. Faces in photographs, luggage, half-eaten meals. Rings. Nothing is ever forgotten, not completely. And if something can be remembered, it can come back.'

THE DOCTOR, *THE PANDORICA OPENS*

'You were there for me when I had a bad day. Always like to return a favour. Got a bit glitchy in the middle there, but it sort of worked out in the end. Story of my life.'

THE DOCTOR, *THE DOCTOR, THE WIDOW AND THE WARDROBE*

LOVE

'Love has never been known for its rationality.'

THE DOCTOR, *DELTA AND THE BANNERMEN*

MARRINER: Without you I am nothing… I am empty. You give me being. I look into your mind and see life, energy, excitement. I want them. I want you. Your thoughts should be my thoughts. Your feelings, my feelings.

TEGAN: Wait a minute. Are you trying to tell me you're in love?

MARRINER: Love? What is love? I want existence.

ENLIGHTENMENT

'Love and hate, frightening feelings, especially when they're trapped struggling beneath the surface.'

THE DOCTOR, *THE CURSE OF FENRIC*

'You know when sometimes you meet someone so beautiful and then you actually talk to them, and five minutes later they're as dull as a brick? Then there's other people, and you meet them and you think, not bad, they're OK. And then you get to know them, and their face just sort of becomes them, like their personality's written all over it. And they just turn into something so beautiful.'

AMY, *THE GIRL WHO WAITED*

'I'm going to pull time apart for you.'

AMY, *THE GIRL WHO WAITED*

AMY: I love you, too. Don't let me in. Tell Amy, your Amy, I'm giving her the days. The days with you. The days to come.

RORY: I'm so, so sorry.

AMY: The days I can't have. Take them, please. I'm giving you my days.'

THE GIRL WHO WAITED

CRAIG: The Cybermen. They blew up. I blew them up with love.

THE DOCTOR: No, that's impossible. And also grossly sentimental and over-simplistic. You destroyed them because of the deeply ingrained hereditary human trait to protect one's own genes, which in turn triggered a... a... a... Yeah. Love. You blew them up with love.

CLOSING TIME

'Better a broken heart than no heart at all.'

THE DOCTOR, *A CHRISTMAS CAROL*

FLIRTING

THE DOCTOR: My dear boy, I could kiss you!

BARBARA: Don't waste it on him, kiss me instead!

THE CHASE

JACKIE: I'm in my dressing gown.

THE DOCTOR: Yes, you are.

JACKIE: There's a strange man in my bedroom.

THE DOCTOR: Yes, there is.

JACKIE: Well, anything could happen.

THE DOCTOR: No.

ROSE

LAZARUS: That's an interesting perfume. What's it called?

TISH: Soap.

THE LAZARUS EXPERIMENT

TASHA: Is that a new body? Give us a twirl.

THE DOCTOR: Tush, this old thing? Please, I've been rocking it for centuries.

THE TIME OF THE DOCTOR

ROSE: OK, so he's vanished into thin air. Why is it always the great-looking ones who do that?

THE DOCTOR: I'm making an effort not to be insulted.

ROSE: I mean, men.

THE DOCTOR: OK, thanks, that really helped.

THE DOCTOR DANCES

'The thrill is in the chase, never in the capture.'

AGATHA CHRISTIE, *THE UNICORN AND THE WASP*

THE BRIGADIER: You may not have noticed, but I'm a bit old-fashioned myself.

SARAH: Oh, nonsense, Brigadier. You're a swinger.

ROBOT

JABE: The gift of peace. I bring you a cutting of my grandfather.

THE DOCTOR: Thank you. Yes, gifts. Er, I give you in return air from my lungs.

JABE: How intimate.

THE DOCTOR: There's more where that came from.

JABE: I bet there is.

THE END OF THE WORLD

THE DOCTOR: I just want a mate.

DONNA: You just want to mate?

THE DOCTOR: I just want *a* mate!

DONNA: You're not mating with me, sunshine!

PARTNERS IN CRIME

'He saved my life. Bloke-wise, that's up there with flossing.'

ROSE, *THE DOCTOR DANCES*

HAWTHORNE: Sergeant, we must do the fertility dance to celebrate.

BENTON: Oh, no, I'm sorry, ma'am. I'm still rather busy.

THE DAEMONS

THE DOCTOR: Your boss, you should just ask her out. She likes you... She said that you were a Mister Hottie-ness, and that she would like to go out with you for texting and scones.

RORY: You really haven't done this before, have you?

THE DOCTOR: No, I haven't.

THE WEDDING OF RIVER SONG

RORY: There are soldiers all over my house, and I'm in my pants.

AMY: My whole life I've dreamed of saying that, and I miss it by being someone else.

THE POWER OF THREE

'My lonely Doctor. Dance with me... There comes a time, Time Lord, when every lonely little boy must learn how to dance.'

REINETTE, *THE GIRL IN THE FIREPLACE*

CLARA: Do you think I'm pretty?

THE DOCTOR: No. You're too short and bossy, and your nose is all funny.

NIGHTMARE IN SILVER

'Nine hundred years old, me. I've been around a bit. I think you can assume at some point I've danced.'

THE DOCTOR, *THE DOCTOR DANCES*

'This is how it all ends. Pond flirting with herself. True love at last.'

THE DOCTOR, *TIME*

THE DOCTOR: Do you mind flirting outside?

JACK: I was just saying hello!

THE DOCTOR: For you, that's flirting.

BAD WOLF

ROSE: You just handed me a piece of paper telling me you're single and you work out.

JACK: Tricky thing, psychic paper.

ROSE: Yeah. Can't let your mind wander when you're handing it over.

THE EMPTY CHILD

THE DOCTOR: We were talking about dancing.

JACK: It didn't look like talking.

ROSE: It didn't feel like dancing.

THE DOCTOR DANCES

K-9: She is prettier than you, master.

THE DOCTOR: Is she? What's that got to do with it?

THE PIRATE PLANET

KISSING

'A Zygon, yes. Big red rubbery thing covered in suckers. Surprisingly good kisser.'

THE DOCTOR, *THE DAY OF THE DOCTOR*

'You're never short of a snog with an extra head.'

THE DOCTOR, *THE TIME OF ANGELS*

KAZRAN: I've never kissed anyone before. What do I do?

THE DOCTOR: Try and be all nervous and rubbish and a bit shaky... Because you're going to be like that anyway. Might as well make it part of the plan, then it'll feel on purpose... Trust me. It's this or go to your room and design a new kind of screwdriver. Don't make my mistakes.

A CHRISTMAS CAROL

RORY: Of course I've got a job. What do you think we do when we're not with you?

THE DOCTOR: I imagined mostly kissing.

THE POWER OF THREE

'We've all got to go some time. There are worse ways than having your face snogged off by a dodgy mermaid.'

THE DOCTOR, *THE CURSE OF THE BLACK SPOT*

JACKIE: What do you need?

THE DOCTOR: Anything with vinegar!

JACKIE: Gherkins. Yeah, pickled onions. Pickled eggs.

THE DOCTOR: And you kiss this man?

WORLD WAR THREE

'Biting's excellent. It's like kissing, only there's a winner.'

IDRIS, *THE DOCTOR'S WIFE*

THE DOCTOR: She kissed me.

RORY: And you kissed her back.

THE DOCTOR: No. I kissed her mouth.

THE VAMPIRES OF VENICE

THE WAR DOCTOR: Is there a lot of this in the future?

THE DOCTOR: It does start to happen, yeah.

THE DAY OF THE DOCTOR

RELATIONSHIPS

'I dated a Nestene duplicate once. Swappable head. It did keep things fresh.'

RIVER SONG, *THE BIG BANG*

'You think you know us so well, Doctor. But we're not abandoned. Not while we have each other.'

BRANNIGAN, *GRIDLOCK*

THE BRIGADIER: Oh dear. Women. Not really my field.

THE DOCTOR: Don't worry, Brigadier. People will be shooting at you soon.

BATTLEFIELD

IAN: Where did you get hold of this?

THE DOCTOR: My fiancée.

IAN: I see. Your what?

THE DOCTOR: Yes, I made some cocoa and got engaged.

THE AZTECS

'I don't care that you got old. I care that we didn't grow old together.'

RORY, *THE GIRL WHO WAITED*

CLARA: Emergency. You're my boyfriend.

THE DOCTOR: Ding dong. OK, brilliant. I may be a bit rusty in some areas, but I will glance at a manual.

THE TIME OF THE DOCTOR

KAZRAN: When girls are crying, are you supposed to talk to them?

THE DOCTOR: I have absolutely no idea.

A CHRISTMAS CAROL

RORY: Amy, I thought I'd lost you.

AMY: What, cause I was sucked into the ground? You're so clingy.

COLD BLOOD

'Let me tell you something about those who get left behind. Because it's hard. And that's what you become, hard. But if there's one thing I've learnt, it's that I will never let her down. And I'll protect them both until the end of my life. So whatever you want, I'm warning you, back off.'

JACKIE TYLER, *LOVE & MONSTERS*

'Sometimes it's like I've lived a thousand lives in a thousand places. I'm born, I live, I die. And always, there's the Doctor. Always I'm running to save the Doctor again and again and again… And he hardly ever hears me. But I've always been there.'

CLARA, *THE NAME OF THE DOCTOR*

'It's the oldest story in the universe, this one or any other. Boy and girl fall in love, get separated by events. War, politics, accidents in time. She's thrown out of the hex, or he's thrown into it. Since then they've been yearning for each other across time and space, across dimensions. This isn't a ghost story, it's a love story!'

THE DOCTOR, *HIDE*

'Hold hands. That's what you're meant to do. Keep doing that and don't let go. That's the secret.'

THE DOCTOR, *HIDE*

THE MOST COMPLICATED RELATIONSHIP OF THEM ALL

'Hello Sweetie!'

RIVER SONG, *SILENCE IN THE LIBRARY*

CHURCHILL: What's she like? Attractive, I assume.

THE DOCTOR: Hell, in high heels.

CHURCHILL: Tell me more.

THE WEDDING OF RIVER SONG

'You know when you see a photograph of someone you know, but it's from years before you knew them and it's like they're not quite finished. They're not done yet. Well, yes, the Doctor's here. He came when I called, just like he always does. But not my Doctor. Now *my* Doctor, I've seen whole armies turn and run away. And he'd just swagger off back to his TARDIS and open the doors with a snap of his fingers. The Doctor in the TARDIS. Next stop, everywhere.'

RIVER SONG, *FOREST OF THE DEAD*

THE DOCTOR: River Song, I could bloody kiss you.

RIVER: Ah well, maybe when you're older.

FLESH AND STONE

'It was never going to be a gun for you, Doctor. The man of peace who understands every kind of warfare, except, perhaps, the cruellest.'

RIVER SONG, *LET'S KILL HITLER*

THE DOCTOR: Doctor Song, you've got that face on again.

RIVER: What face?

THE DOCTOR: The 'he's hot when he's clever' face.

RIVER: This is my normal face.

THE DOCTOR: Yes, it is.

RIVER: Oh, shut up.

THE IMPOSSIBLE ASTRONAUT

RIVER: I'd trust that man to the end of the universe. And actually, we've been.

ANITA: He doesn't act like he trusts you.

RIVER: Yeah, there's a tiny problem. He hasn't met me yet.

FOREST OF THE DEAD

'You, me, handcuffs. Must it always end this way?'

RIVER SONG, *FLESH AND STONE*

'It's a long story, Doctor. It can't be told, it has to be lived. No sneak previews.'

RIVER SONG, *FLESH AND STONE*

THE DOCTOR: Can I trust you, River Song?

RIVER: If you like. But where's the fun in that?

FLESH AND STONE

'Funny thing is, this means you've always known how I was going to die. All the time we've been together, you knew I was coming here. The last time I saw you, the real you, the future you, I mean, you turned up on my doorstep, with a new haircut and a suit. You took me to Darillium to see the Singing Towers. What a night that was. The Towers sang, and you cried.'

RIVER SONG, *FOREST OF THE DEAD*

RIVER: How are you even doing that? I'm not really here.

THE DOCTOR: You are always here to me. And I always listen, and I can always see you.

RIVER: Then why didn't you speak to me?

THE DOCTOR: Because I thought it would hurt too much.

RIVER: I believe I could have coped.

THE DOCTOR: No, I thought it would hurt me. And I was right.

THE NAME OF THE DOCTOR

LIVING LIFE
TO THE FULL

'Living minds are contaminated with crude emotions, organic, irrational, creative, entertaining.'

THE DOCTOR, *ENLIGHTENMENT*

'There is no indignity in being afraid to die. But there is a terrible shame in being afraid to live.'

ALYDON, *THE DALEKS*

'If you're so desperate to stay alive, why don't you live a little?'

THE DOCTOR, *NEW EARTH*

'Letting it get to you. You know what that's called? Being alive. Best thing there is. Being alive right now, that's all that counts.'

THE DOCTOR, *THE DOCTOR'S WIFE*

Chapter Three: The Darkness

'There are some corners of the universe which have bred the most terrible things. Things which act against everything that we believe in. They must be fought.'

THE DOCTOR, *THE MOONBASE*

LONELINESS

'You can spend the rest of your life with me, but I can't spend the rest of mine with you. I have to live on. Alone. That's the curse of the Time Lords.'

THE DOCTOR, *SCHOOL REUNION*

'They leave. Because they should. Or they find someone else. And some of them — some of them forget me. I suppose in the end... they break my heart.'

THE DOCTOR, *THE NEXT DOCTOR*

'If one's interest is held, loneliness does not exist.'

CAMECA, *THE AZTECS*

'I can't stand burnt toast. I loathe bus stations. Terrible places, full of lost luggage and lost souls.'

THE DOCTOR, *GHOST LIGHT*

SADNESS

'Children cry because they want attention, because they're hurt or afraid. But when they cry silently, it's because they just can't stop. Any parent knows that.'

THE DOCTOR, *THE BEAST BELOW*

'I know this great song about this bloke and his girlfriend. She drops the ring he gives her on the railway track, and when she goes back to get it, she's killed by the train and he's really miserable for the rest of his life. Oh, it's fantastic.'

ACE, *THE HAPPINESS PATROL*

SALLY: I love old things. They make me feel sad.

KATHY: What's good about sad?

SALLY: It's happy for deep people.

BLINK

'Happiness is nothing unless it exists side by side with sadness.'

THE DOCTOR, *THE HAPPINESS PATROL*

ENEMIES

'You can always judge a man by the quality of his enemies.'

THE DOCTOR, *REMEMBRANCE OF THE DALEKS*

'Do you know any nice people? You know, ordinary people, not power-crazed nutters trying to take over the galaxy?'

ACE, *SURVIVAL*

LEELA: It is fitting to celebrate the death of an enemy.

THE DOCTOR: Not in my opinion.

HORROR OF FANG ROCK

'If Hitler invaded hell, I would give a favourable reference to the Devil.'

WINSTON CHURCHILL, *VICTORY OF THE DALEKS*

'Am I addressing the Consciousness? … Thank you. If I might observe, you infiltrated this civilisation by means of warp-shunt technology. So, may I suggest, with the greatest respect, that you… shunt off?'

THE DOCTOR, *ROSE*

THE DOCTOR: Mrs Gillyflower, you have no idea what you are dealing with. In the wrong hands, that venom could wipe out all life on this planet.

MRS GILLYFLOWER: Do you know what these are? The wrong hands.

THE CRIMSON HORROR

'Only a fool defends his enemies.'

TEGANA, *MARCO POLO*

'You know, my dear, there's something very satisfying in destroying something that's evil, don't you think?'

THE DOCTOR, *THE SAVAGES*

'Your evil is my good. I am Sutekh the Destroyer. Where I tread I leave nothing but dust and darkness. I find that good.'

SUTEKH, *PYRAMIDS OF MARS*

FEAR

'Fear makes companions of all of us.'

THE DOCTOR, *AN UNEARTHLY CHILD*

'Don't run. Now, I know you're scared, but never run when you're scared.'

THE DOCTOR, *LET'S KILL HITLER*

HOUSE: Fear me. I've killed hundreds of Time Lords.

THE DOCTOR: Fear me. I've killed all of them.

THE DOCTOR'S WIFE

'Safe? No, of course you're not safe. There's about a billion other things out there just waiting to burn your whole world. But, if you want to pretend you're safe, just so you can sleep at night? OK, you're safe. But you're not really.'

THE DOCTOR, *DAY OF THE MOON*

'Some things are better left undone, and I have a feeling that this is one of them.'

THE DOCTOR, *THE TOMB OF THE CYBERMEN*

'You know when grown-ups tell you everything's going to be fine and you think they're probably lying to make you feel better? … Everything's going to be fine.'

THE DOCTOR, *THE ELEVENTH HOUR*

'You must throw off these suspicions. They're based on fear, and fear breeds hatred and war.'

TEMMOSUS, *THE DALEKS*

RORY: I will take you apart cog by cog and melt you down when all this is over.

ROBOT 1: Oh, I'm so scared. Actually, I might be. A little bit of oil just came out.

DINOSAURS ON A SPACESHIP

'One only harms that which one fears.'

MONARCH, *FOUR TO DOOMSDAY*

'Fear itself is largely an illusion. And at my age, there's little left to fear.'

THE DOCTOR, *THE FIVE DOCTORS*

DEATH

'It all just disappears, doesn't it? Everything you are, gone in a moment, like breath on a mirror.'

THE DOCTOR, *THE TIME OF THE DOCTOR*

'It is never easy to die.'

STAEL, *IMAGE OF THE FENDAHL*

'All things pass away.'

CHO-JE, *PLANET OF THE SPIDERS*

'Death is always more frightening when it strikes invisibly.'

THE MASTER, *TERROR OF THE AUTONS*

'Since when did an undertaker keep office hours? The dead don't die on schedule.'

CHARLES DICKENS, *THE UNQUIET DEAD*

'The Church of the Papal Mainframe apologises for your death. The relevant afterlives have been notified.'

COLONEL ALBERO, *THE TIME OF THE DOCTOR*

RORY: What's wrong with you? What's she done to you?

THE DOCTOR: Poisoned me. But I'm fine. Well, no, I'm dying, but I've got a plan.

AMY: What plan?

THE DOCTOR: Not dying.

LET'S KILL HITLER

'With one basic difference, the living are very much like the dead. Who was it said the living are just the dead on holiday?'

THE DOCTOR, *DESTINY OF THE DALEKS*

'If Ben was killed by that damn blasted machine, there'll be anger in his soul. And men that die like that don't never rest easy.'

REUBEN, *HORROR OF FANG ROCK*

'That is the smell of death, Peri. Ancient musk, heavy in the air. Fruit-soft flesh, peeling from white bones. The unholy, unburiable smell of Armageddon. Nothing quite so evocative as one's sense of smell, is there?'

THE DOCTOR, *THE TWO DOCTORS*

'I'll expose him, ruin him, have him arrested, but I won't be his executioner. No one has that right.'

THE DOCTOR, *THE ENEMY OF THE WORLD*

THE DOCTOR: You know, the window's quite out of place. It's not in character at all.

ROMANA: Will you stop babbling about the architecture? We're having a serious conversation about death.

THE DOCTOR: Well, architecture's quite a serious subject.

THE POWER OF KROLL

'It doesn't end there. That is how it all begins again, with a killing. It doesn't end. That ends as it has always done, in chaos and despair. It ends as it begins, in the darkness. Is that what you all want?'

PANNA, *KINDA*

AMY: So, what's wrong with me?

RIVER: Nothing. You're fine.

THE DOCTOR: Everything. You're dying.

RIVER: Doctor!

THE DOCTOR: Yes, you're right. If we lie to her, she'll get all better.

FLESH AND STONE

'Welcome. You are unauthorised. Your death will now be implemented. Welcome. You will experience a tingling sensation and then death. Remain calm while your life is extracted.'

ANTIBODY, *LET'S KILL HITLER*

THE DOCTOR: I know a rogue when I see a rogue and I've no desire to die in the company of a rogue. Have you any desire to die in the company of a rogue?

ROMANA: I'd rather not die at all.

THE DOCTOR: I know that feeling.

THE POWER OF KROLL

THE DOCTOR: Alive isn't sad.

IDRIS: It's sad when it's over.

THE DOCTOR'S WIFE

'That's the charm of a ghost story, isn't it? Not the scares and chills, that's just for children, but the hope of some contact with the great beyond. We all want some message from that place. It's the Creator's greatest mystery that we're allowed no such consolation. The dead stay silent, and we must wait.'

QUEEN VICTORIA, *TOOTH AND CLAW*

DICKENS: This is precisely the sort of cheap mummery I strive to unmask. Séances? Nothing but luminous tambourines and a squeeze box concealed between the knees. This girl knows nothing.

THE DOCTOR: Now, don't antagonise her. I love a happy medium.

THE UNQUIET DEAD

'When it comes to death, quantity is so much more satisfying than quality.'

FENRIC, *THE CURSE OF FENRIC*

'You've been trying to kill me for centuries, and here I am, dying of old age. If you want something done, do it yourself.'

THE DOCTOR, *THE TIME OF THE DOCTOR*

WAR

'The universe is at war, Doctor. Name one planet whose history is not littered with atrocities and ambition for empire. It is a universal way of life.'

DAVROS, *RESURRECTION OF THE DALEKS*

'You don't beg for peace, Princess. You win it.'

MARSHAL, *THE ARMAGEDDON FACTOR*

CONSTANTINE: Before this war began, I was a father and a grandfather. Now I am neither. But I'm still a doctor.

THE DOCTOR: Yeah. I know the feeling.

THE EMPTY CHILD

'A warrior doesn't talk, he acts.'

STAAL, *THE POISON SKY*

'Sir, please do not noogie me during combat prep.'

STRAX, *THE SNOWMEN*

'It is the right of every creature across the universe to survive, multiply and perpetuate its species. How else does the predator exist? We are all predators, Doctor. We kill, we devour, to live. Survival is all, you agree?'

THE NUCLEUS, *THE INVISIBLE ENEMY*

TEGANA: In battle all men face death.

THE DOCTOR: And few expect to meet it, hmmm?

MARCO POLO

'A child is not a weapon!'

THE DOCTOR, *A GOOD MAN GOES TO WAR*

'It used to be the Tiberion Spiral Galaxy. A million star systems, a hundred million worlds, a billion trillion people. It's not there any more. No more Tiberion Galaxy. No more Cybermen. It was effective… I feel like a monster sometimes… Because instead of mourning a billion trillion dead people, I just feel sorry for the poor blighter who had to press the button and blow it all up.'

PORRIDGE, *NIGHTMARE IN SILVER*

'War, a game played by politicians. We were just pawns in the game, but the pawns are fighting together now.'

VERSHININ, *THE CURSE OF FENRIC*

'War is another world. You cannot apply the politics of peace to what I did. To what any of us did.'

KAHLER-JEX, *A TOWN CALLED MERCY*

'A heroic war cry to apparently peaceful ends is one of the greatest weapons a politician has.'

MAVIC CHEN, *THE DALEKS' MASTER PLAN*

'I killed, and I caused to have killed. I sent young men and women to their deaths, but here I am, still alive and it does tend to haunt you. Living, after so much of the other thing.'

PALMER, *HIDE*

'It is not patriotism to lead people into a war they cannot win.'

SELRIS, *THE KROTONS*

'Victory should be naked!'

JOSEPH GREEN, *WORLD WAR THREE*

'You're caught in an impasse of logic. You've discovered the recipe for everlasting peace. Congratulations. I'm terribly pleased.'

THE DOCTOR, *DESTINY OF THE DALEKS*

'What better way to destroy your enemies than to let them destroy themselves.'

IXTA, *THE AZTECS*

THE DOCTOR: They keep coming back, don't you see? Every time I negotiate, I try to understand. Well, not today. No. Today, I honour the victims first. His, the Master's, the Daleks', all the people who died because of my mercy!

AMY: You see, this is what happens when you travel alone for too long.

A TOWN CALLED MERCY

'Strategy is worth a hundred lances.'

SALADIN, *THE CRUSADE*

'You're a man for talk, I can see that. You like a table and a ring of men – a parley here, arrangements there. But when you men of eloquence have stunned each other with your words, we – we the soldiers – have to face it out. On some half-started morning while you speakers lie abed, armies settle everything, giving sweat, sinew, bodies, aye, and life itself.'

LORD LEICESTER, *THE CRUSADE*

AMY: We come in peace!

RORY: When has that ever worked?

LET'S KILL HITLER

'Bullets and bombs aren't the answer to everything.'

THE DOCTOR, *THE SEEDS OF DOOM*

'Weapons. Always useless in the end.'

THE DOCTOR, *REMEMBRANCE OF THE DALEKS*

'Pacifism only works when everybody feels the same.'

IAN, *THE DALEKS*

'I don't think that right is on anyone's side in war, Miss Hardaker.'

REVEREND WAINWRIGHT, *THE CURSE OF FENRIC*

'When you get back to Skaro, you'll all be national heroes. Everybody will want to hear about your adventures... So be careful how you tell that story, will you? Don't glamourise it. Don't make war sound like an exciting and thrilling game... Tell them about the members of your mission that will not be returning... Tell them about the fear, otherwise your people might relish the idea of war. We don't want that.'

THE DOCTOR, *PLANET OF THE DALEKS*

ACE: It's a missile convoy.

THE DOCTOR: A *nuclear* missile convoy.

ACE: How do you know?

THE DOCTOR: It has a graveyard stench.

BATTLEFIELD

'All over the world, fools are poised ready to let death fly. Machines of death, Morgaine, are screaming from above. A light, brighter than the sun. Not a war between armies nor a war between nations, but just death. Death gone mad. A child looks up at the sky, his eyes turn to cinders. No more tears, only ashes. Is this honour? Is this war? Are these the weapons you would use? Tell me!'

THE DOCTOR, *BATTLEFIELD*

IZLYR: We reject violence, except in self-defence.

JO: What about Ssorg's gun? This is supposed to be a peaceful mission.

IZLYR: Unfortunately, in order to preserve peace, it is necessary to survive.

THE CURSE OF PELADON

THE MILITARY

THE DOCTOR: Well quite frankly, Brigadier, I fail to see the value of a lot of idiot soldiers clumping about the place.

THE BRIGADIER: Oh, you've been thankful enough sometimes, Doctor.

THE GREEN DEATH

'I sometimes think that military intelligence is a contradiction in terms.'

THE DOCTOR, *TERROR OF THE AUTONS*

THE DOCTOR: Hello. Who are you?

RESTAC: Restac, Military commander.

THE DOCTOR: Oh dear, really? There's always a military, isn't there?

COLD BLOOD

THE DOCTOR: Never cared much for the word impregnable. Sounds a bit too much like unsinkable.

HARRY: What's wrong with unsinkable?

THE DOCTOR: Nothing, as the iceberg said to the *Titanic*... Glug, glug, glug...

ROBOT

'That's typical of the military mind, isn't it? Present them with a new problem, and they start shooting at it.'

THE DOCTOR, *DOCTOR WHO AND THE SILURIANS*

'Among all the varied wonders of the universe there's nothing so firmly clamped shut as the military mind.'

THE DOCTOR, *BATTLEFIELD*

'The military mind at its most scintillating. Faced with a problem they blast it off the face of the Earth.'

THE DOCTOR, *TERROR OF THE AUTONS*

'Chap with the wings there. Five rounds rapid.'

THE BRIGADIER, *THE DAEMONS*

THE TIME WAR

'The Time War. The whole universe convulsed. The Time War raged. Invisible to smaller species but devastating to higher forms.'

THE GELTH, *THE UNQUIET DEAD*

'Perhaps it's time. This is only the furthest edge of the Time War. But at its heart millions die every second. Lost in bloodlust and insanity. With Time itself resurrecting them to find new ways of dying, over and over again. A travesty of life.'

THE PARTISAN, *THE END OF TIME*

'I've had many faces, many lives. I don't admit to all of them. There's one life I've tried very hard to forget. He was the Doctor who fought in the Time War, and that was the day he did it. The day I did it. The day he killed them all. The last day of the Time War. The war to end all wars between my people and the Daleks. And in that battle there was a man with more blood on his hands than any other, a man who would commit a crime that would silence the universe. And that man was me.'

THE DOCTOR, *THE DAY OF THE DOCTOR*

'For a long time I thought I was just a survivor, but I'm not. I'm the winner. That's who I am. The Time Lord Victorious.'

THE DOCTOR, *THE WATERS OF MARS*

'Everything she did was so human. She brought you back to life but she couldn't control it. She brought you back for ever. That's something, I suppose. The final act of the Time War was life.'

THE DOCTOR, *UTOPIA*

DANGER

'Hello, I'm the Doctor! I believe you want to kill me.'

THE DOCTOR, *SILVER NEMESIS*

ROSE: Mauve?

THE DOCTOR: The universally recognised colour for danger.

ROSE: What happened to red?

THE DOCTOR: That's just humans. By everyone else's standards, red's camp. Oh, the misunderstandings. All those red alerts, all that dancing.'

THE EMPTY CHILD

'The situation, Lavel, is normal. It doesn't get much worse than that.'

THE BRIGADIER, *BATTLEFIELD*

'Arms. Legs. Neck. Head. Nose. I'm fine. Everyone else?'

THE DOCTOR, *MIDNIGHT*

THE DOCTOR: So much fuss over a little water.

PERI: No, but pink water…

THE DOCTOR: Are you frightened it might clash with what you're wearing?

PERI: No, I'm more concerned I might clash with what lives in it.

THE TRIAL OF A TIME LORD: MINDWARP

'Every time, it's rule one. Don't wander off. I tell them, I do. Rule one. There could be anything on this ship.'

THE DOCTOR, *THE GIRL IN THE FIREPLACE*

'A risk shared is a risk doubled.'

THE DOCTOR, *FRONTIOS*

TURLOUGH: We're running out of places to run.

TEGAN: It's the story of our lives.

THE AWAKENING

THE DOCTOR: We're up a gum tree without a paddle.

K-9: Define gum tree.

THE DOCTOR: Well, it's a tree that gives gum.

K-9: Explain use of paddle in gum tree.

THE DOCTOR: You wouldn't understand, K-9.

K-9: Affirmative.

THE HORNS OF NIMON

'We've found something. It looks like metal. Like some sort of seal. I've got a nasty feeling the word might be trapdoor. Not a good word, trapdoor. Never met a trapdoor I liked.'

THE DOCTOR, *THE IMPOSSIBLE PLANET*

'Don't wander off. Now, I'm not just saying don't wander off, I mean it. Otherwise you'll wander off and the next thing you know, somebody's going to have to start rescuing somebody.'

THE DOCTOR, *NIGHTMARE IN SILVER*

'Something's wrong… we haven't been attacked yet.'

THE DOCTOR, *BATTLEFIELD*

'Jamie, we're already in the lion's den. What we've got to concentrate on is keeping our heads out of his mouth.'

THE DOCTOR, *FURY FROM THE DEEP*

VIOLENCE

SEAN: You are so on the team. Next week we've got the Crown and Anchor. We're going to annihilate them.

THE DOCTOR: Annihilate? No. No violence, do you understand me? Not while I'm around. Not today, not ever. I'm the Doctor, the Oncoming Storm... and you basically meant beat them in a football match, didn't you?

SEAN: Yeah.

THE DOCTOR: Lovely. What sort of time?

THE LODGER

'Sad really, isn't it? People spend all their time making nice things, and other people come along and break them.'

THE DOCTOR, *THE ENEMY OF THE WORLD*

BROCK: His scarf killed Stimson!

THE DOCTOR: Arrest the scarf, then.

THE LEISURE HIVE

'Frightening, isn't it, to find there are others better versed in death than human beings.'

THE DOCTOR, *REMEMBRANCE OF THE DALEKS*

'Why can't people be nice to one another, just for a change? I mean, I'm an alien and you don't want to drag me into a swamp, do you? You do!'

THE DOCTOR, *FULL CIRCLE*

'There should have been another way.'

THE DOCTOR, *WARRIORS OF THE DEEP*

THE DOCTOR: When you find something brand new in the world, something you've never seen before, what's the next thing you look for?

STRAX: A grenade.

THE SNOWMEN

ROMANA: You should go into partnership with a glazier. You'd have a truly symbiotic working relationship.

DUGGAN: What?

ROMANA: I'm just pointing out that you break a lot of glass.

DUGGAN: You can't make an omelette without breaking eggs.

ROMANA: If you wanted an omelette, I'd expect to find a pile of broken crockery, a cooker in flames and an unconscious chef.

CITY OF DEATH

'Yes, that's your philosophy, isn't it? If it moves, hit it ... If you do that one more time, Duggan, I'm going to take very, very severe measures ... I'm going to ask you not to.'

THE DOCTOR, *CITY OF DEATH*

'Killing me isn't going to help you. It isn't going to do me much good either, is it?'

THE DOCTOR, *THE FACE OF EVIL*

'You know, I am so constantly outwitting the opposition, I tend to forget the delights and satisfaction of the gentle art of fisticuffs.'

THE DOCTOR, *THE ROMANS*

'If you're bleeding, look for a man with scars.'

LEELA, THE ROBOTS OF DEATH

'I strongly advise the issuing of scissor grenades, limbo vapour and triple blast brain splitters... Remember, we are going to the north.'

STRAX, *THE CRIMSON HORROR*

LITEFOOT: I think this entire enterprise is extremely rash and ill-considered.

THE DOCTOR: My dear Litefoot, I've got a lantern and a pair of waders, and possibly the most fearsome piece of hand artillery in all England. What could possibly go wrong?

LITEFOOT: Well, *that* for a start. It hasn't been fired for fifty years. If you try to use it, it'll probably explode in your face.

THE DOCTOR: Explode? Unthinkable. It was made in Birmingham.

THE TALONS OF WENG-CHIANG

'If there's one thing I can't stand, it's being tortured by someone with cold hands.'

THE DOCTOR, *CITY OF DEATH*

'Whereas yours is a simple case of sociopathy, Dibber, my malaise is much more complex. "A deep-rooted maladjustment", my psychiatrist said. "Brought on by an infantile inability to come to terms with the more pertinent, concrete aspects of life" ... Mind you, I had just attempted to kill him.'

SABALOM GLITZ, *THE TRIAL OF A TIME LORD: THE MYSTERIOUS PLANET*

THE DOCTOR: Hello. I'm the Doctor.

VARNE: Unless you help us, you won't be for very much longer.

ATTACK OF THE CYBERMEN

'How is it wherever I go in the universe there are always people like you pointing guns or phasers or blasters?'

THE DOCTOR, *THE HORNS OF NIMON*

ROSE: Doctor, they've got guns.

THE DOCTOR: And I haven't. Which makes me the better person, don't you think? They can shoot me dead, but the moral high ground is mine.

ARMY OF GHOSTS

'That's what guns are for. Pull a trigger, end a life. Simple, isn't it… Why don't you do it, then? Look me in the eye, pull the trigger, end my life.'

THE DOCTOR, *THE HAPPINESS PATROL*

'Guns can seriously damage your health, you know!'

THE DOCTOR, *THE MARK OF THE RANI*

'Now drop your weapons, or I'll kill him with this deadly jelly baby.'

THE DOCTOR, *THE FACE OF EVIL*

NIMON: Silence. Later you will be questioned, tortured and killed.

THE DOCTOR: Well I hope you get it in the right order.

THE HORNS OF NIMON

THE INQUISITOR: I find primitive physical violence distressing.

THE DOCTOR: So do I, ma'am. Especially when I'm on the receiving end.

THE TRIAL OF A TIME LORD: THE MYSTERIOUS PLANET

STRAX: If she hasn't made contact by nightfall, I suggest a massive frontal assault on the factory, madam. Casualties can be kept to perhaps as little as eighty per cent.

VASTRA: I think there may be subtler ways of proceeding, Strax.

STRAX: Suit yourself.

THE CRIMSON HORROR

'I say, what a wonderful butler. He's so violent.'

THE DOCTOR, *CITY OF DEATH*

'You fought her off with a water pistol. I bloody love you!'

DONNA, *THE FIRES OF POMPEII*

TYRANNY

'Conquered the Earth? You poor, pathetic creatures. Don't you realise? Before you attempt to conquer the Earth, you will have to destroy all living matter.'

THE DOCTOR, *THE DALEK INVASION OF EARTH*

'There are only two sides today, Barbara. Those who rule by fear and treachery, and those who fight for reason and justice. Anyone who betrays these principles is worse than the devil in hell!'

JULES RENAN, *THE REIGN OF TERROR*

THE DOCTOR: I'll say one thing for you, Davros. Your conversation is totally predictable. You're like a deranged child, all this talk of killing, revenge and destruction.

DAVROS: It is the only path to ultimate power.

RESURRECTION OF THE DALEKS

'Krynoid on the outside, a madman lurking inside, not a happy situation.'

THE DOCTOR, *THE SEEDS OF DOOM*

'One man's law is another man's crime.'

THE DOCTOR, *THE EDGE OF DESTRUCTION*

'Bad laws were made to be broken.'

THE DOCTOR, *THE MACRA TERROR*

ROMANA: The Black Guardian's a real threat.

THE DOCTOR: Some galactic hobo with ideas above his station, the cosmos is full of them.

THE LEISURE HIVE

'This is all too easy. A great pity. These facile victories only leave me hungry for more conquest.'

THE MASTER, *CASTROVALVA*

'What is the one thing evil cannot face? Not ever? ... Itself.'

THE DOCTOR, *KINDA*

'Intruders from other planets always say they wish to talk, but all they mean to do is destroy.'

SECOND SENSORITE, *THE SENSORITES*

'Doctor, I offer you power. Power to corrupt, to destroy. Think of the exhilaration of that power. Serve me and live.'

THE CELESTIAL TOYMAKER, *THE CELESTIAL TOYMAKER*

THE NUCLEUS: The age of man is over, Doctor. The age of the virus has begun.

THE DOCTOR: I've heard it all before. You megalomaniacs are all the same.

THE INVISIBLE ENEMY

'Revenge! Best served hot.'

THE MASTER, *LAST OF THE TIME LORDS*

THE DOCTOR: We have the power to do anything we like. Absolute power over every particle in the universe. Everything that has ever existed or ever will exist. As from this moment – are you listening to me, Romana? … Because, if you're not listening, I can make you listen because I can do anything… As from this moment there's no such thing as free will in the entire universe. There's only my will, because I possess the Key to Time!

ROMANA: Doctor – are you all right?

THE DOCTOR: Well, of course I'm all right. But supposing I wasn't all right? Well, this thing makes me feel in such a way I'd be very worried if I felt like that about someone else feeling like this about that. Do you understand?

THE ARMAGEDDON FACTOR

A CARNIVAL OF MONSTERS

'Don't fire until you see the green of its tentacles.'

THE DOCTOR, *HORROR OF FANG ROCK*

ELLIOT: Have you met monsters before?

THE DOCTOR: Yeah.

ELLIOT: You scared of them?

THE DOCTOR: No, they're scared of me.

THE HUNGRY EARTH

LIZ: I deal with facts, not science fiction ideas.

THE BRIGADIER: Miss Shaw, I'm not a fool. I don't chase shadows. What you don't understand is that there might, there is a remote possibility that outside your cosy little world other things could exist.

SPEARHEAD FROM SPACE

'You know, just once I'd like to meet an alien menace that wasn't immune to bullets.'

THE BRIGADIER, *ROBOT*

ROMANA: Are there many creatures like that in other worlds?

THE DOCTOR: Millions. Millions! You shouldn't have volunteered if you are scared of a little thing like that.

THE RIBOS OPERATION

'Makes you wonder what could be so bad it doesn't actually mind us thinking it's a vampire.'

THE DOCTOR, *VAMPIRES OF VENICE*

THE DOCTOR: Any intelligent life form?

TARON: Oh, yes. The Spiridons. They're invisible.

THE DOCTOR: I'd very much like to see one of them.

PLANET OF THE DALEKS

IAN: Maybe we could talk to them, make them understand?

THE DOCTOR: Apart from rubbing our back legs together like some sort of grasshopper, I doubt if we could get on speaking terms with them.

THE WEB PLANET

'Well, I never thought I'd fire in anger at a dratted caterpillar…'

THE BRIGADIER, *THE GREEN DEATH*

COMMANDER: I don't understand. Why was it necessary for him to make himself look human?

THE DOCTOR: Well, if you'd seen a Usurian you'd know what I mean. They look like sea kale with eyes. I mean, would you take orders from a lump of seaweed?

THE SUN MAKERS

'When you've travelled as much as I have, you'll learn never to judge by appearances. These creatures may look like chickens, but for all we know, they're the intelligent life form on this planet.'

THE DOCTOR, *CARNIVAL OF MONSTERS*

BRIAN: Are those pterodactyls?

THE DOCTOR: Yes. On any other occasion, I'd be thrilled. Exposed on a beach, less thrilled.

DINOSAURS ON A SPACESHIP

THE DOCTOR: Excuse me, do you mind not farting while I'm saving the world?

JOSEPH GREEN: Would you rather silent but deadly?

ALIENS OF LONDON

THE DOCTOR: Somehow the Krynoid can channel its power to other plants. All the vegetation on this planet is about to turn hostile.

THACKERAY: You mean like aggressive rhubarb?

THE DOCTOR: Yes, aggressive rhubarb.

BERESFORD: What about homicidal gooseberries?

THE SEEDS OF DOOM

'You really can't go on calling yourself Morbius. There's very little of Morbius left. Why don't you think of another name? Potpourri would be appropriate.'

THE DOCTOR, *THE BRAIN OF MORBIUS*

'We're being attacked by statues in a crashed ship. There isn't a manual for this.'

THE DOCTOR, *FLESH AND STONE*

'As my dear mother always used to say – born under the sign of Patus, middle cusp, she was – if you can help anybody, like preventing them from being eaten by a monster, then do so. They might be grateful.'

ORGANON, *THE CREATURE FROM THE PIT*

RANQUIN: Kroll is all wise, all seeing—

THE DOCTOR: All baloney. Kroll couldn't tell the difference between you and me and a half an acre of dandelion and burdock.

THE POWER OF KROLL

THE DOCTOR: A Nestene is a ruthlessly aggressive intelligent alien life form.

JO: Well, what do they look like?

THE DOCTOR: Well I suspect myself their basic form is analogous to a cephalopod.

JO: What's a cephalopod?

THE DOCTOR: An octopus. I thought you took an A level in science.

JO: I didn't say I passed.

TERROR OF THE AUTONS

DALEKS

'Exterminate!'

THE DALEKS, VARIOUS

COMMANDER SHARREL: You know the Daleks?

THE DOCTOR: Oh, better than you could possibly imagine.

DESTINY OF THE DALEKS

'Advance and attack! Attack and destroy! Destroy and rejoice!'

THE DALEKS, *THE CHASE*

'Daleks are such boring conversationalists.'

THE DOCTOR, *REMEMBRANCE OF THE DALEKS*

'Inside each of those shells is a living, bubbling lump of hate.'

THE DOCTOR, *DEATH TO THE DALEKS*

'You are my enemy! And I am yours. You are everything I despise. The worst thing in all creation. I've defeated you – time and time again I've defeated you. I sent you back into the Void. I saved the whole of reality from you. I am the Doctor. And you are the Daleks.'

THE DOCTOR, *VICTORY OF THE DALEKS*

THE DOCTOR: I thought you'd run out of ways to make me sick … You think hatred is beautiful.

DALEK PRIME MINISTER: Perhaps that is why we have never been able to kill you.

ASYLUM OF THE DALEKS

GILMORE: Doctor, my men have just put three high-explosive grenades into a confined area. Nothing even remotely human could have survived that.

THE DOCTOR: That's the point group, Group Captain, it isn't even remotely human.

REMEMBRANCE OF THE DALEKS

'If you're supposed to be the superior race of the universe, why don't you try climbing after us?'

THE DOCTOR, *DESTINY OF THE DALEKS*

ADAM: Great big alien death machine defeated by a flight of stairs …

DALEK: Elevate!

DALEK

DALEK: Have pity!

THE DOCTOR: Why should I? You never did.

DALEK

'Pity? I have no understanding of the word. It is not registered in my vocabulary bank. Exterminate.'

DALEK, *GENESIS OF THE DALEKS*

DALEKS: Save the Daleks! Save the Daleks!

THE DOCTOR: Well. This is new.

ASYLUM OF THE DALEKS

GILMORE: What am I dealing with? Little green men?

THE DOCTOR: No, little green blobs in bonded-polycarbide armour.

REMEMBRANCE OF THE DALEKS

'It's called a Dalek. And it's not just metal, it's alive … Inside that shell is a creature born to hate. Whose only thought is to destroy everything and everyone that isn't a Dalek too. It won't stop until it's killed every human being alive.'

THE DOCTOR, *DALEKS IN MANHATTAN*

'Never underestimate the Daleks.'

THE DOCTOR, *PLANET OF THE DALEKS*

'One Dalek is capable of exterminating all!'

DALEK, *THE DALEKS' MASTER PLAN*

'It can do many things … But the thing it does most efficiently is exterminate human beings. It destroys them, without mercy, without conscience. It destroys them. Utterly. Completely.'

THE DOCTOR, *THE POWER OF THE DALEKS*

'Today, the Kaled race is ended, consumed in a fire of war, but from its ashes will rise a new race, the supreme creature, the ultimate conqueror of the universe – the Dalek! The action you take today is the beginning of a journey that will take the Daleks to their destiny of universal and absolute supremacy.'

DAVROS, *GENESIS OF THE DALEKS*

'The moment that we forget that we're dealing with people, then we're no better off than the machines that we came here to destroy. When we start acting and thinking like the Daleks, Taron, the battle is lost.'

THE DOCTOR, *PLANET OF THE DALEKS*

'But if I kill, wipe out a whole intelligent life form, then I become like them. I'd be no better than the Daleks.'

THE DOCTOR, *GENESIS OF THE DALEKS*

'The Daleks will triumph. We cannot fail. The Daleks' true destiny is to rule the universe.'

SUPREME DALEK, *RESURRECTION OF THE DALEKS*

THE DOCTOR: The Daleks have failed! Why don't you finish the job and make the Daleks extinct. Rid the universe of your filth. Why don't you just die?

DALEK: You would make a good Dalek.

DALEK

'Sealed inside your casing. Not feeling anything, ever, from birth to death, locked inside a cold metal cage. Completely alone. That explains your voice. No wonder you scream.'

THE DOCTOR, *DOOMSDAY*

'You stupid tin boxes.'

THE MASTER, *FRONTIER IN SPACE*

DALEK JAST: Daleks are supreme. Humans are weak.

DALEK SEC: But there are millions of humans and only four of us. If we are supreme, why are we not victorious? The Cult of Skaro was created by the Emperor for this very purpose. To imagine new ways of survival.

DALEK THAY: But we must remain pure.

DALEK SEC: No, Dalek Thay. Our purity has brought us to extinction.

DALEKS IN MANHATTAN

THE DOCTOR: Dalek hunting is a terminal pastime.

ACE: So what are we doing?

THE DOCTOR: Dalek hunting.

REMEMBRANCE OF THE DALEKS

'We are entombed, but we live on. This is only the beginning. We will prepare. We will grow stronger. When the time is right, we will emerge and take our rightful place as the supreme power of the universe!'

DALEK, *GENESIS OF THE DALEKS*

'The trouble with Daleks is, they take so long to say anything. Probably die of boredom before they shoot me.'

THE DOCTOR, *THE TIME OF THE DOCTOR*

SUPREME DALEK: You are the Doctor. You must be exterminated.

THE DOCTOR: Don't mess with me, sweetheart.

VICTORY OF THE DALEKS

DALEK SEC: My Daleks, just understand this. If you choose death and destruction, then death and destruction will choose you.

DALEK THAY: Incorrect. We will always survive.

EVOLUTION OF THE DALEKS

'The Daleks are never defeated!'

SUPREME DALEK, *PLANET OF THE DALEKS*

'They survive. They always survive, while I lose everything.'

THE DOCTOR, *DALEKS IN MANHATTAN*

'Just touch these two strands together and the Daleks are finished. Have I that right? ... You see, some things could be better with the Daleks. Many future worlds will become allies just because of their fear of the Daleks ... Listen, if someone who knew the future pointed out a child to you and told you that that child would grow up totally evil, to be a ruthless dictator who would destroy millions of lives, could you then kill that child? ... Do I have the right?'

THE DOCTOR, *GENESIS OF THE DALEKS*

CYBERMEN

KRAIL: Feelings? I do not understand that word.

THE DOCTOR: Emotions. Love, pride, hate, fear. Have you no emotions, sir?

THE TENTH PLANET

BENOIT: Have you no mercy?

CYBERMAN: It is unnecessary.

THE MOONBASE

CYBERLEADER: Daleks, be warned. You have declared war upon the Cybermen.

DALEK SEC: This is not war. This is pest control.

DOOMSDAY

'We think of the humans. We think of their difference and their pain. They suffer in the skin. They must be upgraded.'

CYBERMAN, *THE AGE OF STEEL*

CYBERMAN: You know our ways. You must be destroyed.

THE DOCTOR: Yes, well, I was afraid you'd get back to that.

THE WHEEL IN SPACE

'You've no home planet, no influence, nothing. You're just a pathetic bunch of tin soldiers skulking about the galaxy in an ancient spaceship.'

THE DOCTOR, *REVENGE OF THE CYBERMEN*

'Oh, Lumic, you're a clever man. I'd call you a genius, except I'm in the room. But everything you've invented, you did to fight your sickness. And that's brilliant. That is so human. But once you get rid of sickness and mortality, then what's there to strive for, eh? The Cybermen won't advance. You'll just stop. You'll stay like this for ever. A metal Earth with metal men and metal thoughts, lacking the one thing that makes this planet so alive. People. Ordinary, stupid, brilliant people.'

THE DOCTOR, *THE AGE OF STEEL*

'The trouble with Cybermen is they've got hydraulic muscles, and of course hydraulic brains to go with them.'

THE DOCTOR, *REVENGE OF THE CYBERMEN*

THE DOCTOR: That's a living brain jammed inside a cybernetic body, with a heart of steel. All emotions removed.

ROSE: Why no emotions?

THE DOCTOR: Because it hurts.

RISE OF THE CYBERMEN

'It's hard to fight an enemy that uses your armies as spare parts.'

PORRIDGE, *NIGHTMARE IN SILVER*

DALEK SEC: You are superior in only one respect.

CYBERLEADER: What is that?

DALEK SEC: You are better at dying.

DOOMSDAY

CYBERLEADER: If humans had not had the resources of Voga, the Cyber War would have ended in glorious triumph.

THE DOCTOR: It was a glorious triumph, for human ingenuity. They discovered your weakness and invented the glitter gun, and that was the end of Cybermen, except as gold-plated souvenirs that people use as hat stands.

REVENGE OF THE CYBERMEN

CYBERMAN: You are the Doctor.

THE DOCTOR: Correct. And the Doctor always gives you a choice. Deactivate yourself, or I deactivate you.

CLOSING TIME

SONTARANS

'That's a Sontaran spaceship, to be precise, and tremendously powerful for its size, just like its owner.'

THE DOCTOR, *THE TIME WARRIOR*

SARAH: You killed him!

STYRE: That is my function. I am a warrior.

THE SONTARAN EXPERIMENT

'Sontarans never do anything without a military reason.'

THE DOCTOR, *THE SONTARAN EXPERIMENT*

STOR: I am Commander Stor, of the Sontaran Special Space Service.

THE DOCTOR: The SSSS. Isn't that carrying alliteration a little far?

THE INVASION OF TIME

'You have a primary and secondary reproductive cycle. It is an inefficient system, you should change it.'

LINX, *THE TIME WARRIOR*

THE DOCTOR: Sontaran. Clone warrior race. Factory produced, whole legions at a time. Two genders is a bit further than he can count.

STRAX: Sir, do not discuss my reproductive cycle in front of enemy girls. It's embarrassing.

THE SNOWMEN

THE MASTER

'I am the Master, and you will obey me…'

THE MASTER, VARIOUS

'That's my best enemy. He likes to be known as the Master, don't you?'

THE DOCTOR, *THE FIVE DOCTORS*

THE MASTER: I like it when you use my name.

THE DOCTOR: You chose it. Psychiatrist's field day.

THE SOUND OF DRUMS

'We are an explosive combination. One day, one of us might blot the other one out.'

THE DOCTOR, *SURVIVAL*

'Doctor, you're my intellectual equal. Almost. I have so few worthy opponents. When they've gone, I always miss them.'

THE MASTER, *TERROR OF THE AUTONS*

'He's on his last life, fighting to survive. And the science has shown us over and over, in the fight for survival there are no rules.'

THE DOCTOR, *DOCTOR WHO* (TV MOVIE)

'Envy is the beginning of all true greatness.'

THE MASTER, *LOGOPOLIS*

'Life is wasted on the living!'

THE MASTER, *DOCTOR WHO* (TV MOVIE)

THE MASTER: I am the Master!

PERI: So what? I'm Perpugilliam Brown and I can shout just as loud as you can.

PLANET OF FIRE

'I'm indestructible. The whole universe knows that.'

THE MASTER, *THE MARK OF THE RANI*

'I had estates. Do you remember my father's land back home? Pastures of red grass stretching far across the slopes of Mount Perdition. We used to run across those fields all day. Calling up at the sky. Look at us now.'

THE MASTER, *THE END OF TIME*

THE MASTER: Who else is there strong enough to give these humans the leadership they need?

THE DOCTOR: I seem to remember somebody else speaking like that. What was the bounder's name? Hitler. Yes, that's right, Adolf Hitler. Or was it Genghis Khan?

THE DAEMONS

'The drumming. Can't you hear it? I thought it would stop, but it never does. Never ever stops. Inside my head, the drumming, Doctor. The constant drumming.'

THE MASTER, *THE SOUND OF DRUMS*

'I'd like to try and take the Doctor alive if possible. If not, I'll blast him out of space. Pity though… I don't know, rocket fire at long range… somehow it lacks that personal touch.'

THE MASTER, *FRONTIER IN SPACE*

'Where I cannot win by stealth, I shall destroy. That way I cannot fail to win.'

THE MASTER, *THE KING'S DEMONS*

THE MASTER: One must rule or serve. That is the basic law of life. Why do you hesitate? Surely it's not loyalty to the Time Lords, who exiled you on one insignificant planet?

THE DOCTOR: You'll never understand, will you? I want to see the universe, not rule it.

COLONY IN SPACE

THE MASTER: I know this is going to be hard to believe, Doctor, but for once I mean you no harm.

THE DOCTOR: Like Alice, I try to believe three impossible things before breakfast.

THE FIVE DOCTORS

'You're a genius. You're stone cold brilliant, you are. I swear, you really are. But you could be so much more. You could be beautiful. With a mind like that, we could travel the stars. It would be my honour. Cause you don't need to own the universe. Just see it. To have the privilege of seeing the whole of time and space. That's ownership enough.'

THE DOCTOR, *THE END OF TIME*

MEL: How utterly evil!

THE MASTER: Thank you.

THE TRIAL OF A TIME LORD: THE ULTIMATE FOE

HOW INSULTING!

'You're a clumsy, ham-fisted idiot.'

THE DOCTOR, *THE ARK IN SPACE*

'I admire bravery and loyalty, sir. You have both of these. But, unfortunately you haven't any brain at all. I hate fools.'

THE DOCTOR, *THE CRUSADE*

'You swede-bashing cretin.'

COLBY, *IMAGE OF THE FENDAHL*

CHORLEY: There's no sense in us losing our temper, Miss Travers. I'm sorry that my journalistic style doesn't appeal to you, but there are millions of people it does.

ANNE: Yes, the gutter press has a very large following.

THE WEB OF FEAR

'You've been down here so long that you're beginning to think like worms.'

DORTMUN, *THE DALEK INVASION OF EARTH*

'Stubborn old mule'

THE DOCTOR, *HORROR OF FANG ROCK*

'My dear boy, if they had to deal with a man of your talents, they need hardly fear, need they?'

THE DOCTOR, *THE DALEK INVASION OF EARTH*

'They're policemen. We all know they're solid, sterling fellows, but their buttons are the brightest thing about them, don't you agree?'

JAGO, *THE TALONS OF WENG-CHIANG*

'Don't listen to him. It's just the ravings of a demented space tramp.'

ADRASTA, *THE CREATURE FROM THE PIT*

'You weak fool. You craven-hearted spineless poltroon.'

THE MASTER, *THE DEADLY ASSASSIN*

THE DOCTOR: I don't like your tone, sir.

CUTLER: And I don't like your face, nor your hair.

THE TENTH PLANET

'Yes, Packer. Our clever Doctor has outwitted you. Oh, then, that wouldn't be too difficult, would it?'

TOBIAS VAUGHN, *THE INVASION*

'Oh, I do not fear the thunder, you superstitious, dark-dodging decadent!'

HECTOR, *THE MYTH MAKERS*

'You're nothing. Nothing but a mass of superheated junk with delusions of grandeur.'

THE DOCTOR, *UNDERWORLD*

'Do hurry up! A hamster with a blunt penknife would do it quicker!'

THE DOCTOR, *THE ANDROIDS OF TARA*

'You, smart? Krelper, the wind whistles through your ears.'

STOTZ, *THE CAVES OF ANDROZANI*

'Yes, well I'll tell you something that should be of vital interest to you, Professor... That you, sir, are a nitwit!'

THE DOCTOR, *INFERNO*

'For such a little woman your mouth is too big.'

VILLAR, *THE WAR GAMES*

'Yes, let me guess. My theories appal you, my heresies outrage you, I never answer letters, and you don't like my tie.'

THE DOCTOR, *GHOST LIGHT*

'All right. All right, I'll confess... I confess you're a bigger idiot than I thought you were.'

THE DOCTOR, *THE DEADLY ASSASSIN*

'You know, you're a classic example of the inverse ratio between the size of the mouth and the size of the brain.'

THE DOCTOR, *THE ROBOTS OF DEATH*

'If you'd only try and use the little intelligence you have...'

THE DOCTOR, *INFERNO*

'Mickey, you were born in the dark.'

THE DOCTOR, *WORLD WAR THREE*

ROSE: My mother's cooking.

THE DOCTOR: Good. Put her on a slow heat and let her simmer.

WORLD WAR THREE

'You're happy to believe in something that's invisible, but if it's staring you in the face, nope, can't see it. There's a scientific explanation for that. You're thick.'

THE DOCTOR, *WORLD WAR THREE*

'Child, if only you'd think as an adult sometimes.'

THE DOCTOR, *THE DALEKS*

'You craven-gutted factory fodder.'

MANDREL, *THE SUN MAKERS*

'You male chauvinist bilge bag.'

ACE, *DRAGONFIRE*

'I can't decide whether you're a rogue, a halfwit or both!

THE DOCTOR, *THE REIGN OF TERROR*

'Jamie, it's a brilliant idea! It's so simple only you could have thought of it.'

THE DOCTOR, *THE DOMINATORS*

'Don't get all chippy with me, Vera Duckworth. Pop your clogs on and go and feed whippets.'

DONNA, *TURN LEFT*

'You hag! You perfidious hag! You virago! You harpy!'

ADA, *THE CRIMSON HORROR*

'Before we start all that, I just want to say thank you. Thank you, one and all. You ugly, fat-faced bunch of wet, snivelling traitors.'

THE MASTER, *THE SOUND OF DRUMS*

'Harry Sullivan is an imbecile!'

THE DOCTOR, *REVENGE OF THE CYBERMEN*

Chapter Four:
The Universe

'Well, it takes all sorts
to make a galaxy.'

THE DOCTOR, *TERROR OF THE ZYGONS*

THE INFINITE WONDER OF THE UNIVERSE

'We're at the very beginning, the new start of a solar system. Outside, the atoms are rushing towards each other. Fusing, coagulating, until minute little collections of matter are created. And so the process goes on and on until dust is formed. Dust then becomes solid entity. A new birth, of a sun and its planets.'

THE DOCTOR, *THE EDGE OF DESTRUCTION*

'There's always something to look at if you open your eyes.'

THE DOCTOR, *KINDA*

'It seems to me there's so much more to the world than the average eye is allowed to see. I believe, if you look hard, there are more wonders in this universe than you could ever have dreamed of... It's colour. Colour that holds the key. I can hear the colours – listen to them. Every time I step outside, I feel nature is shouting at me – "Come on! – Come and get me! Come on, come on! Capture my mystery!"'

VINCENT VAN GOGH, *VINCENT AND THE DOCTOR*

IAN: Doctor, why do you always show the greatest interest in the least important things?

THE DOCTOR: The least important things sometimes, my dear boy, lead to the greatest discoveries.

THE SPACE MUSEUM

THE DOCTOR: Millions of planets, millions of galaxies, and we're on this one. Molto bene. Bellissimo, says Donna, born in Chiswick. All you've got is a life of work and sleep, and telly and rent and tax and takeaway dinners, all birthdays and Christmases and two weeks holiday a year, and then you end up here. Donna Noble, citizen of the Earth, standing on a different planet. How about that Donna? Donna?

DONNA: Sorry, you were saying?

PLANET OF THE OOD

LIGHT: Everything is changing. All in flux. Nothing remains the same.

THE DOCTOR: Even remains change. It's this planet. It can't help itself.

GHOST LIGHT

'It's a big universe. Everything happens somewhere. Call it a coincidence. Call it an idea echoing among the stars. Personally, I call it a brilliant idea for a Christmas trip.'

THE DOCTOR, *THE DOCTOR, THE WIDOW AND THE WARDROBE*

'Planets come and go, stars perish. Matter disperses, coalesces, reforms into other patterns, other worlds. Nothing can be eternal.'

THE DOCTOR, *THE TRIAL OF A TIME LORD: THE MYSTERIOUS PLANET*

ADRIC: All those stars… Do you know them all?

THE DOCTOR: Well, just the interesting ones.

THE KEEPER OF TRAKEN

'There's all sorts of realities around us, different dimensions, billions of parallel universes all stacked up against each other. The Void is the space in between, containing absolutely nothing. Imagine that. Nothing. No light, no dark, no up, no down, no life, no time. Without end. My people called it the Void. The Eternals call it the Howling. But some people call it Hell.'

THE DOCTOR, *ARMY OF GHOSTS*

KERENSKY: I know what I'm doing. I am the foremost authority on temporal theory in the whole world. …

THE DOCTOR: Well, that's a very small place when you consider the size of the universe.

CITY OF DEATH

'You dreamt of another sky. New sun, new air, new life. A whole universe teeming with life. Why stand still when there's all that life out there.'

THE DOCTOR, *VOYAGE OF THE DAMNED*

'All the elements in your body were forged many, many millions of years ago, in the heart of a faraway star that exploded and died. That explosion scattered those elements across the desolations of deep space. After so, so many millions of years, these elements came together to form new stars and new planets. And on and on it went. The elements came together and burst apart, forming shoes and ships and sealing wax, and cabbages and kings. Until, eventually, they came together to make you. You are unique in the universe.'

THE DOCTOR, *THE RINGS OF AKHATEN*

'Life in some form will always go on.'

THE DOCTOR, *THE MUTANTS*

VINCENT: Hold my hand, Doctor. Try to see what I see. We are so lucky we are still alive to see this beautiful world. Look at the sky. It's not dark and black and without character. The black is in fact deep blue. And over there, lighter blue. And blowing through the blueness and the blackness, the wind swirling through the air and then, shining, burning, bursting through, the stars. Can you see how they roar their light? Everywhere we look, the complex magic of nature blazes before our eyes.

THE DOCTOR: I've seen many things, my friend. But you're right. Nothing quite as wonderful as the things you see.

VINCENT AND THE DOCTOR

'That's two impossible things we've seen so far tonight. Don't you love it when that happens?

THE DOCTOR, *THE LAZARUS EXPERIMENT*

THE INDOMITABLE HUMAN RACE

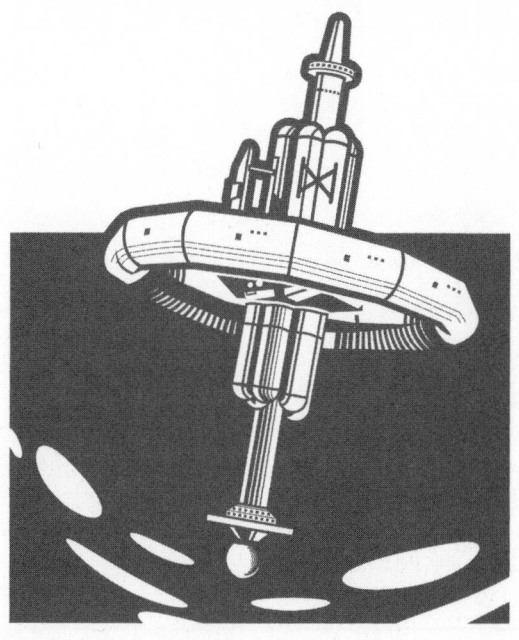

'Homo sapiens. What an inventive, invincible species. It's only a few million years since they crawled up out of the mud and learned to walk. Puny, defenceless bipeds. They survived flood, famine and plague. They survived cosmic wars and holocausts, and now here they are amongst the stars, waiting to begin a new life, ready to outsit eternity. They're indomitable. Indomitable!'

THE DOCTOR, *THE ARK IN SPACE*

'I love humans. Always seeing patterns in things that aren't there.'

THE DOCTOR, *DOCTOR WHO* (TV MOVIE)

'This day is ending. Humankind is weak. You shelter from the dark. And yet, you have built all this… My planet is gone, destroyed in a great war, yet versions of this city stand throughout history. The human race always continues.'

DALEK CAAN, *DALEKS IN MANHATTAN*

'It may be irrational of me, but human beings are quite my favourite species.'

THE DOCTOR, *THE ARK IN SPACE*

'… the great breakout … When your forefathers went leapfrogging across the solar system on their way to the stars. Asteroid belt's probably teeming with them now. New frontiersmen, pioneers waiting to spread across the galaxy like a tidal wave. Or a disease.'

THE DOCTOR, *THE INVISIBLE ENEMY*

'But what I wanted to say is, you know, when you're a kid, they tell you it's all, grow up, get a job, get married, get a house, have a kid, and that's it. But the truth is, the world is so much stranger than that. It's so much darker, and so much madder. And so much better.'

ELTON, *LOVE & MONSTERS*

'Consider the human species. They send hordes of settlers across space to breed, multiply, conquer and dominate. We have as much right to conquer you as you have to strike out across the stars.'

THE NUCLEUS, *THE INVISIBLE ENEMY*

'Funny little human brains. How do you get around in those things?'

THE DOCTOR, *THE DOCTOR DANCES*

'I'm a human being. Maybe not the stuff of legend but every bit as important as Time Lords, thank you.'

DONNA, *THE STOLEN EARTH*

'Don't you see, though? The ripe old smell of humans. You survived. Oh, you might have spent a million years evolving into clouds of gas, and another million as downloads, but you always revert to the same basic shape. The fundamental humans.'

THE DOCTOR, *UTOPIA*

'The nature of man, even in this day and age, hasn't altered at all. You still fear the unknown, like everyone else before you.'

STEVEN, *THE ARK*

'The human race makes sense out of chaos. Marking it out with weddings and Christmas and calendars. This whole process is beautiful, but only if it's being observed.'

THE DOCTOR, *THE RUNAWAY BRIDE*

THE DOCTOR: You know, I'll never understand the people of Earth. I have spent the day using, abusing, even trying to kill you. If you'd have behaved as I have, I should have been pleased at your demise.

PERI: It's called compassion, Doctor. It's the difference that remains between us.

THE TWIN DILEMMA

'Observe humanity. For all their faults they have such courage.'

DALEK SEC, *EVOLUTION OF THE DALEKS*

THE DARK SIDE OF HUMANITY

'Human race, greatest monsters of them all.'

THE MASTER, *LAST OF THE TIME LORDS*

VICTORIA: We've landed in a world of mad men.

THE DOCTOR: They're human beings, if that's what you mean, indulging their favourite past time. Trying to destroy each other.

THE ENEMY OF THE WORLD

'Some of my best friends are humans. When they get together in great numbers, other life forms sometimes suffer.'

THE DOCTOR, *THE INVISIBLE ENEMY*

'These Earth creatures are working to destroy the Sensorite nation. Their pleasant smile conceals sharp teeth, their soft words hide deadly threats.'

THE ADMINISTRATOR, *THE SENSORITES*

MOTHER OF MINE: He didn't just make himself human. He made himself an idiot.

SON OF MINE: Same thing, isn't it?

THE FAMILY OF BLOOD

'Your ancestors have a talent for self-destruction that borders on genius.'

THE DOCTOR, *IMAGE OF THE FENDAHL*

'Your species has the most amazing capacity for self-deception, matched only by its ingenuity when trying to destroy itself.'

THE DOCTOR, *REMEMBRANCE OF THE DALEKS*

'I gave them the wrong warning. I should've told them to run as fast as they can, run and hide because the monsters are coming. The human race.'

THE DOCTOR, *THE CHRISTMAS INVASION*

DALEK SEC: I feel… everything we wanted from mankind. Which is ambition, hatred, aggression. And war. Such a genius for war.

THE DOCTOR: No. That's not what humanity means.

DALEK SEC: I think it does. At heart this species is so very Dalek.

EVOLUTION OF THE DALEKS

DUGGAN: You're mad. You're insane. You're inhuman!

SCARLIONI: Quite so. When I compare my race to yours, human, I take the word inhuman as a great compliment.

CITY OF DEATH

AMBROSE: You could've let those things shoot me. You saved me.

THE DOCTOR: An eye for an eye. It's never the way. Now you show your son how wrong you were, how there's another way. You make him the best of humanity, in the way you couldn't be.

COLD BLOOD

SARAH: Don't you think that people have a right to choose what kind of life they want?

RUTH: People on Earth were allowed to choose. And see what kind of a world they made. Moral degradation, permissiveness, usury, cheating, lying, cruelty.

SARAH: There's also a lot of love and kindness and honesty. You've got a warped view of things.

INVASION OF THE DINOSAURS

EARTH

'I have a place in mind that's on the way, well, more or less, give or take a parsec or two. It's my home from home. It's called Earth.'

THE DOCTOR, *LOGOPOLIS*

ATRAXI: You are not of this world.

THE DOCTOR: No, but I've put a lot of work into it.

THE ELEVENTH HOUR

THE DOCTOR: And where are the Census Bureau going to send you next?

TREVOR: Earth. Have you been there?

THE DOCTOR: Once or twice.

TREVOR: Miserable sort of place.

THE DOCTOR: You're making me feel nostalgic.

THE HAPPINESS PATROL

ROMANA: Earth?!

THE DOCTOR: Well, I thought you'd be pleased!

ROMANA: I might have guessed. Your favourite planet.

THE DOCTOR: How do you know that?

ROMANA: Oh, everybody knows that.

THE STONES OF BLOOD

LIGHT: Earth. Why mention that wretched planet to me … I once spent centuries faithfully cataloguing all the species there, every organism from the smallest bacteria to the largest ichthyosaur. But no sooner had I finished than it all started changing. New species, new sub-species, evolution running amok. I had to start amending my entries. Oh, the task is endless.

THE DOCTOR: That's life.

GHOST LIGHT

SARAH: At least we're on Earth. I mean, just taste that air. I love that fresh smell just after a rain shower.

THE DOCTOR: Yes, it does have that peculiar Earthy smell.

THE ANDROID INVASION

THE HUMAN CONDITION

THE DOCTOR: I'd have to settle down. Get a house or something. A proper house with... with doors and things. Carpets. Me, living in a house. Now that, that is terrifying.

ROSE: You'd have to get a mortgage.

THE DOCTOR: No.

ROSE: Oh, yes.

THE DOCTOR: I'm dying. That's it. I'm dying. It is all over.

THE IMPOSSIBLE PLANET

'I want to sit in a pub and drink a pint of beer again. I want to walk in a park and watch a cricket match. Above all, I want to belong somewhere, do something, instead of this aimless drifting around in space.'

IAN, *THE CHASE*

'If you're going to sit there wallowing in self-pity, I'll bite your nose.'

THE DOCTOR, *THE BRAIN OF MORBIUS*

'Everyone's scared when they're little. I used to be terrified of getting lost. Used to have nightmares about it. And then I got lost. Blackpool beach, bank holiday Monday, about ten billion people. I was about six. My worst nightmare come true… The world ended. My heart broke. And then my mum found me. We had fish and chips, and she drove me home and she tucked me up and she told me a story.'

CLARA, *THE RINGS OF AKHATEN*

BOSS: I will not be angered. I will eradicate anger. It affects efficiency.

THE DOCTOR: Nonsense. Sometimes it helps, you know.

THE GREEN DEATH

'I worked as a waitress in a fast food café. Day in, day out, same boring routine. Same boring life. It was all wrong. It didn't feel like me that was doing it at all. I felt like I'd fallen from another planet and landed in this strange girl's body, but it wasn't me at all. I was meant to be somewhere else. Each night I'd walk home and I'd look up at the stars through the gaps in the clouds, and I tried to imagine where I really came from. I dreamed that one day everything would come right. I'd be carried off back home, back to my real mum and dad. Then it actually happened and I ended up here. Ended up working as a waitress again, only this time I couldn't dream about going nowhere else. There wasn't nowhere else to go.'

ACE, *DRAGONFIRE*

'Oh, come on. Don't be upset. Yes, you failed. You failed, but congratulations – failure's one of the basic freedoms.'

THE DOCTOR, *THE ROBOTS OF DEATH*

'I was born on that planet. And so was my mum and so was my dad. And that makes me officially the last human being in this room. Cause you're not human. You've had it all nipped and tucked and flattened till there's nothing left. Anything human got chucked in the bin. You're just skin, Cassandra. Lipstick and skin.'

ROSE, *THE END OF THE WORLD*

GALLIFREY AND THE TIME LORDS

'The sky's a burnt orange, with the Citadel enclosed in a mighty glass dome, shining under the twin suns. Beyond that, the mountains go on for ever. Slopes of deep red grass, capped with snow.'

THE DOCTOR, *GRIDLOCK*

'A man is the sum of his memories, you know. A Time Lord even more so.'

THE DOCTOR, *THE FIVE DOCTORS*

THE DOCTOR: You can't fight Time Lords, Romana.

ROMANA: You did once.

THE DOCTOR: Hmm. And lost.

FULL CIRCLE

'Oh, you should have seen it, that old planet. The second sun would rise in the south, and the mountains would shine. The leaves on the trees were silver and, when they caught the light every morning, it looked like a forest on fire. When the autumn came, the breeze would blow through the branches like a song.'

THE DOCTOR, *GRIDLOCK*

'They used to call it the Shining World of the Seven Systems. And on the Continent of Wild Endeavour, in the Mountains of Solace and Solitude, there stood the Citadel of the Time Lords, the oldest and most mighty race in the universe, looking down on the galaxies below. Sworn never to interfere, only to watch. Children of Gallifrey, taken from their families at the age of eight to enter the Academy. Some say that's when it all began. When he was a child. That's when the Master saw eternity. As a novice, he was taken for initiation. He stood in front of the Untempered Schism. It's a gap in the fabric of reality through which could be seen the whole of the Vortex. You stand there, eight years old, staring at the raw power of time and space, just a child. Some would be inspired, some would run away, and some would go mad.'

THE DOCTOR, *THE SOUND OF DRUMS*

'And what of the Time Lords? I always thought of you as such a pompous race. Ancient, dusty senators, so frightened of change and chaos. And of course, they're all but extinct. Only you. The last.'

MR FINCH, *SCHOOL REUNION*

IAN: You're treating us like children.

THE DOCTOR: Am I? The children of my civilisation would be insulted.

AN UNEARTHLY CHILD

'Because that's how I see the universe. Every waking second I can see what is, what was, what could be, what must not. That's the burden of the Time Lords, Donna. And I'm the only one left.'

THE DOCTOR, *THE FIRES OF POMPEII*

'In all my travellings throughout the universe, I have battled against evil, against power-mad conspirators. I should have stayed here. The oldest civilisation – decadent, degenerate and rotten to the core. Power-mad conspirators? Daleks, Sontarans... Cybermen! They're still in the nursery compared to us. Ten million years of absolute power, that's what it takes to be really corrupt!'

THE DOCTOR, *THE TRIAL OF A TIME LORD: THE ULTIMATE FOE*

'Smart bunch, Time Lords. No dress sense, dreadful hats, but smart.'

THE DOCTOR, *JOURNEY TO THE CENTRE OF THE TARDIS*

RECEPTION NURSE: Patient's name?

LEELA: Er, just the Doctor.

RECEPTION NURSE: Place of origin?

LEELA: Gallifrey.

RECEPTION NURSE: Ireland?

LEELA: Oh, I expect so.

THE INVISIBLE ENEMY

JOAN: Ever the artist. Where did you learn to draw?

JOHN SMITH: Gallifrey.

JOAN: Is that in Ireland?

JOHN SMITH: Yes, it must be, yes.

JOAN: But you're not Irish?

HUMAN NATURE

INTERN: Tell me, where did you qualify, if I may ask?

THE DOCTOR: A place called Gallifrey.

INTERN: Gallifrey? No, I've not heard of it. Perhaps it's in Ireland.

THE DOCTOR: Probably.

THE HAND OF FEAR

THE DOCTOR: Oh, you shouldn't be worried. Time Lords have 90 lives.

ROMANA: How many have you got through, then?

THE DOCTOR: About a hundred and thirty.

THE CREATURE FROM THE PIT

REGENERATION

'That's the trouble with regeneration. You never quite know what you're going to get.'

THE DOCTOR, *CASTROVALVA*

ROSE: Can you change back?

THE DOCTOR: Do you want me to?

ROSE: Yeah.

THE DOCTOR: Oh.

ROSE: Can you?

THE DOCTOR: No.

BORN AGAIN

'Time Lords have this little trick, it's sort of a way of cheating death. Except it means I'm going to change, and I'm not going to see you again. Not like this. Not with this daft old face.'

THE DOCTOR, *THE PARTING OF THE WAYS*

'The old man must die and the new man will discover to his inexpressible joy that he has never existed.'

CHO-JE, *PLANET OF THE SPIDERS*

'New mouth. New rules. It's like eating after cleaning your teeth. Everything tastes wrong.'

THE DOCTOR, *THE ELEVENTH HOUR*

'I can still die. If I'm killed before regeneration then I'm dead. Even then. Even if I change, it feels like dying. Everything I am dies. Some new man goes sauntering away. And I'm dead.'

THE DOCTOR, *THE END OF TIME*

OTHER WORLDS

'If you could touch the alien sand and hear the cries of strange birds and watch them wheel in another sky, would that satisfy you?'

THE DOCTOR, *AN UNEARTHLY CHILD*

ROSE: If you are an alien, how comes you sound like you're from the North?

THE DOCTOR: Lots of planets have a north.

ROSE

'I have heard Davros say there is no intelligent life on other planets, so either he is wrong or you are lying.'

NYDER, *GENESIS OF THE DALEKS*

ANN: Then where are you from?

NYSSA: Traken.

ANN: Where's that?

SIR ROBERT: Near Esher, isn't it?

BLACK ORCHID

CHARLES: Now then, I'd better attend to that young man. What was his name again?

THE DOCTOR: Adric.

CHARLES: Scandinavian?

THE DOCTOR: Er, not quite. He's Alzarian.

CHARLES: I never could remember all those funny Baltic bits.

BLACK ORCHID

THE DOCTOR: 'If the thraskin puts his fingers in his ears, it is polite to shout.' That's an old Venusian proverb.

JO: What's a thraskin?

THE DOCTOR: Thraskin? Oh, it's an archaic word, seldom used since the twenty-fifth dynasty. The modern equivalent is plinge.

JO: What does plinge mean?

THE DOCTOR: Oh, for heaven's sake, Jo, I've just told you. It means thraskin.

JO: Oh, of course.

THE TIME MONSTER

THE DOCTOR: Florana. Probably one of the most beautiful planets in the universe.

SARAH: Well, count me out.

THE DOCTOR: It's always carpeted with perfumed flowers.

SARAH: I'm not listening.

THE DOCTOR: And its seas are as warm milk and the sands as soft as swan's down.

SARAH: No, Doctor.

THE DOCTOR: The streams flow with water that are clearer than the clearest crystal.

SARAH: No.

INVASION OF THE DINOSAURS

YRCANOS: On my planet of Krontep, a warrior queen fights alongside her king.

PERI: We're not on your planet.

YRCANOS: It doesn't matter. The rule still applies.

THE TRIAL OF A TIME LORD: MINDWARP

RORY: Got any more honeymoon ideas?

THE DOCTOR: Well, there's a moon that's made of actual honey. Well, not actual honey, and it's not actually a moon, and technically it's alive, and a bit carnivorous, but there are some lovely views.

A CHRISTMAS CAROL

'Have you ever looked up at the sky at night and seen those little lights? … They are not ice crystals … I believe they are suns, just like our own sun. And perhaps each sun has other worlds of its own, just as Ribos is a world.'

BINRO, *THE RIBOS OPERATION*

'There are worlds out there where the sky is burning, where the sea's asleep, and the rivers dream. People made of smoke, and cities made of song. Somewhere there's danger, somewhere there's injustice, and somewhere else the tea's getting cold. Come on, Ace, we've got work to do!'

THE DOCTOR, *SURVIVAL*

'No, Amy, it's definitely not the fifth moon of Cindie Colesta. I think I can see a Ryman's.'

THE DOCTOR, *THE LODGER*

AND WHEN YOU'RE HAVING A BAD DAY...

'Over a thousand years of saving the universe, Strax, you know the one thing I learned? The universe doesn't care.'

THE DOCTOR, *THE SNOWMEN*

Chapter Five:
The Journey

'Allons-y!'

THE DOCTOR

THE TARDIS

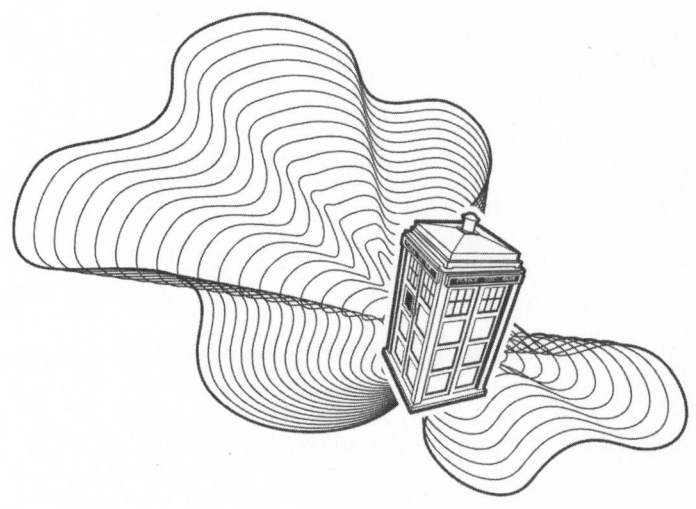

'Let me get this straight. A thing that looks like a police box, standing in a junkyard… it can move anywhere in time and space?'

IAN, *AN UNEARTHLY CHILD*

'Sorry, but you're about to make a very big mistake. Don't steal that one, steal this one. The navigation system's knackered, but you'll have much more fun.'

CLARA, *THE NAME OF THE DOCTOR*

IDRIS: Do you ever wonder why I chose you all those years ago?

THE DOCTOR: I chose you. You were unlocked.

IDRIS: Of course I was. I wanted to see the universe, so I stole a Time Lord and I ran away. And you were the only one mad enough.

THE DOCTOR'S WIFE

IAN: Ship?

THE DOCTOR: Yes, yes, ship. This doesn't roll along on wheels, you know.

AN UNEARTHLY CHILD

'It's my home. At least, it has been for a considerable number of years.'

THE DOCTOR, *THE TOMB OF THE CYBERMEN*

'But I need my ship. It's all I've got. Literally the only thing.'

THE DOCTOR, *THE IMPOSSIBLE PLANET*

IDRIS: You stole me. And I stole you.

THE DOCTOR: I borrowed you.

IDRIS: Borrowing implies the intention to return the thing that was taken. What makes you think I would ever give you back?

THE DOCTOR'S WIFE

THE DOCTOR: We're outside time. Of course, it always seems to take a long time but that depends upon the mood, I suppose.

JO: What, your mood?

THE DOCTOR: No, no, no, hers. No, the TARDIS's.

JO: You talk as if she was alive.

THE DOCTOR: It depends what you mean by alive, doesn't it?

THE TIME MONSTER

'The Type 40 capsule wasn't on the main syllabus, you see... Veteran and vintage vehicles was an optional extra.'

ROMANA, *THE PIRATE PLANET*

'When the TARDIS is on manual, you can't be certain of anything... It's harder to fly than you think. I mean, you don't just flick a switch.'

THE DOCTOR, *CASTROVALVA*

GREG: Well, I thought it'd be a bit more impressive than that.

THE DOCTOR: What did you expect? Some kind of space rocket with Batman at the controls?

INFERNO

RIVER: It's not supposed to make that noise. You leave the brakes on.

THE DOCTOR: Yeah, well, it's a brilliant noise. I love that noise.

THE TIME OF ANGELS

'Now then, you lot. Sarah, hold that down. Mickey, you hold that. Because you know why this TARDIS is always rattling about the place? Rose? That, there. It's designed to have six pilots, and I have to do it single-handed. Martha, keep that level. But not any more. Jack, there you go. Steady that. Now we can fly this thing. No, Jackie. No, no. Not you. Don't touch anything. Just stand back. Like it's meant to be flown. We've got the Torchwood Rift looped around the TARDIS by Mr Smith, and we're going to fly planet Earth back home. Right then. Off we go.'

THE DOCTOR, *JOURNEY'S END*

THE DOCTOR: The parametric engines are jammed. Orthogonal vector's gone. I'm almost out of ideas.

AVERY: Almost?

THE DOCTOR: Well, we could try stroking her and singing her a song.

AVERY: Will that help?

THE DOCTOR: Hard to say. Never has before.

THE CURSE OF THE BLACK SPOT

'This machine is a load of obsolete rubbish.'

STOR, *THE INVASION OF TIME*

STAPLEY: Is that how you travel, Doctor?

THE DOCTOR: Not exactly the first-class end of the market, but a serviceable vehicle, Captain.

TIME-FLIGHT

ANNE: It flies? Through time and space?

VICTORIA: Not exactly flies. Well, it's difficult to explain.

ANNE: Not half as difficult as it is to believe.

THE WEB OF FEAR

TODD: You don't actually go into space in that?

THE DOCTOR: Oh no. That would be completely impossible, wouldn't it?

TODD: Unlikely, anyway.

THE DOCTOR: If not ridiculous.

KINDA

THE DOCTOR: What nobody understands is, the advantage of my antiquated TARDIS is that it's fully equipped and completely reliable.

LEELA: Completely?

THE DOCTOR: Yes, well, almost completely.

THE INVASION OF TIME

BARBARA: Doctor, the trembling's stopped.

THE DOCTOR: Oh, my dear, I'm so glad you're feeling better.

BARBARA: No, not me, the ship.

THE RESCUE

TURLOUGH: Time will tell.

THE DOCTOR: Yes, indeed. Aboard the TARDIS it always does.

WARRIORS OF THE DEEP

'When a TARDIS is dying, sometimes the dimension dams start breaking down. They used to call it a size leak. All the bigger on the inside starts leaking to the outside. It grows. When I say that's the TARDIS, I don't mean it looks like the TARDIS, I mean it actually is the TARDIS. My TARDIS from the future. What else would they bury me in?'

THE DOCTOR, *THE NAME OF THE DOCTOR*

THE DOCTOR: You didn't always take me where I wanted to go.

IDRIS: No, but I always took you where you needed to go.

THE DOCTOR'S WIFE

IT'S A POLICE BOX…

IAN: It's a police box! What on earth's it doing here? These things are usually on the street. Look, feel it. Feel it. Do you feel it?

BARBARA: It's a faint vibration.

IAN: It's alive!

AN UNEARTHLY CHILD

JO: What on earth is he doing inside a horsebox?

THE DOCTOR: It isn't exactly a horsebox. It just happens to look like one.

JO: You mean there isn't a horse inside.

THE DOCTOR: No more than there's a policeman inside my police box.

TERROR OF THE AUTONS

LANE: It's a ship.

PACKARD: What, for midgets?

LANE: Or a coffin for a very large man.

WARRIORS' GATE

THE DOCTOR: I always read the instructions.

IDRIS: There's a sign on my front door. You have been walking past it for seven hundred years. What does it say?

THE DOCTOR: That's not instructions.

IDRIS: There's an instruction at the bottom. What does it say?

THE DOCTOR: Pull to open.

IDRIS: Yes. And what do you do?

THE DOCTOR: I push.

IDRIS: Every single time. Seven hundred years. Police box doors open out that way.

THE DOCTOR'S WIFE

ANDREWS: Are you responsible for this box, sir?

THE DOCTOR: Well, I try to be.

TIME-FLIGHT

BIGGER ON THE INSIDE

'I like the bit when someone says it's bigger on the inside. I always look forward to that.'

THE DOCTOR, *VAMPIRES OF VENICE*

'So we're in a box that's bigger on the inside, and it travels through time and space... How long have Scotland Yard had this?'

CANTON, *THE IMPOSSIBLE ASTRONAUT*

THE BRIGADIER: So this is what you've been doing with UNIT funds and equipment all this time. How's it done? Some sort of optical illusion?

THE DOCTOR : Oh, no, no, no. They come like this. Really.

THE THREE DOCTORS

AMY: I started to think that maybe you were just like a madman with a box.

THE DOCTOR: Amy Pond, there's something you'd better understand about me, because it's important, and one day your life may depend on it. I am definitely a madman with a box.

THE ELEVENTH HOUR

MARTHA: It's wood. It's like a box with that room just rammed in. It's bigger on the inside.

THE DOCTOR: Is it? I hadn't noticed.

SMITH AND JONES

THE DOCTOR: What matters is, we can communicate. We have got big problems now. They have taken the blue box, haven't they? The angels have the phone box.

LARRY: 'The angels have the phone box.' That's my favourite, I've got it on a T-shirt.

BLINK

'Let me stop you there. Bigger on the inside. Don't mind, do you, if we just skip to the end of that moment? Oh, and sorry I lied, by the way, when I said yours was bigger. Kitchen that way. Choice of bathrooms there, there, there.'

THE DOCTOR, *THE CURSE OF THE BLACK SPOT*

THE DOCTOR: It's called the TARDIS. It can travel anywhere in time and space. And it's mine.

CLARA: But it's… Well, look at it, it's…

THE DOCTOR: Go on, say it. Most people do.

CLARA: It's smaller on the outside.

THE DOCTOR: OK, that is a first.

THE SNOWMEN

WELCOME ABOARD

THE DOCTOR: My dear, why don't you come with us, hmm?

VICKI: In that old box?

THE DOCTOR: We can travel anywhere and everywhere in that old box as you call it. Regardless of space and time.

VICKI: Then it is a time machine?

THE DOCTOR: And if you like adventure, my dear, I can promise you an abundance of it.

THE RESCUE

HARRY: Oh, come along now, Doctor. We're both reasonable men. Now, we both know that police boxes don't go careering around all over the place.

THE DOCTOR: Do we?

HARRY: Of course we do. The whole idea's absurd.

THE DOCTOR: Is it? You wouldn't like to step inside a moment? Just to demonstrate that it is all an illusion?

ROBOT

LEELA: Take me with you.

THE DOCTOR: Why?

LEELA: What? Well. You like me, don't you?

THE DOCTOR: Well, yes, I suppose I do like you. But then, I like lots of people but I can't go carting them around the universe with me. Goodbye.

THE FACE OF EVIL

THE DOCTOR: Ace, where do you think you're going?

ACE: Perivale.

THE DOCTOR: Ah yes, but by which route? The direct route with Glitz, or the scenic route? Well? Do you fancy a quick trip round the twelve galaxies and then back to Perivale in time for tea?

DRAGONFIRE

TIME TRAVEL

'So, all of time and space, everything that ever happened or ever will. Where do you want to start?'

THE DOCTOR, *THE ELEVENTH HOUR*

'Time is not the boss of me.'

THE DOCTOR, *THE TIME OF ANGELS*

'The thing is, Adam, time travel's like visiting Paris. You can't just read the guide book, you've got to throw yourself in. Eat the food, use the wrong verbs, get charged double and end up kissing complete strangers. Or is that just me?'

THE DOCTOR, *THE LONG GAME*

'Gosh, that takes me back. Or forward. That's the trouble with time travel: you can never remember.'

THE DOCTOR, *THE ANDROIDS OF TARA*

'I do flit about a bit, you know… I don't seem to be able to help myself. There I am, just walking along minding my own business and pop! I'm on a different planet or even a different time. But enough of my problems.'

THE DOCTOR, *CITY OF DEATH*

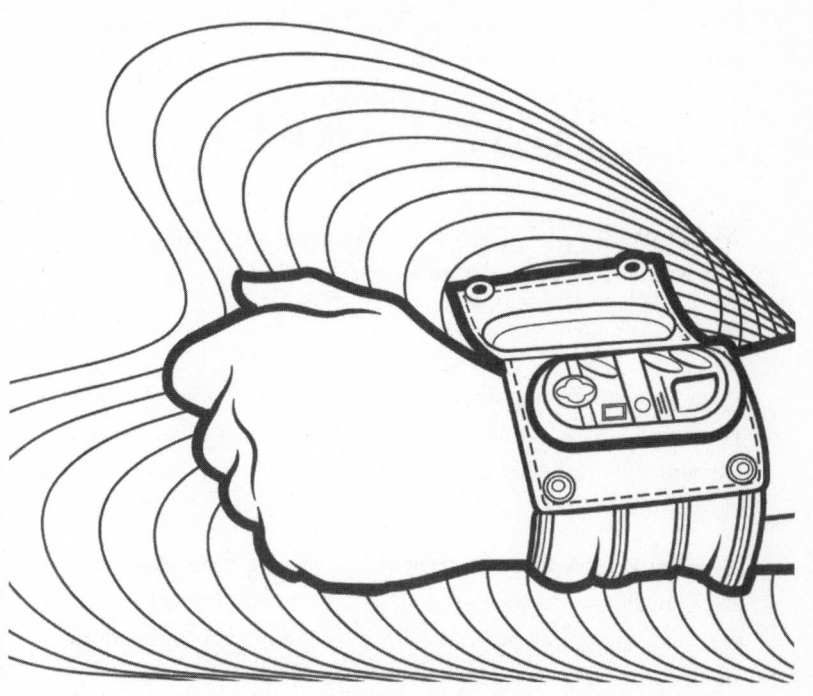

JACK: I used to be a Time Agent. It's called a Vortex manipulator. He's not the only one who can time travel.

THE DOCTOR: Oh, excuse me. That is not time travel. It's like, I've got a sports car and you've got a space hopper.

UTOPIA

'Vortex manipulator. Cheap and nasty time travel. Very bad for you. I'm trying to give it up.'

THE DOCTOR, *THE BIG BANG*

'Christmas. 1860. Happens once, just once and it's gone, it's finished, it'll never happen again. Except for you. You can go back and see days that are dead and gone a hundred thousand sunsets ago. No wonder you never stay still.'

ROSE, *THE UNQUIET DEAD*

'Lots of impossible things happen when you pass through time.'

THE DOCTOR, *THE WAR GAMES*

'You know, the thing about a time machine, though, you can run away all you like and still be home in time for tea, so what do you say? Anywhere. All of time and space, right outside those doors.'

THE DOCTOR, *THE BELLS OF SAINT JOHN*

THE DOCTOR: I also said this ship was generating enough power to punch a hole in the universe. I think we just found the hole. Must be a spatio-temporal hyperlink.

MICKEY: What's that?

THE DOCTOR: No idea. Just made it up. Didn't want to say magic door.

THE GIRL IN THE FIREPLACE

'It's always a big day tomorrow. We've got a time machine. I skip the little ones.'

THE DOCTOR, *THE BEAST BELOW*

'I mean, one minute you're in 1974 looking for ghosts, but all you have to do is open your eyes and talk to whoever's standing there. To you, I haven't been born yet, and to you I've been dead one hundred billion years. Is my body out there somewhere, in the ground?'

CLARA, *HIDE*

'Time travel is damage. It's like a tear in the fabric of reality. That is the scar tissue of my journey through the universe. My path through time and space from Gallifrey to Trenzalore.'

THE DOCTOR, *THE NAME OF THE DOCTOR*

'First things first? ... But not necessarily in that order.'

THE DOCTOR, *MEGLOS*

TRAVEL BROADENS THE MIND

'Isn't it a better thing to travel hopefully than arrive?'

SUSAN, *THE SENSORITES*

'That's why I keep travelling. To be proved wrong.'

THE DOCTOR, *THE SATAN PIT*

'My dear girl, if I stopped to question the wisdom of my actions, I'd never have left Gallifrey.'

THE DOCTOR, *THE TRIAL OF A TIME LORD: MINDWARP*

CRAIG: I'm not much of a traveller.

THE DOCTOR: I can tell from your sofa.

CRAIG: My sofa?

THE DOCTOR: You're starting to look like it.

THE LODGER

ROMANA: Shall we take the lift or fly?

THE DOCTOR: Let's not be ostentatious.

ROMANA: All right. Let's fly, then.

THE DOCTOR: That would look silly. We'll take the lift.

CITY OF DEATH

'It's like I had that one day with you, and I was going to change. I was going to do so much. Then I woke up the next morning, same old life. It's like you were never there. And I tried. I did try. I went to Egypt. I was going to go barefoot and everything. And then it's all bus trips and guidebooks and don't drink the water, and two weeks later you're back home. It's nothing like being with you.'

DONNA, *PARTNERS IN CRIME*

ASTRID: So you travel alone?

THE DOCTOR: All the time. Just for fun. Well. That's the plan. Never quite works.

VOYAGE OF THE DAMNED

'You can't walk into the middle of a Western town and say you've come from outer space! Good gracious me. You would be arrested on a vagrancy charge!'

THE DOCTOR, *THE GUNFIGHTERS*

DONNA: I packed ages ago, just in case. Because I thought, hot weather, cold weather, no weather. He goes anywhere. I've gotta be prepared.

THE DOCTOR: You've got a hatbox.

DONNA: Planet of the Hats, I'm ready. I don't need injections, do I? You know, like when you go to Cambodia.

PARTNERS IN CRIME

'A straight line may be the shortest distance between two points, but it is by no means the most interesting.'

THE DOCTOR, *THE TIME WARRIOR*

'One day we'll know all the mysteries of the skies, and we'll stop our wandering.'

SUSAN, *MARCO POLO*

SUSAN: I never felt there was any time or place that I belonged to. I've never had any real identity.

DAVID: One day you will. There will come a time when you're forced to stop travelling, and you'll arrive somewhere.

THE DALEK INVASION OF EARTH

GETTING LOST

THE DOCTOR: We've come out of the time vortex at the wrong point, that's all. A few years too late.

SARAH: How many?

THE DOCTOR: Thirty thousand.

PLANET OF EVIL

THE DOCTOR: You're never without a sense of direction while there's an air flow. Air flows from A to B. Usually you want to be at B. Or at A.

TEGAN: I don't want to be at A or B, thank you very much.

FRONTIOS

'Oh, well, you weren't too far out, were you? Only about two hundred million miles.

BEN, *THE MOONBASE*

'Well, of course I can control it. Nine times out of ten. Well, seven times out of ten. Five times. Look. Never mind, let's see where we are.'

THE DOCTOR ON THE TARDIS, *THE ROBOTS OF DEATH*

THE DOCTOR: OK, so. Not London 1893. Yorkshire 1893. Near enough.

CLARA: You're making a habit of this, getting us lost.

THE DOCTOR: Sorry. It's much better than it used to be. Ooh, I once spent a hell of a long time trying to get a gobby Australian to Heathrow Airport.

THE CRIMSON HORROR

NYSSA: Where are we?

ADRIC: Earth again.

TEGAN: I did say I wanted to stay with the crew for a while. You can stop trying to get me back to Heathrow.

THE DOCTOR: I have.

TEGAN: You certainly know how to fly this crate, don't you?

BLACK ORCHID

JEFFERSON: You're telling me you don't know where you are?

THE DOCTOR: No idea. More fun that way.

THE IMPOSSIBLE PLANET

THE COLLECTOR: How did you get to Pluto?

LEELA: By accident, as usual.

THE SUN MAKERS

'Even I would find it hard to lose myself in a corridor.'

THE DOCTOR, *THE TRIAL OF A TIME LORD: THE MYSTERIOUS PLANET*

SARAH: We're lost.

THE DOCTOR: Mislaid, possibly.

SARAH: Oh, why don't we just go back to the TARDIS?

THE DOCTOR: For two good reasons. One, that I don't want to leave Peladon without having a word with my good friend, the King.

SARAH: Name dropper.

THE DOCTOR: And second.

SARAH: What?

THE DOCTOR: We *are* lost.

THE MONSTER OF PELADON

'Well, it's called a randomiser and it's fitted to the guidance system and operates under a very complex scientific principle called pot luck.'

THE DOCTOR, *THE ARMAGEDDON FACTOR*

'I always did have a terrible sense of direction. Still as long we keep going down.'

THE DOCTOR, *CASTROVALVA*

SPACECRAFT

'It's a spaceship. Brilliant! I got a spaceship on my first go.'

MICKEY, *THE GIRL IN THE FIREPLACE*

'Rocket. Blimey, a real proper rocket. Now that's what I call a spaceship. You've got a box, he's got a Ferrari. Come on, let's go see where he's going.'

DONNA, *PLANET OF THE OOD*

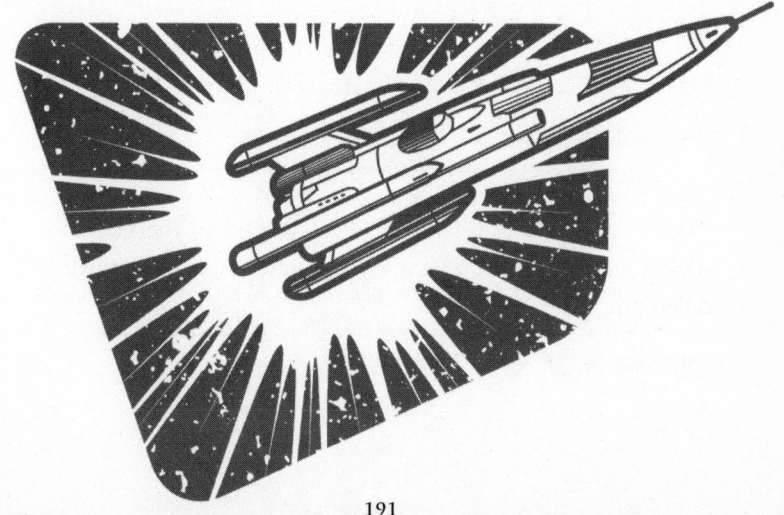

'Brilliant humans. Humans who travel all the way across space, flying in a tiny little rocket. Right into the orbit of a black hole, just for the sake of discovery. That's amazing! Do you hear me? Amazing, all of you.'

THE DOCTOR, *THE SATAN PIT*

'My dear man, I've spent more time in space than any astronaut on your staff. Not, I'll admit, in the rather primitive contraptions that you use, but I'll manage.'

THE DOCTOR, *THE AMBASSADORS OF DEATH*

THE MASTER: Well, that must be them. No other ship would be on a course for Earth at a time like this.

OGRON: We are on a course for Earth.

THE MASTER: Well naturally, because we're chasing them!

FRONTIER IN SPACE

THE DOCTOR: Uncle Josiah knows as much about its secrets as a hamburger knows about the Amazon desert.

ACE: Sounds a bit like you and the TARDIS.

GHOST LIGHT

'My ship's not made of tin like this old trash. Oh, good gracious me! Seems if I cough too loudly, the whole thing'd fall to pieces.'

THE DOCTOR, *GALAXY 4*

JAMIE: A spaceship? Hey, do you reckon that's where the warrior's gone back to?

THE DOCTOR: Well, he didn't come by Shetland pony, Jamie.

THE ICE WARRIORS

'It's funny, because people back home think that space travel's going to be all whizzing about and teleports and anti-gravity, but it's not, is it? It's tough.'

ROSE, *THE IMPOSSIBLE PLANET*

'The wonderful world of space travel. The prettier it looks, the more likely it is to kill you.'

RILEY, *42*

'There's a lot of things you need to get across this universe. Warp drive, wormhole refractors. You know the thing you need most of all? You need a hand to hold.'

THE DOCTOR, *FEAR HER*

ADVENTURE

'Rest is for the weary, sleep is for the dead!'

THE DOCTOR, *ATTACK OF THE CYBERMEN*

'Yes, it all started out as a mild curiosity in a junkyard, and now it's turned out to be… quite a great spirit of adventure, don't you think?'

THE DOCTOR, *THE SENSORITES*

THE DOCTOR: Ah, you want me to volunteer. Isn't that it?

THE WHITE GUARDIAN: Precisely.

THE DOCTOR: And if I don't?

THE WHITE GUARDIAN: Nothing.

THE DOCTOR: Nothing? You mean nothing will happen to me?

THE WHITE GUARDIAN: Nothing at all… ever.

THE RIBOS OPERATION

TEGAN: Anything could be out there.

THE DOCTOR: Yes, and going out is the only way to learn what it is.

ENLIGHTENMENT

'I was imparting a little information. When you ask a question, you should listen to the answer, my girl, otherwise, you will gain absolutely no benefit from being in my company. It is the province of knowledge to speak, and the privilege of wisdom to listen.'

THE DOCTOR, *THE TWO DOCTORS*

MEL: There's the swimming pool, right at the very top of the building. Oh, it's wonderful. I can't wait to have a dip in that. Paradise Towers, here we come.

THE DOCTOR: That's the problem with young people today, no spirit of adventure.

PARADISE TOWERS

'Number one rule of the intergalactic explorer, Doctor. If you hear somebody talking about good vibes and letting it all hang out, run a mile.'

CAPTAIN COOK, *THE GREATEST SHOW IN THE GALAXY*

'And you go with him, that wonderful Doctor. You go and see the stars, and then bring a bit of them back for your old Gramps.'

WILF, *THE POISON SKY*

BEN: Oh, of all the bloomin' fixes to be in.

POLLY: I don't know. I find it pretty exciting.

BEN: Oh, you would.

THE SMUGGLERS

THE DOCTOR: Where's your spirit of adventure?

IAN: It died a slow and painful death when those bats came out of the rafters!

THE CHASE

'Because the thing is, Doctor, I believe it all now. You opened my eyes. All those amazing things out there, I believe them all. Well, apart from that replica of the *Titanic* flying over Buckingham Palace on Christmas Day. I mean, that's got to be a hoax.'

DONNA, *PARTNERS IN CRIME*

'The adventures come without us looking for them.'

BARBARA, *THE ROMANS*

ESCAPE

'There's always a way out. If only we can find it.'

THE DOCTOR, *THE ARMAGEDDON FACTOR*

THE DOCTOR: Right, shouldn't be too far down. Just put your arms over your head, and slide.

PERI: What happens if I get stuck?

THE DOCTOR: I shouldn't advise that. I'll be right behind you.

THE TWO DOCTORS

'The moral is, if you're going to get stuck at the end of the universe, get stuck with an ex-Time Agent and his Vortex manipulator.'

CAPTAIN JACK HARKNESS, *THE SOUND OF DRUMS*

TEGAN: We've got to find the way out.

THE DOCTOR: Well, sometimes it's easier to look for the way in and then work backwards.

FRONTIOS

RORY: Ah, so this is the kind of escape plan where you survive about four seconds longer.

THE DOCTOR: What's wrong with four seconds? You can do loads in four seconds.

ASYLUM OF THE DALEKS

TEGAN: This is ridiculous, running about like rabbits in a hole. If you ask me—

THE DOCTOR: No one is, Tegan, so shush.

FRONTIOS

'Brigadier, I think our past is catching up on us. Or maybe it's our future. Come on, run!'

THE DOCTOR, *THE FIVE DOCTORS*

STRAX: And how will she locate the Doctor?

VASTRA: To find him, she needs only ignore all keep-out signs, go through every locked door, and run towards any form of danger that presents itself.

STRAX: Business as usual, then.

THE CRIMSON HORROR

'There's only one thing we can do... Run!'

THE DOCTOR, *THE SPACE PIRATES*

THE DOCTOR: We can't keep doing this.

RIVER: Any ideas?

THE DOCTOR: Yeah, the usual. Run!

THE ANGELS TAKE MANHATTAN

TEGAN: You mean you're deliberately choosing to go on the run from your own people in a rackety old TARDIS?

THE DOCTOR: Why not? After all, that's how it all started.

THE FIVE DOCTORS

AND IF ALL ELSE FAILS...

JAMIE: Have you thought up some clever plan, Doctor?

THE DOCTOR: Yes, Jamie, I believe I have.

JAMIE: What are you going to do?

THE DOCTOR: Bung a rock at it.

THE ABOMINABLE SNOWMEN

Chapter Six:
The Tools

'If you have a tool,
it's stupid not to use it.'

THE DOCTOR, *INFERNO*

THE SONIC SCREWDRIVER

'It's a sonic screwdriver. Never fails. There we are. Neat isn't it? All done by sound waves.'

THE DOCTOR, *FURY FROM THE DEEP*

JACK: Who looks at a screwdriver and thinks, ooh, this could be a little more sonic?

THE DOCTOR: What, you've never been bored? … Never had a long night? Never had a lot of cabinets to put up?

THE DOCTOR DANCES

'Harmless is just the word. That's why I like it. Doesn't kill, doesn't wound, doesn't maim. But I'll tell you what it does do. It is very good at opening doors.'

THE DOCTOR, *DOOMSDAY*

DONNA: Sonic it! Use the thingy!

THE DOCTOR: I can't. It's wood!

DONNA: What, it doesn't do wood?!

SILENCE IN THE LIBRARY

MARTHA: What's that thing?

THE DOCTOR: Sonic screwdriver.

MARTHA: Well, if you're not going to answer me properly.

THE DOCTOR: No, really, it is. It's a screwdriver, and it's sonic. Look.

MARTHA: What else have you got, a laser spanner?

THE DOCTOR: I did, but it was stolen by Emily Pankhurst, cheeky woman.

SMITH AND JONES

AMY: That is breaking and entering.

THE DOCTOR: What did I break? Sonicing and entering. Totally different.

THE HUNGRY EARTH

'Why are you pointing your screwdrivers like that? They're scientific instruments, not water pistols.'

THE WAR DOCTOR, *THE DAY OF THE DOCTOR*

JACK: OK. This can function as a sonic blaster, a sonic cannon, and as a triple-enfolded sonic disrupter. Doc, what you got?

THE DOCTOR: I've got a sonic, er. Oh, never mind.

JACK: What?

THE DOCTOR: It's sonic, OK? Let's leave it at that.

JACK: Disrupter? Cannon? What?

THE DOCTOR: It's sonic! Totally sonic! I am soniced up!

JACK: A sonic what?!

THE DOCTOR: Screwdriver!

THE DOCTOR DANCES

'Word of advice. If you're attacking a man with a sonic screwdriver, don't let him near the sound system.'

THE DOCTOR, *THE RUNAWAY BRIDE*

'Know what's interesting about my screwdriver? Very hard to interfere with. Practically nothing's strong enough. Well, some hairdryers, but I'm working on that.'

THE DOCTOR, *FOREST OF THE DEAD*

'Even the sonic screwdriver won't get me out of this one.'

THE DOCTOR, *THE INVASION OF TIME*

WHEN SONICS ARE DESTROYED

'I feel as though you've just killed an old friend.'

THE DOCTOR, *THE VISITATION*

'I loved my sonic screwdriver.'

THE DOCTOR, *SMITH AND JONES*

K-9 – A TIME LORD'S (SECOND) BEST FRIEND

THE DOCTOR: Would you like a ball bearing?

K-9: Please do not mock, master.

THE INVASION OF TIME

RIGG: What's that?

THE DOCTOR: Oh, K-9? Well, a computer of sorts.

RIGG: It looks more like a dog. Does he bark?

THE DOCTOR: No. But he has been known to bite.

NIGHTMARE OF EDEN

PROFESSOR MARIUS: That tin thing is my best friend and constant companion. He's a computer. You see, on Earth, I always used to have a dog. But up here, the weight penalty, well, it's just not possible. So I had K-9 made up. He's very useful. He's my own personal data bank. He knows everything that I do, don't you, K-9?

K-9: Affirmative, and more, master.

THE INVISIBLE ENEMY

'K-9 seems to have made up his own mind. I only hope he's TARDIS trained.'

PROFESSOR MARIUS, *THE INVISIBLE ENEMY*

THE DOCTOR: An assistant? Please, sir, on an assignment like this, I'd much rather work alone. In my experience, assistants mean trouble. I have to protect them and show them and teach them and – Couldn't I just... couldn't I just manage with K-9?

THE WHITE GUARDIAN: K-9 is a mere machine.

THE DOCTOR: He's a very sensitive machine!

THE RIBOS OPERATION

K-9: Satisfactory, mistress?

LEELA: Yes, K-9. What do you want, a biscuit?

THE SUN MAKERS

THE DOCTOR: K-9, I don't know how to say this, K-9.

K-9: Master, your concern is noted. Please do not embarrass me.

THE DOCTOR: Good dog.

THE SUN MAKERS

K-9: Predict only sixty per cent chance of success, master.

THE DOCTOR: Tell me, K-9, how is it you always look on the black side of things? Here am I, trying a little lateral thinking, and what do you do? You trample all over it with logic.

NIGHTMARE OF EDEN

THE DOCTOR: We all make mistakes sometimes, don't we, K-9?

K-9: Negative.

THE ARMAGEDDON FACTOR

'K-9, sulking is also an emotional thing. If you cannot wish, you cannot sulk.'

LEELA, *THE INVASION OF TIME*

THE DOCTOR: They can read thoughts. Even encephalographic patterns. That's why I've plugged K-9 into the Matrix instead of me. He's got no brains, you see. Sorry about that, K-9.

ANDRED: Can you trust a machine?

THE DOCTOR: This one I can. He's my second best friend.

THE INVASION OF TIME

K-9: The accuracy of this unit has deteriorated below zero utility.

ADRIC: You mean you're worse than useless.

K-9: Affirmative.

WARRIORS' GATE

THE DOCTOR: Ion drive, or I'm a budgie's cousin.

K-9: Affirmative ion drive. Family grouping negative.

UNDERWORLD

K-9: You have triggered the primary alert function.

THE DOCTOR: Blast!

K-9: Affirmative.

THE ARMAGEDDON FACTOR

'Batteries my exhausted nearly are…'

K-9, *THE PIRATE PLANET*

'Intentions unknown. Hypothesis unfriendly, as K-9 would say.'

THE DOCTOR, *KINDA*

COMPUTERS

'The trouble with computers, of course, is that they're very sophisticated idiots. They do exactly what you tell them at amazing speed, even if you order them to kill you. So if you do happen to change your mind, it's very difficult to stop them obeying the original order, but… not impossible.'

THE DOCTOR, *ROBOT*

'Now, the best thing about a machine that makes sense, you can very easily make it turn out nonsense.'

THE DOCTOR, *THE TOMB OF THE CYBERMEN*

MISS GARRETT: Here we are completely computerised.

THE DOCTOR: Well, never mind.

THE ICE WARRIORS

CLENT: You've worked with computers, I presume?

THE DOCTOR: Ah, only when I have to.

THE ICE WARRIORS

LEELA: What is it?

THE DOCTOR: Number two control room has been closed for redecoration. I don't like the colour.

LEELA: White isn't a colour.

THE DOCTOR: That's the trouble with computers. Always think in black and white. No aquamarines, no blues, no imagination.

THE INVISIBLE ENEMY

'You're still nothing but a gigantic adding machine like every other computer.'

THE DOCTOR, *THE GREEN DEATH*

ROMANA: Well, at least on Gallifrey we can capture a good likeness. Computers can draw.

THE DOCTOR: What? Computer pictures? You sit in Paris and talk of computer pictures?

CITY OF DEATH

HADE: To err is computer.

THE DOCTOR: To forgive is fine?

THE SUN MAKERS

JO: A mind probe?

THE DOCTOR: Oh, you don't want to worry about those things, Jo. As long as you tell them the truth, they can't do you any harm... Well, they're only sort of computers with a few extra knobs on. And you know how stupid computers can be, don't you?

FRONTIER IN SPACE

LEELA: You did say he was the most powerful computer ever built.

THE DOCTOR Yes, and very charming he is too when he wants to be. Marvellous host. I remember once at one of his dinner parties...

LEELA: Doctor, he just tried to kill you!

THE FACE OF EVIL

'Even simple one-dimensional chess exposes the limitations of the machine mind.'

THE DOCTOR, *THE SUN MAKERS*

'Everything in life has its purpose, Drathro. Every creature plays its part. But the purpose of life is too big to be knowable. A million computers couldn't solve that one.'

THE DOCTOR, *THE TRIAL OF A TIME LORD: THE MYSTERIOUS PLANET*

I, ROBOT

'Mankind is not worthy to survive. Once it is destroyed, I shall build more machines like myself. Machines do not lie.'

ROBOT K-1, *ROBOT*

ZADEK: You can't trust androids, you know.

THE DOCTOR: That's funny, you know. That's what some androids say about people.

THE ANDROIDS OF TARA

SARAH: Oh, it's got a brain, hasn't it? It walks and talks like us. How can you be sure it doesn't have feelings too? Are you all right?

ROBOT K-1: My functioning is unimpaired.

SARAH: But you were distressed. I saw that.

ROBOT K-1: Conflict with my prime directive causes imbalance in my neural circuits.

SARAH: I'm sorry. It wasn't my idea.

ROBOT K-1: The imbalance has been corrected. It is not logical that you should feel sorrow.

MISS WINTERS: Really, Miss Smith, this is absurd. I think you must be the sort of girl that gives motorcars pet names.

ROBOT

DRATHRO: I know of values. Is your point that organics are of more value than robots?

THE DOCTOR: Yes. If you want to look at it that way.

DRATHRO: Then why should I be in command of organics if they are of greater value?

THE DOCTOR: But without organics there wouldn't be any robots. There'd be no one to create them.

DRATHRO: Accepted. This shows that robots are more advanced, therefore of more value.

THE TRIAL OF A TIME LORD: THE MYSTERIOUS PLANET

'Robots don't have feelings. It's the people they serve we must hope are friendly.'

THE DOCTOR, *THE ROBOTS OF DEATH*

'You know, people never really lose that feeling of unease with robots. The more of them there are, the greater the unease and of course the greater the dependence. It's a vicious circle. People can neither live with them nor exist without them.'

THE DOCTOR, *THE ROBOTS OF DEATH*

#DOCTORWHO

'You two! We're at the end of the universe, all right? Right at the edge of knowledge itself and you're busy blogging!'

THE DOCTOR, *UTOPIA*

THE DOCTOR: This whole world is swimming in wifi. We're living in a wifi soup. Suppose something got inside it. Suppose there was something living in the wifi, harvesting human minds. Extracting them. Imagine that. Human souls trapped like flies in the worldwide web. Stuck forever, crying out for help.

CLARA: Isn't that basically Twitter?

THE BELLS OF SAINT JOHN

'I bring you to a paradise planet, two billion light years from Earth, and you want to update Twitter.'

THE DOCTOR, *THE GIRL WHO WAITED*

TRANSPORTS OF DELIGHT

'This planet is going to be destroyed and I'm stuck in a traffic jam.'

THE DOCTOR, *DOCTOR WHO* (TV MOVIE)

'We don't walk away. But when we're holding on to something precious, we run. We run and run, fast as we can and we don't stop running until we are out from under the shadow.'

THE DOCTOR, *THE RINGS OF AKHATEN*

ROMANA: For every action, there is an equal and opposite reaction.

THE DOCTOR: That's right.

ROMANA: So Newton invented punting.

THE DOCTOR: Oh, yes. There was no limit to Isaac's genius.

SHADA

ADRIC: So what is a railway station?

THE DOCTOR: Well, a place where one embarks and disembarks from compartments on wheels, drawn along these rails by a steam engine. Rarely on time.

NYSSA: What a very silly activity.

THE DOCTOR: You think so? As a boy I always wanted to drive one.

BLACK ORCHID

'Horse, you have failed in your mission. We are lost, with no sign of Sweetville. Do you have any final words before your summary execution? The usual story. Fourth one this week, and I'm not even hungry.'

STRAX, *THE CRIMSON HORROR*

URCHIN: Turn around when possible. Then, at the end of the road, turn right... bear left for a quarter of a mile and you will have reached your destination.

STRAX: Thank you. What is your name?

URCHIN: Thomas, sir. Thomas Thomas.

STRAX: I think you will do well, Thomas Thomas.

THE CRIMSON HORROR

'And you've got an office on a train. That is so cool. Can I have an office? Never had an office before. Or a train. Or a train-slash-office.'

THE DOCTOR, *THE WEDDING OF RIVER SONG*

MAN: Really, Doctor. A motorbike? Hardly seems like you.

THE DOCTOR: I rode this in the Antigrav Olympics, 2074. I came last.

MAN: The building is in lock-down. I'm afraid you're not coming in.

THE DOCTOR: Did you even hear the word 'antigrav'?

THE BELLS OF SAINT JOHN

SCIENCE AND SCIENTISTS

KALMAR: Doctor? That's a word I've seen in the old records. It's a title used by scientists. Are you a scientist, Doctor, like me?

THE DOCTOR: Well, I've dabbled a bit.

STATE OF DECAY

'We were just wondering if there were any other scientists… You know, witch-wiggler, wangateur. Fortune teller? Mundunugu?'

THE DOCTOR, *STATE OF DECAY*

'Like many scientists, I'm afraid the Rani simply sees us as walking heaps of chemicals. There's no place for the soul in her scheme of things.'

THE DOCTOR, *THE MARK OF THE RANI*

'I had all I can take of that cant in our university days. Am I expected to abandon my research because of the side effects on inferior species? Are you prepared to abandon walking in case you squash an insect underfoot?'

THE RANI, *TIME AND THE RANI*

JANO: I am sorry you take this attitude, Doctor. It is most unscientific. You are standing in the way of human progress.

THE DOCTOR: Human progress, sir? How dare you call your treatment of these people progress!

THE SAVAGES

JANO: We have achieved a very great deal merely by the sacrifice of a few savages.

THE DOCTOR: The sacrifice of even one soul is far too great! You must put an end to this inhuman practice.

THE SAVAGES

ZAROFF: So you're just a little man after all, Doctor, like all the rest. You disappoint me.

THE DOCTOR: You disappoint me, Professor. I didn't think a man of science needed the backing of thugs.

THE UNDERWATER MENACE

PROFESSOR RUMFORD: I warn you, Doctor, he doesn't like scientists.

THE DOCTOR: Well, very few people do, in my experience.

THE STONES OF BLOOD

'There is a difference between serious scientific investigation and meddling.'

THE DOCTOR, *KINDA*

KNIGHT: What's a girl like you doing in a job like this?

ANNE: Well, when I was a little girl I thought I'd like to be a scientist, so I became a scientist.

KNIGHT: Just like that?

ANNE: Just like that.

THE WEB OF FEAR

MISS WINTERS: I suppose it all seems very elementary to a scientist of your standing, Doctor.

THE DOCTOR: Yes, it does rather, but never mind. You've got to start somewhere.

ROBOT

TODD: Which way?

THE DOCTOR: Has anyone ever told you, you ask a lot of questions?

TODD: It's my training. I'm a scientist.

KINDA

'You and I are scientists, Professor. We buy our privilege to experiment at the cost of total responsibility.'

THE DOCTOR, *PLANET OF EVIL*

'Eureka's Greek for this bath is too hot.'

THE DOCTOR, *THE TALONS OF WENG-CHIANG*

KERENSKY: You are stretching me to the limit, Count.

SCARLIONI: Only thus is true progress ever made. You, as a scientist, should be the first to appreciate that.

CITY OF DEATH

KETTLEWELL: For years I have been trying to persuade people to stop spoiling this planet, Doctor. Now, with the help of my friends, I can make them.

THE DOCTOR: Aren't you forgetting that in science, as in morality, the end never justifies the means?

ROBOT

SCIENCE VERSUS MAGIC

'I too used to believe in magic, but the Doctor has taught me about science. It is better to believe in science.'

LEELA, *HORROR OF FANG ROCK*

'The greatest raiding cruiser ever built. And I built it, Mr Fibuli, I built it with technology so far advanced you would not be able to distinguish it from magic.'

THE CAPTAIN, *THE PIRATE PLANET*

THE DOCTOR: What is Clarke's law?

ACE: Any advanced form of technology is indistinguishable from magic.

THE DOCTOR: Well, the reverse is true.

ACE: Any advanced form of magic is indistinguishable from technology.

BATTLEFIELD

'It's not my fault if a bunch of backward savages have turned a Magnum Mark VII light converter into a totem pole!'

SABALOM GLITZ, *THE TRIAL OF A TIME LORD: THE MYSTERIOUS PLANET*

JO: But it really is the dawning of the age of Aquarius... you know, the supernatural and all that magic bit.

THE DOCTOR: You know, really, Jo, I'm obviously wasting my time trying to turn you into a scientist.

THE DAEMONS

'Yes, superstition is a strange thing, my dear, but sometimes it tells the truth.'

THE DOCTOR, *THE SMUGGLERS*

'Everything that happens in life must have a scientific explanation. If you know where to look for it, that is.'

THE DOCTOR, *THE DAEMONS*

JO: How did you do that?

THE DOCTOR: Iron. It's an old magical defence.

JO: But you don't believe in magic.

THE DOCTOR: I don't, but he did. Luckily.

THE DAEMONS

MARTHA: But is it real, though? I mean, witches, black magic and all that, it's real?

THE DOCTOR: Course it isn't!

MARTHA: Well, how am I supposed to know? I've only just started believing in time travel. Give me a break.

THE SHAKESPEARE CODE

THE DOCTOR: I named her. The power of a name. That's old magic.

MARTHA: But there's no such thing as magic.

THE DOCTOR: Well, it's just a different sort of science. You lot, you chose mathematics. Given the right string of numbers, the right equation, you can split the atom. Carrionites use words instead.

SHAKESPEARE: Use them for what?

THE DOCTOR: The end of the world.

THE SHAKESPEARE CODE

'The Minyans thought of us as gods, you see, which was all very flattering and we were new at space-time exploration, so we thought we could help. We gave them medical and scientific aid, better communications, better weapons ... Kicked us out at gunpoint. Then they went to war with each other, learnt how to split the atom, discovered the toothbrush and finally split the planet.'

THE DOCTOR, *UNDERWORLD*

MACHINES THAT GO 'DING'

'Tracked you down with this. This is my timey-wimey detector. It goes 'ding' when there's stuff. Also, it can boil an egg at thirty paces – whether you want it to or not, actually, so I've learned to stay away from hens. It's not pretty when they blow.'

THE DOCTOR, *BLINK*

'It's a machine that goes 'ding'. Made it myself. Lights up in the presence of shape-shifter DNA. Oooh. Also it can microwave frozen dinners from up to twenty feet and download comics from the future. I never know when to stop.'

THE DOCTOR, *THE DAY OF THE DOCTOR*

'Never trust gimmicky gadgets.'

THE DOCTOR, *THE PIRATE PLANET*

'It's for measuring time on 19 different planets … Oh, it can also be used for modifying dythrambic oscillations, cleaning your shoes, sharpening pencils. It can even peel your apples.'

THE DOCTOR, *THE RIBOS OPERATION*

'Oh! Oh, look. Oh, lovely. The ACR 99821. Oh, bliss. Nice action on the toggle switches. You know, I do love a toggle switch. Actually, I like the word toggle. Nice noun. Excellent verb. Oi, don't mess with the settings.'

THE DOCTOR, *HIDE*

WHEN TECHNOLOGY GOES WRONG

YATES: Doctor, suppose this gadget of yours doesn't work?

THE DOCTOR: Then I shall simply turn round and come back, feeling rather foolish.

INVASION OF THE DINOSAURS

THE DOCTOR: Can I get a map of London on this thing? …

CORNISH: That machine will give you surface maps of every surveyed planet, but a map of London? No.

THE DOCTOR: Useless gadgets.

THE AMBASSADORS OF DEATH

THE DOCTOR: What about the colony ship? Must have been brimming with gadgetry.

RANGE: Oh, systems that could rebuild a civilisation for us. Failure-proof technology.

THE DOCTOR: What happened to it all?

RANGE: It failed.

FRONTIOS

'I hate those transmat things. Like travelling in a food mixer, and just as dangerous. I'd be afraid of coming out puréed.'

TEGAN, *MAWDRYN UNDEAD*

'Captain. Your magnifactoid eccentricolometer is definitely on the blink.'

THE DOCTOR, *THE PIRATE PLANET*

'If there's anyone in the emergency control room, would you please answer the phone. Thank you.'

PA, *DRAGONFIRE*

LAWRENCE: You're not proposing to dismantle a piece of equipment worth fifteen million pounds with a screwdriver?

THE DOCTOR: Well, it's not worth fifteen million pins if it doesn't work, is it?

DOCTOR WHO AND THE SILURIANS

THE DOCTOR: Macrovectoid particle analyser. Omnimodular thermocron – there! Megaphoton discharge link.'

PRALIX: What do we do?

THE DOCTOR: Hit it!

THE PIRATE PLANET

ORCINI: We prefer to stand.

KARA: Of course. How foolish. As men of action, you must be like coiled springs, alert, ready to pounce.

ORCINI: Nothing so romantic. I have an artificial leg with a faulty hydraulic valve. When seated, the valve is inclined to jam.

REVELATION OF THE DALEKS

ROSE: Where I come from, Jackie doesn't know how to work the timer on the video recorder.

PETE: I showed her that last week… Point taken.

FATHER'S DAY

'You can't always go by the manuals.'

THE DOCTOR, *FULL CIRCLE*

LEELA: K-9's breaking up, my blaster's finished. What are we going to do?

THE DOCTOR: Shall we try using our intelligence?

LEELA: Well, if you think that's a good idea.

THE INVISIBLE ENEMY

ROMANA: What about the Mandrels? You won't have K-9 or a gun.

THE DOCTOR: I'll have to use my wits.

NIGHTMARE OF EDEN

THE BRIGADIER: Twenty thousand pounds of UNIT money gone up in a puff of smoke.

THE DOCTOR: You've got the mind of an accountant, Lethbridge-Stewart.

THE DAEMONS

LOGIC

'Logic, my dear Zoe, merely enables one to be wrong with authority.'

THE DOCTOR, *THE WHEEL IN SPACE*

'There's too much I don't know. I was trained to believe logic and calculation would provide me with all the answers. I'm just beginning to realise there are questions which I can't answer … What good am I? I've been created for some false kind of existence where only known kinds of emergencies are catered for. Well, what good is that to me now?'

ZOE, *THE WHEEL IN SPACE*

DRATHRO: I have a learning capacity, but my processes of ratiocination are logical. Organics often eliminate such steps.

THE DOCTOR: It's called intuition.

THE TRIAL OF A TIME LORD: THE MYSTERIOUS PLANET

SCOTT: I haven't had much experience of fighting androids.

THE DOCTOR: Oh, they're just like people.

NYSSA: Only they function much more logically.

THE DOCTOR: Which can be their weakness.

EARTHSHOCK

THE DOCTOR: All elephants are pink. Nellie is an elephant, therefore Nellie is pink. Logical?

DAVROS: Perfectly.

THE DOCTOR: You know what a human would say to that?

DAVROS: What?

TYSSAN: Elephants aren't pink.

DESTINY OF THE DALEKS

BAFFLEGAB

'Bafflegab, my dear. I've never heard such bafflegab in all my lives!'

THE DOCTOR, *THE PIRATE PLANET*

THE DOCTOR: With a little bit of jiggery-pokery…

ROSE: Is that a technical term, jiggery-pokery?

THE DOCTOR: Yeah, I came first in jiggery-pokery, what about you?

ROSE: No, I failed hullabaloo.

THE END OF THE WORLD

OSGOOD: What's the principle, sir?

THE DOCTOR: Negative diathermy, Sergeant. Buffer the molecular movement of the air with the reverse-phase short waves. It's quite simple.

OSGOOD: Simple? It's impossible.

THE DOCTOR: Yes, well, according to classical aerodynamics, it's impossible for a bumblebee to fly!

THE DAEMONS

THE DOCTOR: Suppose I reflect a transmission beam off the security shield, feed it back through a link crystal bank and boost it through the transducer?

K-9: Couldn't have put it better myself, master.

THE DOCTOR: I don't think you could.

THE INVASION OF TIME

GRAVIS: I should like to see it, this TARDIS.

THE DOCTOR: Well, it's not all here at the moment, you understand. It's, er, it's been spatially distributed to optimise the, er, the packing efficiency of, er, the real-time envelope.

FRONTIOS

THE DOCTOR: I've switched the Captain's circuits around to create a hyperspatial force shield around the shrunken planets, then I put his dematerialisation control into remote mode … first I dematerialise the TARDIS, then I make Zanak dematerialise for a millisecond or two, then I invert the gravity field of the hyperspatial forceshield and drop the shrunken planets…

ROMANA: Into the hollow centre of Zanak!

THE DOCTOR: Exactly.

ROMANA: What then?

THE DOCTOR: Well, I would have thought that was perfectly obvious.

THE PIRATE PLANET

THE DOCTOR: Right, well tell him to build an EHF wide-bandwidth variable-phase oscillator, with a negative feedback circuit tuneable to the frequency of an air molecule at, um, what is the temperature up at the barrier, Brigadier?

THE BRIGADIER: We've no idea what you're talking about, Doctor. Over.

THE DAEMONS

'Well, I've reversed the polarity of the neutron flow, so the TARDIS should be free of the force field now.'

THE DOCTOR, *THE FIVE DOCTORS*

'New technology dates so quickly these days.'

THE DOCTOR, *THE KEEPER OF TRAKEN*

Chapter Seven:
The Simple Things

'For some people, small, beautiful events is what life is all about!'

APPRECIATING BEAUTY

'Better to go hungry than starve for beauty.'

CAMECA, *THE AZTECS*

'Good looks are no substitute for a sound character.'

THE DOCTOR, *THE PIRATE PLANET*

COUNTESS: I was rather under the impression that Mr Duggan was following me.

THE DOCTOR: Ah. Well, you're a beautiful woman, probably, and Duggan was trying to summon up the courage to ask you out to dinner...

CITY OF DEATH

THE LITTLE PEOPLE

SARAH: I know we're not important …

THE DOCTOR: Who said you're not important? I've travelled to all sorts of places, done things you couldn't even imagine, but you two. Street corner, two in the morning, getting a taxi home. I've never had a life like that. Yes. I'll try and save you.

FATHER'S DAY

'You shouldn't feel ashamed of your grief. It's right to grieve. Your Bert, he was unique. In the whole history of the world, there's never been anybody just like Bert. And there'll never be another, even if the world lasts for a hundred million centuries.'

CLIFFORD JONES, *THE GREEN DEATH*

'Planets and history and stuff. That's what we do. But not today. No. Today, we're answering a cry for help from the scariest place in the universe. A child's bedroom.'

THE DOCTOR, *NIGHT TERRORS*

RELAXATION

'Relax. Relax. More haste, more waste. Pleasure is beautiful.'

THE DOCTOR, *THE MACRA TERROR*

'For me – as for you, sir – sleep is sometimes better nourishment than good red meat.'

THE PORTREEVE, *CASTROVALVA*

'Stupid expression, stands to reason. Why doesn't it lie down to reason? Much easier to reason lying down. Relaxes the cerebellum.'

THE DOCTOR, *THE CREATURE FROM THE PIT*

SANDERS: We've been having fun.

THE DOCTOR: Have you? Oh, good. There's nothing quite like it, is there?

KINDA

GENERAL ADVICE

'Never underestimate plumbing. Plumbing's very important.'

THE DOCTOR, *THE LONG GAME*

'Never trust a man with dirty fingernails.'

THE DOCTOR, *THE TALONS OF WENG-CHIANG*

'Never be certain of anything. It's a sign of weakness.'

THE DOCTOR, *THE FACE OF EVIL*

'Never throw anything away, Harry. Where's my 500-year diary? I remember jotting some notes on the Sontarans. It's a mistake to clutter one's pockets, Harry.'

THE DOCTOR, *THE SONTARAN EXPERIMENT*

'Long acquaintance is no guarantee for honesty.'

THE DOCTOR, *THE DALEKS' MASTER PLAN*

'Nothing's just rubbish if you have an enquiring mind.'

THE DOCTOR, *THE INVASION OF TIME*

'Don't be cool, guys. Cool is not cool.'

THE DOCTOR, *THE TIME OF THE DOCTOR*

'You give a monkey control of its environment, it'll fill the world with bananas.'

THE DOCTOR, *THE TWO DOCTORS*

'If people see you mean them no harm, they never hurt you. Nine times out of ten.'

THE DOCTOR, *THE ROBOTS OF DEATH*

'People who talk about infallibility are usually on very shaky ground.'

THE DOCTOR, *THE MIND OF EVIL*

'When replacing a brain, always make sure the arrow A is pointing to the front.'

THE DOCTOR, *DESTINY OF THE DALEKS*

'Oh, you should always waste time when you don't have any. Time is not the boss of you. Rule four hundred and eight.'

THE DOCTOR, *LET'S KILL HITLER*

'Don't get into a spaceship with a madman. Didn't anyone ever teach you that?'

THE DOCTOR, *JOURNEY TO THE CENTRE OF THE TARDIS*

'Never trust a Venusian shanghorn with a perigosto stick.'

THE DOCTOR, *THE GREEN DEATH*

'Rash action is worse than no action at all.'

THE DOCTOR, *THE EDGE OF DESTRUCTION*

'Don't be a monk. Monks are not cool.'

THE DOCTOR, *THE BELLS OF SAINT JOHN*

'Never ignore a coincidence. Unless you're busy. In which case, always ignore a coincidence.'

THE DOCTOR, *THE PANDORICA OPENS*

'An interested mind brooks no delay.'

CAMECA, *THE AZTECS*

'Don't just be obedient. Always make up your own mind.'

THE DOCTOR, *THE MACRA TERROR*

'Never guess. Unless you have to. There's enough uncertainty in the universe as it is.'

THE DOCTOR, *LOGOPOLIS*

'An apple a day keeps the, er… No, never mind.'

THE DOCTOR, *KINDA*

SHOPPING

'I like the little shop.'

THE DOCTOR, *NEW EARTH*

MEL: A freezer centre? How boring.

THE DOCTOR: Oh, trust not to appearances, Mel. You never know what might be lurking in the freezer chests. Think gothic.

DRAGONFIRE

LANG: I thank you for your offer, Doctor, but frankly, I find you unreliable.

THE DOCTOR: So's most currency. Doesn't stop people spending money wisely.

THE TWIN DILEMMA

'Oh, look down there, you've got a little shop. I like a little shop.'

THE DOCTOR, *SMITH AND JONES*

DONNA: Are we safe here?

THE DOCTOR: Of course we're safe. There's a little shop.

SILENCE IN THE LIBRARY

'I'm the Doctor. I work in a shop now. Here to help. Look, they gave me a badge with my name on in case I forget who I am. Very thoughtful, as that does happen.'

THE DOCTOR, *CLOSING TIME*

HIGH FABSION

FIRE ESCAPE: You we like, Doctor. What you wear is high fabsion and ice hot, for an old one.

THE DOCTOR: Oh, thank you very much. But clothes don't maketh the man, you know.

PARADISE TOWERS

'Bow ties are cool.'

THE DOCTOR, *THE ELEVENTH HOUR*

RIVER: What in the name of sanity have you got on your head?

THE DOCTOR: It's a fez. I wear a fez now. Fezzes are cool.

THE BIG BANG

'I wear a Stetson now. Stetsons are cool.'

THE DOCTOR, *THE IMPOSSIBLE ASTRONAUT*

THE DOCTOR: Ah, there you are, both of you. Well, I don't think I was so far wrong, my boy. What do I look like, my dear?

DODO: You're really with it now, Doctor.

THE DOCTOR: Yes. With what, my dear?

THE SAVAGES

'I don't like this jacket. Not very comfortable. I like a jacket with a lot of pockets, don't you?'

THE DOCTOR, *THE SUN MAKERS*

'Brave choice, celery, but fair play to you. Not a lot of men can carry off a decorative vegetable.'

THE DOCTOR, *TIME CRASH*

'Is nobody going to mention Rory's ponytail? You hold him down, I'll cut it off?'

THE DOCTOR, *AMY'S CHOICE*

'Nothing on Earth changes quite so often as the fashion. You wouldn't believe the way some people look. Some of them even wear safety pins.'

THE DOCTOR, *FOUR TO DOOMSDAY*

POLLY: Hey, you've got your own clothes back.

THE DOCTOR: Yes. Can you imagine, I found them thrown out on the rubbish dump, behind the inn.

BEN: Amazing, isn't it? Well, mine should be dry by now.

POLLY: I liked you better in your dress, Doctor.

KIRSTY: Aye, you made a good granny.

THE HIGHLANDERS

THE DOCTOR: Let's have your tie.

IAN: Well, I haven't got one.

THE DOCTOR: I know you're not wearing one, dear boy, but the one round your middle, hmm?

IAN: I hope my pants stay up.

THE DOCTOR: Yes, well, that's your affair, not mine.

THE WEB PLANET

'Well, you please yourself, I'm no fashion expert.'

THE DOCTOR, *THE STONES OF BLOOD*

'Beau Brummell always said I looked better in a cloak.'

THE DOCTOR, *THE SENSORITES*

PERI: You can't go out dressed like that.

THE DOCTOR: Why ever not?

PERI: You look dreadful.

THE DOCTOR: My dear, that is what people said about Beau Brummell. Remember him?

PERI: Well, he had taste, a feeling for style.

THE DOCTOR: And I don't?

PERI: Not if what you're wearing is an example. It's, oh, *yuck*.

THE TWIN DILEMMA

THE DOCTOR: You look very nice in that dress, Victoria.

VICTORIA: Thank you. Don't you think it's a bit...

THE DOCTOR: A bit short? Oh, I shouldn't worry about that. Look at Jamie's!

THE TOMB OF THE CYBERMEN

'Oh, black tie. Whenever I wear this, something bad always happens.'

THE DOCTOR, *THE LAZARUS EXPERIMENT*

RORY: A poncho. The biggest crime against fashion since lederhosen.

AMY: Here we go. My boys. My poncho boys. If we're going to die, let's die looking like a Peruvian folk band.

AMY'S CHOICE

LEELA: These clothes are ridiculous. Why must I wear them?

THE DOCTOR: Because you can't go walking around Victorian London in skins. You'll frighten the horses.

THE TALONS OF WENG-CHIANG

REDVERS: Please, young lady, you're barely dressed.

ACE: Who's undressed?

THE DOCTOR: Excuse my young friend. She comes from a less civilised clime.

ACE: What do you want me to do, wrap up in a curtain?

THE DOCTOR: Be quiet, noble savage.

GHOST LIGHT

THE DOCTOR: Hey, where do you think you're going?

ROSE: 1860.

THE DOCTOR: Go out there dressed like that, you'll start a riot, Barbarella. There's a wardrobe through there. First left, second right, third on the left, go straight ahead, under the stairs, past the bins, fifth door on your left. Hurry up!

THE UNQUIET DEAD

THE DOCTOR: What do you think of that now, eh? A Viking helmet.

STEVEN: Oh, maybe.

THE DOCTOR: What do you mean, maybe? What do you think it is, a space helmet for a cow?

THE TIME MEDDLER

'I would like a hat like that.'

THE DOCTOR, *THE HIGHLANDERS*

ROMANA: I thought you said external appearances weren't important.

THE DOCTOR: Ah, but it's nice to get them right, though, isn't it?

DESTINY OF THE DALEKS

PHILOSOPHY

ASTRID: Oh, you're a Doctor?

THE DOCTOR: Well, not of any medical significance.

ASTRID: Doctor of law? Philosophy?

THE DOCTOR: Which law? Whose philosophies, eh?

THE ENEMY OF THE WORLD

ORCINI: It is rare for someone in my profession to meet a client on their home territory. Assassins, like debt collectors, are rarely welcome. When we are allowed on the premises, it's usually through the side door.

KARA: He is a philosopher. How charming.

REVELATION OF THE DALEKS

'Is a slave a slave if he doesn't know he's enslaved?'

THE EDITOR, *THE LONG GAME*

'Every problem has a solution.'

DALEK, *THE DALEKS*

'We're all just stories in the end.'

THE DOCTOR, *THE BIG BANG*

'Total takings for the day, one sandwich. Better than no sandwich, of course. Not as good as two sandwiches, or even a chicken.'

WEBLEY, *NIGHTMARE IN SILVER*

'The more you put things together, the more they keep falling apart, and that's the essence of the second law of thermodynamics and I never heard a truer word spoken.'

THE DOCTOR, *LOGOPOLIS*

'I get the impression they don't know where they're heading for. Come to that, do any of us?'

STIRLING, *THE REIGN OF TERROR*

'Everything has got to end some time, otherwise nothing would ever get started.'

THE DOCTOR, *A CHRISTMAS CAROL*

'To the rational mind, nothing is inexplicable, only unexplained.'

THE DOCTOR, *THE ROBOTS OF DEATH*

THE DOCTOR: Nothing's inexplicable.

RIGG: Then explain it!

THE DOCTOR: It's inexplicable.

NIGHTMARE OF EDEN

THE DOCTOR: Ignorance is – what's the opposite of bliss?

CLARA: Carlisle.

THE DOCTOR: Yes. Yes, Carlisle. Ignorance is Carlisle.

HIDE

'Leave the quotes to the expert, Mel!'

Following his sixth regeneration, the Doctor developed a knack for mangling quotes and proverbs. Here's just a selection from his first adventure, *Time and the Rani*.

A bull in a barber shop

Fit as a trombone

A bad workman always blames his fools

Absence makes the nose grow longer

A kangaroo never forgets

The proof of the pumpkin's in the squeezing

Where there's a will, there's a Tom, Dick and a Harriet

All good things come to a bend

Here's a turn-up for the cook

A bird in the hand keeps the Doctor away

Two wrongs don't make a left turn

A miss is as good as a smile

Time and tide melts the snowman

MUSIC

'All we can do now is think, and I think best to music. Now, where is my recorder?'

THE DOCTOR, *THE THREE DOCTORS*

'I should say, this isn't, you know, my whole life. It's not all spaceships and stuff, because I'm into all sorts of things. I like football. I like a drink. I like Spain. And if there's one thing I really, really love – then it's Jeff Lynne and the Electric Light Orchestra. Because you can't beat a bit of ELO.'

ELTON, *LOVE & MONSTERS*

THE DOCTOR: Where'd you learn to whistle?

DONNA: West Ham, every Saturday.

PLANET OF THE OOD

'You want to see Elvis, you go for the late fifties. The time before burgers. When they called him the Pelvis and he still had a waist. What's more, you see him in style.'

THE DOCTOR, *THE IDIOT'S LANTERN*

'Oh, yes. There are no other colours without the Blues.'

THE DOCTOR, *THE HAPPINESS PATROL*

'Klokleda partha menin klatch. Haroon, haroon, haroon. Klokleda sheena tirra nach. Haroon, haroon, haroon. Haroon, haroon, haroon. Haroon, haroon, haroon. Haroon, haroon, haroon. Haroon, haroon, haroon. Well, I must say, you seem quite partial to old Venusian lullabies, don't you, Aggedor, old chap, hmm?'

THE DOCTOR, *THE CURSE OF PELADON*

'It's the first line of an old Venusian lullaby, as a matter of fact. Roughly translated it goes, "Close your eyes, my darling. Well, three of them, at least."'

THE DOCTOR, *THE DAEMONS*

BOOKS AND STUFF

'Books are the principal business of a library, sir.'

SHARDOVAN, *CASTROVALVA*

'Reading's great. You like stories, George? Yeah? Me, too. When I was your age, about, ooh, a thousand years ago, I loved a good bedtime story. "The Three Little Sontarans". "The Emperor Dalek's New Clothes". "Snow White and the Seven Keys to Doomsday", eh? All the classics.'

THE DOCTOR, *NIGHT TERRORS*

'I enjoy the *Strand* magazine as much as the next man, but I am perfectly aware that Sherlock Holmes is a fictional character.'

DR SIMEON, *THE SNOWMEN*

'Books. People never really stop loving books. Fifty-first century. By now you've got holovids, direct-to-brain downloads, fiction mist. But you need the smell. The smell of books.'

THE DOCTOR, *SILENCE IN THE LIBRARY*

'If heroes don't exist, it is necessary to invent them. Good for public morale.'

BORUSA, *THE DEADLY ASSASSIN*

'Well, what's the use of a good quotation if you can't change it?'

THE DOCTOR, *THE TWO DOCTORS*

THE DOCTOR: I love biographies!

DONNA: Yeah, very you. Always a death at the end.

SILENCE IN THE LIBRARY

'You want weapons? We're in a library. Books! Best weapons in the world. This room's the greatest arsenal we could have.'

THE DOCTOR, *TOOTH AND CLAW*

TELEVISION

THE DOCTOR: You say you can't fit an enormous building into one of your smaller sitting rooms.

IAN: No.

THE DOCTOR: But you've discovered television, haven't you?

IAN: Yes.

THE DOCTOR: Then by showing an enormous building on your television screen, you can do what seemed impossible, couldn't you?

AN UNEARTHLY CHILD

THE DOCTOR: Improve what, for instance?

MONK: Well, for instance, Harold, King Harold, I know he'd be a good king. There wouldn't be all those wars in Europe, those claims over France went on for years and years. With peace the people would be able to better themselves. With a few hints and tips from me they'd be able to have jet airliners by 1320! Shakespeare would be able to put *Hamlet* on television.

THE DOCTOR: He'd do what?

MONK: The play *Hamlet* on television.

THE DOCTOR: Oh, yes, quite so, yes, of course, I do know the medium.

THE TIME MEDDLER

BENTON: What are we going to do now?

THE DOCTOR: Keep it confused. Feed it with useless information. I wonder if I have a television set handy.

THE THREE DOCTORS

ROSE: So history's happening and we're stuck here.

THE DOCTOR: Yes, we are …

ROSE: We could always do what everybody else does. We could watch it on TV.

ALIENS OF LONDON

'I hear they rot your brains. Rot them into soup. And your brain comes pouring out of your ears. That's what television does.'

GRAN, *THE IDIOT'S LANTERN*

WINSTANLEY: Are you one of these television chaps then?

THE DOCTOR: I am no sort of chap, sir.

WINSTANLEY: Forgive me, but I thought… Well, the costume and the wig, you know?

THE DAEMONS

THE ARTS

'But a theatre's magic, isn't it? You should know. Stand on this stage, say the right words with the right emphasis at the right time. Oh, you can make men weep, or cry with joy. Change them. You can change people's minds just with words in this place.'

THE DOCTOR, *THE SHAKESPEARE CODE*

'High drama is very similar to comedy. It's all a matter of timing.'

THE DOCTOR, *BATTLEFIELD*

DUGGAN: But it's a fake! You can't hang a fake Mona Lisa in the Louvre.

ROMANA: How can it be a fake if Leonardo painted it?

DUGGAN: With the words 'This is a fake' written under the paintwork in felt tip?

ROMANA: It doesn't affect what it looks like.

DUGGAN: It doesn't matter what it looks like.

THE DOCTOR: Doesn't it? Well, some people would say that's the whole point of painting.

CITY OF DEATH

A WELL-PREPARED MEAL

'I remember saying to old Napoleon. Boney, I said, always remember an army marches on its stomach.'

THE DOCTOR, *DAY OF THE DALEKS*

THE DOCTOR: When did you last have the pleasure of smelling a flower, watching a sunset, eating a well-prepared meal?

CYBERLEADER: These things are irrelevant.

EARTHSHOCK

'Anyone who likes jelly babies can't be all bad, huh? Don't mention this to the Chancellor. He doesn't approve of jelly babies. I think he's frivolous.'

THE DOCTOR, *THE INVASION OF TIME*

CRAIG: So what's the plan tonight? Pizza, booze, telly?

SOPHIE: Yeah, pizza, booze, telly.

THE LODGER

THE DOCTOR: What's for tea?

LOU: Chops. Nice couple of chops and gravy. Nothing special.

THE DOCTOR: Oh, that's special, Lou. That is so special. Chops and gravy, mmm.

PLANET OF THE DEAD

'Oh, look, they've got nibbles! I love nibbles.'

THE DOCTOR, *THE LAZARUS EXPERIMENT*

'If you're calling the butler, I'm very partial to tea and muffins.'

THE DOCTOR, *THE ANDROID INVASION*

TRYST: I am helping to conserve endangered species.

THE DOCTOR: By putting them in this machine?

TRYST: Oh, yes.

THE DOCTOR: Ah, yes, of course. Just in the same way a jam-maker conserves raspberries.

NIGHTMARE OF EDEN

DAVROS: I never waste a valuable commodity. The humanoid form makes an excellent concentrated protein. ...

THE DOCTOR: Did you bother to tell anyone they might be eating their own relatives?

DAVROS: Certainly not. That would have created what I believe is termed consumer resistance.

REVELATION OF THE DALEKS

'Why can't you give me any decent food? You're Scottish. Fry something.'

THE DOCTOR, *THE ELEVENTH HOUR*

ROSE: Oh, can you smell chips?

THE DOCTOR: Yeah. Yeah.

ROSE: Before you get me back in that box, chips it is, and you can pay.

THE DOCTOR: No money.

ROSE: What sort of date are you? Come on then, tightwad, chips are on me. We've only got five billion years till the shops close.

THE END OF THE WORLD

'If you want to know what's going on, work in the kitchens.'

THE DOCTOR, *RISE OF THE CYBERMEN*

THE DOCTOR: You know, I think it was Rassilon who once said, 'There are few ways in which a Time Lord can be more innocently occupied, than in catching fish.'

PERI: It was Dr Johnson who said that, about money.

THE TWO DOCTORS

GROSE: The Doctor said that you'd be fair famished when you woke up, so here's scrambled egg, hot buttered toast, kedgeree, kidney, sausage and bacon.

ACE: Cholesterol city.

GROSE: Oh, no dear. Perivale village.

GHOST LIGHT

THE DOCTOR: Swear to me. Swear to me on something that matters.

AMY: Fish fingers and custard.

THE DOCTOR: My life in your hands, Amelia Pond.

THE IMPOSSIBLE ASTRONAUT

SHOCKEYE: Personally I have never seen the necessity for starting a meal with a, what was your word?

THE DOCTOR: Hors d'oeuvres.

SHOCKEYE: Quite unnecessary, in my opinion. Eight or nine main dishes are quite enough…

THE TWO DOCTORS

'I think I may have accidentally invented pasta.'

THE DOCTOR, *POND LIFE*

'I think I just invented the banana daiquiri a few centuries early. Do you know, they've never even seen a banana before? Always take a banana to a party, Rose. Bananas are good.'

THE DOCTOR, *THE GIRL IN THE FIREPLACE*

'It's a floater, all right. You've got it, guv. On my oath, you wouldn't want that served with onions. Never seen anything like it in all my puff. Oh, make an 'orse sick, that would.'

GHOUL, *THE TALONS OF WENG-CHIANG*

'I've run restaurants. Who do you think invented the Yorkshire pudding? Pudding, yet savoury. Sound familiar?'

THE DOCTOR, *THE POWER OF THREE*

ROMANA: Where are we going?

THE DOCTOR: Are you talking philosophically or geographically?

ROMANA: Philosophically.

THE DOCTOR: Then we're going to lunch.

CITY OF DEATH

'Of course, in primitive times on Old Earth, they ate prodigious quantities of vegetable matter without any apparent harm to their system.'

HADE, *THE SUN MAKERS*

SHOCKEYE: Tell me, on this planet, do they ever eat their own?

THE DOCTOR: I believe in the Far Indies it has been known, but I remember a dish – shepherd's pie.

SHOCKEYE: Shepherd's pie? A shepherd? Can't we walk quicker?

THE TWO DOCTORS

THE DOCTOR: 'Throw in the apple cores very hard, put the lot in a shallow tin and bake in a high oven for two weeks.'

MRS TYLER: That ain't the way to make a fruitcake.

IMAGE OF THE FENDAHL

ARTIE: How can it be your mum's soufflé if you're making it?

CLARA: Because, Artie, it's like my mum always said. The soufflé isn't the soufflé, the soufflé is the recipe.

ANGIE: Was your mum deep on puddings?

CLARA: She was a great woman.

THE NAME OF THE DOCTOR

DORTMUN: Two more pairs of hands. Good.

DAVID: She says *she* can cook … And what do *you* do?

SUSAN: I eat.

THE DALEK INVASION OF EARTH

'Cut out the hard-boiled eggs, I said. Quite apart from their effects on my digestion, they're aesthetically boring.'

GOODGE, *TERROR OF THE AUTONS*

CLARA: OK. When are you going to explain to me what the hell is going on?

THE DOCTOR: Breakfast.

CLARA: What? I'm not waiting for breakfast.

THE DOCTOR: It's a time machine. You never have to wait for breakfast.

THE BELLS OF SAINT JOHN

'The last time I fished this particular stretch, I landed four magnificent gumblejack in less than ten minutes … The finest fish in this galaxy, probably the universe. Cleaned, skinned, quickly pan-fried in their own juices till they're golden brown. Ambrosia steeped in nectar, Peri. The flavour is unforgettable.'

THE DOCTOR, *THE TWO DOCTORS*

'Nothing like sausage sandwiches when you are working something out.'

PROFESSOR RUMFORD, *THE STONES OF BLOOD*

'Did you ever have one of those little cakes with the crunchy ball bearings on top? Do you know those things? Nobody else in this entire galaxy's ever even bothered to make edible ball bearings. Genius.'

THE DOCTOR, *FEAR HER*

SHOCKEYE: Do you serve humans here?

OSCAR: Most of the time, sir. Yes, I think I could venture to say that most of our customers are certainly human.

SHOCKEYE: I mean human meat, you fawning imbecile.

OSCAR: No, sir. The nouvelle cuisine has not yet penetrated this establishment.

THE TWO DOCTORS

'Who was it said Earthmen never invite their ancestors round to dinner?'

THE DOCTOR, *GHOST LIGHT*

'No one loves cattle more than Burger King.'

MISS KIZLET, *THE BELLS OF SAINT JOHN*

'Here, have a jelly baby and don't forget to brush your teeth.'

THE DOCTOR, *NIGHTMARE OF EDEN*

CHEERS!

'You know, one thing you can be certain of with politicians, is that whatever their political ideas, they always keep a well-stocked larder. Not to mention the cellar.'

THE DOCTOR, *DAY OF THE DALEKS*

AMY: And since when do you drink wine?

THE DOCTOR: I'm eleven hundred and three. I must've drunk it some time. Oh, why it's horrid. I thought it would taste more like the gums.

THE IMPOSSIBLE ASTRONAUT

'Patron, three glasses of water. Make them doubles.'

THE DOCTOR, *CITY OF DEATH*

ADRIC: What does that stuff taste like?

RICHARD MACE: Nectar.

ADRIC: Oh. And what does that taste like?

THE VISITATION

'Funny thing. Last time I was sentenced to death, I ordered four hyper-vodkas for my breakfast. All a bit of a blur after that. Woke up in bed with both my executioners. Mmm, lovely couple. They stayed in touch. Can't say that about most executioners.'

CAPTAIN JACK HARKNESS, *THE DOCTOR DANCES*

EMMA: Urgh. I'd rather have a nice cup of tea.

CLARA: Me too. Whisky is the eleventh most disgusting thing ever invented.

HIDE

YATES: Fancy a dance, Brigadier?

THE BRIGADIER: It's kind of you, Captain Yates. I think I'd rather have a pint.

THE DAEMONS

FANCY A BREW?

'Would you care for some tea?'

DALEK, *VICTORY OF THE DALEKS*

ZOE: There's one thing I don't understand.

MILO: Well, you're very lucky, girl. There's about a hundred thousand things I don't understand, but I don't stand around asking fool questions about them, I do something useful. Why don't you do something useful? Why don't you make us all a pot of tea or something?

THE SPACE PIRATES

BRYSON: Excuse me, sir, but are we evacuating or not?

THE BRIGADIER: No.

BRYSON: Oh, well, in that case, sir, what should I do?

THE BRIGADIER: Oh, go and make us all a cup of tea.

INVASION OF THE DINOSAURS

THE DOCTOR: Look, I said I don't want any tea today, thank you.

JO: I'm not the tea lady.

THE DOCTOR: Then what the blazes are you doing in here? … Don't you know this area is strictly out of bounds to everybody except the tea lady and the Brigadier's personal staff?

TERROR OF THE AUTONS

'The coffee's just about as filthy as UNIT tea, if that's possible.'

JO GRANT, *PLANET OF THE SPIDERS*

THE DOCTOR: I don't suppose you can make tea?

ROMANA: Tea?

THE DOCTOR: No, I don't suppose you can. They don't teach you anything useful at the Academy, do they?

THE RIBOS OPERATION

THE DOCTOR: Good. Well, now he's gone, any chance of a cup of tea?

TANE: What?!

THE DOCTOR: Or coffee. My friend and I have had a very trying experience. Haven't we had a trying experience, Harry?

HARRY: Very trying, Doctor.

TANE: Step into the security scan.

THE DOCTOR: What, no tea?

GENESIS OF THE DALEKS

CHANDLER: What be tea?

THE DOCTOR: Oh, a noxious infusion of oriental leaves containing a high percentage of toxic acid.

CHANDLER: Sounds an evil brew, don't it?

THE DOCTOR: True. Personally, I rather like it.

THE AWAKENING

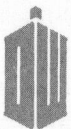

BEING CHILDISH

'What's wrong with being childish? I like being childish.'

THE DOCTOR, *TERROR OF THE AUTONS*

'There's no point in being grown up if you can't be childish sometimes.'

THE DOCTOR, *ROBOT*

THE DOCTOR: Lily and Cyril's room. I'm going to be honest, masterpiece. The ultimate bedroom. A sciencey-wiencey workbench. A jungle. A maze. A window disguised as a mirror. A mirror disguised as a window. Selection of torches for midnight feasts and secret reading. Zen garden, mysterious cupboard, zone of tranquillity, rubber wall, dream tank, exact model of the rest of the house, not quite to scale. Apologies. Dolls with comical expressions, the Magna Carta, a foot spa. Cluedo! A yellow fort.

CYRIL: Where are the beds?

THE DOCTOR: Well, I couldn't fit everything in. There had to be sacrifices. Anyway, who needs beds when you've got hammocks!

THE DOCTOR, THE WIDOW AND THE WARDROBE

'It goes up tiddly up, it goes down tiddly down for only £49.99, which I personally think is a bit steep, but then again it's your parents' cash and they'll only waste it on boring stuff like lamps and vegetables. Yawn.'

THE DOCTOR, *CLOSING TIME*

'I expect chocolate for breakfast. If you don't feel sick by mid-morning you're not doing it right.'

THE GANGER DOCTOR, *THE ALMOST PEOPLE*

THE DOCTOR: Right then, your bedroom. Great. Let's see. You're twelve years old, so we'll stay away from under the bed. Cupboard! Big cupboard. I love a cupboard. Do you know, there's a thing called a face spider. It's just like a tiny baby's head with spider legs, and it's specifically evolved to scuttle up the backs of bedroom cupboards... which, yeah, I probably shouldn't have mentioned. Right. So. What are we going to do? Eat crisps and talk about girls? I've never actually done that, but I bet it's easy. Girls? Yeah?

KAZRAN: Are you really a babysitter?

THE DOCTOR: I think you'll find I'm universally recognised as a mature and responsible adult.

A CHRISTMAS CAROL

'I know you can't wrap your hand around your elbow and make your fingers meet.'

THE DOCTOR, *THE IDIOT'S LANTERN*

'That is the dematerialising control and that, over yonder, is the horizontal hold. Up there is the scanner, those are the doors, that is a chair with a panda on it. Sheer poetry, dear boy. Now please stop bothering me.'

THE DOCTOR, *THE TIME MEDDLER*

'Never knowingly be serious. Rule 27. You might want to write these down.'

THE DOCTOR, *LET'S KILL HITLER*

'Do you have to talk like children? What is it that makes you so ashamed of being a grown-up?'

THE WAR DOCTOR, *THE DAY OF THE DOCTOR*

CHRISTMAS

'A Happy Christmas to all of you at home.'

THE DOCTOR, *THE DALEKS' MASTER PLAN*

'What sort of man doesn't carry a trowel? Put it on your Christmas list.'

BRIAN, *DINOSAURS ON A SPACESHIP*

'Christmas Eve on a rooftop. Saw a chimney, my whole brain just went, what the hell.'

THE DOCTOR, *A CHRISTMAS CAROL*

LINDA: How's the turkey doing?

CLARA: Great. Yeah, yeah, it's doing great. Well, dead and decapitated, but that's Christmas when you're a turkey.

THE TIME OF THE DOCTOR

IDA: Well, we've come this far. There's no turning back.

THE DOCTOR: Oh, did you have to? No turning back? That's almost as bad as nothing can possibly go wrong, or this is going to be the best Christmas Walford's ever had.

THE IMPOSSIBLE PLANET

THE DOCTOR: Father Christmas, Santa Claus or, as I've always known him, Jeff.

BOY: There's no such person as Father Christmas.

THE DOCTOR: Oh, yeah? Me and Father Christmas, Frank Sinatra's hunting lodge, 1952. See him at the back with the blonde? Albert Einstein. The three of us together. Brr. Watch out. OK? Keep the faith. Stay off the naughty list.

A CHRISTMAS CAROL

'It was a present, and it wasn't supposed to be opened till Christmas Day. Honestly, who opens their Christmas presents early? OK. Shut up. Everyone.'

THE DOCTOR, *THE DOCTOR, THE WIDOW AND THE WARDROBE*

AMY: We're about to have Christmas dinner. Joining us?

THE DOCTOR: If it's no trouble.

RORY: There's a place set for you.

THE DOCTOR: But you didn't know I was coming. Why would you set me a place?

AMY: Oh, because we always do. It's Christmas, you moron.

THE DOCTOR, THE WIDOW AND THE WARDROBE

'Back to your mum. It's all waiting. Fish and chips, sausage and mash, beans on toast... no, Christmas! Turkey! Although, having met your mother, nut loaf would be more appropriate.'

THE DOCTOR, *BORN AGAIN*

'That's human Christmas out there! They eat so much. All that roasting meat, cakes and red wine. Hot fat blood food. Pots and plates of meat and flesh … and grease and juice. And baking burnt sticky hot skin. Hot, it's so hot!'

THE MASTER, *THE END OF TIME*

'On every world, wherever people are, in the deepest part of the winter, at the exact mid-point, everybody stops and turns and hugs, as if to say, well done. Well done, everyone. We're halfway out of the dark. Back on Earth, we called this Christmas, or the Winter Solstice. On this world, the first settlers called it the Crystal Feast. You know what I call it? I call it expecting something for nothing.'

KAZRAN SARDICK, *A CHRISTMAS CAROL*

MADGE: No one should be alone at Christmas.

THE DOCTOR: I'm fine. I don't mind. I'm really very good at being—

MADGE: I'm not talking about you, I'm talking about your friends. You can't let them think that you're dead. Not at Christmas.

THE DOCTOR, *THE WIDOW AND THE WARDROBE*

SARDICK: I despise Christmas.

THE DOCTOR: You shouldn't. It's very you.

SARDICK: It's what? What do you mean?

THE DOCTOR: Halfway out of the dark.

A CHRISTMAS CAROL

'Santa's a robot!'

DONNA, *THE RUNAWAY BRIDE*

'I am Mr Copper, the ship's historian, and I shall be taking you to Old London Town in the country of Yookay. Ruled over by Good King Wenceslas. Now human beings worshipped the great god Santa, a creature with fearsome claws, and his wife Mary. And every Christmas Eve, the people of Yookay go to war with the country of Turkey. They then eat the Turkey people for Christmas dinner. Like savages.'

MR COPPER, *VOYAGE OF THE DAMNED*

MR COPPER: Rather ironic, but this is very much in the spirit of Christmas. It's a festival of violence. They say that human beings only survive depending on whether they've been good or bad. It's barbaric!

THE DOCTOR: Actually, that's not true. Christmas is a time of peace and thanksgiving and – What am I going on about? My Christmasses are always like this.

VOYAGE OF THE DAMNED

Chapter Eight:
The Past

'This is what I travel for, Rose.
To see history happening
right in front of us.'

THE DOCTOR, *ALIENS OF LONDON*

FIXED POINTS IN TIME

'But you can't rewrite history! Not one line!'

THE DOCTOR, *THE AZTECS*

'The events will happen, just as they are written. I'm afraid so and we can't stem the tide. But at least we can stop being carried away with the flood!'

THE DOCTOR, *THE REIGN OF TERROR*

'Crossing into established events is strictly forbidden. Except for cheap tricks.'

THE DOCTOR, *SMITH AND JONES*

THE DOCTOR: Are you quite mad? You know as well as I do the golden rule about space and time travelling. Never, never interfere with the course of history.

MONK: And who says so? Doctor, it's more fun my way. I can make things happen ahead of their time.

THE TIME MEDDLER

'Rose, there's a man alive in the world who wasn't alive before. An ordinary man. That's the most important thing in creation. The whole world's different because he's alive.'

THE DOCTOR, *FATHER'S DAY*

'Now listen to me, both of you. There are some rules that cannot be broken even with the TARDIS. Don't ever ask me to do anything like that again. You must accept that Adric is dead. His life wasn't wasted. He died trying to save others, just like his brother, Varsh. You know, Adric had a choice. This is the way he wanted it.'

THE DOCTOR, *TIME-FLIGHT*

'My dear Steven, history sometimes gives us a terrible shock, and that is because we don't quite fully understand. Why should we? After all, we're all too small to realise its final pattern. Therefore don't try and judge it from where you stand. I was right to do as I did. Yes, that I firmly believe.'

THE DOCTOR, *THE MASSACRE*

'This moment, this precise moment in time, it's like... I mean, it's only a theory, what do I know, but I think certain moments in time are fixed. Tiny, precious moments. Everything else is in flux, anything can happen, but those certain moments, they have to stand. This base on Mars with you, Adelaide Brooke, this is one vital moment. What happens here must always happen.'

THE DOCTOR, *THE WATERS OF MARS*

AMY: But it could help us find Rory.

THE DOCTOR: And if you read ahead and find that Rory dies? This isn't any old future, Amy, it's ours. Once we know what's coming, it's fixed. I'm going to break something, because you told me that I'm going to do it. No choice now.

AMY: Time can be rewritten.

THE DOCTOR: Not once you've read it. Once we know what's coming, it's written in stone.

THE ANGELS TAKE MANHATTAN

STEPPING INTO THE PAST

'You may know where you are, my dears, but not when. Oh, I can foresee oodles of trouble.'

THE DOCTOR, *THE SMUGGLERS*

THE DOCTOR: Three o'clock, June the 11th, 1925.

TEGAN: I haven't been born yet.

THE DOCTOR: It's interesting, isn't it? And no jet lag.

BLACK ORCHID

'Time isn't a straight line. It's all bumpy-wumpy. There's loads of boring stuff like Sundays and Tuesdays and Thursday afternoons. But now and then there are Saturdays. Big temporal tipping points when anything's possible. The TARDIS can't resist them, like a moth to a flame. She loves a party, so I give her 1969 and NASA, because that's space in the Sixties, and Canton Everett Delaware III, and this is where she's pointing.'

THE DOCTOR, *THE IMPOSSIBLE ASTRONAUT*

ROSE: It's so weird. The day my father died. I thought it'd be all sort of grim and stormy. It's just an ordinary day.

THE DOCTOR: The past is another country. 1987's just the Isle of Wight.

FATHER'S DAY

'The point of archaeology is to carefully recover the past, not disintegrate it.'

THE DOCTOR, *BATTLEFIELD*

MARTHA: I'm not going to get carted off as a slave, am I?

THE DOCTOR: Why would they do that?

MARTHA: Not exactly white, in case you haven't noticed.

THE DOCTOR: I'm not even human. Just walk about like you own the place. Works for me.

THE SHAKESPEARE CODE

BILLY: Where am I?

THE DOCTOR: 1969. Not bad, as it goes. You've got the moon landing to look forward to.

MARTHA: Oh, the moon landing's brilliant. We went four times.

BLINK

'Roll back time, I see. Can Whitaker really do that? ... Do you realise what'll happen if they succeed? ... There never was a golden age, Mike. It's all an illusion.'

THE DOCTOR, *INVASION OF THE DINOSAURS*

'Don't mess with Egyptian queens.'

THE DOCTOR, *DINOSAURS ON A SPACESHIP*

'Definitely Jurassic. There's a nip in the air, though. We can't be far off the Pleistocene era... It's times like this I wish I still had my scarf. Better watch out for the odd brontosaurus.'

THE DOCTOR, *TIME-FLIGHT*

LYNDA: A hundred years ago? What, you were here a hundred years ago?

THE DOCTOR: Yep!

LYNDA: You're looking good on it.

THE DOCTOR: I moisturise.

BAD WOLF

THE DOCTOR: I'm a time traveller. Or I was. I'm stuck in 1969.

MARTHA: We're stuck. All of space and time, he promised me. Now I've got a job in a shop. I've got to support him!

BLINK

SCARLIONI: Doctor, how very nice to see you again. It seems like only 474 years since we last met.

THE DOCTOR: Indeed, indeed, yes. I so much prefer the weather in the early part of the sixteenth century, don't you?

CITY OF DEATH

YOUNG REINETTE: Monsieur, what are you doing in my fireplace?

THE DOCTOR: Oh, it's just a routine fire check. Can you tell me what year it is?

YOUNG REINETTE: Of course I can. Seventeen hundred and twenty-seven.

THE DOCTOR: Right, lovely. One of my favourites. August is rubbish though. Stay indoors. OK, that's all for now. Thanks for your help. Hope you enjoy the rest of the fire. Night, night.

THE GIRL IN THE FIREPLACE

THE DOCTOR: Oh, smell that air. Grass and lemonade. And a little bit of mint. A hint of mint. Must be the 1920s.

DONNA: You can tell what year it is just by smelling?

THE DOCTOR: Oh, yeah.

DONNA: Or maybe that big vintage car coming up the drive gave it away.

THE UNICORN AND THE WASP

'Oh, the Lake District's lovely. Let's definitely go there. We can eat scones. They do great scones in 1927.'

THE DOCTOR, *THE RINGS OF AKHATEN*

'1979. Hell of a year. China invades Vietnam. *The Muppet Movie*. Love that film. Margaret Thatcher. Urgh. Skylab falls to Earth, with a little help from me. Nearly took off my thumb.'

THE DOCTOR, *TOOTH AND CLAW*

THE DOCTOR: A chemical reaction in a primeval swamp can create life on a planet. Why couldn't the universe be created by a similar chance factor, hmm?

KARI: But exploding fuel in space? It's almost too simple.

THE DOCTOR: It only appears simple because the circumstances were exactly right.

TERMINUS

JAMIE: Ach, here's you saying you're a doctor, you've not even bled him yet.

BEN: What's he on about?

THE DOCTOR: Bloodletting.

BEN: Yeah, but that's stupid.

JAMIE: It's the only way of curing the sick.

BEN: Killing him, more like.

THE HIGHLANDERS

TEGAN: 1851. The Great Exhibition?

THE DOCTOR: All the wonders of Victorian science and technology.

TEGAN: Well, the TARDIS should feel at home.

TIME-FLIGHT

THE DOCTOR: A monastery. Thirteenth century.

AMY: Oh, we've gone all medieval.

RORY: I'm not sure about that.

AMY: Really? Medieval expert are you?

RORY: No, it's just that I can hear Dusty Springfield.

THE REBEL FLESH

THE DOCTOR: I had this friend, once. She called me spaceman.

CHRISTINA: And was she right? Do you zoom about the place in a rocket?

THE DOCTOR: Well, a little blue box. Travels in more than space. It can journey through time, Christina. Oh, the places I've been. World War One. Creation of the universe. End of the universe. The war between China and Japan. And the Court of King Athelstan in 924 AD.

PLANET OF THE DEAD

THE DOCTOR: The Blitz.

LAZARUS: You've read about it.

THE DOCTOR: I was there.

LAZARUS: You're too young.

THE DOCTOR: So are you.

THE LAZARUS EXPERIMENT

CRAIG: Oh, that was incredible. That was absolutely brilliant. Where did you learn to cook?

THE DOCTOR: Paris, in the eighteenth century. No, hang on, that's not recent, is it? Seventeenth? No, no, no. Twentieth. Sorry, I'm not used to doing them in the right order.

THE LODGER

THE DOCTOR: What Paris has, it has an ethos, a life. It has...

ROMANA: A bouquet?

THE DOCTOR: A spirit all of its own. Like a wine, it has...

ROMANA: A bouquet.

THE DOCTOR: It has a bouquet. Yes. Like a good wine. You have to choose one of the vintage years, of course.

ROMANA: What year is this?

THE DOCTOR: Ah well, yes. It's 1979 actually. More of a table wine, shall we say.

CITY OF DEATH

LEELA: In a house this size there must be protection. The professor will have weapons in fixed positions to guard the approaches.

THE DOCTOR: I brought you to the wrong time, my girl. You'd have loved Agincourt.

THE TALONS OF WENG-CHIANG

'Look, sorry, I've got a bit of a complex life. Things don't always happen to me in quite the right order. Gets a bit confusing at times, especially at weddings. I'm rubbish at weddings, especially my own.'

THE DOCTOR, *BLINK*

MICKEY: What's a horse doing on a spaceship?

THE DOCTOR: Mickey, what's pre-Revolutionary France doing on a spaceship? Get a little perspective.

THE GIRL IN THE FIREPLACE

ROMANA: Well, there's one called Zolfa-Thura. That's in the history books.

THE DOCTOR: Well, they're all in somebody's history books.

MEGLOS

NAME DROPPER

GRACE: You know, Freud had a name for that.

THE MASTER: Transference.

THE DOCTOR: Yes, very witty, Grace. At least Freud would have taken me seriously.

GRACE: He'd have hung up his pipe if he'd met you.

THE DOCTOR: Actually, we did meet.

GRACE: Oh, that's right. He's a Time Lord.

THE DOCTOR: We got on very well.

DOCTOR WHO (TV MOVIE)

'Look after this. I love that coat. Janis Joplin gave me that coat.'

THE DOCTOR, *GRIDLOCK*

THE DOCTOR: You know, I haven't seen a coronation since Elizabeth I's. Or was it Queen Victoria?

JO: Name dropper.

THE CURSE OF PELADON

THE DOCTOR: If Horatio Nelson had been in charge of this operation, I hardly think that he would have waited for official instructions.

CAPTAIN HART: Yes... a pretty impulsive fellow. If one can believe the history books.

THE DOCTOR: History books? Captain Hart, Horatio Nelson was a personal friend of mine.

THE SEA DEVILS

'I was on board another ship once. They said that was unsinkable. I ended up clinging to an iceberg. It wasn't half cold.'

THE DOCTOR, *THE END OF THE WORLD*

MORGAN: Something you want, sir?

THE DOCTOR: Yes. A telephone that works. Yours is out of order.

MORGAN: Likely it is.

THE DOCTOR: So is the village call box.

MORGAN: There was a gale last night, sir. Brought all the lines down.

THE DOCTOR: Ah. I always told Alexander Bell that wires were unreliable.

THE ANDROID INVASION

THE DOCTOR: The sun's gone wibbly, so right now, somewhere out there, there's going to be a big old video conference call. All the experts in the world panicking at once, and do you know what they need? Me. Ah, and here they all are. All the big boys. NASA, Jodrell Bank, Tokyo Space Centre, Patrick Moore.

MRS ANGELO: I like Patrick Moore.

THE DOCTOR: I'll get you his number. But watch him, he's a devil.

THE ELEVENTH HOUR

'All I care about is getting back to the TARDIS, where it's nice and warm. No wonder they forced him to sign Magna Carta. Bet there was something in it about underheated housing.'

TEGAN, *THE KING'S DEMONS*

'Agatha Christie. I was just talking about you the other day. I said, I bet she's brilliant. I'm the Doctor. This is Donna. Oh, I love your stuff. What a mind. You fool me every time. Well, almost every time. Well, once or twice. Well, once. But it was a good once.'

THE DOCTOR, *THE UNICORN AND THE WASP*

THE DOCTOR: Attaboy, Charlie.

CHARLES DICKENS: Nobody calls me Charlie.

THE DOCTOR: The ladies do.

THE UNQUIET DEAD

DONNA: No, but isn't that a bit weird? Agatha Christie didn't walk around surrounded by murders. Not really. I mean, that's like meeting Charles Dickens and he's surrounded by ghosts at Christmas.

THE DOCTOR: Well…

DONNA: Oh, come on! It's not like we could drive across country and find Enid Blyton having tea with Noddy. Could we? Noddy's not real. Is he? Tell me there's no Noddy.

THE DOCTOR: There's no Noddy.

THE UNICORN AND THE WASP

SARAH: It's probably been vandalised.

THE DOCTOR: That's a very unfair word, you know, because actually the Vandals were quite decent chaps.

INVASION OF THE DINOSAURS

CORDO: Each Megropolis was given its own sun.

THE DOCTOR: In-station fusion satellites. Galileo would have been impressed.

THE SUN MAKERS

SARAH: Oh, it's no good, Doctor. They won't budge.

THE DOCTOR: Hmm? I used a tangle Turk's Head eye-splice with a gromit I picked up from Houdini. It should work.

REVENGE OF THE CYBERMEN

LEELA: Where did you learn to shoot like that?

THE DOCTOR: Shoot like what? Oh, like that. In Switzerland. Charming man. William Tell, he was called.

THE FACE OF EVIL

STOKER: It's only to be expected. There's a thunderstorm moving in and lightning is a form of static electricity, as was first proven by… Anyone?

THE DOCTOR: Benjamin Franklin.

STOKER: Correct.

THE DOCTOR: My mate, Ben. That was a day and a half. I got rope burns off that kite, and then I got soaked.

STOKER: Quite.

THE DOCTOR: And then I got electrocuted.

SMITH AND JONES

MARTHA: I didn't know you could play?

THE DOCTOR: Oh, well, you know, if you hang around with Beethoven, you're bound to pick a few things up.

THE LAZARUS EXPERIMENT

'I'm telling you. Lloyd George, he used to drink me under the table.'

THE DOCTOR, *ALIENS OF LONDON*

'French picklock. Never fails. Belonged to Marie Antoinette. Charming lady. Lost her head, poor thing.'

THE DOCTOR, *PYRAMIDS OF MARS*

ROMANA: Newton. Who's Newton?

THE DOCTOR: Old Isaac? Friend of mine on Earth. Discovered gravity. Well, I say he discovered gravity. I had to give him a bit of a prod.

ROMANA: What did you do?

THE DOCTOR: Climbed up a tree.

ROMANA: And?

THE DOCTOR: Dropped an apple on his head.

ROMANA: Ah. And so he discovered gravity?

THE DOCTOR: No, no. He told me to clear off out of his tree. I explained it to him afterwards at dinner.

THE PIRATE PLANET

'Pity about the scarf. Madame Nostradamus made it for me. A witty little knitter… Never get another one like it.'

THE DOCTOR, *THE ARK IN SPACE*

THE DOCTOR: I met him once, you know.

SARAH: Who?

THE DOCTOR: Shakespeare. Charming fellow. Dreadful actor.

SARAH: Perhaps that's why he took up writing.

THE DOCTOR: Perhaps it was.

PLANET OF EVIL

COUNTESS: *Hamlet*. The first draft.

THE DOCTOR: What? It's been missing for centuries.

COUNTESS: It's quite genuine, I assure you.

THE DOCTOR: I know. I recognise the handwriting.

COUNTESS: Shakespeare's.

THE DOCTOR: No, mine. He'd sprained his wrist writing sonnets. Wonderful stuff. 'To be or not to be, that is the question. Whether 'tis nobler in the mind to suffer the slings and arrows of outrageous fortune or to take arms against a sea of troubles and…' 'Take arms against a sea of troubles'? That's a mixed… I told him that was a mixed metaphor and he would insist.

CITY OF DEATH

THE DOCTOR: Come on. We can all have a good flirt later.

SHAKESPEARE: Is that a promise, Doctor?

THE DOCTOR: Oh, fifty-seven academics just punched the air.

THE SHAKESPEARE CODE

'Trust yourself. When you're locked away in your room, the words just come, don't they, like magic. Words of the right sound, the right shape, the right rhythm. Words that last for ever. That's what you do, Will. You choose perfect words. Do it. Improvise.'

THE DOCTOR TO WILLIAM SHAKESPEARE, *THE SHAKESPEARE CODE*

'Perhaps it is time we were leaving. We don't want to be blamed for starting a fire, do we? ... I had enough of that in 1666.'

THE DOCTOR, *PYRAMIDS OF MARS*

'And Picasso. What a ghastly old goat. I kept telling him, "Concentrate, Pablo. It's one eye, either side of the face."'

THE DOCTOR, *VINCENT AND THE DOCTOR*

ROMANA: 'To the Doctor. A souvenir with love and thanks for all his help with the Minotaur. Theseus and Ariadne.'

THE DOCTOR: Yes. If I hadn't produced that ball of string to find a way out of the labyrinth, they were going to unravel my scarf, the wretches.

THE CREATURE FROM THE PIT

'I remember watching Michelangelo painting the Sistine Chapel. Wow! What a whinger. I kept saying to him, look, if you're scared of heights, you shouldn't have taken the job, then.'

THE DOCTOR, *VINCENT AND THE DOCTOR*

THE DOCTOR: Poisson? Reinette Poisson? No! No, no, no, no, no way. Reinette Poisson? Later Madame Étoiles? Later still mistress of Louis XV, uncrowned Queen of France? Actress, artist, musician, dancer, courtesan, fantastic gardener!

SERVANT: Who the hell are you?!

THE DOCTOR: I'm the Doctor, and I just snogged Madame de Pompadour.

THE GIRL IN THE FIREPLACE

THE DOCTOR: Oh, it doesn't work like that, Winston, and it's going to be tough. There are terrible days to come. The darkest days. But you can do it. You know you can.

CHURCHILL: Stay with us, and help us win through. The world needs you.

THE DOCTOR: The world doesn't need me.

CHURCHILL: No?

THE DOCTOR: The world's got Winston Spencer Churchill.

VICTORY OF THE DALEKS

THE DOCTOR: Rory, take Hitler and put him in that cupboard over there. Now, do it.

RORY: Right. Putting Hitler in the cupboard. Cupboard, Hitler. Hitler, cupboard. Come on.

LET'S KILL HITLER

GRACE: Did you know Madame Curie, too?

THE DOCTOR: Intimately.

GRACE: Did she kiss as good as me?

THE MASTER: As *well* as you.

DOCTOR WHO (TV MOVIE)

Chapter Nine:
The Future

'I can't tell the future,
I just work there.'

THE DOCTOR, *THE BELLS OF SAINT JOHN*

DAYS TO COME

'Every great decision creates ripples, like a huge boulder dropped in a lake. The ripples merge, rebound off the banks in unforeseeable ways. The heavier the decision, the larger the waves, the more uncertain the consequences.'

THE DOCTOR, *REMEMBRANCE OF THE DALEKS*

'Highness, it is not well to think of the past, there is still the future to make.'

SHOLAKH, T*HE RIBOS OPERATION*

DODO: Doctor, do you think we'll ever see him again?

THE DOCTOR: Well, who knows, my dear? In this strange complex of time and space, anything can happen. Come along, little one. We must go. We mustn't look back.

THE SAVAGES

THE DOCTOR: Our lives are important, at least to us. But as we see, so we learn.

IAN: And what are we going to see and learn next, Doctor?

THE DOCTOR: Well, unlike the old adage, my boy, our destiny is in the stars, so let's go and search for it.

THE REIGN OF TERROR

'Hello, Stormageddon. It's the Doctor. Here to help. Shush. Hey. There, there. Be quiet. Go to sleep. Really. Stop crying. You've got a lot to look forward to, you know. A normal human life on Earth. Mortgage repayments, the nine to five, a persistent nagging sense of spiritual emptiness. Save the tears for later, boy-o. Oh, no. That was crabby. No, that was old. But I am old, Stormy. I am so old. So near the end. You, Alfie Owens, you are so young, aren't you? And, you know, right now, everything's ahead of you. You could be anything. Yes, I know. You could walk among the stars. They don't actually look like that, you know. They are rather more impressive. Yeah. You know, when I was little like you, I dreamt of the stars. I think it's fair to say in the language of your age, that I lived my dream, I owned the stage, gave it a hundred and ten per cent. I hope you have as much fun as I did, Alfie.'

THE DOCTOR, *CLOSING TIME*

'You lot, you spend all your time thinking about dying, like you're going to get killed by eggs or beef or global warming or asteroids. But you never take time to imagine the impossible, that maybe you survive. This is the year five point five slash apple slash twenty-six. Five billion years in your future, and this is the day… Hold on… This is the day the sun expands. Welcome to the end of the world.'

THE DOCTOR, *THE END OF THE WORLD*

'So maybe this is it. First contact. The day mankind officially comes into contact with an alien race. I'm not interfering because you've got to handle this on your own. That's when the human race finally grows up. Just this morning you were all tiny and small and made of clay. Now you can expand.'

THE DOCTOR, *ALIENS OF LONDON*

'There are fixed points through time where things must always stay the way they are. This is not one of them. This is an opportunity. A temporal tipping point. Whatever happens today will change future events, create its own timeline, its own reality. The future pivots around you, here, now. So do good, for humanity, and for Earth.'

THE DOCTOR, *COLD BLOOD*

'People assume that time is a strict progression of cause to effect, but actually from a non-linear, non-subjective viewpoint, it's more like a big ball of wibbly-wobbly, timey-wimey stuff.'

THE DOCTOR, *BLINK*

DESTINY

'Time will tell. It always does.'

THE DOCTOR, *REMEMBRANCE OF THE DALEKS*

'Destiny. Isn't that just a fancy name for blind chance?'

PERI, *THE TRIAL OF A TIME LORD: MINDWARP*

'When faced with the inevitable, don't waste precious time by resisting it.'

THE DOCTOR, *PLANET OF THE DALEKS*

THE DOCTOR: Sometimes knowing your own future's what enables you to change it. Especially if you're bloody-minded, contradictory, and completely unpredictable.

RORY: So basically, if you're Amy, then?

THE DOCTOR: Yes, if anyone could defeat pre-destiny, it's your wife.

THE GIRL WHO WAITED

'You wanted advice, you said. I never give it. Never. But I might just say this to you. Always search for truth. My truth is in the stars and yours is here.'

THE DOCTOR, *THE DALEKS*

'Never mind the mights, my dear, just concentrate on what you're doing.'

THE DOCTOR, *THE CRUSADE*

DAVROS: Do you believe your puny efforts can change the course of destiny?

THE DOCTOR: Well, let's just say I might tamper with it.

DESTINY OF THE DALEKS

'I've never struggled against the inevitable. It's a vain occupation. But I should always advise you to examine very closely what you think to be inevitable. It's surprising how often apparent defeat can be turned to victory.'

TEMMOSUS, *THE DALEKS*

'The universe hangs by such a delicate thread of coincidences. It's useless to meddle with it, unless, like me, you're a Time Lord.'

THE DOCTOR, *DOCTOR WHO* (TV MOVIE)

'There's no such thing as foretelling. Trust a time traveller.'

THE DOCTOR, *THE DOCTOR, THE WIDOW AND THE WARDROBE*

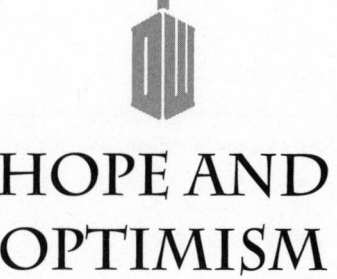

HOPE AND OPTIMISM

'Nothing in the world can stop me now!'

ZAROFF, *THE UNDERWATER MENACE*

'Sit down and write out the menus. First course interrupted by bomb explosion. Second course affected by earthquakes. Third course ruined by interference in the kitchen. I'm going out for a walk. It'll probably rain.'

GRIFFIN, *THE ENEMY OF THE WORLD*

ROMANA: There must be a huge nuclear war going on down there.

THE DOCTOR: Not at all, no.

ROMANA: What else could it be.

THE DOCTOR: I don't know. Probably someone giving a huge breakfast party … Why do you always assume the worst?

ROMANA: Because it usually happens.

THE DOCTOR: Empirical poppycock! Where's your joy in life? Where's your optimism?

ROMANA: It opted out.

THE ARMAGEDDON FACTOR

'Have you ever thought what it's like to be wanderers in the fourth dimension? Have you? To be exiles? Susan and I are cut off from our own planet, without friends or protection. But one day we shall get back. Yes, one day. One day.'

THE DOCTOR, *AN UNEARTHLY CHILD*

'You must travel with understanding as well as hope.'

THE DOCTOR, *THE ARK*

'Nil desperandum, Jo.'

THE DOCTOR, *THE GREEN DEATH*

'No one knows how they're going to be remembered. All we can do is hope for the best.'

THE DOCTOR, *THE UNICORN AND THE WASP*

THE DOCTOR: I don't know, but every single instinct of mine is telling me to get off this planet right now.

CHRISTINA: And do you think we can?

THE DOCTOR: I live in hope.

CHRISTINA: That must be nice.

PLANET OF THE DEAD

'You see, I know that although the Daleks will create havoc and destruction for millions of years, I know also that out of their evil must come something good.'

THE DOCTOR, *GENESIS OF THE DALEKS*

ROMANA: How did you know?

THE DOCTOR: Oh, knowing's easy. Everyone does that ad nauseam. I just sort of hope.

STATE OF DECAY

'Any hope is better than none.'

IAN, *AN UNEARTHLY CHILD*

'When I was a little boy, we used to live in a house that was perched halfway up the top of a mountain. And behind our house, there sat under a tree an old man, a hermit, a monk. He'd lived under this tree for half his lifetime, so they said, and he'd learned the secret of life. So, when my black day came, I went and asked him to help me … I'll never forget what it was like up there. All bleak and cold, it was. A few bare rocks with some weeds sprouting from them and some pathetic little patches of sludgy snow. It was just grey. Grey, grey, grey. Well, the tree the old man sat under, that was ancient and twisted and the old man himself was, he was as brittle and as dry as a leaf in the autumn … He just sat there, silently, expressionless, and he listened whilst I poured out my troubles to him. I was too unhappy even for tears, I remember. And when I'd finished, he lifted a skeletal hand and he pointed. Do you know what he pointed at? … A flower. One of those little weeds. Just like a daisy, it was. Well, I looked at it for a moment and suddenly I saw it through his eyes. It was simply glowing with life, like a perfectly cut jewel. And the colours? Well, the colours were deeper and richer than anything you could possibly imagine. Yes, that was the daisiest daisy I'd ever seen … I got up and I ran down that mountain and I found that the rocks weren't grey at all, but they were red, brown and purple and gold. And those pathetic little patches of sludgy snow, they were shining white. Shining white in the sunlight.'

THE DOCTOR, *THE TIME MONSTER*

THE DOCTOR: Nothing's impossible. There's always an answer if you can find it.

JO: Yeah, such as?

THE DOCTOR: Well, that's the trouble, finding it.

CARNIVAL OF MONSTERS

'It's never too late, as a wise person once said. Kylie, I think.'

THE DOCTOR, *THE IDIOT'S LANTERN*

LITTLE SEEMS TO HAVE CHANGED

LOGIN: A little patience goes a long way.

THE DOCTOR: Yes. Too much patience goes absolutely nowhere.

FULL CIRCLE

JUDSON: Oh yes, the machine can do it. This is the first. In the future there'll be many more computing machines, thinking machines.

MILLINGTON: Yes, but whose thoughts will they think?

THE CURSE OF FENRIC

TEGAN: What year are we in?

THE DOCTOR: Around 2084.

TEGAN: Little seems to have changed since my time.

THE DOCTOR: Absolutely nothing, Tegan. There are still two power blocs, fingers poised to annihilate each other.

WARRIORS OF THE DEEP

'If it is a disease, what has caused it? Once we were farmers and hunters. The land was green, the rivers ran clear, the air was sweet to breathe. And then the Overlords came, bringing Earth's poisons with them, calling it progress. We toiled in their mines, we became slaves. Worse than slaves!'

KY, *THE MUTANTS*

'Well, the Earth these people know now, Jo, in the thirtieth-century empire, is even more grey and misty ... Land and sea alike, all grey. Grey cities linked by grey highways across grey deserts ... Slag, ash, clinker. The fruits of technology.'

THE DOCTOR, *THE MUTANTS*

'Veruna is where one of the last surviving groups of mankind took shelter in the great, er... Yes. Well, I suppose you've got all that to look forward to, haven't you.'

THE DOCTOR, *FRONTIOS*

'Wheel turns, civilisations arise, wheel turns, civilisations fall.'

PANNA, *KINDA*

DONNA: 4126? It's 4126. I'm in 4126.

THE DOCTOR: It's good, isn't it?

DONNA: What's the Earth like now?

THE DOCTOR: Bit full. But you see, the Empire stretches out across three galaxies.

DONNA: It's weird. I mean, it's brilliant, but… Back home, the papers and the telly, they keep saying we haven't got long to live. Global warming, flooding, all the bees disappearing…

THE DOCTOR: Yeah. That thing about the bees is odd.

DONNA: But look at us. We're everywhere. Is that good or bad, though? I mean, are we like explorers? Or more like a virus?

THE DOCTOR: Sometimes I wonder.

PLANET OF THE OOD

ARAK: No more executions, torture, nothing.

ETTA: It's all changed. We're free.

ARAK: Are we?

ETTA: Yes.

ARAK: What shall we do?

ETTA: Dunno.

VENGEANCE ON VAROS

THE BEST LAID PLANS

THE BRIGADIER: It's pretty hard to keep an eye on all these scientist chaps at home, so I had these cubicles put up on several floors. Confined the whole lot to barracks. All my eggs in one basket, so to speak.

THE DOCTOR: That's fine, so long as no one steals the basket.

THE TIME WARRIOR

'You know how it is. You put things off for a day, next thing you know it's a hundred years later.'

THE DOCTOR, *ARC OF INFINITY*

THE DOCTOR: A quarter of a mile straight ahead, and from there we're going to stabilise the wreckage, stop the Angels, and cure Amy.

RIVER: How?

THE DOCTOR: I'll do a thing.

RIVER: What thing?

THE DOCTOR: I don't know. It's a thing in progress. Respect the thing.

FLESH AND STONE

GROWING OLD

JO: How does it work?

THE DOCTOR: Anti-magnetic cohesion, I should think.

JO: Never heard of it.

THE DOCTOR: No, you wouldn't have done, Jo. You were born about a thousand years too early for that.

JO: Oh, I do love being with you, Doctor. You make me feel so young.

CARNIVAL OF MONSTERS

KHAN: Oh, what a trial old age is.

THE DOCTOR: It must be borne with dignity, sir.

MARCO POLO

'I'm old enough to know that a longer life isn't always a better one. In the end, you just get tired. Tired of the struggle, tired of losing everyone that matters to you, tired of watching everything turn to dust. If you live long enough, Lazarus, the only certainty left is that you'll end up alone.'

THE DOCTOR, *THE LAZARUS EXPERIMENT*

'There's no doubt about it, all this rushing around takes it out of you – particularly when you're 1250 years old.'

THE DOCTOR, *THE LEISURE HIVE*

ENDINGS

'The universe has to move forward. Pain and loss, they define us as much as happiness or love. Whether it's a world, or a relationship, everything has its time. And everything ends.'

SARAH, *SCHOOL REUNION*

'Everything has its time and everything dies.'

THE DOCTOR, *THE END OF THE WORLD*

EMMA: What's wrong?

CLARA: I just saw something I wish I hadn't.

EMMA: What did you see?

CLARA: That everything ends.

EMMA: No, not everything. Not love. Not always.

HIDE

'Never let him see the damage. And never, ever let him see you age. He doesn't like endings.'

RIVER SONG, *THE ANGELS TAKE MANHATTAN*

'Why aren't there any lights? I miss lights. You don't really miss things till they're gone, do you? It's like what my nan used to say. You'll never miss the water till the well runs dry.'

RORY, *NIGHT TERRORS*

'My Aunt Vanessa said, when I became an air stewardess, if you stop enjoying it, give it up.'

TEGAN, *RESURRECTION OF THE DALEKS*

'End the day with a smile.'

COLBY, *IMAGE OF THE FENDAHL*

'Time Lord, last of. Heard of them? Legend or anything? Not even a myth? Blimey, end of the universe is a bit humbling.'

THE DOCTOR, *UTOPIA*

'Day I know everything? Might as well stop.'

THE DOCTOR, *THE SATAN PIT*

FAREWELLS

'It's hard to leave when you haven't said goodbye.'

RIVER SONG, *THE NAME OF THE DOCTOR*

'Even after all this time he cannot understand. I dare not change the course of history. Well, at least I taught him to take some precautions. He did remember to look at the scanner before he opened the doors. Now they're all gone. All gone. None of them could understand. Not even my little Susan, or Vicki. And as for Barbara and Chatterton – Chesterton. They were all too impatient to get back to their own time. And now, Steven. Perhaps I should go home, back to my own planet. But I can't. I can't.'

THE DOCTOR, *THE MASSACRE*

'That's right, yes, you're going. Been gone for ages. Already gone, still here, just arrived, haven't even met you yet. It all depends on who you are and how you look at it. Strange business, time … Think about me when you're living your life one day after another, all in a neat pattern. Think about the homeless traveller and his old police box, his days like crazy paving.'

THE DOCTOR, *DRAGONFIRE*

SARAH: Don't forget me.

THE DOCTOR: Oh, Sarah. Don't you forget me.

SARAH: Bye, Doctor. You know, travel does broaden the mind.

THE DOCTOR: Yes. Till we meet again, Sarah.

THE HAND OF FEAR

SARAH: Goodbye, Doctor.

THE DOCTOR: Oh, it's not goodbye.

SARAH: Do say it. Please. This time. Say it.

THE DOCTOR: Goodbye, my Sarah Jane.

SCHOOL REUNION

'If you want to remember me, then you can do one thing. That's all, one thing. Have a good life. Do that for me, Rose. Have a fantastic life.'

THE DOCTOR, *THE PARTING OF THE WAYS*

'One day, I shall come back. Yes, I shall come back. Until then, there must be no regrets, no tears, no anxieties. Just go forward in all your beliefs, and prove to me that I am not mistaken in mine. Goodbye, Susan. Goodbye, my dear.'

THE DOCTOR, *THE DALEK INVASION OF EARTH*

THE DESTINY OF
THE DOCTOR

'On the Fields of Trenzalore, at the fall of the Eleventh, when no living creature can speak falsely, or fail to answer, a question will be asked. A question that must never, ever be answered.'

DORIUM MALDOVAR, *THE WEDDING OF RIVER SONG*

RIVER: There are so many theories about you and I, you know.

THE DOCTOR: Idle gossip.

RIVER: Archaeology.

THE DOCTOR: Same thing.

THE WEDDING OF RIVER SONG

THE DOCTOR: You didn't listen, did you? You lot never do. That's the problem. The Doctor has a secret he will take to the grave. It is discovered. He wasn't talking about my secret. No, no, no, that's not what's been found. He was talking about my grave. Trenzalore is where I'm buried.

CLARA: How can you have a grave?

THE DOCTOR: Because we all do, somewhere out there in the future, waiting for us.

THE NAME OF THE DOCTOR

'So many secrets, Doctor. I'll help you keep them, of course …
but you're a fool nonetheless. It's all still waiting for you. The
fields of Trenzalore, the fall of the Eleventh, and the question …
The first question. The question that must never be answered,
hidden in plain sight. The question you've been running from
all your life. Doctor who? Doctor who? Doctor who?'

DORIUM MALDOVAR, *THE WEDDING OF RIVER SONG*

THE ELEVENTH DOCTOR: I saw Trenzalore, where we're
buried. We die in battle among millions.

THE TENTH DOCTOR: That's not how it's supposed to be.

THE ELEVENTH DOCTOR: That's where the story ends.
Nothing we can do about it. Trenzalore is where you're going.

THE TENTH DOCTOR: Oh, never say nothing. Anyway, good
to know my future is in safe hands.

THE DAY OF THE DOCTOR

'OK, so that's where I end up. Always thought maybe I'd
retire. Take up watercolours or bee-keeping, or something.
Apparently not.'

THE DOCTOR, *THE NAME OF THE DOCTOR*

THE DOCTOR: I could be a curator. I'd be great at curating.
I'd be the great curator. I could retire and do that. I could
retire and be the curator of this place.

THE CURATOR: You know, I really think you might.

THE DAY OF THE DOCTOR

THE DOCTOR: I never forget a face.

THE CURATOR: I know you don't. And in years to come, you might find yourself revisiting a few. But just the old favourites, eh?

THE DAY OF THE DOCTOR

THE TENTH DOCTOR: Trenzalore. We need a new destination because I don't want to go.

THE ELEVENTH DOCTOR: He always says that.

THE DAY OF THE DOCTOR

'Clara sometimes asks me if I dream. Of course I dream, I tell her. Everybody dreams. But what do you dream about, she'll ask. The same thing everybody dreams about, I tell her. I dream about where I'm going. She always laughs at that. But you're not going anywhere, you're just wandering about. That's not true. Not any more. I have a new destination. My journey is the same as yours, the same as anyone's. It's taken me so many years, so many lifetimes, but at last I know where I'm going. Where I've always been going. Home, the long way round.'

THE DOCTOR, *THE DAY OF THE DOCTOR*

FAMOUS LAST WORDS

(WELL, THE ONES WE HEARD ANYWAY)

'Ah, yes! Thank you. It's good. Keep warm.'

THE FIRST DOCTOR, *THE TENTH PLANET*

'No! Stop! You're making me giddy! No, you can't do this to me! No, no, no, no, no, no, no, no no, no, no, no, no…'

THE SECOND DOCTOR, *THE WAR GAMES*

'A tear, Sarah Jane? No don't cry. While there's life, there's…'

THE THIRD DOCTOR, *PLANET OF THE SPIDERS*

'It's the end, but the moment has been prepared for.'

THE FOURTH DOCTOR, *LOGOPOLIS*

'Might regenerate. I don't know. Feels different this time… Adric?'

THE FIFTH DOCTOR, *THE CAVES OF ANDROZANI*

'Carrot juice, carrot juice, carrot juice.'

THE SIXTH DOCTOR, *THE TRIAL OF A TIME LORD: THE ULTIMATE FOE*

'I've got to stop him.'

THE SEVENTH DOCTOR, *DOCTOR WHO* (TV MOVIE)

'Physician, heal thyself.'

THE EIGHTH DOCTOR, *THE NIGHT OF THE DOCTOR*

'Oh yes, of course. I suppose it makes sense. Wearing a bit thin. I hope the ears are a bit less conspicuous this time.'

THE WAR DOCTOR, *THE DAY OF THE DOCTOR*

'Rose, before I go, I just want to tell you, you were fantastic. Absolutely fantastic. And do you know what? So was I.'

THE NINTH DOCTOR, *THE PARTING OF THE WAYS*

'I don't want to go.'

THE TENTH DOCTOR, *THE END OF TIME*

'We all change, when you think about it. We're all different people all through our lives. And that's OK, that's good – you've gotta keep moving, so long as you remember all the people that you used to be. I will not forget one line of this. Not one day. I swear. I will always remember when the Doctor was me ... Hey.'

THE ELEVENTH DOCTOR, *THE TIME OF THE DOCTOR*

APPENDIX

Credit must be given to the many writers and script editors who have put words in the mouths of the Doctor and his friends and enemies over the years. This book is dedicated to each and every one.

WRITERS

Ben Aaronovitch
REMEMBRANCE OF THE DALEKS, BATTLEFIELD

Douglas Adams
THE PIRATE PLANET, CITY OF DEATH (WITH GRAHAM WILLIAMS, AS DAVID AGNEW, FROM A STORY BY DAVID FISHER), SHADA

Christopher Bailey
KINDA, SNAKEDANCE

Bob Baker
NIGHTMARE OF EDEN

Bob Baker and Dave Martin
THE CLAWS OF AXOS, THE MUTANTS, THE THREE DOCTORS, THE SONTARAN EXPERIMENT, THE HAND OF FEAR, THE INVISIBLE ENEMY, UNDERWORLD, THE ARMAGEDDON FACTOR

Pip and Jane Baker
THE MARK OF THE RANI, THE TRIAL OF A TIME LORD: TERROR OF THE VERVOIDS, THE TRIAL OF A TIME LORD: THE ULTIMATE FOE (PART 14), TIME AND THE RANI

Christopher H. Bidmead
LOGOPOLIS, CASTROVALVA, FRONTIOS

Ian Stuart Black
*THE SAVAGES, THE WAR MACHINES
(FROM AN IDEA BY KIT PEDLER),
THE MACRA TERROR*

Chris Boucher
*THE FACE OF EVIL, THE ROBOTS OF
DEATH, IMAGE OF THE FENDAHL*

Ian Briggs
DRAGONFIRE, THE CURSE OF FENRIC

Johnny Byrne
*THE KEEPER OF TRAKEN,
ARC OF INFINITY, WARRIORS OF
THE DEEP*

Chris Chibnall
*42, THE HUNGRY EARTH / COLD
BLOOD, POND LIFE, DINOSAURS
ON A SPACESHIP, THE POWER OF
THREE*

Kevin Clarke
SILVER NEMESIS

Barbara Clegg
ENLIGHTENMENT

Anthony Coburn
AN UNEARTHLY CHILD

Paul Cornell
*FATHER'S DAY, HUMAN NATURE /
THE FAMILY OF BLOOD*

Donald Cotton
*THE MYTH MAKERS, THE
GUNFIGHTERS*

Neil Cross
THE RINGS OF AKHATEN, HIDE

Graeme Curry
THE HAPPINESS PATROL

Richard Curtis
VINCENT AND THE DOCTOR

Russell T Davies
*ROSE, THE END OF THE WORLD,
ALIENS OF LONDON / WORLD WAR
THREE, THE LONG GAME, BOOM
TOWN, BAD WOLF / THE PARTING
OF THE WAYS, BORN AGAIN,
THE CHRISTMAS INVASION, NEW
EARTH, TOOTH AND CLAW, LOVE
& MONSTERS, ARMY OF GHOSTS /
DOOMSDAY, THE RUNAWAY BRIDE,
SMITH AND JONES, GRIDLOCK,
UTOPIA, THE SOUND OF DRUMS /
LAST OF THE TIME LORDS, VOYAGE OF
THE DAMNED, PARTNERS IN CRIME,
MIDNIGHT, TURN LEFT, THE STOLEN
EARTH / JOURNEY'S END, THE NEXT
DOCTOR, THE END OF TIME, PART
ONE, THE END OF TIME, PART TWO*

**Russell T Davies
and Phil Ford**
THE WATERS OF MARS

**Russell T Davies
and Gareth Roberts**
PLANET OF THE DEAD

Gerry Davis
REVENGE OF THE CYBERMEN

Terrance Dicks
*ROBOT, HORROR OF FANG ROCK,
STATE OF DECAY, THE FIVE DOCTORS*

**Terrance Dicks
and Malcolm Hulke**
THE WAR GAMES

**Terrance Dicks
and Robert Holmes
(as Robin Bland)**
THE BRAIN OF MORBIUS

Terence Dudley
*FOUR TO DOOMSDAY, BLACK ORCHID,
THE KING'S DEMONS*

**David Ellis
and Malcolm Hulke**
THE FACELESS ONES

William Emms
GALAXY 4

**Paul Erickson
and Lesley Scott**
THE ARK

David Fisher
*THE STONES OF BLOOD, THE
ANDROIDS OF TARA, THE CREATURE
FROM THE PIT, THE LEISURE HIVE*

**John Flanagan and
Andrew McCulloch**
MEGLOS

Neil Gaiman
*THE DOCTOR'S WIFE, NIGHTMARE
IN SILVER*

Steve Gallagher
WARRIORS' GATE, TERMINUS

Mark Gatiss
*THE UNQUIET DEAD, THE IDIOT'S
LANTERN, VICTORY OF THE DALEKS,
NIGHT TERRORS, COLD WAR,
THE CRIMSON HORROR*

Matthew Graham
*FEAR HER, THE REBEL FLESH /
THE ALMOST PEOPLE*

Stephen Greenhorn
*THE LAZARUS EXPERIMENT,
THE DOCTOR'S DAUGHTER*

Peter Grimwade

TIME-FLIGHT, MAWDRYN UNDEAD, PLANET OF FIRE

Mervyn Haisman and Henry Lincoln

THE ABOMINABLE SNOWMEN, THE WEB OF FEAR, THE DOMINATORS (AS NORMAN ASHBY)

Brian Hayles

THE CELESTIAL TOYMAKER, THE SMUGGLERS, THE ICE WARRIORS, THE SEEDS OF DEATH, THE CURSE OF PELADON, THE MONSTER OF PELADON

Robert Holmes

THE KROTONS, THE SPACE PIRATES, SPEARHEAD FROM SPACE, TERROR OF THE AUTONS, CARNIVAL OF MONSTERS, THE TIME WARRIOR, THE ARK IN SPACE, PYRAMIDS OF MARS (AS STEPHEN HARRIS), THE DEADLY ASSASSIN, THE TALONS OF WENG-CHIANG, THE SUN MAKERS, THE RIBOS OPERATION, THE POWER OF KROLL, THE CAVES OF ANDROZANI, THE TWO DOCTORS, THE TRIAL OF A TIME LORD: THE MYSTERIOUS PLANET, THE TRIAL OF A TIME LORD: THE ULTIMATE FOE (PART 13)

Don Houghton

INFERNO, THE MIND OF EVIL

Malcolm Hulke

DOCTOR WHO AND THE SILURIANS, COLONY IN SPACE, THE SEA DEVILS, FRONTIER IN SPACE, INVASION OF THE DINOSAURS

Matthew Jacobs

DOCTOR WHO (TV MOVIE)

Elwyn Jones and Gerry Davis

THE HIGHLANDERS

Glyn Jones

THE SPACE MUSEUM

Matt Jones

THE IMPOSSIBLE PLANET / THE SATAN PIT

Malcolm Kohll

DELTA AND THE BANNERMEN

Peter Ling

THE MIND ROBBER

John Lucarotti

MARCO POLO, THE AZTECS, THE MASSACRE (FOURTH EPISODE WITH DONALD TOSH)

Tom MacRae
RISE OF THE CYBERMEN / THE AGE OF STEEL, THE GIRL WHO WAITED

Louis Marks
PLANET OF GIANTS, DAY OF THE DALEKS, PLANET OF EVIL, THE MASQUE OF MANDRAGORA

Philip Martin
VENGEANCE ON VAROS, THE TRIAL OF A TIME LORD: MINDWARP

Glen McCoy
TIMELASH

Steven Moffat
THE EMPTY CHILD / THE DOCTOR DANCES, THE GIRL IN THE FIREPLACE, BLINK, TIME CRASH, SILENCE IN THE LIBRARY / FOREST OF THE DEAD, THE ELEVENTH HOUR, THE BEAST BELOW, THE TIME OF ANGELS / FLESH AND STONE, THE PANDORICA OPENS / THE BIG BANG, A CHRISTMAS CAROL, SPACE / TIME, THE IMPOSSIBLE ASTRONAUT / DAY OF THE MOON, A GOOD MAN GOES TO WAR, LET'S KILL HITLER, THE WEDDING OF RIVER SONG, THE DOCTOR, THE WIDOW AND THE WARDROBE, ASYLUM OF THE DALEKS, THE ANGELS TAKE MANHATTAN, THE SNOWMEN, THE BELLS OF SAINT JOHN, THE NAME OF THE DOCTOR, THE NIGHT OF THE DOCTOR, THE DAY OF THE DOCTOR, THE TIME OF THE DOCTOR

Paula Moore
ATTACK OF THE CYBERMEN

James Moran
THE FIRES OF POMPEII

Rona Munro
SURVIVAL

Terry Nation
THE DALEKS, THE KEYS OF MARINUS, THE DALEK INVASION OF EARTH, THE CHASE, MISSION TO THE UNKNOWN, THE DALEKS' MASTER PLAN (WITH DENNIS SPOONER), PLANET OF THE DALEKS, DEATH TO THE DALEKS, GENESIS OF THE DALEKS, THE ANDROID INVASION, DESTINY OF THE DALEKS

Peter R. Newman
THE SENSORITES

Simon Nye
AMY'S CHOICE

Geoffrey Orme
THE UNDERWATER MENACE

Kit Pedler
THE MOONBASE

**Kit Pedler
and Gerry Davis**
*THE TENTH PLANET, THE TOMB OF
THE CYBERMEN*

Victor Pemberton
FURY FROM THE DEEP

Marc Platt
GHOST LIGHT

Eric Pringle
THE AWAKENING

Helen Raynor
*DALEKS IN MANHATTAN /
EVOLUTION OF THE DALEKS,
THE SONTARAN STRATAGEM /
THE POISON SKY*

Anthony Read
THE HORNS OF NIMON

Gareth Roberts
*THE SHAKESPEARE CODE,
THE UNICORN AND THE WASP,
THE LODGER, CLOSING TIME*

Eric Saward
*THE VISITATION, EARTHSHOCK,
RESURRECTION OF THE DALEKS,
REVELATION OF THE DALEKS*

Robert Shearman
DALEK

Derrick Sherwin
*THE INVASION (FROM A STORY BY
KIT PEDLER)*

Robert Sloman
*THE DAEMONS (WITH BARRY
LETTS, AS GUY LEOPOLD), THE
TIME MONSTER, THE GREEN DEATH,
PLANET OF THE SPIDERS*

Andrew Smith
FULL CIRCLE

Dennis Spooner
*THE REIGN OF TERROR, THE
ROMANS, THE TIME MEDDLER,
THE DALEKS' MASTER PLAN (WITH
TERRY NATION)*

Anthony Steven
THE TWIN DILEMMA

Robert Banks Stewart
*TERROR OF THE ZYGONS,
THE SEEDS OF DOOM*

Bill Strutton
THE WEB PLANET

Keith Temple
PLANET OF THE OOD

Stephen Thompson
*THE CURSE OF THE BLACK SPOT,
JOURNEY TO THE CENTRE OF THE
TARDIS*

David Whitaker
*THE EDGE OF DESTRUCTION, THE
RESCUE, THE CRUSADE, THE POWER
OF THE DALEKS, THE EVIL OF THE
DALEKS, THE ENEMY OF THE WORLD,
THE WHEEL IN SPACE* (FROM A
STORY BY KIT PEDLER), *THE
AMBASSADORS OF DEATH*

Toby Whithouse
*SCHOOL REUNION, THE VAMPIRES
OF VENICE, THE GOD COMPLEX,
A TOWN CALLED MERCY*

Stephen Wyatt
*PARADISE TOWERS, THE GREATEST
SHOW IN THE GALAXY*

SCRIPT EDITORS

Douglas Adams
Lindsey Alford
Christopher H.
Bidmead
Peter Bryant
Andrew Cartmel
Richard Cookson
Gerry Davis
Terrance Dicks
Emma Freud

Caroline Henry
Robert Holmes
Brian Minchin
Victor Pemberton
John Phillips
Helen Raynor
Anthony Read
Derek Ritchie
Antony Root
Elwen Rowlands

Gary Russell
Eric Saward
Derrick Sherwin
Nikki Smith
Dennis Spooner
Donald Tosh
David Whitaker
Simon Winstone

THANKS

As always, there are people we must thank for their help, encouragement and support throughout the compiling of this book. Without whom...

The team at *Doctor Who Magazine* – Tom Spilsbury, Peter Ware, Richard Atkinson, John Ainsworth and Scott Gray.

Ben Morris, whose illustrations never cease to take our breath away when a new one drops into our inboxes.

A very special thanks to Daniel Brennan for his continued support, and being an eagle-eared knight in shining armour.

As always, the team at BBC Books who always make a new commission such a pleasurable experience. So to Albert DePetrillo for asking us back, Lizzy Gaisford for keeping us in check (and giving us Christmas!), and the ever-vigilant Justin Richards and Steve Tribe.

And finally, our families for love, support and cups of tea. For Cav – Clare, and his new little *Doctor Who* fans, Chloe and Connie. For Mark – Paula and Oliver.

INDEX

INDEX

INDEX

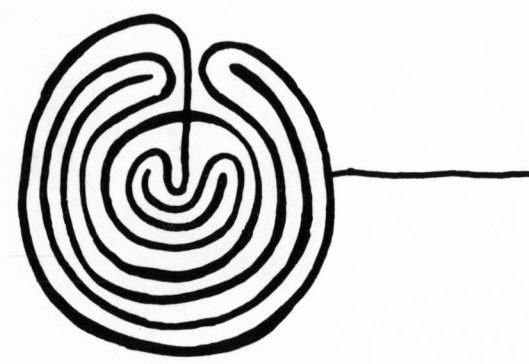

the maze

eileen simpson

SIMON AND SCHUSTER · NEW YORK

S 613 m

Copyright © 1975 by Eileen Simpson
All rights reserved
including the right of reproduction
in whole or in part in any form
Published by Simon and Schuster
Rockefeller Center, 630 Fifth Avenue
New York, New York 10020
Designed by Edith Fowler
Manufactured in the United States of America
1   2   3   4   5   6   7   8   9   10

Library of Congress Cataloging in Publication Data

Simpson, Eileen
   The maze.

   √ I. Title.
PZ4.S6134Maz [PS3569.I489]   813'.5'4   74–23536
ISBN 0–671–21960–X

To R. S.

one

"Benjamin, wake up." Rosy flew out of bed and ran to the window. "We're terribly late."

"Hmmm?" Benjamin said sleepily.

"Assunta forgot to open the shutters." Rosy folded them back on a courtyard blazing with sun. The air was heavy with the odor of garlic cooking in oil. At the window opposite, a canary trilled lustily. Assunta, the Pensione Europa's chambermaid, sang, *"Cuore, cuore 'ngrato"* with passion as she made up the room next door. A radio somewhere blared news of the heat wave that had moved in on Rome during the night. "What a racket! How could we have overslept?"

"Overslept? Impossible. I didn't close my eyes all night."

Picking up the bedding Benjamin had tossed on the floor during the night, Rosy said, "You heard Assunta come in with the tray?"

Benjamin had covered his eyes against the light with his pillow. "She came in?"

"Hours ago."

"I must have been thinking. I had the most extraordinary fantasy. I was dead. Buried. Six feet under. . . ."

"Stone cold." Rosy held her hand against the pot of coffee.

"It wasn't bad, really. I could see what was going on.

7

Take an interest in things. Criticize. Comment. I just couldn't move. I read my obituary. . . ."

"Doesn't sound very dead to me." Rosy removed the pillow from his eyes. "Here."

"Damn those journalists," he said, taking the cup. "They're not asked to invent. *Facts,* that's what's wanted. The obituary was full of errors. I've been thinking: why shouldn't I write my own? Who could do it better? Send it to the *Times*. They're made up ahead, you know. Kept on file."

He's going to be all right today after all, Rosy thought. "I'll wash," she said, taking her coffee to the sink which stood, naked and gawky, in the corner by the window. "Then you can shave."

"Did you hear that bloody fountain last night?"

"Lovely, wasn't it?" Awakened at dawn by anxiety about the coming day, she had been lulled back to sleep by the fountain's soothing *plash plash*. Now, looking down into the courtyard, she could see a waiter from the ground-floor restaurant putting fruit in it to cool for the midday meal. Melons, plums, and peaches danced indolently in the aquamarine water. "I wish I were a peach," she sighed, turning on the faucet.

"Loathsome fountain. Kept me awake all night. I could have sworn it was saying, 'Relax, relax, relax,' like a goddamn physiotherapist. *Me,* relax? Jesus! With my problems? Here we are in Rome without a bean."

> How needful it is to have money, heigh ho!
> How needful it is to have money.

He sang it like a dirge. Yes, decidedly, he was in good humor. It was amazing what a night's sleep could do for him.

"If lunch at the Duchessa's goes well—" Rosy broke off abruptly. If Benjamin caught her worrying about the lunch, he was likely to give her something to worry about. "Your turn. You can shave now."

"Uh-uh. I can't move. I have a rectangular headache. Besides, I can't find my eyeglasses." As Rosy went close to the bed to look for them, Benjamin reached for her hand. "Darling, what do you suppose got into me last night?"

It never ceased to surprise her how green his eyes were. And how weak. Her expression would tell him nothing. Without glasses he saw her as a familiar blur.

He raised his hand as if she might strike him with the truth. "Don't tell me. Booze. That's what got into me. My frontal lobes are swollen with booze."

He had tucked his glasses in one of his bedroom slippers. "Here."

"How clever is the drunk!"

"Now, up."

"Can I finish my coffee?"

"While you shave." Rosy opened the armoire. "What does one wear to the country house of an Italian nobleman? The green shirtwaist, or the polka dot?"

"Oh God, why do I drink?" Benjamin addressed the question to his image in the mirror. "And with such *fools*. You see before you a man about to take the pledge. 'Ireland sober is Ireland free!' "

"What do you suppose the Duchessa will be like? I can't picture her."

"I can. Easily. She's American, remember." Benjamin held his razor poised. "Worthy? Almost certainly." Out of the corner of his mouth, as he stretched the skin on the opposite side, "Pretentious? Probably. A bluestocking? Undoubtedly. I need a new blade. Why do I have to shave?"

"Because you're going out to lunch."

"No, I mean why in general. I know! To celebrate the publication of my book I'll grow a beard. A great big beaver. It will be absolutely splendid! Christ! I've cut myself. Quick, the styptic pencil."

"Where did you put it?"

"How do I know? Hurry. I'm bleeding to death."

"Take it easy. Here it is. What will you wear? I'll get it out. I'm almost ready."

The choice was limited. Benjamin had two suits. "My seersucker."

"Shirt?"

"Blue. Yes, the Duchessa is almost certainly a bluestocking. Heavy ankles. Patronizing too, I dare say." Benjamin was combing his hair. "Will you love me when I'm bald?"

"If you hurry."

"Bald at forty. Still, there'll be the beard."

"This is not the time—"

"All right, all right. You might put my cuff links in. The trouble with the rich, Roxana, is that they no longer know how to be patrons. This duchessa is probably no exception. Now, Willie Yeats—there was a lucky bastard! Where are the Lady Gregorys these days?

> There was a kind lady called Gregory,
> Said 'Come to me, poets in beggary.'

"Of course, if those boobs on the Committee had only given me the grant—not even a grant, mind you, just a bloody *renewal*—we wouldn't have to have lunch with this woman."

Rosy handed Benjamin his shirt.

"You know to whom they give the grants, don't you?"

Rosy knew. She'd heard this before.

"Mediocre professors to study mediocre nineteenth-century poets. That's who gets them. Wait till they begin to study me! Damn, the top button's come off."

"No time to sew it now. I'll get out another shirt."

"The Duchessa . . . Wait. I'm on to something. Yes. Yes, I've got it!" Benjamin did a little leap in the air. "She secretly writes verse. Ha! What do you think she was doing early this morning?"

"Writing her obituary."

"Roxana. You're not thinking. No, she was sitting in bed with a clipboard on her lap, polishing a villanelle she plans to slip Rodney today. I can *see* it. Blue paper—made in England. One version on top of the other. Pages of them. A small, tidy hand. Weak on punctuation. Among other things."

"We have exactly two minutes. The Munsons are sure to be prompt."

"I'm ready. I'm ready. How do I look?"

Rosy took the handkerchief from Benjamin's breast pocket to wipe away the traces of styptic pencil from his cheek. She put it back in place, stood back and looked at him again. How did he look? Like a horse—a high-strung, high-mettled, high-stepping horse, reined in for dressage and ready to dance, or rear up, or gallop away. His eyes darted. His nostrils flared. There was a pulse in his lean cheek. The effect, on the whole, was not displeasing.

"Well?" He smiled his crooked smile at her.

His question, Rosy knew, meant something other than what it asked. Mimicry had served them throughout their marriage as a shorthand for making peace. "Splendid!" she said, with Benjamin's heavy emphasis.

He reached for her hand, "Since you forgive me, I'll tell you something to entertain you. . . ."

"On the way down. You have the key?"

He locked the door. "I'll tell you a *Time* magazine layout on the Duchessa I just thought up. An unflattering photograph . . ."

They started down the stairs.

"She's standing by a flower bed at Roccafalcone, a shepherd's crook . . ."

"A bluestocking with a shepherd's crook?"

"Wait. A crook in one hand, a bound volume of *Ampersand* in the other. She's smiling. Broadly. Shall I have gum showing?"

"No. That's too mean. What about a nervous smile?"

"Good! A nervous, introverted, lady-poet smile. Now for a caption. Let's see. Here: 'No Vittoria Colonna she.' "

They were approaching the ground floor. Benjamin lit a cigarette. "What do you think the plot is for today?"

So he was uneasy about the luncheon too. "Margaret said—"

"That woman! How could Rodney have married her?"

"Benjamin, please. She's harmless—tactless maybe, but harmless. And the point is, Rodney *has* married her."

"If she thinks I'm going to play up to the Duchessa—"

Rosy put her hand up. "Shush."

A Cadillac pulled up in front of Conti's restaurant. Before the chauffeur could get around to open the door for her, Margaret, a plump, well-corseted, stylish woman, got out. She shook hands with Rosy and Benjamin in an energetic, European way. Though Rodney Munson was an old and close friend of Benjamin's from prewar days at Cambridge University, Margaret was new to the Bolds. Not so new, however, that Benjamin had not had time to form an opinion of her. At dinner the night they arrived in Rome, she piqued him by taking it for granted that he knew no Italian (which was not quite true; they had been managing in Italy on his Dantesque vocabulary with mixed success). In the restaurant, when she was not correcting his idioms or countermandering his orders to the waiter ("No, no, no, you don't want zabaione. That's a winter sweet"), she was trying to persuade him to stay at the hotel of her choice. "The Minerva will suit you perfectly." Benjamin protested that they were already installed in the Europa. No matter. Margaret would arrange the transfer. "After dinner we'll walk round to the Minerva. I'll talk to the manager. . . ." Only Rodney's tactful intervention had saved the evening.

"So this is the Europa?" Margaret said, looking for the entrance. "I was telling Rod—wasn't I, dear?"—she called over her shoulder to her husband, who had not yet caught up with her—"that I'd never heard of this hotel. One knows the address because of Conti's. But a hotel? I don't see it. Where is it?"

"It's upstairs," said Rosy.

"Upstairs? Margaret held her patent-leather pocketbook like a visor over her eyes and looked up at the sun-struck façade.

Benjamin dropped his cigarette and crushed it under his shoe. "It's not a hotel, my dear Margaret, but a pensione. On the seventh floor. The elevator, when it works, takes you up, for a token. Never down. The only reading light in the room is a naked fifty-watt bulb suspended from the ceiling."

"You really are comfortable here?" Margaret had been looking the building over, not listening.

"Madly."

Rodney, a bald pink man with a ginger moustache, kissed Rosy and put his hand on Benjamin's shoulder. "How are you both this morning?" he asked soothingly, as if the previous exchange hadn't taken place. If he was distressed that his wife and his old friend were clearly not going to get along, he gave no sign. "Come along," he said, moving them toward the car. "We have one more stop. Ben, will you sit on the jump seat? I'll sit up front with the driver. We're in luck today. Roccafalcone is at its most glorious when Rome sizzles."

"Roxana, I've been trying to think ever since you arrived, who it is you remind me of?" Margaret asked. "It's a cinema star. She wears her hair up," Margaret gestured, "the way you do."

"May Robson?" Benjamin suggested slyly. "She wore her hair up."

"Who? It's just you're blond too."

"Blond. Oh, I know." Benjamin covered his right eye and cheek with his hand to suggest hanging hair. "Veronica Lake."

"Do you really think Roxana looks like her? I don't see that at all. No, it's someone with high cheekbones and—"

"Cheekbones? Why didn't you say so?" Benjamin sucked in his cheeks. "Anna May Wong, obviously."

"No, no, no." Margaret became impatient, as if she had drawn a dull partner in a game. "What's so maddening is that it will probably come to me just before I fall asleep tonight. She's tall, slim, Scandinavian, I think—"

"No, no, no." Benjamin imitated Margaret. "Roxana is pure Pict, a descendant of the Druids. Her ancestors used to dress up in green and dance around in the moonlight when they weren't practicing magic. Like them, she's given to premonitions, intuitions, mystical feelings, sun worship, and, of course, dancing."

Rodney's shoulders heaved up and down with noiseless laughter. "Ben, Ben, you haven't changed. Don't listen to him, Margaret, he's pulling your leg. He knows perfectly well what actress you mean. Roxana must have been told it a dozen times."

"What church is this?" Rosy hoped to change the subject. One never knew when Benjamin's clowning might take a sudden, sharp turn. And even if it didn't, the day would go more smoothly if he didn't begin it on too high a key.

"The Gesù," Rodney said. "We're going to pick up Tullio Fancelli here. Have you ever met him, Ben? He goes often to the States."

"No, I haven't. Nor have I read him. Luckily, Roxana has."

Rosy decided that she would not tell Fancelli how much

she admired his novels. Early in her marriage she had learned how prickly writers were about how they were praised. There seemed to be no way to avoid saying the wrong thing. Either they had come to dislike the book one praised ("It's never been one of my favorites," she heard one say to a gushing fan) or they were put off by its being praised for the wrong reason ("the Affective Fallacy," had said another). What really interested them was the work they were currently engaged on ("It's unquestionably my best"). So she would say nothing. She might just give out a strong feeling. None of them seemed to object to that.

"A miracle," Margaret said. "Tullio's on time."

The man who came toward the car looked like a character out of a Pirandello play. He was dressed in black, his face masked by dark glasses. His heavy suit made no concession to the heat, nor to lunch in the country. He leaned over Rosy's hand, when Rodney introduced them, bending his head of carefully brushed black hair so that she smelled its lemony brilliantine.

"How do you like the heat, Tullio?"

Margaret's question seemingly set a tic in motion in his shoulder. "I'm a Roman," he replied elliptically, and turned immediately to address Benjamin. "Rodney tells me you teach at Harvard."

"Used to."

"But you do know it well. I've been invited to lecture there next spring. Perhaps you can answer some of my questions."

Hadn't the heat last night been suffocating? Margaret turned to Rosy when the men fell into conversation. Incredible for the month of May. At the French embassy, where she and Rodney had dined the previous evening, more than one person had remarked that the atomic bomb was responsible for disrupting the seasons. They were not what they used to be, the seasons. It made it so difficult to know how to dress.

Margaret admired Rosy's dress. Rosy admired Margaret's bracelet which was dangling from the arm she had rested on the open window.

"Yes, it's amusing, isn't it? When Rodney went to Paris for a few days he brought it back to make up for abandoning me." She turned the ruby globe which dangled from a gold band so that it caught the light, and laughed at the idea of being abandoned.

Would Rosy like to go shopping? Margaret wondered. Rome was full of treasures. One had to know where to look for them, of course. There was a man on the via Babuino who made superb shoes and didn't ask the eyes out of one's head. (It was no longer necessary to go up to Florence.) For suits there was a little woman not far from here. Margaret pointed vaguely to the working-class neighborhood through which they were driving.

Margaret's address book was famous. It was said to contain even the names of liberal confessors for visiting Catholics who, for want of such names, had not made their Easter duty at home. By an occasional "Oh, really?" or "That would be lovely," Rosy tried not to show how inappropriate Margaret's suggestions were. She and Benjamin had landed in Rome without, as he put it, a bean. They had planned the trip to Europe confident of the renewal of his grant ("Just a formality," he'd told her). The Committee, which would not be sending out the acceptance notices until the very day of their departure, had given Benjamin permission to call just before sailing to hear their decision. (Their lives were full of such cliff-hangers.) When he heard it, it was too late, of course, to change their plans. Besides, Benjamin had said getting away was a therapeutic necessity: it was Europe or "the loony bin." There could be no rest for him in Cambridge—hounded by shopkeepers for unpaid bills, quarreling with everyone, drinking too much, keyed up and exhausted after finishing his poem. Rodney had guessed their financial situation and was trying to help. The way he had put it was that the Duchessa greatly admired Benjamin's poetry and was eager to meet him. She was known to be generous to writers. If Benjamin was in good form, if the luncheon went well . . .

Reminding herself that she must not worry, Rosy turned her attention to Tullio, who was seated on the jump seat in front of her. When he was amused by something Benjamin said, his mouth made a rectangle, exposing surprisingly small white teeth. The tic had traveled to his cheek. He was probably not easy either, but in a way different from Benjamin. Moody too, but sulky rather than explosive. Perhaps even cold. Only the tics gave him away.

They had been driving through the Campagna for some time when Margaret made signals to catch her husband's eye. "Rod, don't you want to tell the Bolds about Roccafalcone?" In her question there was the note of frustration of a hostess unable to move her guests around, to play Going-to-Jerusalem with them.

"Yes, of course. What should I tell you?" Rodney stroked his moustache between his thumb and forefinger reflectively. It was hard to believe that this man was Benjamin's contemporary. Born avuncular, he had looked, as long as anyone could remember, much as he did today—only a little less round, a little less bald, a little less pink. The ginger moustache, a bristly affair that crowded his upper lip, he had raised during the war and grown so fond of that when it had come time to go back to the Foreign Office he had taken it with him, together with his decorations. His superiors, sympathetic with his literary activities, had sent him to a series of posts which, like Rome, gave him the leisure to put together anthologies of poetry, "fidget" as he called it (although no one was less of a fidget) with his translations, and, for the last two years, edit the Duchessa's magazine *Ampersand*. His well-sheathed nerves, high tolerance for instability in his friends, and fidelity as a correspondent had made him one of Benjamin's closest friends. "Where should I begin?" Rodney wondered aloud.

"With Flossie," said practical Margaret.

"Yes, that's it. I can count on the Duca to tell you about Rocca, but he's not likely to tell you about his wife. She was born Florence Talbot," he began like a kindly uncle telling a fairy tale, "and is called Flossie by a surprising number of people, including the Duca. She grew up in Boston and Pride's Crossing. The year after she came out, she came to visit a maiden aunt in Rome . . ."

"A Miss Barnes she was. Knew absolutely everyone," Margaret interjected.

". . . and met, among a great many other people, the Duca. A widower, he was taken with her, some say, because his first wife had been harrowingly unfaithful . . ."

"You still hear the stories." Margaret made round eyes. "Apropos, Tullio, I must ask you about one I heard last night."

". . . and he saw at once that although Flossie might have faults, infidelity was not likely to be one of them."

"It helped, of course, that she was rich," said Margaret.

Rodney, who had also married a rich woman, seemed to think it over afresh. "Perhaps. But I don't think that was crucial. Flossie's acceptance of his proposal is more mysterious. As you will see, she is as American as corn on the cob— a tall, straight-backed woman, who was undoubtedly as formidable as she was handsome as a young girl. The romantic view, and the one I prefer, is that the Duca took her to see Roccafalcone and when she fell in love with it, as she instantly did, he fell in love with her. They decided on the spot to build a house there."

"Isn't it rather far from Rome?" Benjamin wondered.

"An hour. They have a palazzo in town, but Flossie likes it so little she prefers to have people come out here. I'll show you it one day, Ben, and you'll see why. It's awesomely ugly."

"In the winter she goes off to London," said Margaret.

"Yes. She finds Rome an intellectual desert."

"The Duca doesn't, and neither do I," said Margaret.

"No, they've arranged things very well, just as they have at Rocca. The grounds are his, the house hers. She wanted it to contrast as sharply as possible with the palazzo. I think you'll find it rather American."

"When did she become literary?" Benjamin asked.

"She secretly wrote verse all along," said Margaret.

Benjamin's *"Ha,"* loud but involuntary, made them jump.

"Have I let the cat out of the bag?" Margaret asked blandly.

"It's no secret if you tell us, is it dear?" Rodney said. "To answer your question, Ben, she bought the magazine just before the war, but didn't really get going on it until the late forties. Five or six years ago."

"There's the citadel." Tullio pointed to the left.

Benjamin leaned well out of the window. "Despite the name, I somehow didn't expect it to be a hill town."

"They don't live there," Tullio said. "That was the medieval town. It's inaccessible by road now. They decided to build on the site of the ancient Roman town now that malaria is no longer a threat. These umbrella pines mark one end of the property."

The chauffeur stopped the car. The Duca—it could be no one else—stepped out of a doorway framed in ivy. The women, with covert little gestures, tried to smooth out the wrinkles steamed into their dresses during the trip as they stood next to their cool and impeccably dressed host. Six feet tall, he looked English in all but nose, which was dog-matically Roman. His flannel trousers were thin and chamois-colored with age. His jacket hung with more slack than it had the day it was delivered to him. His hands, so long and thin they seemed to have an extra joint, with flesh the color of his trousers, rested, now that the introductions were over, one on top of the other on a blackthorn. His posture—the bend of his back, both graceful and fragile, which seemed to have been assumed rather than forced on him by age—was full of self-mockery. He encircled his guests with tired black eyes streaked with yellow, like a hunting dog's.

"I suppose you'll want to walk around a bit before lunch," he said in unaccented English. "I warn you, like all guides I'm a bit of a bore. I always tell people more than they want to know. You see, I'm obsessed with the place. Come along. We'll have time for about half what I want to show you before Flossie calls us to lunch."

They followed a wildly rushing stream which wound around the property, past the ivy-covered ruin of a Romanesque apse, across an ancient, moss-covered bridge. From time to time their guide stopped his narration to point his stick up to where the medieval town had been—still populated in his imagination with his ancestors, but marked for the others only by a piece of crenelated tower—or down at the trout in the rushing stream.

"Which one," he asked Rosy, "would you like for lunch? If you put your finger on it, I'll see that it's on your plate. Or would you rather go wading?" he teased, guessing her thoughts.

"Go on," Benjamin coaxed. "Why don't you?"

Rosy slipped her foot out of her sandal and put it in the pewter-colored stream. The water was so painfully cold she drew it back as if it had been burned.

The Duca laughed. "You'd have to be as cold-blooded as a trout to stand that water."

It was, as Rodney had said, a perfect Roccafalcone day. Blistering Rome seemed implausible. It was as though they had moved to another climatic zone. The air was cool and fresh and perfumed, sometimes overpoweringly, by flowering vines and wild flowers. The battle between nature and the Lentini family was still going on. Although malaria was no

longer a threat, one had the feeling that if the gardeners re-
laxed for a moment too long in their chores of pruning and
cutting, one would no longer see the wild flowers along the
stream, nor perhaps even the stream itself, as the weeds and
vines first choked, then buried everything in their weblike
blanket. Roccafalcone was always in danger of disappearing
again.

Trained to live by an American timetable, the Duca
brought his guests in sight of the house as the Duchessa appeared. Benjamin nudged Rosy: he had guessed their hostess
down to her ankles.

Flossie kissed Rodney and Margaret. She turned eyes as
blue and cold as the water of the North Shore on the Bolds
and said she was pleased they had been able to come.

"The Brills are here. You know him, of course, Mr.
Bold? His last novel . . ."

Benjamin was silent.

"We met last night," Rosy said. These were the "fools"
they'd been drinking with, the cause of their quarrel. Toward
the end of a cocktail party given by an Italian journalist to
whom Benjamin had a letter of introduction, they'd found
themselves with their host and the Brills. Jason Brill had
written a serious first novel, but he had long ago "sold out"
to Hollywood. He and his wife, Mimi, were hedonists—the
kind of people who stay suntanned year round by being rich
enough to control their own movements if not the sun's: St.
Moritz, Hollywood, the ranch in Nevada. The visits to Paris
and Rome were in the nature of a business trip, Jason had
said—the business of buying Mimi's clothes.

After the fourth pitcher of martinis, Benjamin and she
had given in weakly when pressed to go on to dinner—Benjamin because he had had more than his share of the last
pitcher, she because the Brills had seemed as exotic as sword
swallowers or aerialists (one didn't meet *their* likes in academic society).

Conti's, the restaurant in the pensione building, turned

out to be a favorite of Jason's. He shook hands with the maître d'hôtel, got the table he wanted, and ordered Soave Bertani as if he were the host. The first three bottles evaporated quickly. Brill suggested three more. Why not? The bill, within easy reach of the others, wiped out their food allowance for a week: that was why not.

The exoticism of the performers had faded long before it became clear that the price of admission had been too high. And there were alarming signs that the gin and wine were turning to bile inside Benjamin. They said good night to the Brills on the sidewalk and turned back to the elevator. It was out of order. An odor of escaping gas permeated the stairwell. They climbed the seven floors in silence. A mean yellow light showed the way to their room. The contrast between the style of life the Brills had been describing and theirs worked like a bellows on Benjamin's temper. He turned on Rosy in fury. What had been her idea in dragging him to dinner with such people? She was amused by Brill's jejune anecdotes, was she? Maybe she should have married a best-seller writer. Skiing in St. Moritz—she'd like that, wouldn't she? (She didn't ski.) Driving a Facel. (She didn't drive.) What difference did it make whether one married a hack novelist or a first-rate poet? Money, that was the difference, he'd shouted.

"That was fun last night, wasn't it?" Mimi said, shaking hands.

"My head was hydrocephalic this morning," Jason said good-humoredly. "How was yours, Bold?"

Benjamin was spared the necessity of answering by a cry that floated across the lawn: "Roxaaaaaana!" Doris Trumbull came running toward them, one hand anchoring a large black picture hat. She embraced Rosy with the passion of a lonely tourist meeting a friend from home. "Sweetie, I'm *thrilled* you're here. I'd lost your address."

"I see you two have already met," said the Duchessa astringently as she turned and led the way in to lunch.

It was easy to see why Rodney found the house American. There were few rooms, no corridors, and a great deal of light. Flossie was heard to say that she had arranged it so that it could be run with a minimum of servants. The main room was high-ceilinged, and served as a living and dining room. Flossie directed them to their places, Jason Brill on her right, Benjamin on her left.

The Duca, removing the bone from his fish with surgical skill, turned to Mimi Brill, "Mrs. Bold is examining her trout to see if it's the one she caught with her bare hands."

"Rocca didn't disappoint you?" Rodney asked Rosy.

Rosy had almost forgotten her uneasiness at dawn. The air of Roccafalcone was not only cool but salubrious. With Benjamin in good humor again, the outcome of the luncheon no longer worried her. At the very least, the Duchessa would give him some editing to do. Their money problems, for the moment, would be solved. "It's a dream," she said lazily, not attempting to express her feeling.

Mimi, blond and bronze, in a dress from the last business trip to Paris, was having less success with Tullio Fancelli than she had had with the Duca. A former model and the wife of a well-known writer, she was used to being looked at if not listened to. Tullio kept his eyes fastened on his plate and responded monosyllabically to her generous openings. When, rather desperate, she asked him if he ever had trouble with his story line (a chronic concern of Hollywood writers if the conversation at Conti's was any indication), he looked past her uncomprehendingly and addressed a question to the Duca in Italian.

Margaret, tougher than Mimi, had blocked an earlier attempt by Tullio and Benjamin to continue their conversation across her. She wanted her turn at Tullio. After gossip, she queried him in French. Fancelli refused to be pumped: "*Je n'en sais rien,*" he repeated, making hard gray pellets with the dough from the inside of his roll. His tics had reached a crescendo.

Jason Brill, a humorously ugly man with a spongy nose and a large loose mouth, was a raconteur who knew how to move into an opening. He seized a lull in the conversation, when the guests were struggling with the small bones of the squab, to expand his audience for the story he had been telling the Duchessa and Doris Trumbull. Their visit in Rome was being spoiled by their unfortunate accident. Mimi, who had been driving the Facel, had knocked down an old lady who'd stepped out from between parked cars the very night they arrived. The woman was now in Salvator Mundi, hovering between life and death. "We divide our days between visits to the hospital to see how she's doing and conferences with her family and our lawyer," he said.

"Who is your lawyer?" Margaret asked.

"Rinaldi."

"Better try Barducci. He's cleverer. You'll need him. I don't need to tell you how it looks—a rich American in a high-powered car and a poor old grandmother on foot."

Jason winced. "No. No need to tell me. It's the American nightmare."

Benjamin, who had heard the story the previous evening, was looking stony. The Duchessa had acted throughout the meal as if it were Brill she had been eager to meet, not him. When at last she turned his way—was it at a signal from Rodney?—she said:

"How do you like Brian MacGrath's new book, Mr. Bold?"

"I don't" was Benjamin's prompt reply.

"Not at all? Oh, come! Aren't you being cavalier?"

" 'Cavalier'?" Benjamin turned it over on his tongue the way he did when one of his students used a word inappropriately. "What most people won't admit, my dear Duchessa, is that at a given time there are very few good poets writing anywhere."

The guests, demanding Flossie's attention, distracted her

from this unpleasant remark which would seem to cut her out. Servants were passing small wicker baskets filled with raspberries that were bedded on fig leaves.

"This is a *spécialité de la maison*," Margaret explained to Mimi and Rosy. "Or I should say, *de la Duchesse*. Flossie raises her own raspberries."

Fancelli, who had been in a ticky reverie, came to life. "Ah, that fragrance! Only at Rocca do raspberries smell as they do in my childhood memory of them."

"*Stupendo!*" Jason exclaimed.

Flossie flushed with evident pleasure. "They are good, aren't they? They're the first of the season."

Rosy, who'd noticed uneasily that Benjamin's mood had changed halfway through the meal, was not reassured to see that during this interlude he had taken on a jaunty air. His head rocked from side to side in shallow arcs, the way the canary's at the pensione window did when he was sharpening his beak on a stone. Benjamin had not touched his berries. He had not even taken up his spoon and fork. The Duchessa, turning back to him to resume her quiz, found him handing her his plate.

"There's a worm in them," he hissed. Pushing his chair out to stand up, he toppled it over onto the stone floor. "A *worm*," he thundered, making for the door.

Wormwormwormwrmwrmmmmmmmmmmm echoed through the high-ceilinged room like the sound of a boulder hurtling down a mountain.

two

Wrenched awake the following morning by a black dream that hovered on the edge of consciousness like a bat in a bedroom, fluttering and diving almost within reach before flying off to some dark corner, Rosy lay rigid, trying to catch hold of it. It was no use.

Five o'clock. She tiptoed to the washbasin, took two aspirin to blunt a pain in her back, and tiptoed back to bed. She lay on her side facing the other bed. Benjamin, in a deep, untroubled sleep, looked almost boyish without his glasses and with a cowlick pushed up by his pillow. As often happened after he had staged a scene, his tension was temporarily reduced.

Not hers. She had not remonstrated with him when they got home. What was there left to say? The worm had been an invention, of course. The Duchessa was more interested in a hack novelist than in a first-rate poet, was she? Well, he'd show her how little willing he was to play up. Only, of course, there was now no question of the Duchessa "doing something" for him. So, no money. Now what?

Now she must think. If Benjamin had come abroad to avoid the "loony bin," she had come abroad to think. To take stock. To view their marriage from a distance. She had tried to tell herself before leaving home that the trouble was Cambridge. What they needed was a change of scene.

The trip had begun inauspiciously. The day of the sailing, while Benjamin waited in line at the phone booth to get the bad news from the Committee, she went aboard with the luggage. At the first warning for visitors to go ashore, Benjamin had not appeared. Nor had he by the second. Fighting her way to the rail, she searched the faces of the passengers late in boarding. No matter how she distorted them, none was his. At the siren's final blast, soul-piercing and ear-splitting as an Old Testament warning of impending doom, terror took root in her heart: the ship was under way.

She raced like a frantic animal loose in a maze, back to the cabin, through the public rooms, up and down stairwells, from deck to deck, from class to class. She finally found him where, had she had her wits about her, she would have looked in the first place: in the bar. The room was blue with smoke and heavy with the odor of Gauloises (her first whiff of Europe). He was sitting at a table against the wall, his coat on, his muffler around his neck, his eyes fixed on a glass with a double martini in it. The way he stared at it, it might have been some vile medicine or poison. A glance told her his mood was dangerous. Better leave him alone. Later, sometime after midnight, she found him again, at the prow of the ship. He threatened suicide (not for the first time, but one never knew) and approached the rail as if to climb it. Experience had taught her not to be an audience for such scenes. It was dawn before he stumbled into the cabin.

Andrew Mallory saved the crossing for them. His note, pushed under the door the next morning, rejoiced at finding the name of his old friend Ben Bold on the passenger list. What about having a drink with him in the tourist bar (his, in cabin class, was "too, too squalid") before dinner? Rich with "bags of gold" he'd earned on his poetry-reading tour of the States, Andrew ordered champagne. They drank to the years before the war in England, at Cambridge University. They drank to Rodney, who had been with them. They drank to Benjamin's new book. To fame that would soon be his.

Benjamin charmed the couple, a maiden lady and her adolescent niece from Nashville, who sat at their table for meals. Although he loathed eating with strangers, his good humor, refueled nightly with Andrew in the bar, spilled over on to them. The niece, a year too young and ten pounds too heavy for the belle she would be the year she came out, began to look at her, Rosy, wistfully. How lucky Mrs. Bold was to be traveling with such an attentive man! The way he broke the lump of sugar for her demitasse. (It's the little things which tell about a marriage.) Brilliant he was, too. And so entertaining!

The object of this envy could only agree. There was no more delightful husband in the world. *This* was the real Benjamin. The previous six months had been but a bad dream. Europe, surely, would work out after all.

But it had not. Oh, not at all. And her excuses for not thinking about the future had now run out. She could delay no longer.

Dressing quickly and quietly, her eyes on Benjamin to be sure he was still asleep, she went out. Up the street from the pensione was the church of Trinità dei Monti. On the congregation side of the altar she sat alone. The childish voices of nuns, unaccompanied, came from behind the grille. A mélange of odors, incense and candle wax, brought back acutely early-morning mass at the school where she had been taken to live following the death of her parents. The school chapel, smaller than this one, had had a ceiling of robin's-egg blue, and white walls punctuated with mahogany confessionals. But the baroque angels, which knelt at either side of the altar, could have been made by the same artisan who had made the ones for this church. On the right, in front of the altar, the convent chapel had also had its Infant of Prague.

In May, when the chapel doors were left open after evening Benediction, the fragrance of incense blended with herbal odors of the kitchen garden. During that month, the month of Mary, a child was selected to carry a rose into the empty chapel, to put it in a bud vase before the Virgin's statue. It was an honor sought after by everyone, but impossible to compete for because it had to do with mysterious qualities of excellence known only to the Mother Superior. Rosy's turn had come near the end of her stay, when she was eight years old. Kneeling to say the Hail Mary, she had felt that she was talking to the Virgin, and had had no doubt that she was being listened to.

Today, unable to do more than repeat the words of the prayers by rote as a background to her thoughts, she was vexed that Benjamin exaggerated her piety. He refused to listen when she explained how variable her feelings were. It suited his passion for extremes to see her as an angel, himself as a devil. Had she lived in a Catholic country, her religious practices would have been taken for granted by Benjamin and her friends. In Cambridge academic circles, their rarity was taken as a sign of intensity. The battle between what was right and what one wanted to do, the frailty and weakness so familiar to any confessor were unknown to them. They would not have understood, or would have been scornful if they had, that she had come to mass this morning quite simply for comfort. But the comfort she sought had become increasingly difficult to find since Theo had come into her life.

Had Benjamin not begun work on his long poem, she might not have gone out on those cold winter evenings, convalescing as she had been, to Theo's lectures. But less than a week after her return from the hospital, Benjamin came into the bedroom, his eyes darting, his voice tense with excitement saying: "I've begun it. *Do you hear?*"

She had not heard. Absorbed in the healing of her body, she had only half taken in that "it" was the subject he had been turning over in his mind for as long as she had known him. When she awakened one night to find him leaning over her with news which couldn't wait until morning, *"I've got it!* I've got my stanza"; and when, a few nights later, after she'd finally fallen asleep to the sound of his furious pacing, he'd shaken her awake with "I'm beginning to sound like *me*. Benjamin Bold. I've found my own voice. Listen!" she *had* listened.

In the beginning she had shared his excitement, and had been grateful to have something rich and warm to put against the harsh sounds of icicles cracking at the window, of the scraping of snow shovels on the sidewalk, of the whine of automobile wheels spinning without traction. But as the poem grew in size and scope and Benjamin stopped eating and sleeping, as day and night became interchangeable and his excitement mounted to hysteria, she began to long for the monotonous but finite sounds of winter.

Was he not going to allow her any time to get well? Pleading with him to let her sleep, to leave her in peace so that she could regain her strength—Did he remember that she was just home from the hospital? No, his eyes told her, he remembered nothing before the beginning of the poem— she saw that, except as an ear, she had ceased to exist for him.

The couch in the living room to which, when she was able, she moved became like an island in a turbulent river surrounded by rapids and whirlpools, which snap down its trees and suck away chunks of its soil. Its boundaries eroded, she contracted into a tight, self-protecting ball. If she was to survive, she would have to get out of the house.

Dr. Gilford, the gynecologist who had operated, looked disapproving when she asked if she could go back to work early. "It's not I who makes the rules," he said sternly. "Six weeks is the prescribed convalescence period after abdominal surgery. Didn't you tell me Mr. Bold agreed to the operation?"

He had agreed.

"He understood its purpose?"

He had understood.

Dr. Gilford toyed with his pen for some time before saying, "Are you sure your husband wants a child?"

Sure? Doubts had added another torment to her convalescence. Fighting back tears, she shrugged her shoulders, as if to say that she was now not sure of anything.

The doctor came around the desk and put his hand on her shoulder. "Yes, go back to work," he said. "Try to take it easy. Loaf on the job. Come to see me again in three weeks. We'll talk more about all this when you're stronger."

The priest, at the epistle side of the altar, read the Introit. The nuns and Rosy echoed his "*Kyrie eleison, Christe eleison, Kyrie eleison.*"

It was not long after she was back at work that Theo arrived. Benjamin, who had known Theo casually in England, accompanied her to his opening lecture. In the auditorium, above eye level, Theo looked, in his brown suede crepe-soled shoes and his heavy Irish tweeds, like a giant towering over a toy lectern. After some shy, whispery opening remarks, acknowledging the flowery introduction, his voice filled the hall without effort. The audience, not at all sure at the beginning that anyone could interest them for six weeks on the subject of Giulio Romano's architecture, stopped coughing and shifting in their seats. Theo ran through his plan for the series, and the mannerisms which would characterize his performance. He rocked the lectern from side to side as if it were made of cork; he ran his hands restlessly through his unruly black hair; he pronounced therefore "tha fore"; he twirled his reading glasses around by one of the earpieces. Swung too energetically near the end of the lecture, the glasses described a leisurely parabola in the air and came to rest, astonishingly, in Rosy's lap. Benjamin, handing them up to Theo (they were seated in the front row), said, "Good shot, Addis," as the audience burst into undisciplined applause.

At the reception afterwards, Benjamin introduced her to Theo with a joke about the intimacy the glasses had already established between them. Theo, apologizing to her, said that while the glasses had always been unpredictable (he never found them where he thought he'd left them), this was the first time they'd openly shown themselves bent on leading a reckless life of their own.

Since it was well known that Benjamin had gone underground to work on his poem, it was she who was paired with Theo at the round of dinner parties given for him. It was he who saw her home. Across the Yard, down Brattle Street, up Memorial Drive, her hand tucked in the arm he offered in support against the icy pavements, they walked companionably through the winter nights. He fed her daydreams of Europe (her soporific against Benjamin's debilitating excitement) with advice about where to go and what to see in Italy. Benjamin should plan a long *séjour* in England, he said. His house, outside Cambridge, could serve as their hotel.

One night, when the air was softer than usual because of the falling snow, Theo walked her home the long way and told her about Vera. He had met and married her when he was doing resettlement work with the inmates—Vera had been one—of Belsen. Six numb years had passed since her suicide. It had done him good to get away from home. He was beginning to feel alive again.

Rosy found herself confiding in Theo about Benjamin. As he pushed to the end of his work on the long poem, his state was becoming alarming. She was beginning to fear for his, always precarious, stability. Night after night now she found him at three and four o'clock asleep in his chair, his fingers burned by the cigarette dangling between them, a ring of burns in the rug beneath his hand.

The evening of Theo's last lecture, at the farewell party given by the head of the department, their relationship, though she had not seen it at the time, had taken a new turn. Benjamin, restless and irritable now that his poem was finished, decided to go with her. A drink or two, he said, might do for him what sedatives were failing to do. From the timbre of his voice in argument with his host, it was clear that the drinks had had the opposite effect. No, he said captiously, when she approached him about going home (only a hard core of drinkers remained), he was *not* ready to leave.

It would require more energy than she had to avoid a quarrel on the way home. The study, where she went to get away from the sound of his hectoring voice, was empty. The room was like many others in houses off Brattle Street where faculty members lived—a well-worn rug on the floor, well-read books in the bookcases, a pair of Windsor chairs from the Harvard Coop decorated with the college seal. She sat on a love seat before the fire, stroking the velours of the cushion in which her hand had just found a worrisome bald spot, when Theo came in.

Although not the giant he had seemed on the platform, he was a big man, with a large head full of bombé surfaces—brow, cheek, and chin. His Levantine eyes were underlined by dark circles which shaded from mauve to black. This evening his eyes looked black rather than brown, and they had lost their luminosity. He looked tired. He took up her hand and folded it into his arm as he sat down. There was just room. Through the sleeve of her blouse she felt the rough tweed of his jacket, which smelled as she imagined peat fires might smell.

He must be glad his lectures were over, she said, realizing for the first time how much she would miss him when he left. He had done more than make tolerable a difficult period; he had become a friend.

"Glad?" he said. "Hardly. Now I have no excuse for

staying on here." He was silent for a moment. "There's something I wanted to say to you, Roxana. You remember when my eyeglasses fell in your lap?"

She laughed at the memory. She told Theo Benjamin had said that since he couldn't go to the other lectures and wouldn't be on hand to play ball boy, perhaps it would be more prudent if she sat farther away from the platform.

"Had he a presentiment of jealousy?" Theo asked.

Benjamin had never been jealous. He had never had reason. "Jealous?"

"He should have been, should be now. . . ."

Without their having heard him, Benjamin had come up behind the love seat. "What are you up to, Addis?" he asked, his voice tight with fatigue and alcohol. "Telling my wife's fortune?"

She became uncomfortably aware that Theo still held her hand. She had not taken it back.

"You came too soon, Bold," Theo answered, as she stood up. "I was about to reveal Roxana's future to her."

"Bad luck, old boy." Benjamin took her arm with a touch of impatience, as if it were she who had kept him waiting. "Catholics aren't allowed to listen to fortune-tellers. It's a sin, you know."

The warning bell, rung by a nun behind the grille, brought Rosy to guilty attention. She knelt up straight, her elbows on the pew in front, her hands pressed against her forehead, to help her pay attention. The priest spread his hands over the bread and wine. *"Hanc igitur oblationem . . ."*

They hadn't met again, she and Theo, until three days later, when he followed her into the subway car at the Harvard Square station. He was out of breath from running. His overcoat was flying open.

"I can't believe my luck," he said, trying to get his

breath. "I've been running to catch you up. I saw you ahead of me." He brushed the snow off his brown Borsalino, which must have been blown off as he ran, and put it on, brim down all around. "Now that the lectures and parties are over, it's not easy to see you. I went round to your office in the Fogg day before yesterday, but you were in the slide room. Yesterday you were out to lunch and I ran into Benjamin instead."

At Charles Street, when the train emerged in the bright winter sun, he pointed to the river, glistening between the slabs of ice. "Put off your errands and come for a walk with me, won't you?"

It was a day of faint false spring after a spiteful winter— a tempting day for a walk. "All right . . . a short one," she said. "Where shall we go?"

"Show me the Public Garden, won't you? It would be a scandal to go back to England without having seen it."

It was she who mentioned the swan boats, said it was a shame they weren't out.

"A pity. Perhaps if we could take a ride, pretend we were somewhere else, I could tell you—" He broke off. "Look here, you have to have lunch somewhere; why not with me?"

Her conscience began to prick her. She had endless errands for which she had taken half a day from work.

"Come along," he said. "The errands will keep. I won't: I go off in two days, you know. What's that Greek place we all went to after Doris Trumbull's party?"

At the Athens Olympia, they were shown to a corner booth. He took her hands, which she had been rubbing, between his. "That's how we warm cold hands," he said. "Now what about a drink?" When their sherry came, he said, "Have you guessed what I started to tell you the other evening?"

As he looked up, she saw for the first time that his chin folded in on itself in a vertical cleft, and wondered at not having noticed it before.

"No, I see you haven't. I told you that getting out of England had done me good. It's done better than that. It's cured me." He took up her ring hand and toyed with her wedding band, twisting it between his thumb and index finger. "I've fallen in love."

The sherry in her glass welled up to one side as she put it down. The thought Please God, don't let me fall in love with this man flashed through her mind. She covered her ring protectively with her other hand.

"I've frightened you. I was afraid I might. But I had to say this before I left." He put his hand in front of her lips to stifle her protest. "No. Don't say anything. All I ask is that you think of me. You'll be in Europe soon. Benjamin told me yesterday he plans a month, maybe more, in England. I'll try to meet you earlier, in Paris, or in Rome . . ."

After lunch she hurried through her errands. It seemed important to get home to Benjamin. When she told him she had had lunch with Theo (less to confess than to convince herself that it had no real importance) he did not look up from the work of cleaning his pipe.

"Beware, darling, beware of jealousy," he said.

She had hoped for a moment he meant his.

"All the women in Cambridge are after Theo. You can't tell me it was Giulio Romano who packed the lecture hall. Uh-uh. It was those sad, Semitic eyes." He filled his pipe and puffed on it to get it started. "You know"—he took the pipe out of his mouth and pointed it at her —"I quite see you married to a don."

Had she been drowning and had Benjamin, instead of coming to her rescue, described to her what drowning was like, she could not have felt more abandoned. No, she could not count on him for help. She would have to struggle alone. When things went well between them, Theo's voice became inaudible; when they went poorly . . .

The priest turned around to give the final blessing. Rosy stood. *"Benedicat vos omnipotens Deus, Pater et Filius et Spiritus Sanctus."* He made the sign of the cross, took the chalice, genuflected, and left the altar. The nuns behind the grille filed out, nunlike, two by two. The one in charge of the altar extinguished the candles.

Rosy put away her unread missal, genuflected, and left the church. It was still early. The morning was fair. The air fresh. The heat had cooled to a summer brilliance. Below, at the foot of the Spanish Steps, flower venders were putting up their parasols and arranging the mounds of roses, carnations, peonies, and gladioli in pails of water.

Benjamin was probably still asleep. Their roles were changing: he had been the victim of nightmares: she the one gifted with tranquil sleep. He might not be up before noon. It would be a long day. In Cambridge there had never been time to think. Today time stretched out before her threateningly, like a sea of quicksand.

thRee

Rosy walked up the Pincio. Except for an attendant who was sweeping the paths, the park was empty. She sat down on a bench overlooking the city and took a brown copybook from her purse. It was a diary, one of a series she had been made to keep as a form of discipline when she was growing up. (She had been a vague and dreamy child; it was hoped that a diary might help her organize her thoughts, sharpen her attention to the everyday world.) Rebelling against the discipline, she had never written a candid word in any of the books until this one. It covered the period just before she met Benjamin and their courtship. After their marriage it was the only one she had saved, putting it in the box with Benjamin's letters. Without asking herself why, she had packed it with her books when they sailed for Europe. This morning she saw it as a bridge over the quicksand, a bridge to the past. It was a way of beginning.

The book fell open to a page marked by an anemone, pink faded to a powdery gray.

JUNE 1: I'm in! Books on the desk. Clothes in the closet. Suitcases under the bed. It's mine. $7 a week. I can almost afford it. Bought a bouquet of anemones at the subway to celebrate my freedom.

Pears. The room—who would have expected it in a hall bedroom in the Village?—smelled of pears. For a long time she had associated Benjamin with their delicate and mysterious odor.

The bouquet had been to celebrate her freedom to live alone, at least for the summer, while Uncle Jim, her guardian, was teaching in Canada.

She turned to the beginning of the book, to January. She and Benjamin had met for the first time when Jane, her closest friend, brought him to a New Year's Day party at Uncle Jim's apartment. There was a long entry about the party, but no mention of Benjamin. Mike (Mike who?) seemed to have been the flame of the moment. It was Jane who set her thinking about Benjamin.

JANUARY 5: To Jane's for the night. Up until 4 a.m. catching up after the holiday. She told me Benjamin Bold had a *coup de foudre* for me. She told him he didn't have a chance, that I was wild about Mike and that in any case I go more for novelists than poets. He supposed I was "crazy" about Thomas Wolfe. (Very sarcastic.) We don't understand why he didn't fall for Victoria, who is crazy about poetry and isn't a virgin. He's not fast exactly, but he says that anyone over 20 still a virgin must be retarded. Not really, of course. Jane told him we all are. Except Victoria.

At the party as I passed him the shrimp, he held on to my hand as well as the dish, and asked whom had I fallen in love with in *War and Peace*—Bolkonsky or Bezukhov? I was so flustered I couldn't remember which was which, so I said Pierre. "Extraordinary" he said in a sort of English accent and looked as if he might give me an F in a little black book.

While I was out with Mike he called twice. Kept calling off and on throughout the holiday. Always at funny hours, like 2 a.m. (which Uncle Jim didn't find at all funny).

Jane said she wasn't jealous because she got over him a long time ago (completely?). She did think it a little tactless of him to take her out and pump her about me. He asked millions of questions. He's glad I'm an orphan (why?). Says he's delighted I'm not crazy like Victoria (who *does* sound more his type) because he's crazy enough for both of us!

What's wrong with liking Thomas Wolfe, I wonder?

There was no mention of Benjamin again until mid-March.

MARCH 10: Benjamin Bold sent me his book! Out of the blue. I rewrote the thank-you note *three* times. It still wasn't right, but I sent it. Must ask Jane who the girl in "Waterloo Station" is.

There was nothing more until June, shortly after the move to the room in the Village.

JUNE 10: B. B. called!! Asked me to dinner. What's there to be nervous about? I do wish I weren't so ignorant.

JUNE 11: Dizzy, headachy, queasy in the stomach. When we met—was it just last night?—he looked quite surprised, as though the wrong girl had come down the stairs. He hadn't remembered my "technicolor beauty." (He made it sound as if he were talking about a harelip or a wart on the end of my nose.) He told me I was taller than he remembered, critically. I turned my ankle. He's shorter than I remembered. (I didn't say so.) If he wore an inverness cape and didn't have a moustache he'd look like W. B. Yeats. Not handsome, but charged with electricity.

It wasn't at all like other dates. He kept talking about how "mobile" my face was and about the "planes" in it. I was starved but couldn't eat. Under the circumstances. He said I was different from what I appeared. That my "Powers Girl smile" didn't fool him. (Shrewd.)

That I was high strung. (I suppose I am.) That no one I've been out with so far has really interested me. (Right.) That I'm looking for someone to "devote" myself to. (?) Jane told him I said I couldn't fall in love with a man who didn't know how to weep (I wish she hadn't. It sounds idiotic), which makes me "quite extraordinary." He thinks I'm very sensitive, but that I don't have a tragic sense of life. (Is that good?) His, it seems, couldn't be more tragic.

All the way home through the park I dreaded what would happen at the door. He said, "A woman who exposes the nape of her neck is longing to have it kissed." So keyed up I couldn't get to sleep. All night I could feel his moustache on my neck.

This morning at 7:30 when I was getting dressed, Mrs. Santini banged on the pipe to tell me I had a phone call. It was B. B. His voice was like a martini on an empty stomach. It made me reel. Mrs. Santini was standing there letting the bacon burn she was so curious. He said he hadn't been to bed. He'd sat up all night in Childs, 42 Street, thinking about me. I couldn't think of anything to say because of the reeling and Mrs. Santini. He said to stop acting as though he were soliciting subscriptions to a magazine, that this was serious. Then he asked if there was a spy listening and I said yes, and he promised to get off the phone if I'd tell him where I worked so he could meet me for lunch.

At the office I made so many mistakes Mrs. Vanderling asked me if I'd had a big night. Somehow Benjamin didn't look so frightening at lunch—just foreign. He wore the some brown gabardine suit and carried an umbrella (it wasn't raining). He wanted to know all about my "work." I said it wasn't "work," just a job, that I was saving money to go to law school. He said that showed I didn't "understand myself," I was not meant to be a lawyer. Besides, he could teach me everything I wanted to know.

I didn't eat again. He asked me for dinner. I told

him I had to go to Granny's. He looked suspicious because Jane had told him I was an orphan. I said I was an orphan, not a foundling, that in fact I had lots of relatives. He looked disappointed. He said Uncle Jim was a "tyrant." I said I was going back to live with the "tyrant" in September when he came back from Canada. He said, "We'll see." What does *that* mean?

Mr. Munroe stopped at my desk and whispered, "Who was that moustache I saw kissing your hand? Isn't that pretty rich fare at lunch time?" I blushed mauve.

11 p.m. Mrs. Santini just banged again. The phone woke her up. He mustn't call so late. He said it would be "very awkward" if I made any more engagements for the next three weeks because we're going to be seeing each other every minute. Tomorrow he's going to meet me before work—lunch time is too long to wait.

JUNE 12: I thought I didn't care very much about being pretty because I wanted to be admired for other things. Now I find I do care. Terribly. It seems I'm not at all his type. He likes women who are short and dark and pale.

Never having been admired, as far as she knew, except for her appearance, and unable to imagine what other qualities she might have which could attract Benjamin to her, she had begun their relationship with a feeling of gratitude, like an ugly girl who has been told that she must be wittier, or more intelligent, or more compliant than other girls if she is to get a husband.

He said this to convince me that his attraction is not just physical, but it made me feel sad.

And that's not all. He doesn't like my name. Wants to change it. And I must stop using words like date, line, crush, flame, wolf. . . . Oh dear!

JUNE 13: On the other hand, no one before Benjamin ever said I was like a character in a novel. He says I'm like Milly Theale—without her dangerous money. I bought *The Wings of the Dove* in a Modern Library. To see. (Of course I exposed the fact that I'd been reading James "chaotically.")

JUNE 14: Each day when I get home from work there's a letter. I wonder they don't burn up the box. He wants me to write him too. I said I have nothing to write (since we meet morning, noon, and night). Well then, I must write what I think before falling asleep.

JUNE 16: My education has begun. He arrived tonight with an armful of books—*Master and Man* and *The Death of Ivan Ilyich,* a fascinating magazine called *Hound and Horn,* a book of poems by John Crowe Ransom, and H. G. Wells's *Experiment in Autobiography.* (I said I didn't like Wells. He said, "Never mind. Read this.") He recited "Sailing to Byzantium." In Childs. What a reader! He makes you *hear* the punctuation. I was embarrassed about the other people hearing, though. B. pretended they didn't exist.

JUNE 19: I'm falling, falling . . .

JUNE 21: If only Jane would come back. I wish I could remember every word she'd told me about B.

JUNE 24: What was life like before Benjamin? I can no longer remember. Being with him is like going on the Steeplechase at Coney Island: I'm nervous waiting. At the beginning it's so calm I wonder why I was afraid. Then POUMB. I hold on for dear life. I get a breath, pray for the end, and POUMB again. But at the end, he urges me to go on again. I resist at first and then . . .

JUNE 25: Is it his intensity that attracts me? Or is it that he talks about love as if it were a subject as worthy of serious attention as poetry? When I asked how he knew he loved me he quoted Santayana—"a deep and dumb instinctive affinity."

JUNE 28: Jane is back. Had lunch at the 8th Street Diner. It was so restful to be away from B, yet I talked of no one else, and now I can't wait to see him this evening. Maybe all spring I daydreamed about the wrong man! It seems there are two Benjamins, this one and Benjamin Warburton. Jane was engaged to B. Warburton after B. Bold (she gets engaged as easily as I blush). Which explains why B. B. is not the divine dancer I thought she said he was, nor the bad drinker who passed out in front of her mother.

Rosy marked the place with her finger, as if afraid of losing it, and looked up. This was the first surprise the diary had to offer—Benjamin's early abstemiousness having been drowned during the intervening years under fathoms of alcohol. It was true. In those days, when they weren't walking, they spent their evenings talking over one glass of beer. Drinking had had no part in their courtship. (It had been one of the many things which had differentiated Benjamin from the other men she knew at that time who still drank with the tedious excessiveness of college boys.) No, drinking hadn't become a problem until after the war—which was why she mistook it for so long for a piece of stage business which Benjamin would use and discard when it lost its dramatic effect.

. . . Hardly drinks at all. But he *is* the one who had the nervous breakdown (too bad that wasn't Warburton too). His half-sister Iphigene told Jane afterwards that it was a rare brain disease, and still later that it was really only a giant temper tantrum. (Iphigene, it seems, is shameless about changing stories.) Whatever it was, it was all the fault of England, and although the scholarship was a great honor, perhaps he never should have gone to Cambridge. Jane says he was impossible when he came home. He had changed fantastically. He was much more serious and always irritable. He'd say "You Americans . . ." as if he weren't one. He hated being back. Everything was "hideous," "vulgar," and "philistine." And he had a beard.

Iphigene's name isn't Iphigene, either. It's Mildred. He got her to change it. He seems to have a thing about names. (I didn't tell Jane he wants to change mine. I'm not crazy about the idea, but after all it's only two letters and if it matters so much to him . . .) Anyway, Mildred-Iphigene is *much* more important than a sister because she half raised B. after his father and their mother were killed (another story which gets changed all the time), when he was 10 and she was 21. They fight like cats and dogs it seems, but Jane said it doesn't mean a thing. They're *thick as thieves*. I knew Iph. was important because he talks about her all the time. Jane says she can be nice or not so nice, depending. When Jane was engaged to Benjamin she was not so. When Benjamin broke off with her for the English girl Phoebe (the one in "Waterloo Station"), Iphigene was very kind and sympathetic. Phoebe came here the year after Benjamin got back and stayed six months. Jane isn't exactly sure what happened (more changing stories), but she suspects Iphigene squeezed Phoebe out. Iphigene is *very* possessive. Sounds dangerous.

JUNE 29: A second date to meet Iphigene broken. Benjamin "didn't feel up to it." What is there to feel up to, I wonder?

JULY 1: Plenty. Wednesday when Benjamin came to pick me up to go to Iphigene's, he asked me to change my dress! I was too startled to refuse. Then on the way he asked me to take off my earrings, and didn't I have on rather too much lipstick!!! I began to feel as if I were going to have an audience with the Pope. I tried to tease him, telling him not to be jittery because I'm the kind of girl all mothers go for. He wasn't teasable. Iphigene was not his mother, and he dared say my experience with half-sisters was limited. (He had never talked to me that way before.)

By the time we got there I was pretty jittery too. Iphigene opened the door—dressed in flowered pajamas, her arms covered with bracelets like a gypsy (me with my earrings in my pocket). She kissed Benjamin as if she hadn't seen him for a thousand years and asked if this was Miss Riordan. Benjamin said: *Of course* it's Miss Riordan. I wasn't likely to have brought some stray young woman. And don't look at her as if she were a painting you had sent home on approval." Iphigene pretended she didn't notice his rude tone and laughed hahahaha, twirling on her heel so that the pajama bottoms flared out.

I can't remember how the conversation went during dinner. There was a lot of talk about the R.A.F. and a friend of Iphigene's pulling strings to get Benjamin to Canada so that he could join—none of which I could follow. Iphigene ignored me except to say, "Miss Riordan, do have some rice." I spent my time watching the candle on the table. I had the feeling I too was melting away.

At the mention of Phoebe I pricked up my ears. (Benjamin had said, to show me how "constant" he is, that he had only been in love once before, with an English girl.) Iphigene asked if Benjamin had had a chance to read the letter that had come that morning, she was so anxious to have Phoebe's news. Benjamin said it was only a book bill from Blackwells. Iphigene said perhaps there had been *two* pieces of mail from England because she was sure she'd seen one of Phoebe's blue envelopes. At this point Benjamin jumped up as if he'd been burned. Why hadn't she steamed open the envelope if she was so curious? She'd done nothing but talk about England all evening. Then *she* jumped up.

She'd only been trying to be helpful. *He* was the one who had talked about nothing but England for weeks. They shrieked at each other. Benjamin yanked me out of my chair where I sat trying to pretend I wasn't there. We were on the street in seconds.

B. "Let's have a drink somewhere. I'm ill with rage."

R. "I want to go home." By this time I couldn't wait to get away from *both* of them. (I'm writing word for word, still trying to make sense out of what happened.)

B. "I never should have taken you there. She was bound to make trouble."

R. "Why?"

B. "Because she'd guessed I'm in love with you. *Do you hear that?*" (Shouting) *"Do you take it in?"*

R. "What about Phoebe?"

B. "What has that to do with us?" (as if my question were at best irrelevant, at worst spying).

R. "I don't understand. You say you're in love with me . . ."

B. "I feel weak" (He says "weak" in a very strong way). "We must sit down. We've walked blocks. I'm *tired,* I tell you. Dead tired." (A loud whine.)

We went into Madison Square Park. Still crowded because of the heat. Groups of people standing around arguing. We sat on a bench by the fountain.

R. "Are you planning to go to England?"

B. "No. Besides, it's quite impossible. There's no way to arrange it."

R. "But if there were a way?"

B. "Idle speculation is tiresome."

R. Summoning my courage, "You're not being candid with me." I felt as if I'd said some terrible thing because he went all queer.

B. "I'm *ill,* I tell you, quite ill." He acted as if he were going to faint—or, I don't know, have a fit maybe. I was frightened to death. But then—and although I've thought about it every minute since, I still don't understand how I dared—I said . . .

R. "You're not ill, Benjamin. You just don't want to talk about Phoebe, that's all." I didn't say it angrily, but as if I were certain. He didn't faint or anything. He didn't say a word. We just sat. After what seemed like hours, he said . . .

B. "You don't believe in me." It sounded more like the voice I knew, crushed maybe, but not that ill-weird voice.

R. Much relieved, "I just don't believe in your illness."

B. "You know nothing about it. The doctors who've been studying it are still mystified. How can you presume . . ."

R. Stubbornly, "I only know what I feel." We sat another long time.

B. "It's easy to simplify, but what am I to do? (Pleading) Phoebe and I were very much in love in England. We were lovers. She came here. We talked of marrying. Didn't. When she went back, we continued to write. Then England went to war. There it is. What more do you want to know?"

R. "Nothing."

B. Benjamin took hold of my wrists. His eyes were darting like shuttlecocks. "Now it's my turn not to believe you. You want to know everything, everything. You're jealous of her. *Ha! Ha!* You're jealous!"

As he said this, jealousy jumped out of the dark like a prowler out of the bushes and got me by the throat. I'd never felt anything like it before, but I knew he was right.

B. "You are, aren't you? Aren't you?" His fingers felt like handcuffs on my wrists.

R. "Yes." I felt as if I'd been in a fist fight and my opponent, holding me down, had said: Give up? Benjamin pulled me closer.

B. "Do you understand what that means, dear silly virginal Rosy? You've fallen in love."

He was jubilant (all recovered)—overpoweringly sure of himself. I broke out of his grasp and ran out of the gate and ran and ran down the avenue and didn't stop running until I was sure I'd lost him.

That was Wednesday evening. Thursday morning I called the office and asked Miss Vanderling if I could take two days of vacation time. She said I could if I promised not to elope. Big joke. Then I told Mrs. Santini I was afraid I was coming down with the flu or something so I was going to stay in bed to sleep it off. To please tell anyone who called that I couldn't come to the phone. Mrs. Santini was suspicious but motherly. She said she'd been worried because I'd been burning the candle at both ends and that probably lowered my resistance.

I slept all day Thursday and all Thursday night as if I really did have a fever. Today I finally wrote to Uncle Jim. It seemed unwise to talk about Benjamin, but on the other hand I didn't see how to account for my time, so I said I'd seen something (understatement of the year) of Jane's old friend who was in New York but who would be going back to Boston soon. Then I wrote all the other letters I owed, did my laundry, straightened my closet and drawers, washed my hair ("Is that wise dear," Mrs. Santini wondered, "with the flu?").

I wrote part of this while my hair was drying and then called Jane to borrow her leghorn hat for Mary's engagement party. Jane's going to meet me with it tomorrow at Grand Central. Iphigene gave her a concert ticket for last night and told her I was "lovely, really lovely . . . but so inarticulate," so Jane guessed it hadn't gone well. I made Jane promise not to tell Benjamin where we're meeting if he should call her (Mrs. Santini is at her wit's end with him).

I'm really looking forward to going to Mary's this weekend.

July 5 Monday: Everything is upside down again. Jane didn't meet me, Benjamin did. A voice behind me said, "Just what do you think you're doing?" and I knew I was trapped. He was holding Jane's hat by the ends of the ribbons, the way a hunter holds a dead bird. At the moment I didn't want her old hat, the traitor. Benjamin said he'd gone to her house when Mrs. Santini said he needn't bother ringing up any more, that I'd gone away for the weekend, because he suspected that's where I was. He simply wore her down (I can believe it) until she told him where she was going to meet me. In any case, I was the criminal, not Jane. Then he asked me again what the "sweet Jesus" I thought I was doing. Thinking. Thinking about what? What was there to think about? I was both cowardly and cruel (that would give me something to confess the next time I went, he said). He'd bought a ticket and was determined to go to Bronxville with me! I got panicky and promised that if he'd just give me the weekend alone I would meet him in the station at 7:29 Sunday night. When I fell into my seat—I was the last one through the gate—I realized he must still be holding the hat. By its ribbons.

In the beginning it was heaven with Mary and her crowd. So easy and familiar and slow motion. I had a big whirl at the dance Saturday night. But somehow by Sunday lunch it seemed *too* slow motion. I began to feel as though I'd outgrown them, that I didn't belong with them any more. They seemed so young, and if Benjamin is too complicated, they're too simple. I was glad the train back was crowded so I could sit with a stranger and not have to talk. It was a pokey train, so I had plenty of time to think. By the time we got to Grand Central I was *wild* to see Benjamin and scared he might have gotten fed up and gone back to Boston. But there he was. He seemed very happy too, and said he had a surprise for me. We took a taxi to the surprise— which is the room he moved into on Macdougal Street. He's not going back to Boston. He's fed up with Iphigene (for the moment), and besides, we can't keep walking all the time or sitting in dreary cafeterias. As usual with Benjamin, everything was going too fast. He told me not to look frightened (why can't I ever hide my feelings?) because he had no intention of raping me. He wants me to be his mistress, but I must decide. He doesn't intend to create any accidental bastards!

Bronxville certainly seemed a long ways away. He brought me home early. He seemed very calm. I'm not.

JULY 6: With Benjamin I always brace myself for the wrong thing. I thought he wanted to marry me, so in a way it's a relief. Although I think I love him, I can't imagine marrying him. (It's so frightening when you think that marriage is *forever*.)

JULY 15: Perhaps because he was raised a Catholic he doesn't talk against the Church. On the other hand, he acts as if the rules somehow shouldn't apply to us. He asked if I'd been to confession lately. I told him even Uncle Jim never dared ask that. But I haven't been. Not since the weekend at Mary's.

Rosy looked up from the page. Her eyes traveled over the city of Michelangelo's dome. That had marked the beginning of her adult life as a Catholic. It was the first of the spiritual tunnels (like the one she was in now, and would remain in until she resolved not to see Theo again), some long, some short, through which she had traveled when for lack of contrition she had not been able to go to confession.

JULY 20: No time to write. The Steeplechase never stops now. It throws me down and then down again.

JULY 24: I've decided. B. says he can have Iphigene's apartment. She goes on vacation at the end of the week.

JULY 28: When I said it was no wonder it had caused so much trouble in the world, he lit a cigarette. The smoke made a screen between us, making him seem far away. He said, *"Post coitus tristis est."*

Sad? How could he be? I wanted to ask what he meant, but was afraid.

It wouldn't have mattered what Benjamin had said. It was too late. She was irrevocably in love with him.

Instead of giving her the long, judicious view she had hoped for, recalling those days had given her a compelling desire to rush back to Benjamin, to tell him that it didn't matter about the Duchessa. He was still overtired, still recovering from the long poem. Yes, that was it. She must be patient. They must both be patient. And as for money? Well, they'd manage somehow. They always had. She would take some bread and cheese and fruit back to the pensione. They would have an inexpensive lunch in the room and together explore their resources.

four

Had she picked the wrong door? Rosy stepped back and looked up to check the number of the room. She was rarely treated to the sight of a picked-up room and a made-up bed. Not only was all in order, but the room was full of flowers. On the dresser there was a small box. Next to it, a note.

At home, she often found notes in the morning which Benjamin, working against a deadline, had written before going to bed:

> Finished a chapter. Let me, I beg of you, sleep. I'll read it you this evening.

he might write. Or in a good period:

> Fed up with work. What about a flic? Marx Bros. at Fine Arts, and a drink at the Lincolnshire. Meet me, 5:30, steps of Widener.

If she left him a suggestion about something he had given her to read, she might find the kind she liked best:

> A very good stroke. I *can* use it. Clever Roxana!

In recent years, as the bad patches grew larger and larger, there was one note repeated so frequently she knew it by heart.

I will be finished. And quickly. And it will not be intolerably bad. Then I mean to take long steps about money, and time. These assurances, to my shame, are all for the moment I can give you—except my psychotic love which, you know, is all yours.

Flowers, a box, a note: a celebration was in the air. What could there possibly be to celebrate? She tore open the envelope.

Darling,
We're rich! I'll buy you a splendid lunch and tell you all about it. Wear this, and come to Rosati's at one.
Your prize-winning husband
B.

She opened the box: the bracelet she had seen in a shop window. How had he known? It was like Margaret's, but the globe was emerald while Margaret's was ruby. She put it on her wrist and twisted the globe the way Margaret had done the previous day, to get the refractions of the light. Her arms fell to her side. How could she be so frivolous? Those terrible windfalls! Since Benjamin had given up teaching they were all they had; yet they continued to behave as they had done when prize money was extra, when they could almost afford to celebrate. Whatever the amount of the prize, they already owed all of it. Unexpected checks only sabotaged her efforts to get Benjamin to think further ahead than the next day. What a luxury it would be to know what they would live on six months ahead! As it was, feasts and famines made Benjamin as improvident as a day laborer. Bills piled up and became more and more unreal as they used up the food and liquor the money had bought, and were in need of more.

Rosy looked at the flowers. She did love flowers. She took a white peony from one of the vases, snapped off its stem and pinned the blossom in her hair. Unfortunately, hers was not a saving nature either. She preferred improvidence to stinginess (as though there were no middle ground), so she was partly to blame.

What to do with the makings of their economical lunch, which were like the good but weak intentions she had heard so much about from the nuns? She was putting the food in the armoire, as one might hide from oneself an inconvenient scruple, when the door flew open.

"*Scusi,*" Assunta said without the least tone of apology. She stood her ground, her shiny black eyes making a quick tour of the room.

"*Prego,*" Rosy replied, and waited for her to leave.

"*Una celebrazione, eh?*" Assunta was in on the party. She had helped *il signore* arrange the flowers. What had been in the box? Obviously, *il signore* hadn't let her in on that. She spied Rosy's wrist and reached out to twist the globe as Rosy had done. "*Ah, che bello!*"

Unarmed before such familiarity, Rosy could do nothing but wait for the inspection to be over. And still Assunta was not ready to leave. She had something on her mind. She came closer, conspiratorially. "*Ha dei bambini?*" she asked, as if the question had been on her mind ever since the Bolds had moved in.

Rosy's nightmare began to come back to her. The bat cruised low overhead again. Something about Dr. Gilford. No, his nurse. She was on the telephone with a message: "Dr. Gilford died in the night. You won't have a baby now," she said as blandly as if she were merely breaking an appointment. "It's too late!"

It occurred to Rosy that Assunta was probably no older

than she was, thirty-five at the most. "No," Rosy answered reluctantly.

Assunta made a noise in her throat, an "Eh," as if to say it was just as she expected. *"Dovemo cambiare. Io ho un bambino, ma non ho marito. E lei ha un marito, ma non ha un bambino."* What a clever trick to play on everyone and, at the same time, what a sensible solution to our predicaments, she seemed to say.

If one didn't speak a language, one was better off not understanding it, Rosy thought as she stood at the door of the armoire, tongue-tied, Assunta's prisoner.

Yes, her baby was in the country, Assunta volunteered. It was a long trip. It spoiled every Sunday, her only day off.

Rosy's silence, far from discouraging Assunta, acted as an invitation to further boldness. She opened the other side of the armoire and ran her hands along Rosy's dresses, as if she knew them well, had perhaps tried them on. *"Tanti, tanti vestiti,"* she said.

Had Rosy's Italian been up to it, she would have protested that she was not a rich American whose husband spoiled her (the dresses were mostly gifts and hand-me-downs from Iphigene), but Assunta had seen the flowers and the gifts, and her mind was made up. Besides, by Assunta's standard she was rich. Or at least not poor, only broke.

Rosy looked at her watch to indicate that she was late. *"Scusi, mi dispiace,"* she finally brought out.

Assunta helped herself to a carnation, and holding it as does a diva who has been presented with a bouquet at the end of the performance, she made a deep reverence. Her laugh, as she turned to leave, was like a hoot in a tunnel, mocking them both.

Benjamin stood up as he saw Rosy approach his table. He looked frisky, like an unsaddled horse about to roll in the sand. He tapped his foot, shook his head from side to side, and sang under his breath:

> How pleasant it is to have money, heigh ho!
> How pleasant it is to have money!

He kissed Rosy on the temple. "You're hideously late. Where the hell have you been?"

"Am I?"

"Six and a half interminable minutes. I never pretended not to believe in the double standard," said Benjamin, who was never punctual. "But I forgive you." He took hold of her wrist. He too gave the irresistible globe a twist.

"How did you know about it?" Rosy asked.

"I always know." Benjamin's tone suggested access to occult knowledge. "And you're not to worry, because while Margaret's probably cost eighteen thousand lire, yours cost eighteen hundred. It's all fake." The waiter hovered. "He wonders what you'd like."

Rosy looked around to see what other people were having.

"I'm having a very bad martini. Join me?" Benjamin said.

"Uh-uh." Rosy shook her head. "Sounds too much like home. Italian vermouth, with a twist of lemon."

Benjamin rapped the side of the glass. "This is my last martini."

Rosy's eyelids blinked. When Benjamin turned over a new leaf it sounded like a screen door slamming in her ear.

"Tell me about the prize," she said.

"What shall I tell you?"

"Everything."

"Wait. Tell me first where you've been. Where did you sneak out to this morning?"

"Mass."

"Let's see. It's not Lent. It's not Sunday. Aha! A holy day. Must have been solemn, high, pontifical—you've been gone for hours."

"Stop teasing, tell me."

"Well, I went to American Express first thing this morning. To tell you the truth, I've been haunting it in hopes of . . . something, anything. . . . And there it was! I see it as a reward for my incorruptibility at the Duchessa's."

Rosy stirred her drink.

"Then I bought the flowers." Benjamin hurried over his false note. "Do you like them?"

"They're lovely."

"I bought the whole stand."

"Without bargaining, I'm sure."

"The flower vender *did* seem surprised. Guess what Assunta was doing when I went back to the room."

"Trying on my clothes."

"No. Tossing the pillow in the air. She was singing— '*Uno, due, tre*'—and clapping her hands like a child, to see how many claps she could get in before the pillow fell. The flowers were more fun than the pillows. She's a bit pushy—mad to see what was in the box, she was."

"She saw. But the prize?"

"I'm coming to that." Benjamin was torn between gaining the maximum in suspense and losing his audience. "It's from the Urbana Poetry Society. Bet you'd never heard of it."

"Had you?"

"Never. It's now my favorite poetry society. The deus ex machina this time is Fanny Brace Houghton. A maiden lady. Was head of the poetry society. More important, was very rich. When she 'passed away,' as the brochure put it, she passed on the dough to those of us less fortunate—from a financial point of view, that is. I'm not laughing at Fanny. I love her. If I still said prayers, I'd say one for the repose of her soul."

"Benjamin . . ."

"Oh, you want to know how much, do you?"

"Desperately."

"Five hundred dollars. Vast, isn't it?"

"Five hundred!" Rosy began to calculate. They had their tickets home, her final salary checks (which Benjamin didn't know about), and about $100 in cash.

"We'll make a budget," Benjamin offered.

Benjamin scorned budgets. She had tried, without success, to institute them in a feeble attempt to control the financial octopus that was always there, threatening to strangle them. She looked at him to judge the seriousness of his promise.

"Yes, we will. And I'll keep to it, you'll see."

"With care we should get by . . . two months?"

"In the meantime . . . can you take some more good news?"

"Easily."

"I'll finish the introduction I promised Harcourt like a shot and send it to *Partisan* or *Southern Review*. That way I'll be paid twice. Look here." Benjamin flashed some sheets of foolscap under Rosy's eyes. She caught a glimpse of his elegant handwriting full of lyric e's and d's. "I had time to kill this morning, so I went to Caffè Greco for coffee. Drafted an outline. In a day or two, I'll have some for you to read."

It would be the first thing he'd given her to read since the poem. It would be calm, well-ordered work for him. Not like the chaos of the winter. She looked forward to it.

"And there's more. Sure you're not feeling overfed on this rich diet of good news?"

"Quite sure."

"While I was waiting for you, guess who came by?"

"Ignazio Silone."

"Close. Tullio Fancelli. He's asked us to lunch at Ostia."

"Just us?"

"Rodney and, of course, Busybody Margaret. Unless I can think of some way to poison her. And—"

"And?"

"He's also asked us to the Strega Prize party. At the beginning of July. They give the awards. There'll be dancing. You'll like that, won't you?"

Rosy calculated. It was the end of May. That would give them at least five weeks in Rome. It would be nice not to have to move again for a little while.

"I'll work mornings, and if it goes well I'll take you sightseeing in the afternoon. There is Doris for company, should you want some. And the Landsdales will arrive before we know it. Rome will be absolutely splendid. There, haven't I arranged things beautifully?"

The diary had done half the work of reconciliation. Benjamin's promise of a budget, more than the gift or the flowers, had done the rest. "Beautifully," Rosy mimicked.

"Where shall we go for lunch?"

"Otello?"

Benjamin paid the bill. "Why not? We can afford it. *Avanti!*"

He linked his arm through Rosy's, meshed their fingers together. They started down the Corso, Benjamin making complicated patterns with his steps—two slow, one quick, and from time to time (it was up to Rosy to guess when it would come, to keep in step) a skip. Benjamin sang:

> How useful it is to have money, heigh ho!
> How useful it is to have money!

five

The Bolds followed Benjamin's plan during the weeks that followed. Rosy left the pensione by nine o'clock each morning, armed with Nagel's *Italy,* a pocket dictionary, and a map of Rome. The important sights—the Forum, the Campidoglio, Saint Peter's—she saved to do with Benjamin in the afternoon. The long and varied list of lesser sights gave her the feeling she need never run out of happy employment. Midmorning, should she tire of walking, there was always a café close at hand where she could have a cappuccino and study her map; or a church in whose dark wintry interior she could rest, cooling her feet on the cold stone floor.

Alone in the room, Benjamin rearranged the furniture for work. He unpacked a footlocker of books he had brought from home and arranged them in an orderly way on the top of the armoire, on the dresser, and on the windowsills. The table he placed by the window to catch what breeze blew. On it he set up his Underwood portable. He covered sheet after sheet of yellow paper with the faultless typing he had taught himself the summer vacation before going to college from a book called *Touch Typing, The Royal Road to Success.*

Lunchtime they went to a workingmen's restaurant (the pensione served only breakfast) in the neighborhood, where they ate pasta and salad washed down with tepid Frascati, unless they had been extravagant at dinner the previous evening, in which case they brought the budget back into line by lunching on cheese and bread in their room.

Rosy succumbed to the national custom and took a siesta after lunch, while Benjamin sat in the sagging easy chair and read. At four o'clock, if Benjamin had not finished his stint for the day, he went back to work, and Rosy went to a tiny wedge of a garden-snack bar below the Pincio where, for the price of an *aranciata,* she was free to sit for the afternoon, to study her Italian grammar book or read.

If the morning's work had gone well, they went on a walking tour. Benjamin, a lively and versatile guide, read to Rosy from Augustus Hare, translated Latin inscriptions, pointed out architectural details, recalled relevant history and mythology, and quoted, from his limitless store, appropriate lines of verse.

Rosy's evening entertainment began with a two-hundred-lire extravagance (only thirty cents, she reminded herself), but a therapeutic necessity after a day of walking—a bath. Signora Schmidt, who regarded baths seriously and wondered at Rosy's promiscuous use of them, led the way down the corridor to the large, bright skylighted room. She opened the door with a key from a bunch attached to her belt; handed Rosy a saucer with a slice of soap on it, together with a coarse, gray bath sheet; and reminded Rosy to lock herself in.

The tub stood on a platform like a prehistoric animal incompletely assembled for exhibition, only the giant claw-shaped feet, the short, stocky, bow legs, and the pendulous belly in place. Hot water belched out of the faucet, spraying the floor and fogging the standing, wood-framed mirror. Rosy lowered herself cautiously into the steam, folded the towel into a pillow behind her head, and gave herself up—her pinched sciatic nerve, her burning feet—to the uterine bliss of the cushioning, faintly chlorinated water.

While Rosy dressed for dinner, Benjamin fixed them

each a drink of Italian brandy with water—it was cheap, and palatable without ice—before going to the Albrecht for dinner. They were not fond of the Albrecht (the germanized Italian food and steins of beer seemed a flat note in Rome), but it was within their budget, and the light, while excessively bright for dining, was ideal for illuminating the pages of the books they read until bedtime.

Occasionally, to vary the routine, they looked for a film or a concert after dinner, but since the Roman season was over and the tourist season had not yet begun, they more often than not settled for an espresso in an outdoor café in whatever neighborhood they found themselves in, and walked home, arm in arm, in the soft June night air.

One evening, as Rosy was drying off after her bath, Assunta rapped on the door: Signora Bold was wanted on the telephone.

"Roxana? Can you hear me?" Doris Trumbull shouted into the mouthpiece. "I don't trust these Roman phones."

Rosy held the receiver away from her ear. "Clearly. How are you?"

"I would have called earlier, but I thought I'd see you at dinner with the Brills."

"You've been seeing them?"

"Since Rocca. I'm crazy about them. You turned them down?"

Rosy and Benjamin had decided they couldn't take the financial (or emotional) gamble of another Brill evening. "Benjamin is working," Rosy said, giving the blanket excuse which no one they knew ever questioned.

"Sweetie, I'm dying to see you."

Rosy suddenly realized that she hadn't talked with a woman friend since she'd been in Europe. "What about lunch?"

"Tomorrow?"

"Fine. Where can we meet? Nothing too posh." Rosy had the budget in mind; it didn't allow for extravagances.

"Suits me. I've never *been* so poor."

Doris's part-time job as a Harvard secretary was a time-filler. She had an income, "a tiny, tiny income" from an inheritance, which permitted her to spend her vacations in Europe and generally live above the standard of the academics with whom she associated. A Yankee at heart, she enjoyed practicing little economies, and if the check from her trust fund was late, she might even, for a day or so, *feel* poor.

"What about the Frascati on the via Floria, near my hotel?" Doris suggested.

Rosy arrived at the restaurant early. The waiter showed her to a side table for two. He propped up one of its legs with an empty matchbox and handed her an illegible menu mimeographed in purple ink. Doris would almost certainly be late. Uncle Jim's rigid training in punctuality had resulted in the waste of hours, days, weeks even, of waiting for a world of people not so trained. Today Rosy didn't mind. Sitting had become an exquisite pleasure. She nibbled a *grissino* and made notes about what she'd seen in the morning.

Twenty minutes after the appointed time, Doris parted the beaded curtains. She stood at the door, waiting for her eyes to accommodate to the interior light. She was hatless today and wore a beige piqué dress which set off her small, almost boyish figure and blended with her biscuit-color skin and hair. This dress, like Mimi Brill's, was from Paris, but unlike Mimi's it was a year old. Each summer Doris had two or three ensembles made by a Paris dressmaker. In order to avoid being too boldly ahead of Cambridge fashions, and because she enjoyed saving, she kept them in her closet—which was where Rosy had seen this one before—for a year. She was no more tempted to wear them immediately (she'd told Rosy, who had asked how she resisted) than she would have been to dip into capital.

The two women worked in the Art History department at Harvard, moved in the same circles, and from time to time had lunch to discuss the resistance of Richard to the marriage that Doris, approaching thirty, was impatient to celebrate. Despite his professions of love, Richard showed a distressing reluctance to ask his wife, from whom he'd been separated for years, for a divorce.

"Oh, sweetie, *there* you are," Doris called across to Rosy. All heads in the restaurant went up on the word "there." Doris covered her mouth with her hand. "Was I shouting again?" she asked in an Irish whisper. "The Duchessa gave me the ice about that the day at Rocca, didn't she? Wasn't it *incredible* our meeting there? I mean one expects to run into Cambridge people in Paris and Rome. But Roccafalcone? It really *is* a small world." She kissed Rosy, pulled out a chair opposite her, and sat down. "As I said, I'd lost your address. I was afraid I'd have to wait until the Landsdales arrived . . . Any word from them?"

"Not yet."

". . . to find out where you were staying. Am I terribly late?"

"You've been to the hairdresser?"

"Right. Trapped under the dryer. I'm burning up. Let's have some white wine, *subito*. With ice. O.K.? Roman wine is never cool enough, have you noticed?"

Rosy who'd been inhaling the aroma of garlic and mussels from a neighboring table, said, "Let's order first, then talk."

"You're getting a lovely color, Ro. Is it the Roman sun? Do you understand any of this?" Doris meant the mimeographing.

"I'm having cannelloni and salad," Rosy said. "I see now what it is, Doris. I knew there was something different—you've changed your hair."

Doris told the waiter she'd have what Rosy had ordered.

"Do you like the bangs? I do hope it doesn't detract from the *jolie-laide* effect." This expression, learned ten years earlier when she spent her junior year in Paris, had helped Doris to come to terms with her gothic nose and the beige-blue eyes that somewhat crowded it.

"It's very becoming. Where did you have it done?"

Doris took out her compact to check for herself. "Margaret Munson's hairdresser."

"Margaret? You've been seeing her too?"

"She was sweet that day at the Duchessa's. When she heard I was alone in Rome, she offered to take me shopping —Wait till you see the shoes I'm having made!—and when I said I was looking for a hairdresser gave me the name of her man. I'd give it to you, but I'm afraid you'd find him too expensive." Doris had her ideas about what people without an income, be it ever so tiny, could afford. "Besides, your hair is so curly you don't need to have it done." Doris played with her new bangs. "The thing is, will Richard like it?"

"Tell me, what's happened since February? Your parting remark was 'I may have big news for you in Rome.' "

"Big news!" Doris snapped her compact shut. Powder flew out from under the lid in a little puff. "Ro, if I'd found anyone to be unfaithful with at home I would have been. I mean it. Just to scare him. It would have been so much cheaper than taking a leave of absence. *And* more agreeable. Theo Addis—now, if he'd stayed around! Wouldn't you just love to cheer him up? He sometimes looks so . . . *triste*. And yet such sex appeal!"

Rosy felt herself coloring. There had been a letter from Theo that morning. He had some work to do at the Uffizi near the end of the month, he said. He hoped it would give him a chance to see her between his train and plane in Rome. She had decided she would not meet him. Things had been going so well with Benjamin she had all but put Theo out of her mind.

"Tell me about your trip," she said to Doris. "What kind of a time have you been having?"

"It's been sheer hell."

"How long have you been here?"

"Forever. If I could have stayed in Paris . . . The thing is, one can't stay too long without people catching on that something is wrong. You can't *look* as if you're staying on, if you know what I mean. I saw all my friends, went to the dressmaker, saw all the exhibitions. Finally, with no progress on the home front, I decided to come here. How I hated Rome! I was so *mizzerable*." Doris's speech was like a line of baroque music, full of grace notes, shakes, and trills. "Cheese?"

"Thanks."

"There wasn't a soul here. I kept trying to tell myself it was the monuments that counted, not people. I walked my feet off every day. . . ."

"It's the getting lost." Rosy could sympathize.

"*And* being misdirected. *And* the closing hours."

"How did you spend your evenings? Wine?"

"Love some. The evening? Night after night I sat alone in a trattoria."

"Aren't they bright?"

"Like operating rooms. Try looking inconspicuous when you're alone in one of them! And yet I sat and sat, because afterwards there was nothing but the four walls of my hotel room. I wrote Richard—how I missed him!—trying not to talk about why didn't he *do* something, filling up page after page with the *marvelous* time I was having. Lies, lies, lies. Then one day I tried to get into Sant' Ivo for the tenth time . . ."

"I finally got in yesterday."

"You're lucky. When I found it closed *again,* something inside me snapped." Doris's caesura here was to allow Rosy to hear the echo of the snap.

"Poor Doris. What happened?"

"I walked around to a café in the Piazza Navona, ordered a Campari and *burst into tears*. I was about to send a telegram to Richard saying I was flying home when Flossie's note came."

"How did you know her?"

"She and Aunt Lucy spent summers together at Pride's Crossing as children. I wrote her a note, enclosing one from Aunt Lucy. I knew if I could get to one of Flossie's luncheons I'd meet people and be all set. Never have I been so thrilled to receive an invitation, I went through my wardrobe three times trying to decide what to wear." For a moment Doris lost momentum. "When I saw Flossie in that shirtwaist . . . Do you suppose she writes home to Peck & Peck for them? Never mind, she *rescued* me."

"Will you stay on now?"

"You bet. With you here, and the Brills—they're great fun—and the Landsdales arriving any day, I know I'll make it now." Doris took out her compact. She blotted her lips on her napkin and applied fresh lipstick. "What about you, Ro? As usual I've done all the talking. I gather Benjamin got his grant, because here you are. I told you not to be such a worrier."

"It was a renewal, not a grant. He didn't get it."

The compact snapped closed again. *"He didn't?* How did you get to Europe? Have you had an inheritance? Shall we have some more wine?"

"Yes to the wine. No to the inheritance."

"Ro, I know you're terribly, terribly clever about managing—I don't see how you do it without financial backing—but what, if I may ask, are you living on?"

"Benjamin's grant didn't run out until last month, so we had that to go on."

"Should you have come abroad?" Doris's disapproval was undisguised.

"It probably was a mistake," Rosy acknowledged, "but

here we are. And since this is my first time in Europe, I'm trying to enjoy myself and not worry too much about the future."

"But what about the fall?"

The fall. Rosy didn't like to think about it. She drank some wine. "I don't know. Benjamin is obviously hoping something will turn up."

"I never understood why you allowed Benjamin to give up teaching. No one believes you can earn a living by writing these days. And Benjamin is hardly the man to make compromises. . . ."

No. He certainly was not. But as to allowing Benjamin to do anything . . . Besides, his gesture hadn't been as cavalier as it appeared. The fact was he had not been reappointed. A brilliant teacher he certainly was; it had not been a question of that. It was simply that his appointment had been up. Occasionally an exception was made. Benjamin, sanguine when he ought not to have been, had counted on that. But he had never toadied to his head of department (there were those who said he had been dangerously unpolitical), so the termination of his contract came as a surprise to no one but him. The day he heard—it was five years ago now—he came home dancing with false animation.

"I'm free. Free, do you hear? No more bloody papers to read. No more classes."

For once she had not fallen in with his mood. She had not been able to hide her apprehensiveness. What would they do?

"Do? Do? I'll live as a writer. That's, after all, what I am. Why should I have to pose as a teacher to earn a living? And you're not to worry, darling. Now that I don't have to teach I can do a thousand things. I'm bursting with ideas. I have a story in mind. And there's my play."

That, as he well knew, was not what worried her. He

always had more than enough things in mind. But none of them paid.

"Who can tell? I might even make a killing with my play."

She could tell. The play might get written. Might even be first rate. But a killing? Benjamin frightened her when he talked this way. It showed how little, to quote one of his phrases, he understood himself. She didn't doubt for a moment that one day he would be famous. But that he would make a living by writing . . .

He knelt by her chair and looked up at her, anguish written on his forehead, which was waffled and beaded with perspiration. He couldn't bear her to resist him, especially when his enthusiasm masked fear. "You wouldn't want me to look for another job? Would you ask me to go through that again?"

She took his head in her hands and kissed his brow to avoid seeing the peeled, pleading look on his face. No, she would not ask him to go through that again. The first time he had been jobless they had been married little more than a year. The students had begun to be drafted in large numbers. Faculty members without permanent tenure were let go. Benjamin went to Washington, hoping to get into intelligence work. Rejected by the OSS because of poor vision, and undraftable because of the nervous breakdown he'd had when he returned from England, he decided they'd better move to New York; jobs would be easier to find there. The economy was booming, so the daily paper told them, but there seemed to be no work Benjamin could do. He called on friends, went to agencies, waited for phone calls, hung on a bit of encouragement here, a new lead there. The leads dried up during that hot, blank summer one after the other, forcing Benjamin to look for jobs less and less suitable to his temperament. One day, when he broke down weeping, she found he had been trying to sell encyclopedias. His tears were not because he felt the job was beneath him—he was beyond that. He was asked to sell to people so poor, so eager for information, and so ill equipped to extract it from what he had to offer that he couldn't in conscience make a sale.

In September, offered a teaching job in a second-rate preparatory school, he leaped at it. The boys were unruly, the other masters stupid, the paperwork unending. He was up half the night preparing Latin and Algebra, two lessons ahead of his pupils, grateful to have narrowly escaped an assignment to supervise the track team. And then their luck changed: Harvard called him back to teach the Navy.

"Things do turn up," Rosy said defensively, in answer to Doris's question. "Benjamin just won a prize." She was about to name the "vast" amount when it occurred to her that it might be somewhat less than the check Doris received each month from her trust fund. "And there's my job. Did I tell you I got a raise? What about a dessert?"

"Eat, drink and be merry?" Doris gestured as if it were all beyond her comprehension. On the one hand she admired the "gallantry" of people like the Bolds; on the other, she worried lest they become borrowers, or burdens to the community, like welfare cases. "You have something, Ro. Something nice and gooey for both of us. Rome is ruining my waistline. I may lose Richard in the end for turning into a fat girl."

Doris reached for the bill when it came. "It's mine," she said, "You paid last time."

It was not true. Each one had, as usual, paid her share. Rosy too put her hand on the bill. "Let's go *alla romana*."

"Is that what it's called in Italian? Well, in that case, 'When in Rome . . .' "

Doris tactfully gave in.

SIX

Benjamin and Rosy had finished a walking tour at the Castel Sant' Angelo and were crossing the Ponte Vittorio Emmanuele. "I must say, I don't get it," said Benjamin. "Why is Fancelli putting himself out to be agreeable? The Strega invitation, the 'little lunch' he's planning for us next week, and here we are on the way to look over his library." They stopped walking and were looking down into the muddy Tiber water churning under the arches of the bridge.

"Why does that surprise you?" Rosy asked.

"Why? Romans are no more famous for being hospitable than are Parisians. Besides, Fancelli is famous."

"Ambivalent Benjamin! If you're not instantly recognized as a genius and treated as one you're furious. If you are, you become uneasy."

"I never pretended not to be ambivalent. How could I? It's the core of my nature, and no amount of psychoanalysis will change *that*. Sickness, Death, Ignorance, Concupiscence. What about Ambivalence? There's a result of original sin the Church Fathers slipped up on. You know, I used to be ambivalent about fame too. Not any more. Uh-uh. I'm fed up with being so *little* known."

"*Pazienza!*"

"I've been patient for twenty years."

"It won't be much longer."

"The proofs will be here any day."

Rosy's heart sank. "So soon? It's been so peaceful, hasn't it?"

Benjamin wasn't listening. "A cold eye and a warm ear, that's what I'll need. Hear it again. Check the details. Is it as good as I think?"

"It's a masterpiece," Rosy teased, trying to recapture her previous mood.

"Thanks. Advance copies should go out by September. God, it's slow!"

"Who'll write the blurbs for the book jacket?"

"I wonder. They sent it out to some big names. Hmm. Why shouldn't *I* write them?"

"Like your obituary?"

"Exactly. How about: 'While others of his generation hurried into print, Bold held off until he could give us a masterpiece.' "

"Not bad."

"Listen to this one: 'A poet's poet, Bold has cleared a path which others will now follow.' "

"Follow, boys, follow."

"Or: 'His technical subtlety . . .' "

"You're in form today."

"I'll tell you one thing." Benjamin's eyes followed the cigarette butt he had flicked into the Tiber. "I don't want my name writ in water, muddy or otherwise."

"Lights?"

"Not necessarily. But not water either. Keats admonishes the poet to make a bow to Fame and forget her. All very well when you're twenty. At forty, one can't help casting a backward glance to see if the old girl is *there*."

"Did it ever occur to you when you were younger that you might not become—"

"It used to race across my mind like the shadow of a rat slithering across a dark alleyway."

"It's such a chancy thing."

"Chance. That old bitch! I might be run down by a crazy Italian driver; nearly was yesterday. Or I might jump into the river. When I was younger I was afraid I'd die of a stupid disease."

"Keats."

"No. *No!*" Benjamin cried out, as if someone had threatened his life. *"I won't have it.* I'm agile enough to dodge the crazy drivers. And I won't jump, *or* slit my wrists, or shoot myself . . ."

"Is that really all over?" Rosy, serious now, turned to look at him.

"And as for dying—I don't plan to. I *refuse*. I have the constitution, as you so inelegantly put it, of a horse."

"I wonder if you'll be any happier when you're famous?"

"You wonder . . ." Benjamin seemed astonished. "Skeptical Roxana!"

"Maybe this is the best period. Now. Before the book comes out, before the splash, when you're certain of it and still don't have it. . . . Won't fame bring with it a whole new set of problems?"

"It may. Still, I'm willing to risk it."

"I wonder how it will change you?"

"So, you've been brooding about that, have you? I should think that from your point of view any change would be for the better. I can't go anywhere but up. I'll be more solvent, for one thing."

"No more financial crises? Now it's my turn to say hmmm."

"O.K. Fewer."

"But will you become—"

"Vain?" Benjamin imitated the dreamy, speculative voice Rosy had been using.

"No. I mean something more complicated. Take Tullio. He undoubtedly was more interesting when he was young and unknown, before he developed the façade. Or take Hemingway . . ."

"Now, wait. I'll never be *that* famous."

"No, I know, but—"

"You're afraid I'll become a parody of myself, is that it?"

"I would like to have known Fancelli and Pound and Eliot and all the others before they became famous, when they were—"

"Young and ardent?" Benjamin only smiled at Rosy this time. He put his arm across her shoulders. "We better go. We'll be late."

At Tullio's house, on the via di Sant' Eligio, they were unable to find a light in the somber vestibule. Benjamin lit a match to look for the bell. "Damn it. I've burned myself." He danced up and down and licked his finger.

"Here. Let me try," Rosy said. She found the bell and rang it. They stood in the dark and waited.

"Ring it again," Benjamin said. "I feel like a trespasser." They stood in the dark, unable to make out more than the outline of a wall mirror and a table under it. "Sure you didn't mistake the day or the hour?"

"Oh, dear. I hope not," said Rosy, losing confidence with the passing minutes. "Let's go outside. It's so gloomy in here."

"Bold?" They heard a voice call. "Up here." They looked up to see Tullio's dark glasses at the fifth-floor window. "Sorry to have been slow. I couldn't find the key. I'll throw it down."

The envelope fell at their feet. "I have it," called up Benjamin. "Quite a system," he said to Rosy on the way up the stairs. "Not overmechanized, are, they?"

"Here I am," Tullio called. "It's quite absurd," he said, shaking hands with Benjamin, "but our *portiere* is ill. Forgive me for not coming down for you. I'll lead the way."

They followed Tullio down a long hallway. It was decorated with garnet velvet draperies tied back with heavy

75

passementerie, family portraits, and heavy dark furniture. "My mother is not very well," he said as if to explain the closed doors and the reason they wouldn't meet her. "Here are my quarters." He stood aside to let them go in. "Please."

The room had more light than the others they'd seen off the corridor, but the same bourgeois style hung heavily over it. A young woman who had been sitting on the window seat came toward them, her hand extended. "Elvira Ascoli," Tullio said, introducing them. "Elvira pretends she doesn't remember a word of English. It's not true, of course. She's timid about speaking it."

Signora Ascoli would have been called pretty but for a darkness which had to do with mood rather than color. Her frown deepened at Tullio's remark.

"I wish timidity were my only problem," said Benjamin. "It's maddening how little help reading Italian with ease and even being capable of making a creditable translation are when it comes to speaking it."

"You're probably too modest about your Italian. However, if you're more comfortable in French you'll find that everyone at the luncheon next week speaks it. Will you have a drink? Or shall we look at the library?"

"The library," Benjamin said.

Tullio and Benjamin went into the next room, through the open door of which were visible a large desk and floor-to-ceiling bookcases. A ladder, with a platform for reaching the books on the upper shelves, was placed against the opposite wall.

Rosy and Elvira, left alone, smiled at each other uncertainly. "You've been in Rome since how long?" Elvira began.

"Three weeks. It seems much longer."

"It pleases you?"

"Enormously." A bout of shyness made Rosy effusive. "It's always like that. Visitors love Rome. They don't see how difficult life is here." The difficulties of life were etched on Elvira's face. Rosy wondered what they could be. Surprised at being taken seriously, Elvira gave a little flute note of a laugh and said, "It's a pretty view, no?" She led Rosy to the window. They looked out at a dome in the foreground and the Tiber behind it. "The dome is by Raphael."

"It's very satisfying," said Rosy, thinking how agreeable it would be to look out on this view every day. "What church is it?"

"It's not used as a church any more. It's a . . . fraternity?"

Elvira was asking Rosy about M.I.T., where her younger brother hoped to go to graduate school, when Tullio came out of the library. Benjamin followed with an armful of books.

"Sure you won't have a drink? Or will you join us with some friends we're meeting at Rosati's?"

"Many thanks, but we're dining with Rodney. Margaret has gone to London to see her sister."

"We'll drop you there. No, it's no inconvenience. Elvira's car is just at the door."

Rodney was standing at the door of the embassy when they arrived, looking through a pair of binoculars.

"Spying?" Benjamin called, getting out of the car.

"On birds," said Rodney, waving to Tullio and Elvira as they drove off. "Margaret tells everyone we have nightingales. For the first time I thought I heard one. Of course, by the time I got my glasses it had stopped singing. Let's have a drink in the garden, shall we?"

He led them to the back of the house. On a flagstone terrace there were deep wicker chairs painted white, with cushions covered in blue linen, glass-topped coffee tables, and hydrangeas the color of the cushions in white jardinieres.

Glasses and bottles had been set out on a tea wagon. A servant brought a silver bucket of ice. "What can I give you?" Rodney asked, dismissing the servant.

"I would like one brilliant martini," said Benjamin. "Roxana, you're not to take it that I'm breaking my rule. We're not in Italy, but at the embassy. It's an extraterritorial martini."

"Then I'll have one too," said Rosy.

"Let's pull these together." Rodney meant the chairs. "Tell me whom you've met," he said as they sat down with their drinks.

"Tullio's mistress," said Rosy.

Benjamin laughed. "Roxana's very prompt with that because in Protestant Cambridge a mistress is as rare a bird as a flamingo."

"Does he have a wife too?" Rosy asked.

"You see, Rodney? Roxana is much interested in these arrangements. It gives life more complexity. At home the only complication occurs when a member of the faculty falls for a Radcliffe girl, in which case he leaves his wife, gets a divorce, and remarries. *Does* Fancelli have a wife?"

"Yes. It's the old Italian story. An early marriage . . ."

"I take it he comes from an upper-class family. Was it arranged?" Benjamin asked.

"No, but favored. To an extremely attractive, intelligent woman, I hear. I've never met her. She lives in Rome too. Has her own arrangements."

"Is that why Elvira looks so unhappy?" Rosy asked.

"Heavens, no. She too is separated. There's no question of remarriage for these people."

"And they accept it?" There was a note of rebellion in Benjamin's voice.

"Completely. I'm not sure they're any less happy than your Cambridge friends who divorce and remarry. If Elvira looks unhappy it's because Tullio is a difficult man."

A servant came to announce dinner. "I hope I'm not

rushing you to the table?" Rodney said. "The cook rules our lives."

"Do diplomats ever get loaded?" Benjamin asked.

Rodney's shoulders bounced. "Not the way poets do— at least, not before dinner. When I'm in London I'm always astonished at how different the routine is at Andrew's house. If you want to get 'loaded' you'll have no trouble there. They have a docile Italian maid who just keeps the meal hot until Andrew is ready to leave the pub."

A small table had been set up in one corner of the dining room, facing the terrace. A silver candelabrum gave the only light. "Roxana, won't you sit here? I hoped I'd be able to see much more of you two, but I'm racing to get this anthology together before my deadline. Next week we must plan some outings. You've not been bored?"

"You mustn't feel sorry for Roxana," Benjamin said. "Every day someone else arrives from home. Harvard people are funny. By the end of the academic year they can't wait to get away from one another. But no sooner are they in Europe than they seek each other out. In Rome they cluster around Paul Landsdale and his wife, who always travel with an entourage."

"The art historian? I didn't know you knew him. He's at Harvard now?"

"Has been for five years. We not only know him, he's Roxana's boss."

"Is he! I greatly admire his work, especially the book on piazza space. Although he's often in Rome, I somehow have never met him."

"Then you *must*," said Benjamin, who had a boyish eagerness for his good friends to like each other. "Nothing is easier. We're going to Tivoli with them tomorrow. We'll arrange it then."

"They've been on leave this semester, in Greece," Rosy said, "so we're eager to see them."

"You're close, are you?" Rodney asked.

"Quite. Roxana and Paul's wife, Erika, see a good deal of each other. She's a doctor, the daughter of a famous German publisher who was driven out by Hitler. You'd know the name, which for the moment escapes me. Through Paul we've met a group of people I call the Happy Extroverts—"

"Who are neither as happy nor as extroverted as Benjamin paints them," interrupted Rosy.

"They've rather changed our lives. You see, before we met Paul we never went out. I kept Roxana under lock and key like a jealous Arab, and sulked around frightening off invitations."

Rodney looked at Rosy. "It's true," Rosy said; "he did."

"Paul was so charming and so hospitable that I couldn't refuse. He has a big house, enough money to entertain frequently, and he surrounds himself with young people. What I liked was that we met all sorts of people there: not just academics and writers—God, I get sick of them!— architects, lawyers, businessmen. There was dancing for Roxana, and perhaps too much drinking for me."

"Yes. And they spoil Benjamin dangerously. They humor him, flatter him, forgive him when he behaves badly," said Rosy.

"Why not?" Benjamin asked as they walked back to the terrace to have coffee. "Am I not worth humoring? Do I not entertain them? Divert them? Instruct them? And as for the drinking—we can hardly blame them for that. It's an occupational disease," he said dropping into a chair.

"Have you finished that introduction?" Rodney handed him a demitasse.

"To tell you the truth, I'm marking time, waiting for my proofs. I can't really think about anything else."

In the dark, deep in her chair, a corkscrew twist of anxiety made Rosy sit forward, on guard. Against what?

Her back? An old ailment, which she'd been trying to ignore, was acting up again. The wicker chair gave a promise of comfort it didn't fulfill. The days of sightseeing, which she had kept at more energetically than she would have liked in order to leave the room free for Benjamin, had begun to take their toll. She had been telling herself that Benjamin would soon be finished with the preface, that she would be able to stay in the room, to rest a little.

"Still obsessed, Ben?" Rodney said.

"Still, still, *still*. Will it never end?"

"I urged you to come here because I hoped Rome would offer you the diversion you needed. I don't like to think what you must have been like when you were working on the poem. The letter you sent with it gave a hint of the—"

"Madness? Is that the word you're looking for? I can tell you that afterwards it was even worse. I went through a postpartum psychosis."

"Like your protagonist, Daphne?"

"I was as much Daphne as Flaubert was Emma. I'm still working my way out of it."

"Since you survived, since you're here and not locked up in an asylum, I can say it was worth it. This is it, Ben. Like it or not, this is the end of being an obscure poet. Won't you say a stanza or two?"

Rosy pressed back in her chair, as if she were being cornered. This was what she was afraid of: the poem. As Benjamin's voice began to fill the night air, she blocked her ears against his recitation. When would she be able to listen to it again without flinching?

It had been worse, in a way, after the poem was finished because they had both expected that life would go back to what it had been before. They celebrated the end with champagne (bought on credit). Five uncanny days followed during which Benjamin slept around the clock like someone in a coma. He awakened restless, irritable, empty. Nothing filled the void the poem had left. Dead-of-night phone calls replaced the sound of pacing. He read the poem to friends in distant cities, begging them to share his excitement: It was a masterpiece, wasn't it? She became increasingly afraid he was going to have a breakdown. In the end it was she who had become hysterical. In a fight for self-preservation, she told him he'd have to go away, anywhere, leave her in peace.

"All right, I'll go," he said, abruptly calmed by her hysteria. "But where? Where can I go?"

She didn't know where. All day at work she turned it over in her mind. To friends? She ran down the list. Who could stand it? No one. By the end of the day she had it: Atlantic City. The grotesqueness of the suggestion would appeal to Benjamin. Out of season it would be easy to get a room, and cheap. He could walk himself exhausted on the boardwalk, shout his poem to the sea. The salt air would help him sleep. He could see his publisher in New York on the way home.

Benjamin leaped at the idea. "Oh, clever Roxana! Oh, brilliant Roxana! What genius! Atlantic City!" Seeing the relief on her pinched face, he was overcome with remorse. "Darling, what have I been doing to you? I'm killing you." It was as though he were seeing her for the first time since her operation, since he'd begun his poem. "When did you lose all this weight? You're so thin! You must *eat*!" He grabbed her and held her, as if she might evaporate before his eyes. "I'm a monster, a monster," he said, rocking her in his arms. "Flaubert was right. Writers are all monsters. We shouldn't be allowed to marry. How can you stand it?"

"I can't," she admitted, laughing with nervous fatigue. "That's why I'm packing you off." In the past just his awareness of what it had been like for her would have been enough. Now she needed more. She needed peace. She needed to be away from him.

Benjamin fell in with the arrangements for the trip like a child going to the beach. He'd get his ticket, if she'd find a place for him to stay. He couldn't face having to do that at the other end. By telephone, she found him a small hotel on a side street, very cheap. Benjamin packed a suitcase of books and a sweater. They went to the station together. "To be sure I get on the train?" Benjamin asked. She nodded. They both laughed. "I'll come back as tranquil as a turtle. You'll see."

He stayed away five days (she had hoped for a week) and called, always in the middle of the night, to report how *good* he was being. He was eating again.

Obviously not sleeping.

Oh yes, he had found he was able to sleep during the day. No, the nights were still difficult.

Alone in the apartment, she took her evening meal to bed on a tray, washed down a sedative with a glass of milk, and fell asleep, counting the days—forty-two, forty-one, forty—until they would leave for Europe.

"You know, Roxana," Rodney said when Benjamin finished his recitation, "you need never starve. If poetry goes out of fashion . . ."

"Oh? Is it in?" Benjamin asked.

". . . Ben can always earn a living as an actor. Olivier couldn't have read those lines better."

"I'm not sure I'd like to be married to an actor," Rosy said, standing up to go.

"The trouble is," Benjamin said, coming over to put his arm around Rosy, "that although nothing could be worse than being married to a poet, I've taken care to unfit Roxana for marriage to anyone else. What would she do for excitement? *Think* how dull life would be."

seven

Signora Schmidt and Assunta paused at a discreet distance. Their shopping baskets on their hips, they watched the Bolds, who were getting into a car—which while not chauffeur-driven, was, like the Munsons' car, a Cadillac. Assunta escaped from Signora Schmidt's restraining hand and came close to the car window.

"*Buon giorno, Professore, buon giorno,*" she said, the greeting an excuse to look over the Landsdales.

Paul Landsdale, in the driver's seat, looked into the rearview mirror before pulling away from the curb. He caught Benjamin's face in a grimace of suppressed laughter. "What's up?" Paul asked. "You two seem vastly amused."

"Who are your rustic friends?" Erika Landsdale asked.

"The saucy one, the one who spoke up, is Assunta. She's the maid who does our room. The older woman is the owner of the pensione," Rosy answered. "Benjamin is killing himself because they've just collected another bit of evidence that we're rich. What they can't make out is why we're staying in the Pensione Europa."

"They clearly don't know how contemptuous you are of academic titles," said Paul. "Of course they mean to flatter you."

"I don't mind being called professor," said Benjamin.

"It's simply that I don't want to *be* one. I must say, Paul, your car seems to have grown."

"It's the same old bus I drive in Cambridge. We bring it over on the boat every year. I'm too big for Italian cars and too old to pretend not to be."

Erika leaned over and stroked Paul's cheek. "Poor Paul. Since his illness he thinks he is very old. You see how his color has changed? That's the hepatitis."

Benjamin leaned forward and patted Paul on the back. "I must say, old boy, that aside from your Oriental color, which rather becomes you, you look quite well. I didn't know what to expect. Two months in the hospital. What rotten luck!"

"It was ironic that the night the ship docked at Piraeus, I told Erika I had never felt so well on a trip. No tummy trouble, nothing. Next morning I woke up looking like a jack-o'-lantern."

"How lucky you didn't get it too," Rosy said to Erika.

"Thanks God!" said Erika, getting the idiom a little wrong as she sometimes did. "And you two?" Erika turned around. She was a handsome woman, fifteen years Paul's junior, with a face for which intelligence and beauty had contested. Intelligence had won, but not by much. She had a high wide brow, a strong nose, and lively speckled green eyes. "Let me look at you." Her eyes, a sharp diagnostic tool, played quickly over Benjamin and Rosy, as if looking for symptoms. "No, you both look well. Rozan is more than ever the color of a *pêche-abricot*."

"She is, isn't she?" said Benjamin. "Someone the other day tried to say Roxana looked Scandinavian. Can you imagine?"

"And you, Benjamin, even you've put on a little weight. Europe does you good. And what about your trip?"

"You can't imagine Roxana's excitement," Benjamin said. "She wept, literally wept, when we landed at Le Havre."

"Not surprising," said Paul. "With all your talk about Europe for years now. You built up her hunger for it."

"In Paris I showed her *everything*," said Benjamin. "Quite wore her out."

"Zo. You were Rozan's cicerone," said Erika. "That was good for you. It calmed you down."

"Not noticeably," said Benjamin, dryly. "I had a pretty rocky time until we got to Rome. I think—I hope—I'm coming out of it now."

"We were so worried," Erika said. "Everyone wrote that you were working too hard."

"It was a bitch of a winter," said Benjamin.

"Does one dare ask what the new poem is about?" Paul asked. "Everyone you read it to—"

"There is *nobody* to whom I didn't read it—even the little bald man at the Harvard Provision Shop."

"They all rave, but no one was very clear about the subject," said Paul.

"So it goes." Benjamin's lips tightened. "They rave, but they don't know what it's about. I can tell you this much: it's about women."

"Ah! That's interesting," said Erika.

"And about one woman in particular. I missed you, Erika. I needed your help with medical details."

"Is it clinical?"

"You'll see," said Benjamin.

"It sounds like a subject which should certainly increase your audience," said Paul. "Don't women love to read about themselves?"

"In the *Ladies' Home Journal* perhaps. Not if they have to work for it the way I make them work. The trouble is, people only read a poem once. Once! And the poet is supposed to be grateful for that! What can they learn on one reading?"

"You'll have a wider audience, in any case."

"My audience will be much the same—other poets, former students, old girl friends. A few more libraries will order it. My friends will buy it; make a stab at it—once; keep it on display for a few weeks. The only real difference will be that the other poets are likely to have the tops of their heads blown off by it. Ha!" Benjamin rubbed his hands together in anticipation. "And it should be reviewed more prominently."

"The front page of the *Times* and the *Tribune*?" Paul was eager for Benjamin's success.

"It will be lucky if it gets one of them."

"And will you read it to us?" Erika said.

"At the drop of a hat. You're lucky I didn't bring it with me today."

"No, first we must catch up the Cambridge gossip." Erika turned to Rosy, her eyes dancing with malice, her lips parted over slightly protruding upper teeth. "Any scandals?"

"Before the scandals, check the map a minute," said Paul.

Erika looked out the window. "It's still the via Tiburtina? Yes. You're O.K." Erika turned back to Rosy. "Yes?"

"No scandals big enough to interest you." Rosy laughed.

"The only ones were those I made," said Benjamin with a certain pride. "For months I behaved like a firecracker, as you must have heard. Either I was a dud, or I went off like all the sparklers, Roman candles, Catherine wheels in the box."

"I heard Addis's lectures were a great success," said Paul.

"They certainly were with Roxana," said Benjamin. "She insisted we go to Mantua to see the Palazzo del Te as a result of them."

"And Sabbioneta?" said Paul.

"Yes, that too. The bus ride there, over dirt roads, was memorable. Yes, Addis has given Roxana a taste for architecture."

"Benjamin is jealous if someone else is your teacher,

eh?" Erika said to Rosy. "Tell me, why didn't anyone make some excitement with Doris and Theo Addis? Isn't that a good idea? At least they could have had a flirt. I'm so tired of Richard and his delays."

Rosy, blushing, was glad Erika's shrewd eyes were facing forward.

"Uh-uh." Benjamin said after a moment. "No good."

Paul looked at Benjamin in his mirror again. "Why no good?"

"Doris is not Addis's type," said Benjamin.

"You sound as if you had a theory about him," said Paul.

"I have. He has a big rescue complex."

Erika laughed. "Now Benjamin becomes more Freudian than Freud. I was never sure that psychoanalysis was good for you."

"Look at the evidence," said Benjamin. "There is the work Addis did at Belsen at the end of the war. Now he goes up to London once a week, he tells me, for some sort of rescue-and-relief mission. There is the woman he married—wasn't he trying to rescue her? What do you think of my theory, darling?"

The cat had Rosy's tongue.

"If anyone could have arranged the match between Theo and Doris," Benjamin went on, not waiting for Rosy's response, "it was Roxana. She's thick with both of them."

"I'm no matchmaker," said Paul, "and I waited a good long time before marrying myself, but the last time I saw Addis in England I thought he seemed lonely. Too bad she's not his type. He'd make some woman a splendid husband."

"So what we have to find for him is a damsel in distress?" said Erika, who was a matchmaker.

"That's the ticket," said Benjamin.

"And for Doris? What can we do about this Richard?"

"*Sentite,*" Paul interrupted, quieting them with his hand.

"We're almost there—this is the Ponte Mammolo—and I haven't told you that Doris is joining us today. She may be here already. A young man named Kline is driving her out. Have you met him?"

"Kline? Who is he?" asked Benjamin.

"A Prix de Rome composer at the Academy. A Californian. A nice lad. Said to be very talented."

"Park in the shade of those trees," Erika said. "It's not bad now, but by noon the car will be grilled. What will you wear against the sun?" Erika asked the Bolds. "I have my parasol. Paul has his straw hat."

"Roxana never wears a hat except for church," said Benjamin, "and I left the only one I had on the Havre–Paris boat train."

"The porkpie?" said Paul laughing. "The one Roxana had so lovingly rolled and twisted into just the right shape?"

"What if I make you a hat," said Erika, "out of yesterday's *Corriere della Sera*? Look. I fold it like this." She folded a sheet of the newspaper in half. "Then I turn down the ears like this. Then I fold up the bottom. You see? It's a Napoleonic hat. Did you wear one like that when you were a boy?"

"Of course! Let me have it," Benjamin said impatiently. He put the hat on. "How do I look?" He jumped out of the car and marched around, his right arm flexed as if he were shouldering a gun.

"I can't believe my *eyes*." Doris Trumbull's voice came from an approaching car. "Don't move," she said. "I must have a picture of you like that." Doris readied her camera at the window. "Hold still."

"No. Wait! Wait!" shrieked Benjamin in mock horror, tipping the hat down over his face. "Not here. I'll find a suitable place in the villa."

"Promise?"

"I promise. One can't be too careful about snapshots.

One never knows where they'll turn up. I can see Doris's in *Time* with the caption: 'In a less tragic mood, poet Bold frolics at Hadrian's Villa.' "

A young man dressed in a flowered shirt open at the neck, khaki-colored army slacks, and espadrilles got out of the car behind Doris.

"What's this, Kline?" Paul eyed with disapproval the bottle swinging from Mel's index finger. "You've fortified yourself with Chianti, have you?"

Mel brushed his crew-cut hair with his free hand. "You mustn't look at me as if I were an alcoholic, Professor Landsdale. It's water. I was out here two weeks ago and it was like a dust bowl."

"Alas, it's true," said Paul. "Hadrian's pools are bone dry these days. There's a reconstruction plan being worked on now, but that will take years. Today you'll have to take my word for what it was like."

Dressed like a traveler from the twenties, in a Norfolk jacket and a panama hat, Paul guided them through the ruins. He sketched in walls where only a few stones remained, paved streets, planted gardens, and filled the pools with water and fish, to help them to see what he saw—what had been there in Hadrian's time.

Like all tourists they exclaimed about the vastness of the site, whose size caused them to cluster together. From time to time, as the sun rose and the hot, still air buzzed with insects, they sought shelter in the shadow of an ancient wall or under an umbrella pine. They were grateful for Mel Kline's foresight.

Doris admitted to being disappointed. "It's all so *ruined!*" she exclaimed.

Benjamin, on the other hand, was exhilarated. As was his habit when he was with an expert, he became an attentive, even greedy student. He wanted to know everything Paul knew, and pressed him for more and more detail.

In a niche meant for a statue, Benjamin posed in his paper hat for Doris's camera. He played Lear to them in the theater, so that they could test the acoustics. He imitated the other tourists who crossed and recrossed their paths: an English schoolmaster, a German university student, a French couple who vied with each other to recall the history they had learned in school. He was—the hat had something to do with it—indefatigable.

By noon the heat had become crushing. They were covered with a fine dust raised by their feet on the dry paths. Mel's bottle was empty.

"Enough, enough. I have had enough of Hadrian," cried Erika. "My parasol is going to catch on fire. I am ready to sit down." It was only at such moments, or when one walked by her side, that one remembered that Erika was lame. Her "rotten leg," as she called it, a residual of infantile polio, was a burden she carried as if for a lesser, frailer spirit, as she might have carried a package for an elderly lady. She was a passionate sightseer, her curiosity and enthusiasm far outdistancing her physical strength. (She did not take well to restraint. "I fall down? Zo. Always there is someone to pick me up," she would say when a friend preached caution. "That's how I met Paul. And once in Yucatán, on the pyramids, I fell and an Indian—such pretty knees he had!— came and picked me up.")

"I have it!" said Benjamin. "Kline and I will make a chair and carry you back." Benjamin locked wrists with Mel and started toward Erika.

"What a good idea!" said Erika. "You play at being my slaves?" She put one hand on each of their shoulders as if she would sit down. "Paul do you think I can trust them not to drop me?"

"Not for a minute. Take my arm, dear. It's far more reliable."

Mel's Topolino, which looked like a toy next to Paul's

car, led the way to Tivoli. They passed workmen on foot and on Vespas on their way home for the midday meal. At the Sibilla restaurant they found they had the place to themselves. They reassembled in the garden, washed and dusted, and went to look over the ravine while Paul ordered lunch.

"That's the Anio." Benjamin was looking at the map. "And there's the Sibyl's temple."

"I'll take a commemorative photo there after lunch," said Doris.

"Is there time for a visit to the Grotto of the Sirens before lunch, do you think?" Benjamin wondered.

"I can't make another step without food," said Rosy.

Paul hit the side of a glass with a spoon. *"Ragazzi, vino,"* he called.

They sat at a trestle table under grapevines and ate olives and bread while they waited for the pasta.

"No wine for you, Paul?" asked Benjamin.

"Not for some months," Erika said. "One can't drink after hepatitis."

"Pauvre Paul, mes condoléances!" said Benjamin.

"And it's so deliciously cold," Doris said. "Have you told Benjamin and Rosy the plans?" she asked Erika.

"No, I haven't. We were too busy catching up on Cambridge on the way out."

"There's a cocktail party at the Academy tomorrow," said Doris. "It's sort of for Paul."

"Any excuse for a party," Paul laughed.

"Good," said Benjamin. "I'll get my old friend Rodney Munson invited if he hasn't been already. I want very much for you to meet him."

"Munson? I'd like very much to meet him. Someone told me he could introduce me to the Duca di Lentini. He has an early drawing of the Piazza Navona I need to see."

"He's a sweetie, the Duca," said Doris.

"You went out to Roccafalcone for lunch, didn't you? And what about his wife? I hear she's charming," said Paul.

"Hmmm," said Benjamin.

"Benjamin didn't like her?" Erika asked Rosy in an aside.

"More important than the cocktail party is Punza," said Doris.

"Ponza, Doris, not 'Punza.' You pronounce it like a Neapolitan," said Paul. "We were telling Doris last night that we are thinking of going to an island off the coast of Formia for two weeks or so."

"What?" Benjamin objected. "When you've only just arrived? Are we not to see you at all?"

"You will if you agree to come with us," said Paul.

"The doctor says that Paul must take it easy some more weeks. Rome is too exciting for him. I know he'll overdo," said Erika.

"I've found a pensione which is inexpensive and probably empty at this time of year," Paul said.

"My proofs are coming any day," said Benjamin.

"I can't wait," said Doris. "I'm longing to swim."

"What about you, Mel?" Paul asked politely.

"It's nice of you to include me, sir," said Mel, falling into an undergraduate tone. "Can I think about it and let you know?"

"Do. Maybe you can all let me know at the party tomorrow. I should call the pensione about the reservations. We plan to go in three or four days. And don't decide against it, Benjamin. We'll talk about it further on the way home. But children, you must finish your coffee. It's time for the Villa d'Este. We don't want to squander the afternoon."

Benjamin jumped up and put on his hat. *"Avanti!"* he cried.

The entrance to the Villa d'Este, dark, dank and as uninviting as a cellar, was a shock after the dry heat of the morning and the airy coolness of the Sibilla. It was as if the long empty rooms through which one had to pass before getting to the gardens had been arranged to give the tourist a jolt, to keep him from sliding passively from one marvel to the other. Once they were on the sun-warmed terrace, however, the overwhelming spectacle had its effect. They stood for some time, leaning over the parapet, letting their eyes take it in.

"You won't need my help now," said Paul. "Erika and I will stroll up here—we've seen it many times—while you young people go exploring."

The gardens were a perfect contrast to Hadrian's Villa —compact where the other had been limitless, verdant where it had been dusty, watery where it had been arid, the fantasy as explicit as it had been hidden in what remained of Hadrian's plan. As the agoraphobia of the morning had held them together, the intimacy of the gardens made them separate. High above them they saw and lost Paul and Erika, her parasol tilted back over her shoulders now that the sun was less of a threat, her body moving up and down next to Paul's with that special rhythm dictated by her shorter leg. The "young people" wandered up and down, meeting, pointing out to one another things not to be missed, separating, posing for Doris's camera.

They converged, as if by design, at a spot where Benjamin stood, his paper hat tipped rakishly over one eye, his body poised—a leader ready to be followed. Wordlessly they fell in behind him. They tried to imitate the runs, skips, and stops of his walking games. When he was sure that they were able to keep up, he quickened his pace. He became more daringly inventive. Should they, laughing and panting, fall out of line, he called commands to bring them to order. He grimaced back at the grotesques. (They had to follow suit.) He pinched the stone breasts of the sphinx. He jumped into and out of the rainbow spray at the fish pools. As they approached the Ovata fountain he shouted, "An orgy of water! An orgy of water! Suddenly he faced ahead like someone pursued by the Furies. When they caught up with him, he had disappeared behind the waterfall.

Mel, Doris, and Rosy stopped and looked at each other with bewilderment. The game had got out of hand. It had become, even, a little sinister.

Somewhere above the fountain they heard Paul's voice. They looked up to see him before a low-hanging cloud which rested heavily on top of the cypresses. He waved, "Rain . . . run for it . . . tomorrow . . . Ciao" was all they heard.

Drops of rain fell on their upturned faces. All at once, a wall of water came down on them as if a celestial but malicious giant, jealous of the man-made wonders of the Villa d'Este, had spitefully kicked over a monstrous pail.

Mel recovered first. "Let's go," he shouted. "Get Benjamin." He took Doris's hand and started up the stairs.

Rosy cupped her hands and called to Benjamin, who was still on the other side of the waterfall. He grinned crazily and threw his legs around wildly in a demonic dance.

"We must go with the others," Rosy shouted. "Please, Benjamin!" She gestured to reinforce her plea.

Benjamin stopped dancing. He saw that the game was over, that she was in earnest. He seemed to think it over. He shook his head, "No," and started dancing again.

Rosy brushed back her hair from her face. It was raining so hard she could scarcely see. The water hit the ground and bounced up again. She gestured that she was leaving.

At the top of the first flight of stairs she parted her hair again and looked to see if Benjamin was following. Her dress clung to her body like classical drapery. She caught sight of Benjamin's seersucker jacket, the gray stripes gone violet with wetness. He caught up with her and together they ran up the watery levels, panting and slipping, to the exit.

The others were waiting in the car. "Paul and Erika?" Rosy asked, getting her breath.

"They've gone ahead," Doris said. "Erika was anxious to get Paul home. She said she'd call you tomorrow."

The windows of Mel's car had been left open. They sat on what felt like bags of wet sand. The rain had felt warm as it fell, but sitting in their wet clothes, their shoes oozing water, they shivered and sneezed and tried to keep their teeth from chattering.

Mel was forced to drive slowly. Lightning occasionally illuminated the sky. They drove in silence, their eyes fixed on the road. At the Porta Tiburtina the rain turned to hail. It hammered the hood and the roof of the car.

"I didn't think it *ever* rained here in June." Doris's wail extracted one more laugh from them. It died quickly. They were impatient now for the outing to be over.

Rosy walked back to their room after a hot bath and a brisk rubdown with the coarse towel, planning a cozy evening indoors. She stood before the dresser mirror and made a turban with the towel to cover her wet hair. "I'm not sure I can face the rain again, can you?" she said to Benjamin's reflection. He was sitting in the easy chair. "We could make do with the food I have in the room, and afterwards put our pillows at the bottom of the bed under the light and read. I've just begun *I, Claudius*."

Benjamin didn't answer. His reflection didn't move. Rosy turned to see if he had heard. The light hit the thick lenses of his glasses. They looked like blank windows. There was a slight tremor in his head. His shoulders were hunched as if he were collecting himself for some great effort.

"Stop trying to control me!" he slammed at her, hard, like an aced tennis ball.

The unfinished turban slipped. "Control you?" She was shocked, but only as she might have been had she been hit accidentally, as if she had not been aware that the game was on. "When?" It was a misunderstanding that could easily be cleared up.

"When? When?" Benjamin mimicked Rosy's question with a disagreeably plaintive note.

"What are you talking about?" Whatever was wrong would not easily be made right, but Rosy's tone was still vague. She was stalling to give herself time to run through the events of the day, as a practiced dealer flips through a deck of cards before cutting them. "On the ride back? At Tivoli? Do you mean when it began to rain?" That was it. "But Benj—"

Benjamin catapulted himself from the chair to the door. "Stay in if you like, but be so good as not to make plans for me." The clack of the door punctuated his sentence. He was gone.

Rosy's protest, barely formed, died on her lips. She sank down on the bed, the towel in her hand, her hair dripping on her shoulders. With the other hand she impatiently brushed away tears which had sprung to her eyes (they seemed always to be there, premade, ready to flow. How they bored her!), as if she needed to keep her vision unblurred.

Where had Benjamin gone? She was not tempted to run after him, as she would have done in the days when she still hoped to bring him around by reasoning. He would be on his way to the Albrecht. Or was already there. Seated at their table, a stein of beer before him, untouched. His head would still be trembling like a plucked harp string, the long horizontal trough above his upper lip beaded with perspiration, the shirt he'd changed into as wet as the one he'd taken off. With an unsteady hand, he would light a cigarette. He would be as astonished as she was at the violence of his feelings. Or if not at the violence (he must be inured to that), at the suddenness with which they had overtaken him.

From what had they sprung? Was it his hypersensitivity to abrupt changes in the weather? Keats and other poets had suffered from it. Or had the rain been a drenching reminder that time does not stand still? Then there had been her invitation to an evening of intimacy. Panic. *But why?* He didn't know.

Nor did she. Years of diligent study of the way his mind worked—a mind like a house full of hidden stairways, trapdoors, sliding walls, and secret drawers—did not help her. If she fixed her attention on a panel in the wall, a trapdoor opened under her; if on the trapdoor, a panel slid open behind her.

It was not peace she had been enjoying these past weeks, but a cease-fire. The war was on again.

eight

Benjamin burst into the room late the following afternoon brandishing a package. "They've come!" His voice was shrill with excitement. Through half-opened eyes Rosy saw him put the package on the table with both hands, carefully, as if it contained an explosive.

"Why are you in bed?" he asked sharply.

"The wet ride home yesterday didn't do my back any good. I thought I'd rest before the cocktail party."

"What cocktail party?" Benjamin looked up from sorting the mail. "I hope you didn't accept for me."

"Paul mentioned it yesterday."

"You go. I want to get at the proofs."

"Paul had Rodney invited."

"Blast! I did promise to introduce them. Hmmm." Benjamin adjusted his eyeglasses, pushing them back on the bridge of his nose. "All right. We'll have one drink, come straight back."

Rosy got up and began to dress.

"Guess whom I met at American Express," Benjamin asked.

"Someone from Harvard?" This was an old game of theirs: guessing. They played it with greater or less sprightliness depending on how things were going between them. Benjamin's question was stiff, Rosy's answer listless.

"The Ritchies."

"Who are they?" Rosy asked without interest.

"Our table companions from the boat—the maiden lady from Nashville and her niece Charlotte. I've asked them to tea tomorrow. They were the very portraits of American innocence and confusion. They haven't a clue about how to read a map, for one thing."

"Do we want to have tea with them?" Rosy was incredulous. This was the kind of social engagement she had long ago learned to spare Benjamin. Social life was enough of a strain without imposing polite obligations on him.

"If I can take time from my work"—Benjamin paused—"surely it isn't too much to ask you to take an hour from your sightseeing."

Benjamin's tone, which rang as irritable as an alarm clock, warned Rosy to drop the subject. Still she wondered: what was this about the Ritchies? Benjamin's streak of Galahadism? Charlotte Ritchie's wide-eyed admiration? Did he imagine that one day when he was famous the Ritchies would get out the photograph album of their European tour and, pointing to the snapshot they'd taken of him at Le Havre, tell their friends how kind, how very kind he had been to them, how he had given them tea in Rome?

"Mostly bills." Benjamin finished the sorting. "A letter from Iphigene. From the heft of it, it's one of her single-spaced, ten-page numbers. Oh yes, there was also this." He took a telegram from his pocket and handed it to Rosy.

It was from Theo. He would have an hour between train and plane and hoped to see them. The letters floated around the page as if in an alphabet soup.

"It's tomorrow. You go," Benjamin said. "Explain that my proofs have—"

"Can't you take time?" It seemed important—crucial,

even—that Benjamin go with her. On the ride to Tivoli she had wondered at his talk of Theo. Had there been a touch of malice in it? Was he suspicious? The idea frightened her. And yet she hoped for it. "You have to have lunch anyway," she said, trying to sound matter-of-fact. "He gets in at noon."

"Not possibly. I can't break into my morning."

"It's not the morning," Rosy said stubbornly. "It's noon."

"I'll see him in London. Find out if he's still eager to have us stay with him. Might not be a bad idea. Unless something turns up soon our money will be, to say the least, low."

"You're taking time for tea with the Ritchies," Rosy begged.

"Look here, Roxana. This Academy party comes at a very awkward time for me. If you expect me to go to it, don't waste my time arguing. Let's get there and get it over with."

Rosy had the sensation of falling through space with a parachute on her back which refused to open. On the ride up the Janiculum while Benjamin read aloud the letter from Iphigene, Rosy made up her mind that she would not go to meet Theo alone.

The common room at the Academy was already crowded when they arrived. The windows which gave on the terrace were open to the gray sky and the cool damp air which had been ushered in by the previous day's storm. The noise level was high. Higher still was the report of American laughter.

"Sweeties. Here you are," said Doris coming up to them. "Paul was afraid you'd forgotten. It's a terrific party. *All* Rome is here."

Doris led them over to where Paul was standing with Mimi Brill and a group of young men, fellows of the Academy. On the way she turned to say, with some excitement, "Will Hendy is here. See him?" Doris pointed. "Do you know him?"

Benjamin balked. He pulled his head up. The muscles

of his neck knotted, like those of a frightened horse about to bolt. Doris turned to see if they were still following. "Do you?" she asked again.

"No. I'm *longing* to meet him." Benjamin burlesqued her.

Hendy, a poet half a generation older and far better known than Benjamin, might pretend not to have heard of him, or, suspicious of a growing rival (had he heard of the new poem?), might be provocative and aggressive. Benjamin would not have chosen to meet him on the edgy eve of seeing his new work in proof; nor at a cocktail party.

"Ro, don't miss Mimi Brill's cape. It's from Balenciaga. She claims she got it *en soldes*. She must have paid a fortune for it."

"Ah, here you are!" Paul came toward them, his arms open in an expansive welcoming gesture. The color of his skin, which looked like a fake suntan in the evening light and gave his hair an artificially bleached appearance, made him look more theatrical than ever. He was dressed all in white with a colored handkerchief hanging out of his breast pocket. He looked as if he might have been invited to the party to perform as a magician, or to demonstrate his talents as a mesmerist. "Mrs. Brill was just telling us a story about Proust." Paul, who knew about literary matters only what Benjamin had taught him, lowered his voice. "Come rescue me, Benjamin. I'm out of my depth already."

He led Benjamin and Rosy to the group.

Doris stood behind Mimi and directed Rosy's eyes to the cape to be sure she was taking it in. She was. It was copied from a shepherd's cloak, seamed with cunning, and of an uncommon blue. Mimi's arms were folded across her waist, a hand resting on either arm, as if to excuse herself for wearing the cape indoors, as if even with it on she were still chilly.

Benjamin accepted Paul's introduction to Mimi as if he couldn't quite place her.

"I hope I didn't tell this story the night we had dinner at Conti's?" Mimi said, as if to refresh his memory. "We had gallons of wine that night and my memory of our conversation is foggy."

Benjamin made no reply.

"No, you didn't," said Rosy, whose memory for the events of that evening was still sharp.

"There's not really much to tell." Mimi lost confidence before Benjamin's blank stare.

"Do go on," said Paul. "I'm sorry to have interrupted you."

"It's just that Jason and I were very lucky last time we were in Paris. We had a letter to a woman, a comtesse, who was the model for the Duchesse de Guermantes."

"Oh?" Benjamin said dubiously.

"Yes. It's well known. She asked us to tea. Just the three of us. Jason was thrilled because he's such a Proust fan."

"How old is she?" asked one of the young men.

"It's hard to say. Seventy-five? If you didn't know she had a title you'd take her for a *femme de chambre*—hair knotted on top of her head, a dowdy dress—until she speaks, of course."

"The French aristocracy is like that," said Doris. "They play everything down. What did you have for tea?"

"Madeleines."

"How Proustian!" Doris sighed appreciatively. "Wouldn't you have been fascinated to meet her?" Doris meant her remark as an aside to Rosy, but Benjamin answered.

"Nothing could interest me less."

"You're anti-Proust, Mr. Bold?" one of the young men asked.

"Proust? Proust interests me greatly, but this woman . . ."

The young man smiled at the others in the group. "But surely in a *roman à clef* . . ."

Benjamin brought his hand up to his eyeglasses, as if to bring his interlocutor into sharper focus. "Ex*cuse* me," he said with heavy emphasis, "but this talk displays a touching naïveté about the nature of fiction. This Comtesse de . . . Chose is no more the Duchesse de Guermantes . . ."

"But she is," Mimi insisted, wounded. "She *is*."

". . . than Elizabeth Peabody is Miss Birdseye."

The young man smiled more broadly. "She's not? William James thought she was."

"Well, William was wrong. You may remember that Henry wrote him that he borrowed from Miss Peabody nothing but her habit of gesturing with her glasses. 'Miss Birdseye,' he said, 'was evolved, like all my characters, from my moral consciousness.' "

"Henry James took another view of the matter when someone put *him* in a novel," the young man insisted.

"It's the characters that have passed through the author's imagination that I want to meet," Benjamin continued, ignoring the young man. "And when I do, I know where to find them—and it's not at a tea party. So, to paraphrase Henry James, let us have as little as possible of its being Mrs. Thing or Comtesse Chose."

"Hear, hear!" Rodney joined the group, patting his hands in gentle applause. "What is this, Ben, a lecture?"

"Tell me . . ." Benjamin turned to Rodney as if he'd dismissed his class. "Have you ever read the novel supposedly about James by that woman who lives in Florence—what's her name?—Lee, Vernon Lee."

"No, I haven't. I didn't even know until recently that Lee was a she."

Paul, who had detached himself from the group some time before to greet people, caught Benjamin's eye.

"Paul, Rodney. Sorry." Benjamin said, taking each of them by an arm. "Here I have you both and I had forgotten what it was I'd come to the party for. It's monstrous that you two have never met."

Rosy looked over the room. There were just enough

Romans to keep the Americans from feeling they had not traveled in vain. Occasionally an Italian word was heard over the roar of English, and a few Italian women, elaborately coiffed and dressed in summer black, gave the party an exoticism it would not have had at home.

Margaret was back. She was talking to the Duchessa and the big, rawboned man Doris had pointed out as Will Hendy. Hendy must have said something flattering to the Duchessa. She was looking up at him, smiling almost coquettishly, her cheeks slightly flushed. Would he do the editing Benjamin was to have done? The Duca was in a corner talking to Tullio. Rosy went to join them.

"Roxana." Margaret intercepted her. "You give me a bad conscience. I'm afraid I've rather left you on your own in Rome after proposing to take you shopping. But now I'm back. What was it we said we'd do together? Shoes?"

"There's something you could tell me," said Rosy, remembering that Margaret was the woman to know. "I need the name of an orthopedist."

"Nothing serious, I hope?"

"I'm having back trouble." The afternoon in bed had not noticeably diminished the pain.

"Your back?" Margaret, whose well-padded back had the look of performing its job admirably, looked shocked, as if Rosy had said she was having trouble with her brain. "It's those wretched pensione beds. I told Rod that place would not do. Why not change to the Minerva? That would suit you better. Still, you probably should see a doctor. Let me think, now," Margaret said, warming up. "Is Agnelli an orthopedist? I think he is. He's at Salvator Mundi."

Rosy looked in her pocketbook for something to write on and found Theo's telegram. Margaret dictated the information.

"He speaks some English, but I'll be glad to go with you. Shall I do that?"

"I'm sure I can manage," said Rosy.

"You'll call me if you need help? Promise?" Margaret said, going back to the Duchessa and Will Hendy.

Rosy felt an arm encircle her waist as she got a great smacking kiss on the cheek. "Hector Bates!" she said. Hector, a tall slim man with a face shaped like a badge, was Paul's protégé and assistant. "When did you arrive?"

"This instant. Roxana, you—look—magnificent." He spaced his words for emphasis. "You've changed. What is it? Let's see." He stood off and squinted one eye at Rosy as if he were studying a painting. "That's it," he snapped his fingers. "You look European. Italian even. North Italian, of course. Your hair is the color of *giallo antico*. It's incredible how quickly Europe changes women. It's all that attention from men that does it. Had your bottom pinched recently?"

"Can't say that I have."

"You will. Unless, of course, you go around looking forbidding, as you sometimes do."

"Do I?" said Rosy, amused and surprised by this tone of intimacy. This must be the Italian Hector Bates. Their relationship seemed to have developed since February, like a culture prepared in a test tube and left alone. Or was Hector simply tight? When he put his arm around her waist again, Rosy was sure he must be.

"Will you come for a Roman walk with me one day?" he asked, in a confidential tone. "I can show you things you'll never find in a guidebook."

"For instance?" Rosy asked, laughing and inching out of his grasp.

"A secret tower. Don't laugh," he said, looking wounded and more familiar. "I can show you Hilda's tower."

"Doves and all, Bates?" Benjamin came up behind them, his voice rich with scorn.

How many martinis had *he* had? In the mood he was in, two would be sufficient to poison him.

"I'll thank you to take your arm from around my wife's waist—unless, of course, she likes it." Rosy too was given a dose of scorn. "Why not introduce her to the son of the Faun? She was always curious about the Faun's sex life. Did he—"

Rosy put her hand on Benjamin's arm. "Shouldn't we go?"

Benjamin flicked it off. "Go? Go where? We're going to dinner with the others. You don't mind if *I* decide occasionally what we'll do, do you?" Benjamin's voice was loud and combative. Not without a pang of conscience, Rosy abandoned Hector to him. Without her as audience, Benjamin might calm down.

"Rozan, Doris said you were here but I couldn't find you in this mob," said Erika. "And how did you make out yesterday? You understood about our leaving? I had to get Paul home."

"How is he really?" Rosy asked. "He looks well, except for the jaundice."

Erika fanned her hand. "One day good, the next not so good. That's why we go to Ponza. You must come."

"I don't think Benjamin will."

"Where is he?"

"Over there." Rosy gestured.

"I hear him. He's up?" Erika meant high.

Rosy nodded.

"Take him away. Make him eat."

"I tried."

"Zo. He's in a not so good mood. How he changes! Yesterday he was so charming. I wish I could help you, but Paul is making a sign to go. He tires so quickly." It was Erika at the cocktail parties at home who got Benjamin to go out for dinner when she saw trouble coming. "I'll call you tomorrow. We'll have Paul convince Benjamin about Ponza. We go day after tomorrow."

Doris came up as Erika went off. "Now, Ro, you're not thinking of going home. Come to dinner with us."

"I'm sorry to say Benjamin has decided we will join you after all. Can't we go soon? The party is thinning out."

"Now, Ro, relax. The party is good for *hours*. What's the hurry? What you need is another drink."

"I've had hundreds," Rosy said. It was not true. She had stopped drinking, as she often did when Benjamin drank too much, in an absurd long-distance attempt to control his consumption.

Hector came up with a drink and handed it to Rosy. "You look as if you need this," he said. "And let's not have any talk about breaking up the party. It's just getting cozy."

"I'll take the drink if I can have a chair too," said Rosy with resignation. "I can't stand another minute."

"Here. Mel, give me a hand with this." Hector and Mel pulled a pair of overstuffed chairs together. "Is something the matter?" Hector asked. "You look worried."

"Too much sightseeing, I guess." Rosy slumped down in the chair.

"All the more reason to come to Ponza."

"You're going too?"

"Erika urged me to. I'll do a little work with Paul so he won't get restless. It'll be fun. Do come."

"Benjamin has to work. His proofs have just come."

"I don't give a damn about Benjamin. And I'm sick of his poem. Let him work. You come."

Rosy was listening to Benjamin across the room in a noisy exchange with Will Hendy. "What did you say?" she asked, realizing that Hector had said something to her.

"Why don't you give it up?"

"Give up what?"

"What you're doing now."

"What's that?"

"Being a psychiatric nurse."

Rosy now gave Hector her full attention. "How do you mean?"

"That's what you are, you know." Hector seemed pleased with his insight and the arresting effect it had on Rosy. "A psychiatric nurse. You're not a wife. But then, he's not a husband."

Rosy put her hand up in front of Hector's mouth. "Wait, wait, wait!" She tried to stop him. He was decidedly drunk.

"Oh, no!" Hector pulled her hand down. "You're not going to shut me up. I've been watching you for years. Surprised, aren't you? He's the great man. He makes a mess. You clean up after him. Why? Is the care and feeding of poets so damned interesting? I doubt it. And as for his compulsive sleeping around . . ."

Rosy knocked over a drink as she stood up. Her face on fire, she hurried across the room.

"Hey, there." Rodney caught her at the door. He held her still. "Where are you going?" He gave her a look as if to say, No matter what it is, you don't want to go flying off like this. "We're all going now," he said, still calming her.

Not trusting her voice, Rosy made no reply. She allowed Rodney to lead her to the door. The Brills were getting into their car. "Will you take Roxana with you?" Rodney urged Rosy into the back seat, not waiting for an answer. "I'll bring Benjamin with me. We'll follow you down." Will Hendy came to the door. "You'll go in this car, Hendy? You know the Brills?"

Will Hendy lowered his enormous frame gingerly into the front seat. "You won't believe it," he said as he did, "but we're old friends. Brill here"—he took a jab at Jason's arm—"writes the lousiest novels in the world, but he's the damn best shot I know. And besides, he's the *only* writer, good or bad, who comes anywhere near Hairpin, Nevada."

"Who's the canary in the back seat?" Will asked Jason, as the car started down the hill.

"I'm so sorry," Mimi spoke up. "It never occurred to me you didn't know each other."

Will reached around, in a double-jointed movement, and crushed Rosy's hand in his paw. "Has anyone ever told you what a pill you're married to? A pill," he repeated with satisfaction, as if he'd found *le mot juste*.

The contrast between the large man and the small noun forced a gasp-laugh from Rosy, as a blow on the back might do to someone holding his breath. "Will you be good enough to drop me by Conti's?" Rosy said.

"You're not coming with us for dinner?" Mimi asked.

"Not on your life," Will said. "Don't let the canary out. We need her. Have to have a canary." Will leaned over and whispered to Jason, "She thinks she's going to slip away to a late date with some Eyetie and leave us with Mr. Pill?"

"No point in going home," Jason said. "Rodney's taking Benjamin to the restaurant with him."

"Give it the gas, will you, Jason?" Will said. "I'm late as hell. My bride, my young and beautiful bride, will be as mad as an unfed baby. I'm testing her love for me." Will struggled out of the front seat when they stopped at the Hotel Eden. "The first of many tests."

"He's an hour late," said Mimi. "I'd kill any man who did that to me. And on his honeymoon!"

"Luckily, you're not married to him," said Jason, still smarting from Will's brutal dismissal of his work. "Next time we go hunting I'm going to sink a bullet into his thick hide. Who would believe that that big slob could write such delicate lyrics?"

"It's wonderful what drinking does for people, isn't it?" Mimi remarked to Rosy.

The hotel door opened and out came Ann on Will' arm. They made a comical pair. Ann was small and delicate Will, big and tough. "But Baby," Ann was protesting.

"Come on, love, hop in," said Will, "or we'll nibble a your flesh we're so hungry."

"Isn't he outrageous?" Ann asked, smiling tolerantly. "I've been waiting for hours."

"Beauty and the Beast, Mrs. Bold." Jason said by way of introduction as Will and Ann got into the car.

"How are you?" Mimi asked Ann. "What kind of a trip have you been having?"

"Divine. I adored Paris. Must show you what I bought."

"And London?"

"We haven't been yet. Will has a reading at the BBC in July, so we'll go then."

"The Bolds are going then too," said Mimi, trying to include Rosy in the conversation.

"Where'd you get the tan, Beauty?" Jason asked.

Will growled and made as if to bite Ann's bare shoulder. "Doesn't it look good enough to eat?"

"We've just come from Porquerolles. You know the island? It's a paradise. Baby hated it."

Baby, his skin a midwinter gray, was scowling. "A loathsome place. Full of lizards, jellyfish, and sea anemones."

"Will always thinks the French are laughing at him because of his accent," said Ann.

"They probably are," said Jason, whose French was good.

At the Piazza Sant' Ignazio the waiters were discussing how to accommodate those who had come down from the Academy. Rosy and Ann were left alone when the others went to join the discussion.

"Are you from Nevada too?" Rosy asked, making conversation.

"Philadelphia. I met Will when he came to Swarthmore to teach creative writing. It will be fun being a faculty wife. I'm curious to see what it's like from the other side."

"Have you been abroad long?"

"Two months. I'm loving it, but in a way I'll feel more married when I get home."

"You married just before you came abroad?"

"The day before. I can't wait to get back and unpack my china and set up housekeeping."

Rosy looked over at Will. Would he be able to keep the promise of permanence implicit in Ann's dream of domesticity? Probably not. And yet she felt a twinge of envy. It was not Will she envied Ann, but their marriage just beginning; they had not yet had time to make major mistakes.

Rodney brought over an Italian who'd come with his group from the party. "This is Professor Ricci of the University of Rome. Mr. Hendy is for dining outdoors. Professor Ricci is for inside. How do you ladies feel?"

Professor Ricci, a thin man with hooded eyes, dabbed the tip of his ibislike nose with a gray handkerchief he held rolled into a ball. "It's going to rain," he predicted in a timid, nasal voice. Professor Ricci was a sharp reminder that not all Italian men are handsome, or concerned with *bella figura*.

The waiters moved the tables outdoors. "My Will seems to have had his way," said Ann.

Rodney tried to organize the anarchic group. "Roxana, come sit down. If we do, maybe the others will follow."

The baroque piazza was empty—the other diners, as Professor Ricci pointed out to no one in particular, were, sensibly, indoors—except for their long table, which had been placed perpendicular to the restaurant. The church was dark and locked for the night. A sullen sky hung low over the undulating façade of the palazzo.

"It's going to rain." Ricci, seated next to Rosy, was still trying to get someone to listen to him.

"Perhaps not until we've finished dinner," said Rosy, who would have welcomed a downpour. Benjamin, seated next to Margaret—how had that happened?—was already disputing with her.

"Paul said to be sure to have the scampi," Mel reminded them as they studied their menus.

Will Hendy, bracing his large hands on the table, heaved himself to his feet as if he were going to make a speech. Hands went out on all sides to steady the rocking wineglasses and jigging silver. Will removed his jacket and snapped his suspenders—red ones—smartly. "I can lick anyone in the square." No one contradicted him. "In Rome. In Italy. In Europe. In"—he swayed gently like prairie grass in a light wind—"in the universe."

" 'Course you can, Baby," said Ann.

Will, reassured, sat down. Professor Ricci was not quick about his glass. Wine splashed out of it, making a puddle at his place.

"Ben. Come on, stop arguing," Jason called down the table. "Everyone's ordered but you."

Benjamin looked at Jason glassily. "My name is Bold. My wife and friends call me Benjamin. My school friends— and you're not among that lucky number, Brill—call me Ben."

"Cut the lecture. You'll lose us the waiter," Jason said irritably. Margaret, also concerned that the waiter would leave before Benjamin made a choice, signaled him to her side and ordered for Benjamin.

Rosy tried, hard, to concentrate on what Ricci was saying. He taught Modern American Literature—was especially interested in poetry, American poetry—was planning a visit to the United States next year, in preparation for a book of translations he was putting together. He had come down with the others from the cocktail party because he had heard—was it from Mr. Munson?—that there were poets in the group. Important poets he might put in his book. Could Mrs. Bold point them out?

Sometime after the waiter had brought their orders, Rosy interrupted Ricci, who was telling her his theory about *Hiawatha,* to say, "That's one of them."

Will had heaved himself to his feet again. Holding his glass up as if for a toast, he declaimed, "O Ben! O Bold! O

113

Bacchus!" He drained his glass, put it down on the table, and as if taking in the name for the first time said, "Bold . . . bold. A silly name, Bold. Sounds made up to me." He put his fists in front of his face and assumed a comic boxing stance. "If you're so bold, why don't you fight me. I can lick you."

"Baaaby." Ann drawled the "a" affectionately. "Have some scampi. They're yummy."

What was Ricci saying? Rosy's head pounded so hard she couldn't hear him.

"On your feet, Bold," said Will, dusting the tip of his nose with his thumb.

Benjamin started to his feet. Margaret plucked at his sleeve, to pull him down. "Your lovely fish is getting cold."

"Fish?" Distracted from Will, Benjamin put his head down close to the fish. "Poor fish, getting cold," he crooned to the sole on his plate. He took a napkin and blanketed the fish with it, gave it a tender pat as if it were a doll. Then, remembering that he wanted more wine, he reached for the fiasco.

"Here. You don't want any more of that." Margaret tried to move the wine out of his reach.

Benjamin, moving nimbly, grabbed it. "You're so wrong, my dear Margaret." He swung the fiasco over her head. *Ego te baptizo*"—chanting ceremoniously, he poured the wine— *"in vino . . ."* It had been aimed at Margaret's head, but it was Doris who, because Benjamin lost his footing, was baptized instead.

In an instant Rosy was at his side. *"Now* are you ready to go," she said, shaking with rage.

They walked swiftly and silently, the commotion at the table following them. Soon there was only the sound of Rosy's heels echoing in the maze behind the palazzo. They had not got very far before Benjamin threw his head up. He split the air with an unearthly shriek. The street light hit his eyeglasses. His eyeballs looked as if they had floated loose from their sockets. His lips were drawn back in a gash, his teeth bared in a grimace of pain. He looked like a frantic horse tethered in a burning barn, threatening to break loose and trample anyone nearby. He raised his arm and struck out.

Rosy jumped back. Her arm, raised in reflexive self-defense, caught the blow. "Benjamin," she screamed. "Are you mad?" Then, after a moment of paralysis, she turned and ran. She ran and ran, pursued by a lunatic voice shouting incomprehensible words. Her shawl fell off. She had to backtrack to pick it up. Her sandals slipped from her heels. As she stopped to adjust them, she heard a pumping noise, grotesquely magnified in her ears. It was her heart. She started to run again.

Abruptly she was out of the maze. She found herself on a broad, banal street. There was no sound now but the click of her heels. The street was lined with shops, inhospitably sealed by metal doors. The city wore an alien, unfriendly aspect at this hour. She had never been out alone at night in Rome. It was late. How long had it been raining? She would take a taxi. Her purse? She had left it on the table at the restaurant. In her hand was a paper napkin, kneaded into a ball. Across the street a man eyed her, kept pace with her. She gathered her shawl close. She had no idea where she was. A car followed her slowly, as large fish follow small fish looking for food, taking their time. She counted her steps— one, two, one, two. Her heart beat a syncopated rhythm with her feet. A prostitute appeared from a doorway. She grazed Rosy's shoulder as she passed and hissed something. The woman smelled of stale garlic and dead gardenias.

Blisters on her toes, made by her sandal straps, slowed her pace. She tried to avoid pushing against the straps, but the blisters stuck to the leather. She stopped to wedge pieces of the paper napkin between the blisters and the straps. A few yards of walking dislodged them. At last, in the distance, she saw the first building she recognized, the Victor Emmanuel monument. She was no longer lost.

She thought back to the Piazza Sant' Ignazio. Doris? Tomorrow she would make light of what had happened: "Oh, Ro, forget it. It was an accident." People did that with Benjamin, giving the lie to his blurred memory. In the end he never knew for sure what to feel guilty about. Margaret and Rodney? Margaret resolute, Rodney worried. Professor Ricci? An introduction to Contemporary American Poetry. No need to worry about the Hendys and Brills; Hollywood and Hairpin made people tough. The only grave damage, in the end, was in her relationship with Benjamin. With a tongue honed to a rapier sharpness, and a pen to serve his animus and rage, he had never, until now, needed physical violence. Other men might strike their wives when drunk, but for Benjamin to do so was as out of character as if he had threatened her with a switchblade. It could only mean that the fissure between them had terrifyingly deepened.

She was home. The waiters in the restaurant were stacking tables. She took off her sandals and leaned against the cold, damp wall of the stairwell to get her breath. There was the familiar smell of gas. She climbed the stairs barefoot. The cold stairs anesthetized her burning feet. At the entrance to the pensione she stood holding her shoes as she used to, a girl, coming in late after a dance, hoping to slip to her room unnoticed. A pinpoint bulb burned on Signora Schmidt's desk. Rosy ran on tiptoe to her room, closed the door behind her, and fell face down on the bed.

She would have to get up again to undress. That would mark the beginning of the vigil. She wanted to delay it as long as she could—to be grateful, simply, that the walk was over, that she was home. With a corner of the sheet she dried her face. Her face felt feverish, her hands clammy. The gate-door of the restaurant clanked as it was locked for the night. Now silence. Only the fountain's *plash plash, plash plash, plash . . .*

nine

Rosy shuddered awake, cold. Three o'clock. She undressed hurriedly and got into bed: to wait. Years ago she had left Benjamin on the street the way she had this evening. It was at the end of spring vacation. They had met at Iphigene's apartment after doing last-minute errands separately, before going back to Cambridge. On the way to Grand Central, Benjamin began to make a scene, to shout, to gesticulate, to clown—not with the high-spirited clowning of the morning at Hadrian's Villa, but crazily, so that he attracted the attention of a policeman and passersby. (What had been the cause that time?) Her attempts to get him to stop had made him worse. In the end, exploding in anger, she had left him to take the train alone. Late that night when he arrived at the apartment in Cambridge, he accused her of having abandoned him. But the next day, reasonable again, he said she had done the right thing: there was no telling what he might have done had she stayed to watch the performance. She could not count on that kind of reasonableness when he came in tonight.

Footsteps in the hall. Rosy sat up—relieved, but braced. Benjamin was all right, then. But in what state? The footsteps continued past her door. It was Luigi, the pensione factotum, making his rounds. Rosy turned on the light. To help pass the time, she would read. She turned it off and huddled down on the bed again. Better feign sleep. Avoid a confrontation when Benjamin came in. There had been the happy years, then the years of confrontations, and now the months of avoiding them.

A current shot through her body, making her jackknife up, rigid, as if she had touched an exposed wire with a wet hand. Hector's unpleasant words. Was it possible that Benjamin had staged the scene in the square (how good an actor he was Rodney did not begin to guess) to break up the party, to get free of her so that he could meet someone?

It had begun, as far as she knew, the first summer they went to Maine. It was the last year of the war. Ruth's invitation had come when, dead broke, they had seen no possibility of getting out of steaming Cambridge. Ruth had a large house, she wrote, and Annie to help with the work. Wouldn't they come for two weeks? Benjamin, who had met Ruth a couple of times casually, was vague about her. A mother figure, he thought, but well intentioned. She specialized in underweight poets, if he remembered correctly. She was trying to write herself. Would undoubtedly make him sing for his supper. It would be worth it, to get away.

Little Gull was more remote than ever in those days. Most of the rambling frame houses were shuttered for the duration of the war. The beaches were deserted. Ruth's house was large and well run. If anything could have spoiled the vacation—they hit a streak of brilliant weather: the water and sky mirroring each other, competing in blueness; the air as crisp and sharp as a tart apple—it would have been Benjamin's quarrels with Ruth ("If she poses as an intellectual she'll have to learn to take it") and with her ten-year-old daughter, Wendy ("Don't defend her when I tick her off. She's a very rude little girl and needs someone to tell her so").

At the end of their stay, the day before they were to leave, Ruth took Benjamin off to go over her poems. Wendy, threatening to have a temper tantrum at being left behind, jumped at Rosy's suggestion that the two of them go for a walk. Wendy skipped ahead, leading the way through the woods. The sun filtered through the pine trees. The surf pounded in the distance. They picked mushrooms and spied on a family of blue jays. They lay on the ground, face down, to breathe in the aroma of pine needles roasted in the sun, to store the memory of their fragrance against the coming winter.

The morning flew by. Late for lunch, they raced each other home. Benjamin and Ruth had not come back. The maid fed Wendy and grumbled about how lunch would be spoiled if the others didn't get back soon. Her vexation turned into apprehension as it grew later and later: something must have happened. Wendy said she knew where they had gone. She would show Rosy.

They took a shortcut through the salt marshes to a farmer's shack. Halfway there, the child abruptly changed her mind: they wouldn't be there after all. Better try the beach. The previous year another guest had gone off like this with Ruth, and had almost drowned because of the undertow. One of Benjamin's games was to swim too far out. They ran to the beach, not playing now. Ruth and Benjamin were not there, of course.

"How silly of you to have worried," Ruth said blandly when she and Wendy got back and found them already at lunch. "It was a very profitable morning. We simply forgot the time."

At the moment Rosy had felt only the rebuke (once the fear was removed, her alarm *had* seemed foolish), but afterwards . . . Had precocious Wendy understood more quickly than she Ruth's price for hospitality?

Rosy thought back to the faces around the table at the restaurant. With whom had Benjamin gone off this time? He had been disagreeable to Mimi at the cocktail party, but that was sometimes his way of beginning. Not Ann. He had never met her before, and she had eyes only for Will. Margaret? Ridiculous. Or was it? Benjamin liked to sing

> *Mille e tre, mille e tre!*
> *V'han fra queste contadine, cameriere, cittadine;*
> *V'han contesse, baronesse, marchesane, principesse*

as he showered. Rosy felt the blood rush to her face: it was Doris. He had spilled the wine on her. But Doris was *her* friend. The protest died in her throat. "A disguised form of incest" Benjamin had once called it, to explain away an earlier episode (and as if to analyze it excused it). And hadn't Doris said she was looking for someone to be unfaithful with, to punish Richard?

Rosy fell back on the bed, limp. This dead-of-night paranoia! What if she were imagining it all? In the end it would be possible to forgive Benjamin all the rest; but this would be hard—these doubts, these degrading suspicions.

If Benjamin was not with Doris or one of the others, where could he be? In Cambridge there was always someone to drop in on at any hour. He was clever at finding people to humor him. They were flattered. They could dine out on it the next evening: "Benjamin Bold woke us at four in the morning. In bad shape. Wanted a martini." "At that hour?" "Wild-eyed, but, brilliant. Told his Pushkin story. And a bawdy limerick about Byron and Shelley. Very funny. Wish I could remember it. At dawn he was finally willing to go. Says he doesn't feel safe going to sleep before there's light in the sky—the result of childhood nightmares."

In Rome there was no one to drop in on. Rosy got up and walked back and forth between the bed and the window. What if Benjamin didn't come back by morning? How long should she wait before calling for help? Who was there to call? She stood at the window and butted her head softly against the shutters. It was madness to have come abroad. What if Benjamin, drunk as he was, stepped out in front of a car, like the old woman Mimi ran down? He could be lying in the street at this moment, in a grotesque position. Or be stretched out on an examining table, under a blue-white hospital light. He could be . . .

The door banged open. Rosy wheeled around. Benjamin hung on the doorframe. His suit was covered with chalk. His tie was missing. His face was gaunt and looked twice its length, as if distorted by a trick mirror.

"I can't see," he cried. "My glasses . . . horrible . . . glasses . . ."

Rosy ran to him. "What is it? Where have you been?" How had he got home without his eyeglasses?

He dropped to his knees and clutched at Rosy's legs. "A fight . . . They took my glasses . . . The police . . . You deserted . . ."

She had abandoned him and something ugly had happened. A moment ago she had wished him dead. Now she said a prayer of thanksgiving that he was alive. "Come to bed," she said, pulling him to his feet.

"I can't *see*. I can't *see*." Benjamin threw his arms around spastically.

Rosy dragged him over to the bed. He fell on it, sobbing. She took off his suit and shoes, and covered him with a blanket. "Try to get some sleep," she said. Before she had finished the phrase, he was breathing deeply and rhythmically.

Rosy lay on her bed, on top of the covers, to wait for morning. She kept her eyes on Benjamin's back, not trusting his sleep, still on guard. The night dragged on. There was only the sound of the fountain and Benjamin's breathing.

When at last she heard Assunta and smelled the breakfast coffee and the burnt milk, she got up and dressed. She emptied the pockets of Benjamin's suit. His watch was there, the glass broken, and his wallet, empty. She rolled the suit into a ball to take it to the cleaners.

After listening at the door, she slipped into the hall and walked to the stairs quickly and stealthily, like a thief. An arm reached out of a shadow, the frames of Benjamin's glasses resting on the palm of its hand. Rosy jumped back and dropped the suit. Luigi followed his arm out of the gloom. He stood before her like a blind man offering useless waves. He had been waiting for her, his patient posture seemed to say. Rosy took the frames, trying not to touch his hand. Luigi picked up the suit, now unrolled and exposed. He handed it to her wordlessly, with a gesture as rich as a mime's. Rosy backed into the wall, whirled around, and raced down the stairs.

On the way to the *tintoria* she caught a glimpse of a strange face in a shop window. It was white around the eyes and mouth, like the negative of a photograph: it was hers. She put the suit on the counter, pretended not to understand the raised eyebrows and tongue-clicking at its deplorable condition. The shopkeeper pointed out a rip in it. *"Lavare a secco,"* Rosy repeated again and again, as if the shopkeeper were deaf, and fled without getting a ticket for it.

A car swerved to avoid her as she crossed the street. A woman grabbed her arm to pull her to safety. The woman said she must be more careful. She must. She must get control of herself. It would be a long day. Benjamin would lie in one of his mute, motionless states, closer to coma than to sleep, until evening. She would not go back to the pensione before tea with the Ritchies. (Would he remember?)

Worse almost than the white nights were the gray, purposeless days. A woman whose husband or lover is being operated on walks the streets, often in strange parts of the city where she normally would not go, unable to follow her normal occupations, observing those who do like figures in a silent movie. Rosy, like this woman, floated, dispossessed, between those who went about their daily routines and an etherized Benjamin.

At a café, she ordered a *cappuccino* and a roll. When they came, she looked at them bleakly. The gin and cigarettes, the night's anxiety had left her without appetite. She picked up a discarded newspaper left on the next table. Benjamin's sightless face, as he had looked when he stumbled into the room, projected itself on the newsprint. The police had brought him home with broken glasses and an empty wallet. Any scenario she could make up to account for the hours during which he had been missing was disagreeable. She put the paper down, paid the waiter, and left the restaurant.

She walked without direction. A church. She tried the door. Locked. She walked on. The Via Veneto. Fashionable couples out promenading. A holiday was in the air. A single woman among couples, she felt lonely, exposed, out of place. Was this what it felt like to be unmarried? Or rather, still married but separated? At the Borghese Gardens, she sat on a bench. Someone, a man, sat down beside her. Too close. Said something. She moved on.

At the gates of the zoo—how had she got there?—she wondered whether or not to go in. Why not? Kill time. See the animals. The zoo was lively with parents and children, celebrating the holiday together. An adoring papa held his doll-like daughter up to see the baby zebra. The child squealed her superiority at the zebra, which was unrealistically frisky on shaky legs.

How it smelled, the zoo! The dampness brought it out. It was another gray day. Rosy sat at a table in the restaurant and made another stab at breakfast. No use. The roll tasted of elephants. She found an empty bench, apart from the crowd, and sat down, her frame slack. In front of her was a cage of parrots. A bilious green one screeched, *"Pericolo, pericolo."* She wished it would stop. A big man, English from the cut of his suit, came between her and the cage. He posed his children for a snapshot. He wore brown suede shoes. Like Theo. Theo! She started to her feet. How could she have forgotten? This was the day Theo was to arrive. His telegram was in her other purse, left at the restaurant. She was sorry not to have it. To reread it. Just to reread it.

Her winter walks with Theo. The tip of his nose and his rounded cheek used to show between the brim of his hat and his turned-up coat collar. Their footsteps crunched in the snow in unison. Their breaths made little balloons of fog in the air as they talked. She had always hated the cold, and yet it was on these walks that she had begun to get well. When Theo took off his glove and held her hand to say good night at the door of her apartment, she had felt strength and warmth flow from his hand to hers. A longing—it was almost like homesickness—filled her to see him. Why not go to the station? If she missed him (it was almost noon now), it would mean she should not have gone. If he was there . . .

She hailed a taxi. An extravagance, and perhaps a wasted one, she thought, getting in. The thought calmed her. Before long, the taxi slowed down. It stopped dead. They sat. The driver swore. They heard the sound of repair work. The driver got out to investigate. A pneumatic drill, close by, danced on Rosy's skull. The driver got back in, backed up, and swung the car around in a wild curve. Horns protested on all sides.

The taxi turned down a narrow side street. In a matter of minutes they stopped again. A truck, loaded with cases of Pellegrino, blocked the way. Its driver was making deliveries to a restaurant. He carried the cases two at a time. At the rate he was going, he had half a day's work. He didn't respond to, didn't even seem to hear, the blasts from the taxi's horn. The driver leaned out the window, called the delivery man a *"deficiente,"* and asked if he was going to be allowed to pass.

The Pellegrino man put his cases down with excessive care. He folded his arms. No, he wouldn't let any *"testone"* pass.

The "fathead" jumped out of the taxi and shook his fist at the Pellegrino man, whom he now called a *"cocciuto."*

"Fifone."

"Cornuto."

The owner of the restaurant left his patrons to join the fight. The air was heavy with invective. Rosy's watch said 12:05. The meter ticked away, and her heart with it.

At the railway station, she asked for the track and raced to it. She had been directed to the train departing for Florence. By the time she found Theo's train, it was empty. The quay was deserted except for a cleaning man who was sweeping the platform with a long-handled broom. He said the train had arrived five minutes early, and made a joke about how the service was even better than it had been in Il Duce's day.

"I'm safe," Rosy said aloud.

The man nodded his head, sagely, as though he understood and agreed. He went back to his sweeping.

Rosy stood there, dully. She had not thought what to do next. There were still hours and hours to kill. The cleaning man stopped sweeping and looked at her. He said something and pointed behind her. She didn't understand. She gave him a vague smile and, turning to go, turned square into Theo.

Her feet left the ground. Her ear, a stethoscope against Theo's heart, heard it pound. His raincoat was damp and cool to her cheek.

"I was putting my bags in a taxi when I saw you get out of yours. I've been chasing you ever since," he said.

Her feet touched the ground again. They felt numb, untrustworthy. Theo put his hand under her chin and lifted her face. He looked at her lips. His eyes made them feel swollen. "Benjamin?"

"Not coming."

"You got my telegram?"

"He did."

Theo tried to read what that meant. "Let's go," he said, putting his arm around her shoulder. "You can tell me about it in the taxi."

In one of those English trench coats which are all buttons, belts, and buckles, he seemed taller than she had remembered. His hair was longer and more unruly. He ran his hand through it as if she'd commented on it.

"A violinist, would you have said?"

"More like a Shakespearean actor."

"Which would you prefer as a husband?"

The sentence made a word salad in Rosy's ear. She couldn't make sense of it, yet it frightened her.

Theo waved to his taxi driver, who was looking around apprehensively. "Where shall we go?" Theo asked Rosy. The driver turned for directions. Theo made a fanning motion with his hand and told the driver to go ahead; he'd tell him where to go in a minute. "I can't think," he said to Rosy.

"Neither can I."

"Are you hungry? Do you want a drink?"

Rosy wasn't hungry. She felt as if she'd had a drink. "A museum?" she suggested, and then immediately, "No, Rome is suddenly full of Harvard people. We'll run into someone."

"Where have you not been with Benjamin? There must be . . . What about the Palatine?"

"Let's go there."

Theo told the driver. "Now tell me everything," he said, settling back and taking her hand in his. "Did you go to Mantua? And what about Strà? And did you stay at the Fenice?"

This was the companionable Theo of their winter walks. Rosy grew calm as she talked about her trip. At the gates of the Palatine, Theo told the driver to wait. They walked up the hill, their arms linked. At first Theo took long, deep strides and Rosy short, nervous ones, but soon they found their old rhythm. The ground underneath their feet was spongy from the rain. It gave up an odor of damp leaves and moist earth. Occasionally a root in the path threw them into each other and their thighs brushed.

The threat of rain had kept people away. They were alone as they walked around Livia's house. Theo picked a poppy, which had grown up between the cracks in the floor mosaic, and gave it to Rosy.

"Was it Benjamin who took you away from Paris when I wrote that I was coming?" He led her over to a low wall, to sit down.

"My doing."

"Yet you came today. Have you thought about us?"

"I've tried not to."

"Benjamin doesn't deserve such fidelity."

Her fidelity had never been tested until now. In the past, when in anger she wished she could wound Benjamin with revengeful infidelity, or when, fleetingly, she permitted herself to think of leaving him, what held her back was that while he had ceased to be a husband except in name, he had remained—there was no word in the language to describe the kinship—her closest relative: the father who had died when she was a child; the brother she had never had; and most binding of all, the teacher who had formed her. How could she be unfaithful to or separate herself from all of them? "I suspect my fidelity is a burden to him," she said, as if she were talking to herself.

"Then why? . . . I know why. Benjamin keeps you so busy being apprehensive about him that you never have enough peace of mind to think what *you* want, what you need. I offer you a life radically different. And I'm sure

I could make you happy. I would look after you. Would you miss the excitement? I don't think so. A don's wife has an agreeable life in Cambridge. Should we want to get away, I have a bachelor flat, a small one, in London. Between terms, when I'm working, we would be here, in Italy. My work, while not as glamorous perhaps as Benjamin's, will interest you, I know it will."

Theo's voice was even and low-keyed, as if he wanted to state his case fairly, neither over- nor underplaying it. While he talked, a yellow butterfly with black markings fluttered around the wild thyme and poppies which grew around the ruin. From below came the whoosh of traffic, and the occasional *clop clop, clop clop* of a horse carriage on its way to the Colosseum.

"Religion will be a problem for both of us," he said. "At the moment I don't see the solution to yours, but I'm stubborn enough to feel sure there is one. I know a good many people at the Vatican who might help us. As for me, I'm not devout, but my parents—or rather, my mother is. It will be a blow to her to have me marry a Gentile. I can't deny that."

Rosy felt Theo's eyes on her. She could imagine their blackness and the mauve circles under them. She stared at the vibrant velvet petals of the poppy so hard a green after-image came before her eyes.

"And I would like to have a child," he said.

The butterfly alighted on a thyme blossom. Its black markings looked smeared.

Theo took hold of Rosy's chin and lifted her head, as he had at the station. "You are so unhappy," he said. "Is it because of Benjamin?"

Rosy dropped her arms. The poppy fell from her hand. "Everything."

"He's draining you dry. You have no idea what a price you're paying. Who are you? What are you—besides Benjamin's wife? You don't know because you've completely submerged your personality to his. Do you realize you're trapped?" Theo's tone was no longer dispassionate. "If you stay with Benjamin while you try to decide, you'll never get free. Never. He has no intention of letting you go. He tries to hold you by whipping up excitement about his work. When that fails, he reminds you how much he needs you, how he needs to be looked after, doesn't he?"

He stood up and lifted Rosy with him. "What about what *you* need? Come with me. Now. Today. Don't go back. You can stay in the flat I mentioned in London. I promise not to press you. You can be by yourself there to think." He was leading Rosy along the path they had come up. (How long had the taxi driver been sounding his horn?) "We'll get another ticket at the airport. You can have your things sent. When we get to London you can call Benjamin—"

A high, sustained one-note cry, plaintive as the sound of an oboe, escaped from Rosy. She threw herself against Theo as if he were a wall which would be impervious to her pain. Remembering, as his arms enfolded her, that it was he she feared, she pounded his chest with her fists. "Please, please go," she pleaded, pulling away.

He still held her. "If you won't come with me now, promise me you'll go away by yourself, to think. Will you?"

"Yes, yes," Rosy promised frantically, urging him down the hill toward the taxi driver, who'd come looking for his fare. "I promise."

"Write me. Or better, telephone. You have my number. I'll come for you whenever you say."

When the rain came down, hard and cold, Rosy sought shelter in one of the Farnese birdhouses. She felt bone tired and empty, as one feels after a protracted fever. It was clear that she must get away. She would write Benjamin a letter, asking him to think what he wanted for the future, pointing out that their marriage couldn't continue like this. Then she would go away. Her last paycheck (what better use for it?) would take her to Ponza with Erika and Paul. She would lie in the sun, away from both Benjamin and Theo, and think.

Rosy found a telephone. Erika was not in; Doris was. Good. No time to change her mind. "Doris?"

"Sweetie, where *are* you? You sound as if you're calling from Memorial Hall."

"I've decided to go to Ponza."

"I'm thrilled. Benjamin too?"

"No. He's working."

"He won't mind your leaving?"

"It's just for a few days."

"That's true. I'll tell Erika and Paul. I'm having dinner with them this evening. We go by boat from Formia at a grim hour. They're picking me up at five-thirty. And I mean *a.m.* We'll stop for you a few minutes later."

"I'll be down at the door."

Buoyed up by her decision, Rosy had forgotten to brace herself for her meeting with Benjamin. As she came into the pensione, she heard Signora Schmidt pronounce the name "Bult." She was talking to Assunta and Luigi. When Anglo-Saxons, like Il Professore, had trouble with the police, it was never serious, she was saying. Il Professore had probably been drunk, that was all, so the police had escorted him home. Assunta and Luigi were not to gossip about it. The best thing was to act as if nothing had happened. Assunta was dissatisfied with the Signora's explanation. She was for a more dramatic interpretation of the evidence. The Signora was firm.

As Rosy passed, the Signora gave her employees a model for their conduct. *"Buona sera,"* she said in a workaday voice.

Luigi and Assunta fell into line. *"Sera,"* they repeated.

Benjamin had not forgotten the Ritchies. He was dressed and waiting for her, pale and contrite. "We won't speak of last night now," he said, "with only a quarter of an hour before we go out. I can't find my extra eyeglasses. Will you help me? I know I brought them, but I can't find them."

"The footlocker," said Rosy.

"Of course! Where is it?"

"We'll have to get Signora Schmidt. It's locked in the storeroom."

"You needn't worry about her," Benjamin said, seeing Rosy hesitate. "She didn't see me. Only Luigi."

Tea at Babington's went smoothly, thanks to Benjamin. In his silver-rimmed glasses (which he hadn't worn in years and which looked too small for his face) and his seersucker jacket, the arms of which seemed to have shrunk from the rain at Tivoli, he more closely resembled the boy in his First Communion photograph than the man who had come in sobbing at dawn. With maps and guidebooks spread over two tables, he planned the Ritchies' trip north through Italy to Paris. Rosy used the time to draft in her mind the letter she would leave him.

Miss Ritchie and the wide-eyed Charlotte could not express their gratitude enough. Their only hope was that the Bolds would give them the extreme pleasure of being their guests soon in Nashville. Shaking hands in farewell, Benjamin promised the visit soon, very soon. At the moment he was convinced that nothing would be more agreeable.

The Bolds followed the disappearing Ritchies with their eyes until they were out of sight, to delay as long as possible the moment when they would be alone together. When it came, they turned to walk to the pensione.

"What can I say about last night?" Benjamin asked. "That I was insane? But that hardly needs saying. What does is that I beg forgiveness. Can you, again, give it to me?"

"We won't talk about it now," she said. "I'm going away tomorrow."

Benjamin turned his head around sharply. "Where? With whom?"

"To Ponza. With Erika and Paul."

"Of course. I forgot they were going. How long will you be away?" And then, as if he had to have an excuse for asking, "We promised to go to the Strega party."

"I'll come back that morning."

They were standing outside of Conti's. Benjamin brought the cigarette which he held deep between his fingers up to his face. His nicotine-stained fingers trembled. He took his hand away, exhaled the smoke, and squinted one eye at her. "What about a posh dinner tonight? We might have a drink at Rosati's and then go—well, wherever you like."

It took Rosy a second. "I think I'll coast on the tea," she said, "to pack and get to bed early."

"You must be tired."

"I leave at dawn. Don't get up with me."

"I won't insist. I know how you hate being seen off." He pulled her to him and held her. She felt his body tremble. He rocked her in his arms. "Can you believe I love you?" He held her off to see what she could believe. They looked at each other searchingly a moment and kissed goodbye.

ten

By the time the steamer *Nettuno* docked in Ponza harbor, the members of the Landsdales' party, the only tourists aboard, were wondering why they had left Rome. Their departure had been jaunty, despite the early hour, but the Formia fishermen to whom they had waved goodbye were barely out of sight before the sea's spray, at first playful, became rude. They were forced into the cabin. The odors of fuel oil and fish drove them out. The spray forced them in again. The odors out. Pinned between sea and sky, they had had time to ask themselves how, so recently healthy, they could now feel so ill. It had been a long and agitated crossing.

Ponza town was like a house whose invited guests arrive, through some misunderstanding, a day early. Despite feverish activity, there was nobody on hand to extend a greeting, or to take the luggage. The travelers stood blinking in the sun, swaying on sea legs.

"Five hours for a *ferry* ride." Doris was indignant. She untied the kerchief from around her head, and studied herself in the mirror of her compact. "My bangs, my beautiful bangs. Where have they gone?" she wailed.

"Blown to bits." Hector sat on a bollard, his head in his hands.

"In the planning stage a boat trip always seems so

agreeable." Paul, whose complexion had turned verdigris, was trying to sort things out. "I think they might consider putting a more substantial vessel on this run. I'm frankly relieved that we made it."

"It's no wonder Ponza is unspoiled," said Mel Kline.

"Where is the pensione, Hector?" Doris was still worrying her bangs with a comb.

"How should I know?" Hector didn't trouble to look up.

"Hector Bates! You said you knew Ponza."

"From books." Hector had been actively ill the whole way. He was in no mood to be nagged.

"I'll go scout," said Mel. "Hold this, will you?" He handed Doris the portfolio which held the music he'd brought to work on.

"Rozan, please. Sit on my suitcase," Erika said, coming to life. Rosy hesitated. "Sit, sit, sit," Erika urged Rosy down. "You are so bent over to one side, it hurts me to look at you. We must get you better, or Benjamin will be angry at us for taking you away."

Rosy sat. Now that she no longer had to battle seasickness, she was filled with misgivings about her impulsive decision to leave Rome. Doris had seemed edgy with her on the drive to Formia, fanning Rosy's suspicions about her to life again. Hector, embarrassed about what he'd said to her at the Academy party, gave her shifty glances. Above all, there was the gnawing concern about Benjamin's reaction to her letter.

"God, I'm hungry," said Paul. "I hope they'll have a meal ready for us at the pensione."

"What do I hear?" Erika was incredulous. "That's the first time you've said you were hungry since Greece. Now I remember why we came!"

Mel returned eating a tomato he'd picked up in the market. "Is this place *primitivo*!" he said, the tomato juice running down his chin. Doris blotted it with her handkerchief. "Mmmm. Thanks. The pensione is there in Santa

Maria"—he pointed—"not far, as you see. There's one taxi, but it's on the other side of the island today. We can walk or go by donkey."

"Why don't you all take our luggage on the donkeys," Paul suggested. "Roxana and I will walk."

"You won't have any trouble finding it. Take the main street until there's a fork. The beach is off to the left. You go right," Mel said. "We'll go along the quay."

Ponza's main street, on a terrace above the quay, overlooked the harbor. It was composed of eight shops, only one of which had any pretensions to having been fixed up for tourists. There was a café, empty at this hour, with a few metal chairs and tables in front of it. .

"I do hope those herbal odors I smell are seasonings for our lunch," Paul said as they approached the pensione.

They were. Signora Todi, the owner of the pensione, suggested they sit down to lunch immediately; it would give her time to make a bed for Rosy, for whom no reservation had been made. After lunch, she took them on a tour of the rooms. Paul and Erika were given what had been the main bedroom before the house had been turned into a pensione. Doris and Rosy, below them, would have the former living room, which had a grand piano and a bed on the ground floor and a second bed on a balcony half a flight up. Hector and Mel were in the *dependenza* across the court.

The little group visited from room to room, studying the views from one another's windows: from one, a slice of the harbor; from another, the hill which rose behind the town; from still another, the church bell tower. They tried the various mattresses, borrowed from one another objects they'd forgotten to bring, and swapped books, like students the first day of the new term. Since it was too late to do more with what remained of the day than unpack and take a siesta, it was agreed that they should meet in the courtyard for drinks at six.

"Ponza is thought to be ancient Aeaea," Paul said. He was making martinis with gin Hector had brought from the mainland. "The magical island Homer conjured up for Circe—remember?"

"I can't say I do," said Doris, taking the drink he offered her, "but how romantic!"

"It's been a place of banishment for political enemies since Roman days. Mussolini filched the idea from Tiberius and Caligula."

"I wouldn't mind being exiled here," said Mel.

"I wonder if you realize we're sitting on Roman mosaics." Hector pointed to the courtyard surface.

"Ponza is a *'ridente borgo,'*" Erika read from the Touring Club of Italy's *Lazio*. "There seem to be many ruins to visit . . ."

"*Ragazzi,*" Paul said, bringing them to order. "We must make a plan, who will do what and when. Tomorrow I'll stay in my room and try to do a little work."

"I want to see about renting a boat to go around the island," Mel said.

"I plan to lie like a lizard on the beach," said Rosy.

"Mel will play for us one evening. Did you try the piano?" Erika asked.

"It's not badly out of tune," said Mel. "Yes, we'll have a concert."

"Saturday let's have dinner in town," Doris said. "Signora Todi said lots of Romans come in on yachts for the weekend. It might be fun to see them."

"And Sunday, while Rozan is still with us, maybe we can hire the taxi to take us to the other side of the island, which the book says is worth seeing," said Erika.

The following morning, Mel and Erika were already getting information from Signora Todi when Doris and Rosy joined them.

"Zo, Rozan, we'll go to the beach without Hector. Poor

thing is in bed. He's afraid he is sick not from the crossing but from food poisoning."

"Chiaia di Luna is on the other side of the island," said Mel. "You two take the donkeys. If Doris and I get a boat, we'll come around and join you."

"I've never ridden a donkey." Rosy had been dreaming of an easily accessible American beach. "Is this the time to begin, do you think?"

"Look how cute they are!" Erika pointed through the courtyard to where the donkeys were waiting. "With those straw hats on their ears, don't they look like Cambridge ladies dressed for a lecture?"

"They look sweet, but how do they feel?"

"Ride sidesaddle, Roxana; it won't be too bumpy." Mel helped them to mount and gave the well-trained animals a slap on the flank to start them off.

Chiaia di Luna, through the Roman tunnel and a narrow underpass so low they had to dismount and walk bent over, was a dazzling crescent at the foot of a sheer white-faced cliff. Erika and Rosy stood taking it in. "The tunnel and then this—it's baroque, isn't it?" Erika said. They picked their way over the hot stones to the edge of the water. "Orange peels, of course, and no sand! That's the Mediterranean."

"On the other hand, there are no people. Let's go straight in," said Rosy.

They swam out, churning up the still green water— Erika well in the lead, her arms more than making up in power what she lacked in her crippled leg. The water was transparent and unusually buoyant. They turned on their backs and looked at the beach.

"*Che messa in scena!*" Erika exclaimed. The cliff rose two hundred feet to meet the sky.

"I'd like never to move again." Rosy lay with her arms outstretched, her eyes closed. "Wouldn't it be nice if one could just float and drift indefinitely?" Rosy said. "It's too bad Paul didn't come with us. Wouldn't it have done him good to have a swim?" Rosy asked.

"One has to be careful with the sun. It's bad for the liver. And he was tired from yesterday's trip." They swam to shore, spread out their towels on the stones, and sat down. "Rozan, would you believe it? I'm ready to go home?"

"To Cambridge? No. I wouldn't."

"It's true in some months I will be restless for Europe again. But we've been away a long time. I miss my work. I miss the hospital. Apropos hospital . . . Rozan, do I dare ask . . ."

Rosy, who'd been making designs in the sand, looked up.

". . . Your letter was full of Benjamin's poem. Not a word about your operation. You had it?"

Rosy nodded.

"And?"

Rosy looked out at a passing boat. "It was a mistake."

"How's that possible? A mistake? Gilford is first rate." Erika was shocked.

"Technically it went well. It was pointless, that's all. Gilford thought he should do it, to remove a shadow of a doubt—"

"That the trouble was with you? And now he thinks it was not."

Rosy held a small round stone the size of a marble in her crooked forefinger. She shot it with her thumb. "Benjamin began work on the poem almost as soon as I got back from the hospital. It was a nightmare period. It went on and on."

"And you mean he has been in a bad shape ever since?"

Rosy didn't answer.

"Zo. He doesn't want a child."

"I thought at first his beginning the poem just then was a coincidence. Now . . ."

It wasn't until the war was over that she had become importunate. When the sleepy, monastic life of Cambridge was shattered by the noise of the returning veterans—men now, with wives and babies—to talk of cannon fodder (which had been Benjamin's way of dismissing the question of having a child) when they who had fought seemed not only willing but impatient to risk producing it seemed inappropriate and out of date. They met the Landsdales and the Happy Extroverts, who were "breeding like rabbits," as Benjamin had said with distaste. She had given Benjamin all sorts of absurd promises it would have been impossible to keep: it would not change their lives; he would not have a rival (how had she thought to arrange that? Oh yes, it would have had to be a girl); she would continue to work, so they could manage financially. In the end Benjamin had agreed. Or so she'd thought. His objections, concealed, gone underground, became as disruptive to their marriage as moles to a lawn. When he heard he wouldn't be reappointed, he decided to live by writing. They needed her job more than ever. Slowly he began to reverse day and night (with no classes to meet that was easily arranged), working while she slept, sleeping while she worked. The depressions and periods of nervous exhaustion which he hadn't had since their marriage came back so severely he began seeing a psychiatrist.

". . . Now I think he doesn't want another area of vulnerability in his life," Rosy said.

Erika was silent. "Perhaps when he's older, when he's better established."

Rosy shot another stone, making the one it hit jump. "I too will be older."

"It's true." Erika said, taking it in. "But you have time yet. And one never knows. Maybe it's for the best this way."

"That's what Dr. Gilford said. I had a dream about him when we first arrived in Rome."

Erika drew her head back and smiled, showing her teeth, as she did when she listened to a piece of gossip. "Zo, you had a flirt with Gilford? All women fall in love with their gynecologists."

"I dreamt he was dead."

Erika's smile faded. She started to say something, thought better of it, and said, "Why wouldn't we go for another swim?"

They dived in and out of the shallow water to cool off. Then Rosy went to the beach to get her hat—a gondolier's hat of beige straw, trimmed with a blue ribbon, which she had bought in Venice. She put it on and came to sit in the water on the sandy bottom opposite Erika, who said, "I was in love once with a novelist, a very known one in Germany. What a man he was! So ego-selfish, so unstable!" Erika said almost with admiration.

"What happened?"

"I was eighteen. He was fifty. My father sent me to Switzerland. I threatened suicide. In six months I was in love with another man. You know, Rozan, with artists it's always difficult. One has to make allowances for them. And yet, have you noticed how women are attracted to them?"

"Mmmm."

"No, I mean even if they're not so attractive as Benjamin. My novelist, he was so ugly. You wouldn't believe how ugly. And he wore . . ." Erika searched for the word she wanted in English. As often when she couldn't find it, she gave it in French, not German. "He wore *pantoufles*! At eighteen I would have made such fun of any other man who did that. What *is* it with them? Women always think they'll understand them so well."

"Wait till you read Benjamin's new poem. He told you the other day that it was about a woman. What's interesting is that it's about a woman who thinks she's barren, but finally conceives. The child is born in the poem. Benjamin acted as if *he* were having a child."

"No!"

"I went to the hospital for the operation, and he had the baby. He even talks about the postpartum psychosis he went through afterwards."

"Now, that's bizarre. What a strange man Benjamin is! And so changeable! One minute he's a darling, then next minute he's a devil. Isn't it so? You know how fond of him we are. It's for that that we worry so about—you don't mind if I say this?—about his drinking. It's so bad for him. Can't you make him stop?"

"How? You must see how little one can make Benjamin do anything he doesn't want to do. Not that I haven't tried, foolishly."

"Is he an alcoholic?"

Rosy raised her shoulders and dropped them in a gesture of impatience.

"I'm sorry," said Erika.

"I don't mind your asking. It's just that it's so complicated. What *isn't* Benjamin? He's so many different things. Poets have always gone in for excesses. Byron and Shelley drank brandy and took laudanum. For Benjamin's generation it's gin. His excuse for drinking at first was that he needed it to help him when he was with people."

"To pick him up?"

"To calm him down after the excitement of writing. Writing, writing, writing." Rosy splashed her hand in the water with irritability and stood up. "That's all he cares about."

"No, there you exaggerate," said Erika, following her out of the water. "He loves you. And he cares enormously for his friends. And for his students—when he had them."

"I don't mean he lacks feeling for people, or can't be interested in them, even passionately so. But writing is the only passion that isn't transitory. Everyone to whom Benjamin is close must sooner or later serve it."

"But the drinking . . ." Erika tried to bring Rosy back

to her concern when they were lying on the beach again.

"Yes, that's all part of what I'm saying. First the need was superficial, playing a role. Now it's real enough. It's one of the prices he pays for his ambition."

"He is very ambitious? He would like the Nobel Prize one day?"

"I think he'd accept it." Rosy laughed. "Not, mind you, that he'd do anything to get the prizes, anything politic. He wants them for the poetry alone—as a long-overdue payment for the years of obscurity. His private ambition is what takes it out of him. When he began to see clearly what he needed in order to write as he wanted to, he also took in that he would have to pay a heavy price. He pays it in anxiety."

"Yes, one sees, one even feels his *Angst* sometimes."

"The trick is to write as he does and not go mad."

"And if he fails?"

"Benjamin courts, even collaborates with disaster. He has a very limited tolerance for happiness. I sometimes think that if he felt he wasn't paying a high enough price for his gift he would get panicky, afraid that his talent might dry up. So he keeps the turbulence going all the time."

"Is it worth it?"

"He has no choice."

"He has the luck to have married someone like you, Rozan, who understands so well."

"Is that lucky? Benjamin once said that what he needed was a mud hut of a wife, someone who wouldn't budge when the hurricanes blew, someone who couldn't be picked up and spun around by his tornadoes. I've become a lean-to, trembling at every breeze." Rosy stood up.

"You're still standing." Erika put her hands on Rosy's shoulders, to straighten them.

"Only just."

eleven

Chiaia di Luna was deserted the next day. The sea was as dead as glass. There was no movement in the air. Rosy lay on her beach towel. The sun or the hot stones burned into her back as she turned from side to side. She tried to keep her mind a blank, or to think only of the sun, the stones, the heat—her cure—as she sank deeper and deeper into a torpor more restful and agreeable than sleep because it was conscious. From time to time her donkey made a nasal "Keekaw, keekaw," and the sea gulls, high on the cliff, called, "Cau, cau."

When the heat became intolerable, she put on sandals to walk to the water's edge and lowered herself into the cool green sea cautiously, as if to avoid fracturing the glass. In a dead man's float she opened her eyes. Tiny particles of white sand made a unified and unblemished background for the electric-blue fish which swam by. They were in a great hurry. Their darting about seemed frantic, aimless. She was not in a hurry. She had the whole day. Treading water, she made gentle circles with her hands as she looked up at the white cliffs, the gliding sea gulls and the almost brutal cloudlessness of the July sky.

At noon, hungry, she took out the lunch the pensione cook had prepared for her: coarse Ponza bread cut in a generous wedge, a piece of goat cheese, a tomato, and an orange. She ate them slowly, savoring each bite, each texture distinct, each flavor discrete. Afterwards she put on her straw hat and rested on her elbows to watch the passing fishing boats. Her eyelids began to droop with drowsiness. She rolled herself in her towel, pulled the hat over her eyes, and, hypnotized by the sun filtering through the straw, fell asleep.

She awoke with an aching sense of loss. In a dream, they had been dancing, she and Theo, in an enormous empty room. There were no other couples. It was not clear where the music was coming from. Perhaps there was no music. They pivoted around, faster and faster, keeping a precarious balance, excited, laughing, their heads thrown back, their mouths open. A wind, hot and mechanical as if made by a machine, began to blow. They felt themselves being pulled apart, sucked separate by air currents. Their arms were still extended but empty. They no longer touched each other. Each effort they made against the wind caused them to lose ground. With their eyes they held each other as long as they could. Theo was sucked into the corner of the room and disappeared. She was alone, shivering. It had turned cold.

There was no sun coming through her hat now. She lay still, waiting for the ache to let up, trying to recapture the mood of the morning.

"A penny for your thoughts."

Rosy looked up.

Hector was standing there. At home, dressed in a gray flannel suit and a hat which hid what he called his "high forehead," he often passed for an undergraduate. In a terry-cloth robe and hatless, he looked older than his thirty-five years. "What happened to the sun?" she asked.

"Gone. It's behind the cliffs now. Erika was beginning to worry. She sent me to look for you. I hope I'm not intruding."

"I must have slept. I'm wide awake now."

"What a beach! I'm glad I didn't know what I was missing on my bed of pain yesterday," said Hector.

"All better?"

"Completely. Glad you came?"

"Very."

"Roxana, about the cocktail party. I'm sorry I said—"

"We were all high. I don't remember any better what you said than you do."

"Did anyone ever tell you you were a peach?"

"As a matter of fact, someone did. A beau of mine once made up a poem about my uncle calling him a lemon. And there was a niece/peach rhyme in it somewhere."

"So I'm not even original. Was it always poets who attracted you?"

"He was hardly a poet. No, his charm was that he was six feet two and the best dancer around that season."

"I'm six feet two and not bad on the dance floor either. He put his hand on her arm and dropped his bantering tone. "Give me a chance, will you, Roxana?"

Disconcerted, Rosy began to collect her things. "It's tonight Mel's going to play for us after dinner, isn't it? Shouldn't we start back?"

"That's what girls always say to me. No, I don't think we should start back." Hector was on the edge of a sulk. "But we will."

After Mel's concert and after a nightcap, Doris and Rosy straightened their room. They draped the fringed shawl over the piano again, emptied ashtrays, rinsed out glasses, and went to bed.

It was a hot night. Mosquitoes buzzed in the air. Two men on their way home from town argued incomprehensibly as they passed under their windows. The orchestra across the harbor played "Lili Marlene" as though it were a Neapolitan song, thumping it out.

"Ro?" Doris called down from her bed on the balcony.

"Hm?"

"You asleep? Can I talk to you? I hoped it would go away . . . that it wouldn't come to this. . . . Are you listening?"

The suspicion of the white night: was this going to be a confession? "I'm listening."

"I'm miserable, Ro. I need your help. It's about . . . well, it's about . . . Mel," she brought out.

"Mel?" The gun pointed at Rosy's heart hadn't gone off. Hadn't even been a gun.

"Yes, Mel. You sound surprised. I know he's young. . . . You didn't guess?"

"No, I must say I didn't."

"Remember I said I'd have an affair to spite Richard if I could find someone to have it with?"

Rosy remembered clearly.

"Well I've found him. Damn Richard. It's his fault. He shouldn't have let me leave. His so-glad-you're-having-a-good-time letters! I want him to be *sick* that I'm having a good time, sick the way I was before you and the Landsdales showed up. It all happened that day at Tivoli. Remember?"

Rosy had no trouble remembering that either.

"Mel took me dancing that night. And the night of the cocktail party we slipped off together after dinner . . . You listening?"

Doris damp with wine? "Carefully."

"Well, to be blunt about it, Mel wants me to go to bed with him."

Rosy could now concentrate her attention on Doris's problem. "And you?"

"I don't know. Mel is here. He's an angel. Ponza is beautiful. I'm fed up with Richard and his stupid wife. What am I to do?"

Across the harbor the crooner groaned, *"Anima e cuore."*

"How often do you write Richard?"

"Every day. Why?"

"Don't write."

"At *all*?"

"Not a word."

"For how long?"

"Give it two weeks."

"Two weeks! It will be agony." Doris struggled with herself. "O.K. It's worth a try. I've done everything else." Silence. "Ro?"

"Yes?"

"One more thing. Come with us tomorrow, will you? I'd rather not be alone with Mel." Doris yawned. "I'm *so* relieved. I've been out of my mind with nervousness. You sleepy?" Doris was already half asleep. "Night, sweetie."

The dream Rosy had had on the beach leaped up at her like a dog that had been deserted and locked in all day, demanding attention, clamoring to be let out. She reran it, trying to control the dance, to keep it going, to keep herself spinning with Theo. But the air currents pulled them apart —their bodies, then their arms, until their fingertips were grasping at the air. They held each other with their eyes. Then, the current grew stronger. It sucked Theo away. She was alone again, with the aching sense of loss.

Doris was up and dressed for the boat trip when the maid came with the breakfast the next morning. "I think I'll go tell Mel I asked you to come with us," she said to Rosy.

"Why not get him to ask Hector too, so I won't appear too transparently a chaperone."

"Mel looked bruised," Doris said when she came back, "but better now than . . . He knows about Richard, of course, but I don't think he took in *how* important he is. I must say I can't wait to not write Richard. What do you think he'll do?"

"It's hard to say. He'll delay as long as he can, probably, and then write you as if you've just been too busy to write him. When he becomes alarmed, he may cable."

"What will the cable say?" Doris asked as if Rosy were a clairvoyant.

"Ah, you must wait and see." Rosy teased.

Weighed down with virtue and impatience, Doris gave a theatrical sigh.

The boat was waiting for them at the Santa Maria beach. Stefano, proud of his outboard and suspicious of Mel's talent with it, instructed him in its working. He told him of the danger of rocks along the coastline, and warned him to watch the wind which could blow up without warning and make the sea as turbulent as it had been the day of their arrival.

After a few abortive attempts to get the motor going, they waved back at the uneasy Stefano, who continued to shout instructions and prohibitions. Mel turned the boat in close to land when he was safely out of sight, so that Doris and Rosy could look for beaches while Hector, at the bow, watched the shallow water for rocks.

The coastline was a series of sculptural fantasies—arches, boulders, and grottoes of black volcanic rock, whose sizes, shapes, and density were infinitely varied. What looked like attractive beaches, however, invariably turned out on closer inspection to be beds of seaweed, or anemone-covered rocks. Mel shouted that they might have to swim from the boat. Doris and Rosy shook their heads: they wanted a beach. They sloshed suntan lotion all over themselves as the sun rose overhead, and put on hats against the heat and the glare. As they rounded the tip of the island, Hector signaled to Mel to cut the motor. They saw their beach.

Beneath a cliff of limestone and streaked lava was a stony cove, the water a limpid aquamarine.

"This is it, don't you think?" said Hector.

"No question," said Mel. He rowed between *faraglioni* into the cove. "I'm glad the famous wind isn't blowing. We'd never get in here without scraping against the rocks."

When they could see the bottom, Hector jumped out and guided them in. Doris and Rosy collected the baskets of lunch and bathing gear. "Give the wine here. I'll bury it in the stones underwater. By the time we're ready for lunch it will be cool," Hector said.

"There's a cave back here," Doris called. "No one-eyed monster, but there *is* a boat. I do hope the owner doesn't come back." They left the lunch in the damp coolness of the cave and went immediately for a swim.

"I wonder if the water here isn't more beautiful than at Chiaia di Luna," Rosy said. She was gathering cupfuls in her hands, spilling it down her sunburned face.

"It's the white and yellow rocks just under the water that give it that incredible color," said Mel.

Hector came back from burying the wine saying they must take turns borrowing his snorkel. "I've never seen such fish. Schools of silver-gray ones, pursued by something I couldn't see, and hundreds of brilliant blue-and-gold ones. There are underwater islands of grass and then patches of carefully waved white sand. Just lie in a float," he said, putting the mask on Rosy. "The only thing to beware of is the anemones, but the water is so clear you can't miss them. Just don't put your feet down."

They took turns exploring and swimming until it was time for lunch. "Do you realize how boring most beaches are?" Hector asked as he poured the Ischian wine. "There's nothing to see but the sea, whereas here we have the tips of the cove in the foreground, the *faraglioni* in the middle ground, and Palmarola in the distance. What makes this beach so attractive, of course"—he got up to gesture with the chicken leg he was chewing on—"is the sulphur yellow running down the limestone . . ."

"And the butterflies," said Rosy.

"And that delicious fragrant herb growing out of the limestone. Wonder what it is?" said Doris.

149

"What goes on on Palmarola?" Mel wondered.

"Much less than on Ponza I imagine, because the state never used it for prisoners. If we were here for a couple of weeks it would be fun to investigate it."

"I'm ready for a siesta," said Doris, yawning. "I was so thirsty I drank too much wine."

"Siesta? You're mad. We have hours of exploring ahead. Come. On your feet." Hector came to give Doris a hand.

"No. Why don't you two go? Ro and I will stay and do the dishes."

"Roxana?"

"I'm afraid I've had all the sun I can take."

The two women moved up under the shadow of the cliff to take a nap. The sound of the outboard motor had not long faded before Rosy, dozing, heard the by now familiar "Ro? You asleep?" of her roommate. "Mel's sweet, isn't he? But he is a *tiny* bit young for me." Doris seemed pleased to have found a concrete reason for being virtuous. "How old would you guess?"

"He was in the war, but maybe only just. Twenty-six or so?"

Doris took out her compact and studied her worried image. "You see what's happening to me, don't you, Ro? I'm becoming an older woman. There are no men left around, just boys. It's too *triste*." Doris gave a *triste* little sigh and rested her chin on her fists. "How did you get Benjamin to marry you?"

"I didn't, actually."

"You mean he simply fell into your trap?"

"If it was a trap we fell into it together. Neither of us wanted to marry."

"You *didn't?*" Doris sat up with disbelief. "Weren't you in love?"

"Desperately. We'd known each other a year. After a summer together we hated to be separated, and neither of us earned enough to make the trip between Boston and New York possible more than once a month."

"Why did you wait?"

"Marriage was such a serious step for both of us. Benjamin wasn't sure he should marry, and I worried—"

"Oh, Ro, you *are* a worrier. Did he propose in verse?"

"No, in a railway station, halfway between Boston and New York."

"Oh, I get it, symbolic. Doesn't it seem silly that you worried, now that it worked out so well?" Doris was intent on a happy ending. "Benjamin is difficult, of course—we all see that—but he's quite marvelous too. Remember that poem he wrote me—'a roofer' he called it—after the weekend you spent at Pride's Crossing? I was *thrilled*." Doris sang a grace note on the word. "You're probably blasé about having poems written to you, but that's the first and probably the last one I'll ever have." Doris turned over on her back and folded her hands under her head. "Ro? What's it really like being married to a poet?"

"Really like?"

"I mean in comparison with being a professor's wife, say, or a lawyer's."

"I don't know. It's probably more like being married to an explorer. In between voyages an explorer's life is not so different from a professor's. There's a long period of study and preparation which his wife is likely to hear about step by step, and maybe even help with. She enjoys this time and wishes that it could go on, that her husband didn't have to go wherever it is—to the top of Everest, or to the bottom of the Red Sea. There's no question of his not going. She gets detailed accounts of the trip in the beginning and can't help catching the excitement of it. At the crucial moment, when all his forces are engaged, there's likely to be a total breakdown in communication. She can do nothing but sit it out, and pray that he'll come back safely, whole. If he does, there's the thrill of success and the adulation, which she shares. After a period of letdown and restlessness, which he's bound to feel with ordinary life, he settles down. If she's lucky. Until the next time."

"I wouldn't like it," said Doris promptly. "I used to envy you, Ro, and wish I could be married to someone creative, but I know it's not for me. I'm too selfish. I don't want to live in a hovel—not that Prescott Street is a hovel, but you know what I mean: bookcases made out of bricks and boards, bits and pieces of hand-me-down furniture, on a shoe-string. Of course, you have other gratifications. There's always so much excitement in your life. And then, Benjamin *adores* you."

That evening, on the way into town for dinner, Hector said to those who hadn't been on the outing, "We found a Roman bath—a pool, almost intact, with mossy steps leading down into it."

"That must have been the Grotta di Pilato, the sacred eel pool," said Paul.

"Eel pool!" Doris and Rosy chorused.

"There aren't any eels now, I'm sure. The Romans bred moray eels for divination," said Paul.

"Look, look. Ponza has been discovered," said Erika.

The population of the town had doubled overnight. The main street and the café were crowded with Romans over for the weekend.

"I'll join you at the table," said Rosy. "I must send Benjamin a telegram about when I'm getting in."

Coming out of the stationery store, Rosy collided with a man who looked like Tullio, but who was dressed all in white. It *was* Tullio. He smiled his rectangular smile at the tall blond girl he had on his arm. Was it this girl who had so preoccupied him that day at Roccafalcone when he made little mounds of bread crumbs at the table?

"What's up, Roxana? Seen a ghost?" Hector stood up and pulled out a chair for her.

"Just dazed from the problems of sending a telegram. I have no confidence that it will go off."

"Why not stay a little longer?" Hector said.

"You could call Benjamin," Paul suggested.

"No, we mustn't urge Rozan. Benjamin will be cross with us," Erika said.

The service was slow and the pasta tepid at the café restaurant, but they had a view of the harbor, and felt part of the weekend excitement. After dinner, they walked up the hill to the outdoor nightclub. Fashionable Romans who'd come in on yachts were sitting around languidly, smoking and gossiping. Tullio, deep in a corner with the blond girl, had his back to them.

"There's the Principessa Gozzi," said Doris, trying and failing to whisper. "You've seen her photograph a thousand times in *Vogue*. Don't they make you want to throw all your clothes away and get new ones? And then spend a day at Elizabeth Arden?"

"Not a bad combo," said Hector. "Come on, Roxana, let's dance." On the floor he said, "We don't dance enough in Cambridge. Next fall, let's do it more regularly. We don't have to wait for a big party at Paul and Erika's. There's plenty of room in my apartment. I've got lots of records from my dissolute undergraduate days. . . ."

"Mind if I sit?"

"I'm boring you," Hector said, sulkily.

"No, it's just—"

"Your back? Erika said it's been giving you trouble."

"It's better. I don't want to push my luck."

On the walk back to the pensione, the voice of the crooner followed them:

Quando sorge la luna a Marechiare,
Persino i pesci tremano d'amore.

"What's he saying, Mel?" Doris asked.

"He's saying that when the moon rises even the fish make love."

"Oh, dear. I suppose they do."

Sunday Mel played the organ at the mass Rosy went to. During the long and passionate sermon Father Rinaldi preached to the wives of the fishermen, Rosy gave up trying not to think about Benjamin. It seemed to her she had been away a long time.

In the afternoon Stefano appeared with his old touring car, the top down, and took them on a tour of the island. Since Rosy was leaving early in the morning, she said good-bye to her friends after dinner. Paul kissed her and told her to take care of herself. She and Erika made a date for lunch in Rome.

"Hector disappeared because he didn't want to say good-bye," Doris said, while Rosy packed. "He probably feels you're breaking up the party, so he's sulking. I think maybe he has a *tiny-tiny* crush on you." Doris sighed. "I wish you weren't going. I'll miss you."

"My protection?"

"Partly. But it's been so cozy here. We've seen more of each other in Ponza than we would in a semester in Cambridge."

There was a discreet rap at the door the next morning soon after Rosy's alarm went off.

"Hector. What are you doing up?" Rosy whispered. "It's five o'clock."

"I'm hungry, so I thought I might as well walk you to the boat. I can carry your bag."

"You shouldn't have gotten up, Hector. I'm not very good at being seen off. I get jittery."

"Calm down, and hand me your suitcase. You shouldn't lift it."

They walked past the church and the Santa Maria beach through the tunnel into town.

"How long will you stay in Rome?" Hector asked.

"I don't know. We're supposed to go to England sometime, but Benjamin hasn't decided when."

They sat in the deserted café, the chairs still stacked on the tables, and drank coffee left over from the previous evening. "The espresso machine isn't working, so I said we'd take this," said Hector, "It's not bad with milk. It's a long time till Formia, so eat heartily."

"What about you? What are your plans?" asked Rosy.

"I've work to do in Siena for Paul in August, and then some friends to visit in Genoa, so I'll sail from there. Is that all you're going to eat?"

"I think I'd better go."

"You've got ten minutes."

"I told you I was a nervous traveler."

"Come on, then." Hector put Rosy on board and asked one of the sailors to take her suitcase off for her in Formia. "I hope you have a better crossing this time," he said.

"Erika gave me a Dramamine to take."

"Have you something to read?"

"Paul gave me the carbon of the chapter Erika typed yesterday." Rosy gave Hector a peck on the cheek. "You're a dear for getting up at this hour." She stood at the rail. Hector turned once to wave. "See you in Rome," she called.

It was a smooth crossing. Nevertheless, Rosy found she couldn't read. Her thoughts went back to the morning when she had tiptoed around the pensione room, dressing to leave for Ponza. She had put the letter on Benjamin's night table where he couldn't miss it. She had kissed the part of his cheek that was not covered by the sheet, and had turned the door-knob carefully to let herself out. Had he heard her alarm? And followed her movements around the room? He might have waited for her to be safely away and then, feeling in his bedroom slippers for his eyeglasses, put them on to see what she had put on the table. He would have picked up the letter, felt it, put it down again, suspicion covering him like a rash. No, he would not read it! He had lost one day on his proofs (never mind whose fault) and couldn't risk another. Whatever the letter had to say could wait. After the proofs were corrected and in the mail? Rosy's stomach rolled. This time the sea was not to blame.

At Formia there was just time for a sandwich. In the hot, crowded train she sat, knee to knee, with a pair of lovers. The man had his arm around the girl's shoulder. He whispered to her and bit the lobe of her ear. The girl smiled at their secret.

Rosy's impatience to see Benjamin became intractable. Would he meet the train? She hadn't asked him to, and ordinarily she preferred not to be met, but if he was there it would be a good sign. If not? Well, if not, it might mean that he hadn't had her telegram. Or that he was waiting for her at the pensione, restlessly pacing the room, smoking, no better able to read than she was.

It seemed like weeks since she had seen him. But then, she was the one who had gone away. For Benjamin, in Rome, it might have been barely time to take in what she had written.

twelve

The room was as dark as it had been the morning Rosy had left. Benjamin was asleep. It was as though she had never been away. She put down her suitcase and looked around in dismay at the disorder. Benjamin's clothes were everywhere. The stale odor of cigarettes filled the room. Had Assunta stopped coming altogether?

"Roxana, darling! Oh, no, *no!*" Benjamin cried as if in pain. "You're not here already? The bloody alarm didn't go off. Or I didn't hear it. And I was going to meet you. Come here. Let me kiss you."

Rosy went over and sat on the edge of Benjamin's bed.

"What unholy hour is it?" he asked.

"Noon."

"Eeeeee!" Benjamin swung his legs out of bed. "I have hours of work before I go."

Rosy went to the window and opened the shutters. It gave her something to do. "Go?"

"I'm taking the six o'clock for Paris. Tonight." Benjamin was looking for his glasses. "I'm wild to get out of Rome."

Rosy sat down on her bed, facing Benjamin's back, waiting.

"How about you?" he asked.

"How do you mean?" Rosy's stomach rolled as if she were still on the boat.

"Of course. You don't know yet. Here's the plot. Andrew has rescued us. Asked us to London for the weekend. Their top-floor flat is free—they're trying to rent it—so we can stay there until Monday. After that, they'll find us a place nearby over a pub where we can get bed and breakfast. 'Bed and breakfast,' do you hear?" Benjamin danced over to Rosy. He stopped when he saw her expression. "What's up? Aren't you pleased?"

Rosy looked up at his seemingly innocent eyes. She would not speak of her letter first. "I'm trying to take it in," she said.

"Well, hurry and take it in. And give me a hand. There's work to be done. I take the luggage on the night train. I decided you shouldn't sit up all night—How is your back, by the way?—so I bought you a plane ticket. We'll meet in Paris tomorrow night, stay the night, and go to London the next day. You're worrying about missing the Strega, is that it?"

Rosy had forgotten about the party.

"I've done all that. I talked to Tullio before he went off somewhere. . . ."

"To Ponza."

"No! You saw him?"

"With a big blonde."

"*Tiens*! Old Tullio leads quite a complicated life, then," Benjamin said with admiration. "Rodney we'll see in London. They go home on leave soon. You can call them to say goodbye after I leave." Benjamin was dressed. "I'll write letters if you'll pack for me. See if you can find Assunta and get my laundry. That one! She made up a new song:

> *Non c'è male*
> *Ma non è per me*

Benjamin sang in falsetto. "Isn't that cheeky? She meant *me!*"

Benjamin spent the afternoon in a fever of typing. He answered all the letters which had accumulated since they'd been in Europe. Change, almost any change, gave him a temporary feeling of euphoria. He read the manuscripts sent him by former students and admirers, and wrote long careful letters of criticism and encouragement. To Iphigene, he wrote a detailed account of their stay in Rome. He felt, as he told Rosy when she came back with a sandwich for his lunch, hopeful. Looking ahead to London was like looking to the year ahead on his birthday or New Year's Eve. What was ahead always looked better to him than that which was just behind. The old year was always "a bitch" of a year, well to have done with and out of the way. The old place—Cambridge, New York, and now Rome—was used up like the daily newspaper, which, except for literary purposes, could be left behind without nostalgia. He looked ahead.

Rosy, thought to be optimistic by nature, took the contrary view. She always remembered the past as having been happier than it had been, and looked forward to the future with apprehension. When she left a place, she left feeling as if she were leaving part of herself behind.

For the most part, the history of their marriage had confirmed Rosy's and not Benjamin's view. But having no immunity to Benjamin's moods, good or bad, and interpreting his silence about her letter as a good sign (he was thinking seriously about their future), she packed the footlocker and the suitcases cheerfully.

The letters finished, Benjamin took them to the post office. He paid the bill, shook hands with Signora Schmidt, and tipped Assunta, who looked, he said, as if she might nudge him in the ribs with her broom handle.

He and Rosy took a taxi to the Stazione Termini. In the evening light the station had the cinematic, romantic air

European stations have for Americans. The atmosphere was mauve, and hazy with puffs of steam rising from the tracks. Vacations were beginning. The quay was crowded with travelers and porters carrying luggage. They dodged the wagons loaded with wine, panettone, chocolate, brandy, coffee, and unwrapped, aromatic salami sandwiches.

By the time they had found the third-class compartment and installed Benjamin's belongings, he was as excited as a provincial going to the metropolis for the first time. "It won't be bad," he said, striding up and down the platform. "I have my Dante here." He patted his pocket. "And I may even sleep. Having written those letters, my conscience is as clean as a baby's. What a relief! Why don't I write them more often?" They separated to let a cart of trunks go by. "Do you know how long it is since I've seen England?" he asked, as he took Rosy's hand again without breaking his stride. "Sixteen years! If anyone had told me when I went down from Cambridge that it would be that long . . . ! Not, mind you, that I wasn't wild to get away. God, what a mess I was in! My book bills were grotesque. My tailor was howling. Phoebe and I quarreled constantly. . . ."

They'd quarreled constantly, had they? This was news. Phoebe, his first love, the girl he'd almost married. Of the women he had known, only Phoebe had made Rosy deeply jealous. The others were names in a catalogue: once listed they were forgotten. Not so Phoebe. Unquestionably Benjamin had loved her. In the myth he had created about her she was the paragon of all the virtues a poet could look for in a wife. Until this moment he had always given Rosy to believe that their relationship had been idyllic.

"I loathed my tutor, passionately." Benjamin laughed as if that sort of thing were all well in the past.

"That's your train they're calling." Rosy turned Benjamin back to his compartment.

"You remember where we're to meet?" he asked.

"La Coupole. Six o'clock."

"If I'm not there, don't worry. It means the train has been delayed. Take a book with you. Order yourself a drink."

Benjamin pulled Rosy toward him and kissed her. He took the steps of his car in one upward leap. He disappeared and then reappeared at the window of his compartment. "You have your ticket?"

Rosy nodded.

"And the money?"

She nodded again.

The train lurched. It began to move slowly. Benjamin did a Chaplinesque jig and blew a kiss. As the train picked up speed, he leaned farther and farther out of the window, blowing kisses with both hands.

Rosy stopped laughing and called, "Pull your head in, idiot."

Benjamin didn't hear. The kisses were now caught by the small audience which had gathered around Rosy. "They think . . ."—the wind held Benjamin's words an instant before releasing them—". . . that I'm your loooooover."

thirteen

Benjamin's euphoria held through the all-night train trip from Rome (an *instituteur* from a Neuilly lycée with a portable chess set, and a flask of brandy bought at a station en route proved agreeable companions), and even the intervening day in Paris. By the time the couple had boarded the boat at Calais, it had given way to a series of shallow highs and lows, like the movement of the ship through the rising and falling Channel swells.

"I wonder if the Mallorys really want us." Benjamin addressed his doubt to the sea rather than to Rosy, who stood beside him on deck.

This was not the remark for which Rosy had been bracing herself. During the silent trough which had immediately preceded it, she had suspected, watching the way her husband's jaw ground the stem of his pipe, that he must be framing an answer to her letter. Her mood, a mirror image of Benjamin's, had followed his rapid dips and lifts as a good dancer follows a familiar but unpredictable partner, until this moment. Instead of dipping, she lurched. Had Benjamin, in his eagerness to get out of Rome, simply invented Andrew's letter?

"Didn't they invite us?" she asked with alarm.

"Andrew did. I have his letter here." Benjamin, reading her thoughts, tapped his breast pocket. "Still . . ."

"Still what?"

"We don't know Imgard. She may take a dim view of having us."

"Surely they would have discussed it," Rosy said without conviction. From what she'd learned of Andrew during the crossing from New York, she knew him to be an impulsive man: he was quite capable of responding to some hint in Benjamin's letter without consulting his wife.

"The English are different, you know. Andrew's 'Do come for the weekend' might have been disingenuous."

Rosy turned her back on the sea. It had all been arranged too hastily. She should have written Imgard, to be sure. Nevertheless, it was dangerous to agree with Benjamin when he threatened to get worked up. He might suggest they bolt back to Calais. Or even Rome. "Have you noticed," she said, "that all the other passengers on board are either children or nannies?"

Benjamin looked around, mildly interested. "Curious. So they are. That could make the beginning of a play." He dragged on a dead pipe. "A very bad one." He hit the bowl of the pipe on the rail. "I don't know whether it's the threat of siblings that's done it, but I find I've a sharp appetite. Shouldn't we go in for tea before the little bastards get their sticky fingers on everything?"

"Weak tea, thick mugs, soggy sandwiches," Rosy said, as these were assembled in front of her by a waitress. "I feel as if I were back at boarding school after the holiday. Whatever happend to summer?"

"Poor Roxana. You're missing the sun, aren't you?" Benjamin was eating like a schoolboy. "The marmalade cake, please. Never mind, you'll love London, you'll see. And I dare say you'll find the Mallorys' not a bit like school."

Rosy, who was not eating, said, "*If* Imgard lets us in."

Benjamin seemed not to have heard. He stirred his tea vigorously, as if it were in some way resisting him. "I suppose we'll see Phoebe while we're in London."

Rosy's heart tripped. Yes, of course, Benjamin would want to see Phoebe. Phoebe, to whom he'd dedicated his first book. Phoebe, the subject of their first quarrel, the woman who had taught her what jealousy was. Phoebe, who had never married and was said never to have got over Benjamin.

And there was Theo. She must write him as soon as they got to the Mallorys'.

By the time they were in a taxi crossing London, reasons for apprehension had sprung up around them like mushrooms in the forest.

"What actually do we know about Imgard?" Benjamin reviewed for the examination they were about to take.

Rosy pressed back against the brown leather upholstery of the taxi for warmth and comfort. "Nothing," she said uncooperatively.

"Not true. Come, we must marshal our facts. *Primo,* she's half Danish. *Secundo,* she was an actress." Benjamin bent back the fingers of his left hand with his right, ticking off the facts—his imitation of a pedantic schoolmaster. "*Tertio,* something went wrong with her career, for which she blames the war. And perhaps Andrew? . . .

"They have a child, don't they?"

"There! You see? You knew more than you thought you did. Tonkey—what a ridiculous name to give a girl!"

"How old?"

"Hmm. Eleven? Twelve? A wildly unattractive age. Pray her boarding school hasn't let out yet."

The taxi made a sharp turn, drove into a crescent of Regency town houses, and stopped. Rosy felt a pang of regret: self-absorbed, she hadn't once looked out at London on the way.

A Junoesque woman in a loose-fitting, flowered peignoir opened the door. Her copper-colored hair was dressed *à la grecque.* A thin pink line crossed her brow where the edge of a hair net had been burned into her pale skin by a hair dryer.

"Ben, thank God you're not late," she said familiarly, as if they were old friends. "Andrew, the wretch, is. Caterinaaaa," she sang up the stairwell. "*Ecco i signori.* We won't have a minute together before the party," she went on to the Bolds. "We're having our big do of the year tonight. Be poppets and toddle up to the flat. I'll send you a scratch supper on a tray. Guests arriving at nine. Don't keep Caterina. She still has yards of sandwiches to make."

Caterina, who looked like a half-grown child next to Imgard, bobbed her head up and down in a shy greeting. With surprising strength, she picked up their suitcases before Benjamin could help her, and led the way up the stairs.

"We're in!" Benjamin mimed and danced his way up behind her. "And we've already escaped!

"Not bad, do you think?" he said, when Caterina had gone. "After months of hotels, a real bedroom is a relief."

"It feels almost warm," said Rosy.

The flat, made over from what had previously been servants' quarters, had an attic coziness about it. The beds and windows were covered in blue-and-white chintz. There were a small writing table; a couch and reading chair covered in red leather, the color dark with use; and a night table between the beds on which stood a bowl of roses, some of whose petals had fallen on the current issue of the *Times Literary Supplement.*

Benjamin inspected the bookcases which lined the walls. "Overflow from Andrew's library," he said. He pulled one book out and pushed another in to straighten a row. "Trollope." He took a book bound in blue leather, one of a series, and blew along the top of the pages before opening it. "I think I'll read nothing but Trollope while we're in England. How pleasant it will be to read Trollope!" He took the book with him to the bathroom and ran water for a bath. "I get first crack at the tub. I'm as dirty as a chimney sweep. When we're rich let's have a hotel room with a bath." He came back to get his shaving kit. "Aren't you going to take your coat off?"

Rosy had been standing in the middle of the room, hugging her arms. She was waiting to warm up. Her coat still on, she bounced on the bed, testing the mattress.

"How is it?" Benjamin asked, going back to the bathroom.

"Better than either the one in the pensione or the one in the hotel in Paris." Rosy got up and unpacked. "Mind if I hang out my dress for the party?" she said, opening the door on the steamy bathroom. Benjamin didn't hear. He held his book up in front of him with the flat of one hand, as a singer holds his music, and wiped the steam from his glasses with the other. "Delicious!" he cried. "Listen, listen to this. . . ."

Rosy turned off the water, which was rising dangerously high. "Wasn't that a knock?"

It was Caterina with a tray. She bobbed and said, "Prego, prego," as Rosy took it from her.

"Sherry," Rosy called to Benjamin, "and"—she lifted a quilted rabbit's head (a relic of Tonkey's nursery days?)—"hard-boiled eggs and"—she peeled back the corner of a sandwich—"watercress and cucumber and"—she lifted the lid of the teapot—"black China tea."

"Bring me a sherry, will you, darling? You see," he said when Rosy handed it to him, "I told you it wouldn't be a bit like boarding school."

At eight thirty they heard Andrew. "Come down instantly, you two, so we can have a quiet drink before the hordes descend."

Benjamin put his book down stoically. "I dread this party." Seeing Rosy's expression, he said, "Now, look here, Roxana, don't *you* get shy too. I have all I can do to cope with my own timidity without worrying about yours. It's my fault. I shouldn't have frightened you about Imgard." He gave Rosy his hands and pulled her to her feet. "What you need is a stiff drink."

"Well, you old pirate," Benjamin called down when he saw Andrew's face at the foot of the stairs. One could easily imagine Andrew, a handsome man with wild, wavy black eyebrows, wearing a red bandanna around his head, or a gold earring in one ear and a patch over one of his fierce blue eyes.

"If I'm a pirate, then Roxana's a Gypsy. Look at her. Ruffles, flounces, dangling earrings (he flicked one of them with his index finger) and skin the color of tawny port." He whirled her around in an embrace. "How did you get so brown?"

The men threw their arms around each other. "What's this I feel, flesh?" Andrew cried carnivorously. "My God, Ben, you've put on weight." He roared with laughter. "Wouldn't it be a hoot if you turned out to be a fat man?"

Andrew led them into the living room, where a bar was set up for the party. "Everything all right up there?" He indicated the flat. "Wish we were rich enough not to have to rent, so you could just stay on. But tomorrow Imgard will find you something nice nearby. She's a wizard at that sort of thing." Andrew lowered his voice, "I had a drop on the way home. Bit nervous always at the beginning."

"You too? Let's fortify ourselves with a little gin," suggested Benjamin.

"That's probably Molly," Andrew said when the doorbell rang. "She always comes early." He returned with a tiny, frail woman who fluttered at his side in a long gauzy gown. Andrew's mock-deferential attitude toward her suggested that this guest was a personage, and that he was on terms of intimacy with her. "Our houseguests, Mr. and Mrs. Bold; Mrs. Curtiss-Grey. Benjamin Bold it is, Molly. A famous American poet." Andrew winked at the Bolds with the whole right side of his face. "Bet you never heard of him, did you? The truth, now, Molly."

Mrs. Curtiss-Grey took up her rope of amber beads,

almost as long as she was tall, and twisted them, her gauzy arms fluttering. "I love to catch you out, Andrew darling." Her voice, which sounded as if it had been wrecked by cigarettes and malicious laughter, cracked appealingly on the "darling." "Of course I know who he is." She turned her chin up to Benjamin and angled her head to show him the best-preserved features of her ruined beauty. "Unlike most novelists, I do read poetry." She slipped her hand out of Andrew's arm and gave it to Benjamin. "I'm so happy to have a moment alone with you before the others arrive. Come sit by me—it's barbarous the way we're all made to stand at parties these days—and tell me what you're working on now."

Other guests followed quickly. Rosy stayed close to Andrew. When they had a minute alone, she said, "I can hardly believe it. I thought Mary Curtiss-Grey died years ago."

"Died?" Andrew exploded with laughter. "She's only just stopped taking young men, preferably poets—that's why she reads them—to bed with her. Look at them."

They looked over at Benjamin, who was leaning forward, gesturing excitedly, while the famous novelist lay back on the chaise longue like a faded *maja,* twisting and untwisting her beads and wiggling her toes in her little silk slippers. "I'd keep my eye on Ben if I were you. Molly's an outrageous woman. I wouldn't trust her even now. And"— another guest arrived—"you better be especially nice to me" —Andrew gave Rosy a familiar slap on the bottom—"or I'll tell her what you said and she'll scratch your eyes out."

Imgard came by in time to see Andrew's gesture. "For God sakes, Andrew, behave yourself tonight, will you? And remember they're *your* guests as well as mine. I'll take care of Roxana. You see to the door."

Imgard led Rosy to the other room. "The house covers in England. We don't introduce the way you Americans do. Just talk to anyone, and I'll find you when I have a minute."

It was a big "do," all right. The living room and library

were quickly filled with Andrew's literary friends and theater people Imgard knew from her prewar career. All London, as Doris would have said, was there. Rosy wandered around looking and listening for a time. No better able to tolerate standing than Molly, and timid about talking to strangers she hadn't been introduced to, she found an empty chair in the library and sat down.

A bald, ectoplasmic man appeared from nowhere as if he were meeting her by arrangement to continue a long, intense, and incomprehensible story. He did not say his name, or give a synopsis of the past action. "You must, I mean you simmmmmply must meet Brenda. She's so . . . sort of . . . I mean . . . she's really quite quite extrrrrrrraordinary. You'll simply love her."

Earlier something frightful had happened. To whom? To him? And who was Brenda? It was very confusing. Rosy was taken with the narrator's trick of flicking his cigarette ash into his trouser cuff, and his affectation of a stutter. He held on to some letters and swallowed others whole. Had he been at Cambridge with Andrew and Benjamin? Stuttering had been fashionable there in Benjamin's time. The story went on and on. Rosy thought of slipping away, but the crowd was too thick and the effort too great. Imgard, in the end, set her free.

"Tony Curtiss, I need you." Imgard pounced on the storyteller. She forced an empty platter into his hands. "Be an angel. Take this down to Caterina and ask for more sandwiches."

Tony, who knew he wasn't likely to find another ear all evening, looked despairingly at Rosy. "Dddddddon't go," he pleaded. "I'll be strrrrraight back. We were having such a jolly chat," he said petulantly to Imgard.

"Poor Roxana," Imgard said after he left. "Not much fun for you. You got the whole saga, did you? 'Extrrrraordinary woman; why did she leave me?' All that? He's a pederast, of course. That's why. Tony was naughty and careless. Brenda found him in her bed with a boy. A bit much. He's too boring when he's drunk, Tony. Sober he's really quite nice. Lives next door. Molly's illegitimate son."

"Mary Curtiss-Grey's?" This more than made up to Rosy for her captivity.

"Ummmm. Molly was that generation. They all had to have an illegitimate child. The thing to do. Just one, not to carry it too far. To show they didn't need a man. Except to get it started, of course. They tell me Tony is clever at the BBC. Sharp. A driver. Saves the whining for women. You better fly away before he comes back. I'm off to the loo. Been trying to get there for hours."

Rosy wandered into the entrance hall. Andrew and a group of cronies were clustered around the stairs singing at the top of their lungs. With the long spoon from the martini pitcher as a baton, Andrew urged the chorus on to greater volume. They were straining to a glorious finale of a war song. Still singing, Andrew came down the steps toward Rosy. He grabbed her hand, reeled her in to him, and twirled her around. Simultaneously with the final note, he brought her down with him on the bottom step, sharply. There was an explosion of applause.

Rosy, her head bent to her knees, hid her face in her hands. A flash of pain, blinding and jagged like lightning, tore through her spine. Someone began another song. Andrew stood up to lead them.

> No cares have I to grieve me,
> No pretty little girls to deceive me.
> Happy as a king, believe me,
> As I go rolling, rolling home.

Rosy tested her legs when the pain subsided. They worked. She reached for the banister and stood up. She had to move quickly to escape Andrew's reach.

"All right, then," he called after her, "but come right back."

Rosy talked to herself as she climbed the stairs. "Don't panic. Get into bed. Lie still. Oh, please God, make it go away!" In the room she started to undress, realized she couldn't. She lay down on the bed.

There it was again, an electric saw going through her spine more slowly, more deeply this time. "Oh, no. *Please!*" she pleaded, grabbing a clutch of bedcovers in her fists. Slowly the saw was drawn back and out of her body again. Rivulets of sweat coursing down her face and under her arms felt like scurrying ants. "Now I'm really trapped," she said to the wall. It was a slipped disk, unquestionably. The sickening pinch of nerve, once you knew it, was unmistakable.

It would be hours before Benjamin came up. What could he do, anyway? Tell her she was wrong, that it was not the disk. She wouldn't believe him, but it would be a comfort to hear it.

Molly must have left. There was Benjamin's falsetto. He and Andrew were singing a duet:

I'm just a sherry party girl.

Damn Andrew! If he had been a little less drunk . . . If it hadn't been Andrew, it would have been something else. A sneeze, they said, could do it. Ponza had merely delayed what was inevitable.

For half an hour now there had been no pain. Rosy moved her legs cautiously. No, no pain. Perhaps she had exaggerated. Just nerved up: Benjamin's silence about her letter. Phoebe. Theo (she must write him tomorrow). A day in bed might do the trick. Awkward in someone else's house, of course (especially with people coming to see about renting the flat), but not serious. She stood up to test it, and lay down again. No, no pain.

Downstairs there was a crash of glass. Andrew shouted at someone. The front door slammed. Then Imgard, announcing that she was going up to bed.

"Don't sit up all night, you two," Imgard's party-weary voice called.

"Up in a minute," Andrew promised.

Rosy stood up again, this time to undress. As she reached her dress over her head, there it was again and she was begging for mercy: "Oweeeeee." She promised not to test it again, if only it would go away. Eventually it did.

Benjamin was being Bessie Smith now. He knew her every inflection.

If you get good lovin' don't go and spread the news
Or your man will leave you with those empty bed blues.

A long silence. The men must have gone down to the kitchen for more drink. The night dragged on. Sometime after the hall clock struck four, she heard them coming up to bed. No, to Andrew's study on the floor below. Of course: there was no possibility of Benjamin's going to bed until he had said his poem. Would Andrew, who had heard it on the crossing once with wild enthusiasm, and then again, let Benjamin go to the end? Benjamin would be standing in the middle of the room, his face pale and damp, his hands icy now as he came to the last stanza.

There was a short, not quite respectful, silence before Andrew said in his public reading voice, "And now, I have an early Bold I would like to read to you. Ah yes, here we are." Andrew's voice, even bigger than Benjamin's, rumbled like stones echoing down a well.

The bloody head rolled . . .

Rosy was surprised to hear herself laugh. It was a schoolboy poem of Benjamin's. Where had Andrew found it? It was his revenge for having been made to listen to the long poem again.

"Traitor! Spy!" Benjamin shouted. "Stop. Not fair! My turn. Here. Here we have an early Mallory, ladies and gentlemen, listen.

> Her neck, white-green and glistening
> Like a latrine

"Liar! Tin-eared paraphraser!" Andrew shouted. Benjamin was gagging and Andrew exploding with laughter as they mocked each other's vernal efforts.

Light was coming through the curtains when Benjamin began to tell his bee story: the end was near.

". . . and tell Roxana," Andrew called after Benjamin as they separated, "that I say she's a frightful little sneak, going off like that."

"Andrew says to tell you that you're a sneak," Benjamin delivered the message as he came into the room. "Yes, a little sneak. Why did you leave? We had a lovely time after the guests left."

"I've hurt my back," Rosy wailed. "This time I'm sure it's the disk."

Benjamin stumbled on his way over to Rosy's bed. "Sorry," he apologized to the chair. "Unfamiliar terrain." Then he patted Rosy's foot. "Poor Roxana. Don't worry. It will go away. Got to get some sleep now. It's late. Very, very la . . ." Benjamin fell face down on his bed and was instantly asleep.

Rosy lay awake, vigilant, lest an unguarded movement cause the pain to return. At last, hearing Imgard's bedroom door open and close, she put on her robe and went down to the basement kitchen.

fourteen

Imgard, in a faded pink wrapper, her copper-colored hair hanging down her back, looked like a worn-out Valkyrie. She sat at the kitchen table, holding her head up with one hand. With the other she had a cup of coffee.

"Morning," she said to Rosy. "Coffee?"

"Please."

"Egg?"

"No, thanks."

"I won't ask you how you slept. How could anyone sleep with those two shouting? Ben read some damn poem as long as *Kristin Lavransdatter*. They must have heard him down in Kent. And Andrew . . . oh those tiresome Eighth Army songs!" Imgard talked with the resignation of a laborer's wife, making common cause with a neighbor over their husbands' payday excesses. "The drink does it to him every time. Reminds him of his freedom and the lovely drunks they used to have during the war. Only improvement now is he doesn't smash furniture as I hear he used to."

"There was one crash."

"Not Andrew, worse luck. One of my friends—a man Andrew detests—broke a vase which belonged to Andrew's mother. It will put him in a beastly temper if he sees it this morning. I'm going to duck out with it first thing, take it to be repaired, as soon as I finish my coffee. Another cup?"

"Thanks."

Imgard poured them each a second cup. "When the sleeping bards come down, remind Andrew that he has a program this afternoon, will you? He might take it into his head to go off larking with Ben. And hold on to Ben. We'll go look for a room when I get back. You won't mind more or less looking after yourself? It's likely to be a bit of a circus today—people coming to see the flat . . . I say, would you mind awfully not jiggling like that?"

Rosy's leg, dancing with pain, made it impossible for her to sit still any longer. "It's a terrible bore, I'm afraid," she said, standing up, "but I'll have to see a doctor today. I've hurt my back."

"You've done *what?*" Imgard banged her cup down on its saucer. Her arms fell limply by the sides of her chair. Then, suspicious, she leaned forward. "Just come on you like that, did it?"

"Not quite. It's been troubling me since we've been in Europe. Just recently I thought it was better. Last night something really went out."

Imgard braced her elbows on the table and squeezed her head between her taut fingers, as if to keep it from expanding. After a few minutes she said, "Look here, it's not your fault. How could you have known what a frightful time it is for me to have guests? The flat to let, Tonkey coming home from school, the two of us to be got ready to go to Denmark. With Andrew being left behind, that means preparing the house for a blitz. The last time I came back it looked like the sack of Rome. . . . I say, you are rather listing to one side, aren't you," she said, taking in Rosy's posture. "I'm sorry. Go back up to bed. I'll send Caterina up with a hot-water jar and some aspirin. That may be just the job. There's nothing we can do in any case until the bards wake up. After they've had breakfast, we'll see about a doctor."

By the time Rosy got up to the room, the pain had become tyrannical.

"Roxana." Benjamin jolted awake. "What is it?"

"The pain," Rosy cried. "It's getting worse. Please get me a doctor."

"At this hour?"

"It's after ten."

"Imgard?"

"Out on an errand. Get the name of a doctor from her as soon as she comes back and call him. Tell him I must have something for the pain. If it's the disk I'll have to go to the hospital, and the sooner the better."

Benjamin, who didn't like to be confronted with problems before he'd taken the measure of his hangover, dressed, looking bleak. "I'll get someone. I'll be back. Try to sleep if you can."

At noon he returned to tell Rosy that Dr. Dinglefoot was coming as soon as she could get away. His first conversation with her—yes, a woman—had not gone well. When he mentioned the disk, she asked him to be good enough to leave the diagnosing to her.

Benjamin looked at Rosy reproachfully. "How can you be ill when you look so rosy?" he said. "It's hard to believe there's anything the matter with you. Imgard, now, who's probably as strong as a peasant, has blue pouches under her eyes and is pale with fatigue." They heard Imgard on the landing. "Here's Tingleass now," said Benjamin, grimly.

"Please, Benjamin, Dinglefoot," Rosy said severely.

"She may be exaggerating, Wilhelmina," they heard Imgard say to the doctor. "She's American, you know."

Dr. Wilhelmina Dinglefoot marched into the room, swinging her little black bag smartly. Her stocky figure was wrapped in gray flannel. She was wearing a tie. Her hair, cut short all over, was like a skullcap of steel wool. "So, you've already diagnosed your trouble," she said to Rosy in a scrubbed-up voice. "You've gone through the list and hit on the most serious, have you?"

"I've had this before," Rosy said.

"I suppose you want to go to hospital, too." Dr. Dinglefoot dropped her bag with ill-disguised irritability. "Our hospitals are chockablock full of Americans, every last one of them pretending to have come as tourists when it's our public health service they're after. Dishonest, that's what it is, coming sick and expecting us to take care of you. Get your own health service, I say."

Rosy flushed with anger. "I want to be hospitalized as a private patient." She had had time during the long morning to remember that her hospitalization insurance would cover her in England.

Dr. Dinglefoot was not mollified. "Stand up," she said. "I want to examine you."

As Rosy turned over to get up, the pain began again. "I can't," she cried out.

"Try."

Benjamin, who had been standing at the door trying to act as if he were not there, rushed forward. "Now, look here, Dinglefoot. Stop lecturing my wife. If you're not competent to examine her, say so, and I'll get someone who is." Benjamin and Wilhelmina glared at each other with undisguised hostility.

"I was merely pointing out the difficulties." A bully, Dr. Dinglefoot saw she had met her match.

"You needn't. They're crystal clear."

"If you'll be good enough to leave the room, Mr. Bold, I'll examine your wife."

At Rosy's imploring look, Benjamin left. The doctor helped Rosy to turn over. She probed her back. "Did this ever happen before?"

"Six years ago."

"You should have said so in the first place." With Benjamin out of the room, Dr. Dinglefoot was back in character.

Rosy's rage came out in tears.

"No need for tears. You'll have to show a little courage. I'll give you an injection of morphine and leave you some tablets. One every three hours. No sooner." The doctor called Benjamin back. "Your wife is to stay in bed, flat. She's not to sit up for meals. I want her to use a bedpan. Come around with me to my house and I'll give you one. You're to look after her."

"I can't stay here." Rosy found her voice. "Can't you get me to a hospital?" But Dr. Dinglefoot was out of the room, followed by stony-faced Benjamin. On the landing, she told Imgard it looked serious: she would try to get an orthopedist. What Americans didn't seem to understand was that it took time to arrange about a hospital, should it be necessary—the hospitals being, as she had said, so full of their compatriots.

Rosy, who had been dozing from the injection, woke when Benjamin thundered into the room, carrying the ill-disguised bedpan.

"That bitch! That monstrous bitch! How can Imgard use her? (Did you sleep? Good.) If we don't get another doctor soon I'm likely to kill this one." He sat on the edge of Rosy's bed and took the hand she held out to him. "I had a rather satisfying fantasy on the way back," he said. "I set a bomb under Tingleass's desk. Well out of danger, but close enough to watch, I listened for the blast. *Brooooooom*. Then a shower of dismembered pieces of the late but easily recognizable doctor—arms, legs, the decapitated head, its gray stubble rigid, the eyes popping in horror." Acting out the fantasy, Benjamin let the bedpan clatter to the floor.

"You needn't worry about that thing," said Rosy. "I have no intention of using it. There will be quite time enough for such indignities when I get to the hospital."

"You sure?"

"Just put the dope she left within reach and keep after Dinglefoot about the hospital." Overcome with frustration, Rosy said, "Oh Benjamin, I wish I were home."

"It's rotten bad luck." Grateful to be relieved of his nursing duties, Benjamin kissed Rosy's hand. "Try to go back to sleep. I'll go out with Imgard to look for a room, so she won't think she has us on her hands for life. We'll be back in a little while."

It was late afternoon when Benjamin came in again. He threw himself down on his bed. "I've done a fair day's work," he said with obvious satisfaction. "First, we found a place— a clean, well-lighted room over the Ram's Head, bed and breakfast thirty shillings. To make us both feel as though things were still going along as planned, I paid a deposit. Imgard was still so low—I knew something was up—that I thought a drink might help. At the Rose and Thistle, over a glass of Sancerre, I did some high-powered marriage counseling. I'm really rather good at it, I find. Perhaps I should have been an analyst. God knows it's a damn sight better paid than poetry. I just may have averted a major crisis in the Mallory household."

"What about the orthopedist?"

"No luck, darling. He's away for the weekend. Tingleass says we can do nothing until Sunday evening."

"Is Imgard frantic about the room?"

"She was rather hoping you'd be well enough to get up tomorrow, but Wilhelmina told her you're not to budge. Is it any better?"

"Uh-uh. I wish she'd left me more pills. They never last three hours."

Benjamin got up and lit a cigarette. "Aren't you curious about the crisis? Or would you rather go back to sleep?"

"No. I wasn't sleeping. Tell me."

"Was Imgard disagreeable to you this morning?"

"She acted as if I'd brought cholera into the house."

"She'd been suspicious for some time, but this morning, going through Andrew's pockets—women!—she discovered a letter from some American girl. Obviously not the first. The girl seems to be making plans to come over."

"A student?"

"How did you guess? Pamela Something. Andrew met her when he read guess where?"

"Bennington."

"Right. She followed him all over the country—the mid-winter work period, I believe they call it. What made Imgard especially furious is that Andrew came back from his reading tour saying that American women were so unattractive—so 'cas*trat*ing!' to use Imgard's pronunciation. Andrew really is behaving very badly," Benjamin said sententiously.

"Do you think it's serious?"

"Hmmm. I'll tell you what I think. This girl is one of those poet-followers—God protect us from them! She's young, undoubtedly pretty, obviously not opposed to a little free love. More important, she's a fresh ear for the stories and songs Imgard has heard a million times: in short, a new audience. Andrew probably sees her as the subject of a new series of poems—'Love in the New World,' or 'America the Beautiful.' " Benjamin laughed dryly.

"Your advice was?" Rosy was curious.

"To sit tight. Wait for it to blow over. For all we know Andrew may already be trying to shake the girl. As I told Imgard, it will take a little correspondence back and forth—creative writing, it's called at Bennington."

"Will Imgard listen to you?"

"Don't know. It's curious. I began by feeling very sorry for her. At the end when she said, looking rather hard, 'I have no intention of giving Andrew up. None. It doesn't at all suit my book,' it was Andrew I felt sorrier for."

"Ben?" They heard Andrew call from the floor below.

"Right down," Benjamin called back. "They want me to go out to dinner with them. You don't mind? Caterina will bring you up a tray. I do feel they rather need me as a buffer."

Three times a day Caterina brought up trays. She looked at Rosy with spaniel-like eyes, moist with sympathy, and sighed, *"Poverina, poverina."* The hall clock sounded the hours. The front door opened and closed as Imgard, Andrew, and Benjamin came in and went out. Imgard showed what she could of the flat. Rosy ate, dozed, took her medicine, and watched the light change through the part of the window she could see out of. Rose petals covered the *Times Literary Supplement.*

Monday Imgard followed Caterina in with the lunch tray and sat down on Rosy's bed. "It's really no better? No, I can see it isn't. Ben isn't much when you're sick, is he?"

"There's nothing he can do," Rosy said.

"You don't have to defend him to me. They're washouts when you're sick. Andrew won't even come up to pay you a polite visit. He acts as if you have cancer of the face. Luckily, I'm as strong as a horse. I've never been sick except when I had Tonkey. And then Andrew behaved like a devil. He would have it that *he* was having the baby. Morning sickness, the lot. The 'couvade' he called it. Endless talk about primitive tribes and so on, which, as I kept pointing out, we were not members of. You should thank God it's your back, not a baby. I tricked Andrew into the pregnancy —he was dead against it—and I've never stopped paying for it. Well, I didn't come to tell you my troubles, but to say that Wilhelmina just called. She talked to Dr. Birdbyle, the orthopedist. He will meet you at the hospital. He seems to agree with you that that's where you may have to be for a bit. Wilhelmina will come around this afternoon to arrange the move."

"Any luck renting the flat?" Rosy asked. "I'm terribly sorry . . ."

"It's done. A young couple. They'll move in tomorrow." Imgard stood up. "We never have trouble renting. It's a cozy room, isn't it? Molly Curtiss-Grey lived here, you know. We bought from her. She wrote most of her novels in this room. Funny she didn't use the one Andrew uses downstairs. She said she was afraid of being distracted by the view of the park."

It was after four when Rosy heard a commotion in the downstairs hall. Dr. Dinglefoot was giving orders like a general. Benjamin appeared at the door. "They've sent an ambulance," he said, looking funereal.

Two orderlies came in with a stretcher. "I don't need that," Rosy protested. "I can walk."

" 'Ere now, Mrs.," one of them said, "leave it to us. Doctor's orders."

Benjamin was asked to wait downstairs with the doctor. The orderlies lifted Rosy by the head and feet, like a rolled-up carpet, and lowered her onto the stretcher. They folded a tan blanket with a Greek key–motif border on it around her, exchanged signals, and picked her up.

The descent began slowly and spasmodically, like a roller-coaster car in an amusement park which gives its passengers a backward-and-forward tug before hurling them down the chute. Benjamin, Imgard, and Dr. Dinglefoot, at the bottom of the stairs, their mouths open to help them crane their necks, looked dwarfed and dull-witted. As the stretcher rounded the first curve, the orderly in front stumbled. Rosy, her hands bound in the blanket so that she couldn't hold on, felt as if she were being pitched over the railing. Was it she or Benjamin, or the two of them in unison, who cried, "Aaaaaaa"?

Benjamin had covered his face with his hands.

"Steady," Dr. Dinglefoot called out sharply.

Imgard, white from holding her breath—it was, after all, her entrance hall into which Rosy would have been spilled—recovered as the stretcher was carried past. She felt for Rosy's arm under the blanket and gave it a squeeze. "Don't go into a funk, now, will you?" she said. "I'll be around to see you soon. University College Hospital is first rate."

fifteen

How odd, thought Rosy, as the ambulance drew up beside a solemn-faced bobby, solemnly directing the early-evening traffic: how odd to be seeing London for the first time upside down. Any sadness she felt at the obliqueness of this view of the city was tempered by her overwhelming relief to be out of the Mallorys' house. It gave her, for the moment, a false sense of freedom. She had exaggerated her symptoms (the stretcher and ambulance had made her feel that). Dr. Birdbyle might find nothing more serious than a severe muscle spasm, in which case she would be released from the hospital after a few days' rest. Even the trip to Cambridge did not seem out of the question.

"Curious," Benjamin, sitting on a jump seat next to the stretcher, said, "but I have a triangular pain in my right shoulder." Benjamin went in for geometric pains. He had suffered rectangular headaches, octagonal heart spasms, hexagonal stomachaches, and even, on one occasion, a trapezoidal intestinal cramp. "I think I'll ask Birdbath to look at it."

Distant but sympathetic at the Mallorys', Benjamin was giving Rosy notice that his tolerance for her illness had reached its limits. And by what more dramatic way than to suggest that *he* was the one who needed a doctor's care? Rosy kept her head turned toward the window.

"Byle, not bath," she corrected—"as in unpaid." Though she would not look at Benjamin's appeal for attention, she could imagine him kneading the muscles in his shoulder with one of those theatrical gestures which had a way of drying up her sympathy. He might even be looking at her accusingly, as if she had shot an arrow into his shoulder and had left it there, quivering.

"I haven't had a chance to tell you how good a letter it was you left me. When you went to Ponza." Benjamin aimed an arrow of his own, and sank it deep into its target.

Now? Rosy shrieked to herself. Of course now. Benjamin's impeccable sense of timing. She kept her eyes resolutely fixed on the passing scene: double-decker buses, fanlights, cornices, a bottle-green park.

"I read it with care," Benjamin went on. "You're quite right, of course. We must think of the future. I am not lacking plans, as you must know. But the things I'm working on, and will do, are not likely to bring in money. The application for a renewal of the grant was my effort at that, you remember." He paused. Then, with abstract interest, "What had you in mind?"

That brought Rosy's head around. "I? Surely it's not up to me to have something in mind."

The glass window which partitioned the driver's seat from the stretcher squeaked open. " 'Ere we are. You 'op out, sir. Almost there, Mrs. Wasn't too bad, now, was it?"

A door lettered boldly in red, EMERGENCY; an antiseptic odor which protested too strongly that it had nothing to hide; a silence in the elevator as if a corpse were a passenger; Benjamin seen from below looking like a pallbearer: this was University College Hospital.

"I'm Sister Logan, the head nurse," a face set off by a starched white cap, absurdly shaped and set on the head at a precipitous angle, said. "Mrs. Bold for Dr. Birdbyle? Come this way."

Sister Logan led the way down yet another corridor. Unlike the noisy extroversion one finds in American hospitals, here all was closed doors and discretion. Rosy had the uncanny feeling she might be the only inmate.

"Mrs. Bold? Birdbyle." The doctor held out and down a dry hand with spatular fingers for Rosy to shake. From her supine position she saw a vast brow, corrugated like tin; small, close-set eyes; and an undershot jaw (had the family got its name from this physical anomaly?). The doctor was wearing an old-fashioned high white collar and a long white coat which gave off the sickly-sweet smell of ether.

"Now, then, Mrs. Bold." Dr. Birdbyle began his examination as soon as Rosy had been moved to the bed. "Will you be good enough to show me how high you can raise your right leg? Is that as far as it will go? And the left. Now, as I run this pin down the outside of your legs will you tell me if you have more sensation in one or the other."

"More in the left."

"Now, in the left, is there a difference between the inside and the outside?"

"It's less sensitive on the outside."

"Sister Logan, will you help us to a sitting position?" the doctor asked, as if he too had been lying down. "Just dangle your legs freely." He hit each of Rosy's knees a smart blow with his mallet. "Shall we try the left again?" The left leg was recalcitrant. "We'll stand up now, Sister. Can you straighten any more than that, Mrs. Bold?"

Rosy tried.

"Cough. Does that hurt?"

"Not really." Feeling that she was not performing well, Rosy began to dissimulate. Was there no chance left of going to Cambridge?

"Everett." Dr. Dinglefoot marched in and verbally saluted her colleague. "Your impression?"

"Acute herniation," Everett Birdbyle said, shaking on it. "Sister Logan, we can lie down now. That will be all for today. We'll x-ray tomorrow." He wrote out a prescription for the x-rays. "As you undoubtedly know, Mrs. Bold—this is not your first herniation, is it?—the history will tell us more than the x-rays. I understand from my colleague Dr. Dinglefoot that you are tourists. You're wondering about your plans." The doctor's lower lip vanished in a pale smile. "No more sightseeing for you, I'm afraid. The likelihood is that you'll be with us for three weeks. Longer, of course, if surgery is required. We'll watch you closely for the next few days. In the meantime, Sister Logan, see that the patient is completely immobilized. No pillow. No sitting up for meals. Bedpan. The usual. How severe is the pain now?"

"Not at all," Rosy flatly lied—a last attempt to escape as Dr. Birdbyle's net billowed down around her.

"We'll see that you have some injections," he said, not taken in.

Benjamin, forgotten during the examination, pushed his way between the doctors. "Roxana," he cried, grabbing her arm. "Let's get out of here. Let's go home. *Please*. Come with me," he pleaded. His wild eyes darted as if their lives were at stake, as if he knew (and she did not) that they were in the hands of sinister people who meant them harm.

Benjamin's appeal was so compelling, his fear for their safety so palpable, that for one crazy moment Rosy saw them escaping—fleeing hand in hand, past the doctors, down the corridors, and out the door marked EMERGENCY to freedom. She must have made a movement in his direction, because in an instant the doctors were at either side of the bed, restraining her.

"I don't understand, Mr. Bold," Dr. Birdbyle said with shocked incredulity. "You mean to the United States? Don't you understand that any movement at all is contraindicated?"

"Couldn't she be taken to a plane on a stretcher?" Benjamin said, as if remembering something he'd seen in a movie.

"You don't seem to understand"—Dr. Birdbyle spoke

very slowly—"that at the moment we prefer for your wife not even to raise her head. We cannot take the responsibility if you move her. There is the possibility of permanent nerve damage. Of lameness. We can look after her as well here as they could in the United States. All that's required, you know, is bed rest."

"You mentioned surgery," Benjamin pounced.

"There's always that possibility, but there's no need to rush ahead like that." The doctor put his mallet away and snapped shut his bag. "Why not go ahead with your sightseeing as planned, Mr. Bold? There are a great many things to see in London." In went his lower lip. "Or why not go to Stratford? It's Shakespeare's—"

Benjamin had been looking at Birdbyle murderously. "*I hate Shakespeare,*" he spat out.

Birdbyle exchanged glances with his colleague and gave a nervous little laugh: this man was unstable enough to need humoring. "Oh well, go to Brighton then." The doctors left the room.

Sister Logan, zealous to lose no time in carrying out the doctor's orders, pulled the pillow from under the patient's head.

"May I come in?" another nurse said at the door. "Supper tray."

"I'm not hungry," Rosy said rebelliously.

"She'll want glass straws," Sister Logan said, ignoring the willful child. "This is a complete-immobilization case."

Transfixed where the doctors had arrested him, Benjamin looked at Rosy as if he had caught her in the act of infidelity. She might have become, from the way he stared, so disfigured by corruption as to be unrecognizable. "I'll go." He raised a hand in abdication, "I'll go . . ."

The nurse who had brought the supper tray came back with the glass straw. "Come, now that your husband has gone, let me feed you some of this lovely soup," she said.

Her jaw locked, her eyes fixed on the ceiling, Rosy protested with her head. She must not, must not, must not cry until she was alone.

At last, when the nurses could find nothing further to do, and Sister Logan had given her an injection and flicked out the light, Rosy turned over on her side and covered her face with her hands. The lump in her throat had turned to stone. Her dry, gritty eyes ached with impotence. Her tear ducts, which burned hotter and hotter, seemed to have forgotten their function. Tears, which had flowed so ungovernably and treacherously all her life, refused to come. She rolled from side to side and, making dry moaning noises, pounded the mattress with clenched fists. After a while her body stopped rocking, her fists unfurled, and the injected morphine came over her like a black spongy mask.

By the time Benjamin called the next morning, Rosy felt that she had already spent a lifetime at University College. Early-morning tea, Dr. Birdbyle, an injection of morphine, the cleaning woman, breakfast, a sponge bath, and a trip to the x-ray room had all come and gone. The private room, a luxury she had longed for in Boston the previous winter, was like a tomb. She found herself wishing for the vulgar conviviality—the clanking carts of fruit juice; the parade of the ambulatory in various states of deshabille; the visits of interns, laboratory assistants, and doctors; the blare of radios; the nagging conversation of roommates—which had so repelled her in the Boston hospital.

Benjamin said when he telephoned that he could tell by her voice that the medication was taking effect; she was in less pain. He was grateful to be given practical errands. He would collect the books she asked for, borrow a radio from Imgard, and come by with them in an hour.

The lunch tray, when it came, offered little diversion. The food was uniformly farinaceous and bland. Why hadn't she been hospitalized in Rome? Rosy asked herself. At Salvator Mundi she would have been wheeled out on a sunny terrace (her narrow view of the outside world showed her a silver tinsel of drizzle), the food would have been palatable and accompanied by wine, and she would have had a relay of friends to distract her.

The nurse who had brought the lunch tray came back at three with another injection. "It makes a long day if you have no visitors," she said. "Are you alone in London?"

"No, my husband is here," said Rosy.

"Pity, then, he didn't come to feed you lunch. That's what they usually do in immobilization cases."

"He'll be in this afternoon," Rosy said defensively, her resentment at Benjamin's lateness making her retort sharp. Oh, the hateful passivity of waiting! Benjamin knew how poorly she tolerated it. They had been over it all in January. She never asked him to stay long (he was too obviously ill at ease beside a hospital bed), but she did want him to come when he said he would.

At seven o'clock, when for an hour she had been telling herself that she didn't care if she ever saw him again, Benjamin came in. He used his umbrella as an extra and steadier limb. His head was cocked in a mixture of bravado and guilt.

"Where have you been?" she burst out. "The day has been an eternity."

Benjamin stood at the foot of the bed, both hands resting on the handle of his umbrella. "So, you greet me with reproaches, do you?" His tongue was thick with ale.

"Oh, Benjamin." Rosy hit her hand down on the bed with frustration. "Why can't you . . ." Their eyes met as they took in at the same instant that he didn't have the books and radio.

"Christ! I must have left them in the pub." Benjamin said. "They'll keep them until tomorrow."

"No hurry. Tomorrow. The next day. Next week. Anytime. . . ."

"You think you've had a long day. What do you imagine it's been like for *me?*" Benjamin flared out. "I too have had to get through it. I'm a writer, for Christ's sake"—his voice climbed—"not a visiting nurse or a bloody social worker."

Forgetting the doctor's orders, Rosy sat up. "Shu—"

"Can't you get that through your *head?*" With vicious force he hit his hand against his temple.

"Stop shouting," Rosy said between clenched teeth. "Get hold of yourself."

"Don't tell me what to do." Benjamin's umbrella clattered to the floor. A vein, knotted like a piece of blue rope, cut a sharp diagonal across his brow as his head jerked up violently. From deep in his throat came a blood-chilling "Aiiiiii."

It was the night of the Academy party again, the maniacal scream she had run away from. There was nowhere to run now. She could do nothing but clamp her hands hard against her ears. She was powerless. Or was she? A glint of metal drew her eye to the saltcellar on the supper tray. Her hand went toward it. How cold! A thrill shot through her body as she hurled it through the air.

"Get out! Go away!" she shouted over the sound of crashing dishes, as she threw one object after another until the tray was empty.

Benjamin backed out of the room as if from a crazed animal which might break out of its cage.

Rosy fell back on the bed. It seemed no longer to be there. Down and down she tumbled, weightless and without volition as if she were being rolled by a giant breaker. It pulled her up, up, up, arrested her an instant in midair, then pounded her down again. A dragging undertow sucked, churned, boiled her up again, twirled her in its vortex like a broken toy. This was not like other waves she'd learned, during the course of her marriage, to take. It was no kin to the slow green breakers which, curling back on themselves in a ruffle of white foam, fulfilled their promise of a long exhilarating ride, to be taken with abandon, hands extended, head down, the kind one wishes would never end and, when it does, makes one scramble up and hurry out again, greedy to catch the next. Nor was it like those for which she had not been quite ready, those she had learned from experience to take with her body turned sideways so that they washed past her. Nor was it even like the walls of water she had learned to dive into or duck under and which, when occasionally she misjudged, had ground her in the sand. Never had there been anything to compare with this—this ground swell before which she had had time to do nothing but swallow her breath in terror. In an instant of searing clarity—such as has been reported by those on the verge of drowning—she knew that Benjamin had been trying to say, "I want, I need, I will choke, I will smother, I will die if you don't let me go. I must be free. *Free.* Do you hear?" Then the waves came slamming down again and washed her up, limp and mindless as a clump of seaweed, on a foreign strip of shore.

sixteen

There could be no question who it was when the telephone rang before early-morning tea. Rosy jumped as if there were an electrode on her heart, controlled at a distance by Benjamin. She let the phone ring and ring while she strengthened her resolve.

"Where were you?" Benjamin sounded as if he'd been afraid she'd escaped during the night. "They didn't want to put me through at this hour. I told them it was urgent. It is. Oh, darling, please, *please* forgive me."

"We were both overwrought," Rosy said with synthetic calm.

"I've never seen you like that—you didn't shed a tear."

"I've been thinking, Benjamin. Birdbyle is right. Why don't you go away for a few days? Go up to Cambridge."

"We were to have gone together. You so looked forward to it."

"Just leave me the books and radio."

"I know I'm not much help when you're sick . . . especially as I was yesterday. I promise to behave."

"Please go."

"You really want me to? I don't like leaving you alone. Imgard's gone to get Tonkey, so you couldn't even call her."

"There's nothing I need."

"Are you sure?"

"Quite sure."

"When should I go?"

"Today. This morning."

"Hmmm. Perhaps I will after all." Benjamin was making his voice gloomy to compensate for the rise in his spirits. "All right. As soon as the pubs open I'll get the radio and books and come straight to the hospital. I promise not to have a drop."

"Don't come up with them."

"You're still angry." Benjamin was alert and alarmed.

"No."

"You *do* forgive me? You're not just sending me away?"

"I just want to be left in peace." Rosy squeezed out a laugh.

"Of course. And you must have it to get better. I'll call you from Cambridge this evening."

"No, don't call. They give me an injection so early."

"That's true. I might disturb your sleep. I'll be back Sunday evening. Be good. Hear? And do as the doctor tells you, so he'll let you out of jail very soon. Bless you."

Benjamin—she could deny it no longer—wanted to be free. The signs, written in giant letters, had been everywhere, but until now she'd been afraid to read them: his silence about her letter and bland "What had you in mind?"; his behavior after the Academy party, after Tivoli, at the Duchessa's; his pushing her toward Theo; his threat of suicide the day they sailed.

She had told herself she had come to Europe to examine the state of their marriage. Instead she had seized every pretext to reassure herself that there was nothing to examine: Benjamin was overtired, overwrought. All that was required of her was patience. She had been as unwilling to translate his screams and decode his signals as, in the beginning, she had been sluggish to understand that theirs would not be, could not be a conventional marriage.

After the wedding, and a weekend honeymoon in New York, he had taken her to live in his bachelor apartment in Cambridge. His salary, which had barely supported him, would not feed two. She found a job in the registrar's office at Harvard, one she would have hated had she had time to think of anything but Benjamin. He prepared for classes, lectured, read papers. Evenings and weekends were theirs. On the long walks they took around Cambridge, Benjamin talked about his students, about the verse play he was turning over in his mind (it had an Irish subject; he was writing it as a wedding present to her), about the future and the fame that would one day be his. When it grew too cold for walking, they stayed indoors. Her education began in earnest. He read to her, gave her books to read. When they tired of reading, they listened to music. Sometimes they sat up until dawn, talking, filling in the past for one another.

For months they were as isolated as if they had been on an island in Maine out of season. Orlando, Benjamin's closest friend, a poet and a colleague at Harvard, telephoned one day when she was home and Benjamin was meeting a class. "How's the phantom bride?" he asked with some amusement. "You're married to a madman—you know that, don't you, Rosy? He's trying to hide you. He can't keep refusing invitations forever. He offends people who are trying to be kind. Make him bring you to the Coopers' on Saturday. Remind him that one doesn't refuse an invitation from one's head of department."

Had he been refusing invitations? she asked Benjamin when he came home.

"It's over now," he said with resignation. "I suppose no woman could live as I've lived. You'd like to go to the Coopers', wouldn't you? I'll take you. With a caveat: novels may grow out of social life, but poetry requires solitude."

It hadn't been the beginning of the Coopers' kind of life, as Benjamin had feared it might be. The war, making entertaining difficult, had been on his side. They saw no one but Orlando. They drank inexpensive sherry (and very little of that). The men talked poetry, read, criticized, applauded each other's work. In good weather she and Benjamin took picnics to the James plot in Mt. Auburn, or to Walden Pond. When there was something to celebrate—an act finished, a poem written—they went into Boston to the Lincolnshire for a drink, or to dinner at the Athens or Jacob Wirth's.

The first break in their self-absorption came after Benjamin finished his research for the play. He began to write. At night? she asked him, trying to pull him back to bed. He kissed her and, folding her arms under the covers, said, "Did you imagine we could go on forever living like ordinary husbands and wives? A writer covets the long silent hours of the night. It's only then he's free to brood, to write. I warned you you would have a rival."

How dangerous, how implacable a rival she had not understood until later when it became clear that Benjamin was willing to sacrifice everything for his work. But by that time he had convinced her that he couldn't live without her. She was essential to his happiness, he used to say, "the pivot around which my life gyrates."

"So you're happy with your genius?" Uncle Jim said, seeing it plainly on one of his visits. (Uncle Jim had not approved of the marriage. "What has this man to offer you?" he'd asked. "He has no money, his teaching job barely supports him, he has no family, no name." "He has genius," she had said, defiantly.)

Yes, she was very happy. She was learning what it was like to be married to a genius—its disciplines, its rewards.

"Wait," Uncle Jim said. "If after a few years you're ten percent happier than you were before you married, you can count yourself blessed."

The percentage had been so much higher that she had often felt she was getting more than her share. She had had more in those years than most people have in a lifetime.

It was after the war, when they'd been married six or seven years, that their problems began. Orlando, running into her one day in the Harvard Coop, said, "I've been hoping to have a chance to talk to you alone about your crazy husband." (Orlando used the word "crazy" fondly; he was "crazy" too.) "You must *make* Benjamin publish. He has enough poems for two books. He must do it to bolster his academic career if for no other reason. His term is up next year. Reappointment is by no means automatic. Get after him."

Benjamin knew instantly who'd put her up to it when she asked that evening at dinner why he didn't publish. "Don't listen to Orlando. Nor to Iphigene. One of the things I love about you is that you aren't ambitious for me. I can't be a careerist like Orlando. I hate the intrigue which he loves. I'll publish when I'm ready. And as for my academic career . . ."

His academic career had ended shortly thereafter. Before long, lack of money began to make trouble between them. Just when they needed to be more economical than ever if they were to get by on her salary and the odd check Benjamin received from magazines, he became more extravagant. At first blush his requirements were modest—books, records, a little sherry, theater tickets if he was working on a play. Iphigene had warned her not to be deceived. He was not a bohemian. His extravagant nature was as cleverly disguised as a monk's gluttony by loose brown robes. The records required a first-rate phonograph, his appetite for books was insatiable, the sherry turned into gin.

And by that time there was the psychiatrist to pay. The strain of living by writing ("It won't work, Benjamin," Orlando had said. "Nobody can do it these days. If that's what you wanted, you should have married for money, not love") was taking its toll. He drank more. Insomnia, anxiety attacks, nightmares, which he claimed she'd cured him of, began to devil him again. "Occupational hazards," he said. "To be tolerated with little complaint—unless they interfere with my work."

They interfered with their lives but not with his work. He published his first book of poems. His articles and reviews appeared in the literary magazines. His second book was a critical success. He was invited to give readings. With fame, modest though it was, came other problems. They came to a head the summer a bicycle accident put her to bed with a back injury (the same disk trouble that had felled her at the Mallorys'). The pain, without morphine, had been grueling. For some time she hadn't known or cared that Benjamin had withdrawn from her. A robot resembling him came to stand at the door of her room. He looked at her, as if through a visor, with narrow, reproachful eyes. Why have you deserted me? they seemed to say. Why do you torture me with your pain? After the acute phase had passed, she took in that he wore another look, guilty and evasive. He was revenging himself on her: he had begun an affair.

What did it mean? Was he merely angry at her for being sick? Or was he restless, straining against the years of marriage? She had given him more freedom than most women grant their husbands. Had it not been enough?

It meant nothing, he said, when she confronted him. It was over. He was depressed, remorseful. It would be easy for her to forgive his infidelities . . .

This girl. Ruth. What others?

. . . if she understood how little they had to do with love. Love? Why, they were more like pitched battles. His behavior with other women was *pathological*. Dr. Sage had made him see that. And having seen it . . . it would not happen again.

He was convincing. She believed him. There followed,

as so often after a violent eruption, an idyllic period. It was during this time that she made the mistake of pressing for a child. If only . . . if only . . .

If only she had been more successful at growing a skin against his infidelities. For, of course, they continued. During white nights following quarrels that became more and more frequent, she imagined that if their marriage ended it would be because Benjamin asked for a divorce to marry a Radcliffe student. Or a poet-follower like the ones that clustered around him after public readings. Like the one who was after Andrew.

There was no woman now. She was sure. She knew the signs. Benjamin had been right all along: it was not women but poetry that was her rival. It was for the sake of his work that he wanted to be free. The publication of the long poem would mark the end of an era. He wanted to be free to begin a new one. To begin a new creative cycle. How was it Yeats had put it?—to look for new metaphors.

If this was true—and the more she thought about it the more certain she was—why, instead of staging scenes, hadn't he told her so? Or, if he found the idea of telling her too painful (how explain a need so abstract to a wife? How much easier it would have been to be able to say he loved someone else), if this was it, why hadn't he simply left her, gone away?

It was possible that Benjamin didn't see it clearly himself. Brilliant as he was, he was often surprisingly lacking in insight. And then there was his ambivalence, his terrible ambivalence: I want . . . I do not want; I need . . . I do not need; it would be better . . . maybe it would be worse. And his fear. He, no less than she, would be afraid to face the numbness, the loneliness, the lovelessness that would follow.

For Benjamin, who, where work was concerned, not only had a limitless capacity for stoicism but actually *sought* suffering, there was something more. What if he was making a mistake: this was not the beginning of a new cycle? What if, once alone, he found his talent had dried up? What if, without her, he found he couldn't write? The source of inspiration being so mysterious, he invested everything connected with writing—his pen, the old Underwood typewriter, the chair he sat in—with magic. If she was his muse, his mage, as he had often said, what a dangerous thing it would be to leave her! If, on the other hand, she left him, the spirits that govern the flow of inspiration—this was the way his mind worked—would not punish him, a passive victim, would they?

Occult hocus-pocus. She didn't believe in this rubbish. Why should she fall in with his fantasies. His art. His gift. His work. She was sick of the words. Sick to death of them. She had survived many crises. She would survive this one. Perhaps she had been distorting, exaggerating the whole thing. Immobility did that to one. He hated her being sick, had had too much to drink, had become hysterical. Nothing more. Hadn't he tried to get her to leave the hospital with him, to fly home? Hadn't he been genuinely remorseful before she went off to Ponza (and even anxious to know with whom she was going, afraid it might be Theo)? What about the peaceful weeks they'd had together before Tivoli? Didn't they count for something?

After she was discharged from the hospital, they would continue as before. They would tour England. When it was time, they would go home. He would find some work to do. Or get an advance from his publisher. The book would come out. . . .

Yes, and the quarrels would get worse and worse, the scenes, the screams, the nightmares, the threats of suicide, the push toward madness. Whether from lack of inspiration or resentment, he would be unable to write. She claimed she didn't care about his work, but could she imagine him without it? He would be like someone lobotomized, decapitated. It would not be *he*.

The difficulties of living with a man of his temperament, which had been bearable when she was convinced of his love, of his need for her (Theo had seen how important that was), would become intolerable. He would grind her down and down. Eventually—how long would it take, a year? two?—he would come to hate her. And she him.

So, during the days while Benjamin was away, Rosy went round and round like someone lost in a maze near closing time. A maze such as one sees in Italian gardens. A maze full of false clues, ingeniously contrived cul-de-sacs, crisscrossed and mislabeled paths. While her immobilized body was washed, fed, injected and examined, her thoughts raced in panicky disorder down one path and then another. From time to time, worn out, hopelessly lost, she cautioned herself to slow down. To think, decide, plan. Instead, she fell into anxious ruminating until, imagining she heard the jingling of the guardians' keys as he came to lock up for the night, she began again trying to find her way out, first calmly, then frantically, panic once more engulfing her.

The door of the room was flung open. Benjamin came rushing to her side. "Darling. Has it been hideous?" He buried his face in her gown.

She stroked his head. Lifted it. Looked into his eyes. The pupils were doing their ceaseless nystagmic jig, a reminder of the roiling activity that went on behind them. How he suffered! She ran her hand down his cheek. Could she really come to hate him?

"You're looking at me reproachfully," he said.

She shook her head: No. It took a minute to find her voice. "Pull up a chair," she said.

"Birdbyle isn't a bit pleased. He says the spasm is as tight as if you'd been running the whole time I was away. Did it seem long?"

"A lifetime."

"I never should have left you." Benjamin's reservoir of guilt was always full to the brim; one added drop and over it spilled. "Look," he said, as if suddenly remembering that he was not all bad. "See what I brought you? Some little presents. First, a map of Cambridge. Isn't it pretty, with the greens and blues? It will help you see where everything is— Trinity, Kings. Then there's this." He undid a piece of brown paper. "A Shakesperean coin. The real thing. See the date? I found it in an antique shop. And, something I suspect will please you most of all." He drew out of his pocket a bar of chocolate. "There is a tiny bite missing. I got terribly hungry on the train. Is the food frightful?"

She couldn't remember having eaten. "Tasteless."

"Puddings and brussels sprouts. I bet they're strong on brussels sprouts. How shall I entertain you? Shall I tell you about Cambridge?"

It was not scenes that she would have to guard against now, but sweet talk. If he suspected for a moment . . .

"Tell me, what was it like?" she said.

"How I wished you were with me! It was *so* beautiful. More even than I remembered. What a neurotic idiot I was to be unhappy there! I don't see now how it was possible. The first day I just walked and walked, relieved to find it all there, the way I'd left it. No bomb craters like London. I was like a mother nervously going over a child who's been in an accident to see if everything is there. All the fingers and toes. And everything *was* there. Not even a tooth missing. The lawns! There never were such lawns! Do you realize there are no lawns in Italy? And that combination of gray walls, ivy, and flower beds full of geraniums. You mustn't get the idea that it's pretty. Not at all; the scale saves it from that. It's noble. Grand. After hours of walking I went to Kings Chapel. I'm as gothic, I decided, as you and Paul are baroque. It suits my temperament better. Someone was practicing Bach on the organ. I sat and listened, drenched in nostalgia.

That evening I went to a messy old Indian restaurant I used to eat in. You're not tired?"

"What did you do the next day?" Rosy pressed him to go on, afraid of blurting out what was raging in her mind if he remained silent for even a moment.

Benjamin jumped up with remembered excitement. "I went punting on the Cam. It's slim and willowy—rather like you. And the Backs! And the bridges! In memory I'd made them fewer. The weather was rather like you too. Sunny and clear one minute, then showers, then sun again." Benjamin smiled happily at the fleetingness of his wife's moods, so unlike his. "Each time it rained I'd hide under a bridge, smoking. Before I'd finished my cigarette the sun was out again."

He began to pace the floor between Rosy's bed and the door. "You won't guess whom I saw on the way here," he said after some time.

"On the way to the hospital?" A change in Benjamin's voice made Rosy alert.

"No, not exactly. When my train got in from Cambridge it was your dinner hour—or I thought it must be. Having time to kill, I decided, on the spur of the moment, to telephone"—Benjamin tried, unsuccessfully, to make his tone suggest that praise would be in order for his resourcefulness —"Phoebe."

Phoebe. Rosy felt a distant yet piercing stab of jealousy somewhere, as a patient with an amputated leg feels pain in the phantom limb.

"I looked her up in the phone book. There she was. Same number, same address. You know, she still hasn't married."

Beautiful, brilliant, much-sought-after Phoebe had never married. Benjamin's specter always intruded between her and her suitors. Or so Benjamin used to say to Rosy in the days when, after a quarrel, he was afraid of losing her. "Don't think I don't know what it's like living with me," he used to say. "No woman could bear it. But you mustn't leave me. Should you, you would find that after me no other man would satisfy you." Did he regret having taunted her this way, now that he wanted to be free?

"What's extraordinary is that she's become a psycho-analyst."

"I thought she was a dancer." She had always pictured a Vivian Leigh in tutu. How will Benjamin describe me to my successor? she wondered. She would undoubtedly become more beautiful, more mysterious, wittier, wiser as she drifted off into a fog of myth and fantasy. Cold comfort.

"She was, and a good one. Very. Of course, it's been years. I shouldn't have been so surprised at the change. Actually, Phoebe always had the makings of a headmistress. It's curious"—Benjamin stopped pacing—"her ankles have thickened."

So, the interview had not gone well. Benjamin had a keen eye for ankles, but ankles, unlike waists, don't change. Was he punishing Phoebe for damaging the image he'd carried around all these years?

"She had me know that she's a great success, with a very lively practice. So lively, in fact, that she hasn't time for any but professional reading." Benjamin looked up with a pinched, humorless smile. "You won't believe it. She didn't know I'd been publishing."

Phoebe's revenge. Had she done nothing since the day she sailed back to England but study how to wound Benjamin, she could not have done better. He had been at pains to have what he wrote published in London, had counted heavily on her reading him. "Fame is hollow," he was fond of saying. "All a writer can hope for"—and he was only half joking—"is for his wife and one or two old flames to read him with devotion." There went one.

"She's become quite formidable." Benjamin laughed dryly. "I must say I'm glad she's not *my* analyst. She's eager to meet you, by the way."

"Injection time." A nurse burst into the room without knocking. "Oh, sorry. I didn't know you had a visitor." The nurse seemed as embarrassed as if she'd caught the Bolds in bed.

"This is my husband," Rosy said, relieved that Benjamin would have to go now.

"I'm sure Mrs. Bold will sleep well tonight, now that you're back," the nurse recovered coyly. "I'm afraid I must ask you to leave now. It's lights out."

"I'm off." Benjamin came to kiss Rosy. "Shall I leave you *The Eustace Diamonds*? I finished it on the train coming down. Marvelous writer, Trollope. I'm thinking of doing a piece on him. I'll ring you first thing in the morning." Benjamin stopped at the door. "Oh. I forgot. Guess whom I met on High Street?"

"Quiller-Couch." Rosy strained to keep up her act for another moment.

"Uh-uh. Someone you know. A hint: he lives near Cambridge."

"I give up."

"Theo Addis. With a woman. There! Don't I bring interesting things to tell you? His father just died. They buried him that morning, I think."

"Mr. Bold, it's time," the nurse said.

" 'Hurry up please. It's time.' " He mimicked. To Rosy he said, "Theo's leaving tonight to take his mother—who has rather gone to pieces, I gather—to Canada to be with her sister. He says we must go to his house when you get out. His sister will look after you. Won't that be nice?"

The nurse was still holding the hypodermic needle.

"I'm off." Benjamin waved. " 'Good night, ladies, good night, sweet ladies, good night, good night.' "

seventeen

Imgard came to visit the day Rosy was permitted to sit up for the first time. Imgard was sorry not to have come sooner. Had it really been two weeks? Getting ready for vacation had taken all her time. She was worn out. God, what a job it was! *She* could do with a spell in the hospital. Not a bad life: breakfast in bed, lovely flowers (she took in the roses Theo had sent), a round of visitors. Frankly, she couldn't wait to get to Denmark. Her mother would spoil her a bit. She could do with a little spoiling.

Imgard looked more haggard than she had the morning after her party. She seemed edgy, as if she had something on her mind. She had. What would Rosy think of going back to her house when she was discharged from the hospital? "You and Ben could have our room. Andrew can sleep in his study. It would be nice to think you were there, to sort of see to it that Andrew didn't burn the house down."

The second invitation. Theo had called from the airport, the night Benjamin returned from Cambridge, to urge her to go to his house. His sister not only would look after her, but also would hold on to her until he got back from Canada. He would leave his mother as soon as he decently could—in two weeks if all went well.

"I'm afraid we can't," Rosy answered Imgard. "I—"

Imgard gave up the pretense of a polite invitation. "Has Benjamin told you about Andrew's beastly girl? I suppose he has. To be quite candid, I thought if you'd move into the house it would at least make it damned inconvenient for the two of them. Andrew has no tact. None. It's not beyond him to put that girl in my bed."

Benjamin, suspecting that Imgard was working on a counterplot, had warned Rosy that this invitation might be forthcoming. The beastly girl was indeed in the wings, waiting to come on stage as soon as Imgard made her exit. Benjamin was packed, ready to move to the pub, to give his old friend a clear field. In the two weeks that Rosy had been in the hospital and Benjamin had lived with the Mallorys, he had been won over entirely to Andrew's side. The affair with the Bennington girl was not serious, but Andrew's rebellion against Imgard's "domination" was. According to Andrew, the marriage was "a living hell," and had been for years.

Rosy wondered about Imgard. If what Andrew said was true, why did she hang on? Had she become inured to a loveless marriage? She was tough (according to Benjamin), tougher far than Rosy. She could tolerate living in a battleground. Perhaps, when there was no serious threat like this girl, she even enjoyed the power struggle. And there was Tonkey.

And Andrew? Both weaker and stronger than Benjamin, he would neither leave Imgard nor drive her away. His fame had come early. Since then he had published little. He was coasting on his reputation. If he accomplished less than Benjamin, as seemed likely, he would also suffer less. Much less.

"I was waiting to hear what the doctor would say after his examination this morning," Rosy said to Imgard, "so I haven't told Benjamin yet: I plan to fly home as soon as I'm discharged."

"Isn't that risky?"

"Not, it seems, if I agree to stay here an extra week, and go harnessed in a steel brace."

"God! You have to wear one of them?"

"According to Birdbyle."

"And you don't want to see something of England?"

"Sightseeing is 'contraindicated.' England will have to wait until another time."

Rosy rang for the nurse to lower her bed. She had looked forward eagerly to sitting up; had counted on the change of posture to still the thoughts that sang round and round in her head, off-key, whining, perseverative, like the tune of an amusement-park calliope; but after an hour she was so tired she longed to lie down.

"I told you so," the nurse said. "You feel as if you'd been digging ditches, don't you? Wait until you try to walk for the first time and feel your legs go all rubbery under you. I won't lower the bed just yet, though." She handed Rosy a card. "Visitors, like muffins, come in batches."

"Ivy Griffen," Rosy read aloud the name on the card. She ran her finger over the engraving, as if that might give her a clue. "I don't know anyone . . ." Ivy Griffen. Of course. That was Phoebe. The name Ivy hadn't suited Benjamin, so he'd changed it. "Tell her . . ."

Too late. There was a knock on the half-open door. "I hope I'm not intruding. You're Roxana?" She shook hands. "You don't look at all as I expected."

Nor, as Rosy saw when Ivy/Phoebe came into the room, did she look as Rosy had expected. Phoebe was wearing a tweed skirt, a twin sweater set, and brown brogues. Her black hair was pulled back in a bun the way ballet dancers wear theirs, but tighter, with a schoolmistress's severity. Large gray eyes were her most striking feature. She was not conventionally beautiful, nor even pretty, but short and dark; she was, Rosy remembered with another twinge in the phantom limb, what Benjamin had described as his "type."

"Won't you sit down?" Rosy indicated the chair Imgard had vacated.

Phoebe sat very straight, her legs crossed at the ankles (which were not thick). "Benjamin said you wanted to see me?"

"That *I* . . . ?" Rosy laughed at Benjamin's outrageousness. He had told each the other wanted to see her.

"I came because I took it your request was not based on vulgar curiosity." Phoebe looked directly at Rosy. Phoebe's patients must feel the penetration of those gray eyes. "And it occurred to me that you must be alone in London," she added, softening a little. "Do you know anyone here?"

"Just the Mallorys. Benjamin tells me that the Munsons and other people we saw in Rome are arriving in a few days."

"It must be hard to have only Benjamin to rely on. He went up to Cambridge the first weekend you were here, didn't he?"

"I sent him off. I needed—"

"What you needed, what any woman in hospital needs is to have her husband be attentive. Passive-dependent men like Benjamin go to pieces as soon as their spouses are ill." Phoebe said this objectively, as if she and Rosy were discussing a case.

The conversation was moving too quickly for Rosy. And in a direction she didn't like. She wasn't up to it. She wished, above all, that she could lie down. How trapped one was in a hospital! "Will you have some tea?" she stalled, when the maid appeared with a tray.

"I'd love some. I didn't have time for lunch today." Phoebe accepted a piece of cake. "It's always been more or less up to you to look after Benjamin, hasn't it?" she asked when the nurse left. "You've had to be . . . well, nurse, mother."

Hector's words: "a psychiatric nurse." From wife to nurse: When had the transition taken place? "It's not mothering Benjamin wanted. He's had more than he could take of that from Iphigene."

"Iphigene! That was smothering not mothering. Was

there ever a more poisonous, castrating, hateful woman?"

"Hateful? I don't know. Her greatest sin is loving Benjamin too much."

"So much I wonder at her letting him marry you."

"She came to see me as an ally." When Iphigene decided that Rosy was "good" for Benjamin, she had become less possessive. In the end the two women had become friends.

"I lived with them for six months, so there's little about her I don't know. She was very kind at first. Gave Benjamin and me two rooms in her apartment. I admired her lack of hypocrisy . . ."

"Anything for Benjamin."

"Yes, I suppose that was it. And then she must have decided I was not good for him."

Just what Iphigene had told Rosy: "Phoebe is a brilliant girl. Charming, too. She was not for Benjamin, though. Too intransigent. It would have been a terrible mistake for them to have married."

Phoebe put her cup back on the tray. "No, thanks. Nothing more. By the time I left New York, I was in such a state my family had to send me to Germany for a cure. I had a breakdown. A physical one. I did a lot of thinking at the spa. I came to realize how lucky I was to have escaped from the two of them with my life."

Rosy wished she could be candid enough, since candor was in the air, to ask Phoebe why she'd never married. Instead she said, "Benjamin says you've become an analyst."

"Yes. After I came back from Germany, cured but at loose ends, a woman I knew who'd been analyzed by Jung gave me his books to read. She was the one who urged me to study. It was too late to go to medical school, but I found I could become a lay analyst." And then, as if she'd guessed Rosy's unasked question, "You can't imagine how absorbing my work is. And how demanding. It quite fills my life."

Phoebe was not convincing. While she had been talking, Rosy had been trying to imagine the girl Benjamin had fallen in love with in Cambridge. The woman who sat opposite her bore so little resemblance to the one she had been jealous of that she could not put the two together. It was not simply that Phoebe had changed with the passing years. Rather, it was that today she was using her clinical manner as a façade to cover her real feelings. It had taken courage for her to come to see Rosy.

"Forgive me. I'm due at Tavistock Clinic," Phoebe said, looking at a gold watch which hung from a chain around her neck. "I wanted to be sure there was time for something else I wanted to say. Frankly, I'm concerned about Benjamin. It strikes me he's not at all well. Are you aware how manic he is?"

"He was. I thought he had calmed down."

"The night he came to see me he talked wildly about a poem he'd written. He went on and on, with no awareness of my lack of interest. I only just escaped having to listen to it by pretending an evening engagement. He needs treatment. To reduce his hostility, if for no other reason."

"He doesn't want it reduced. He has a theory that animus generates creative energy."

"That's splendid for him. What about you? Treatment would also help him come to terms with his incestuous feelings. I see you shaking your head. You're opposed to psychoanalysis?"

"Benjamin knows all that. He's read everything there is to read. He's been to a psychiatrist."

"Ah. He kept that dark the other evening. And it didn't help?"

"It helped as much as he wanted to be helped. It got him to send out poems, let him deal with the mechanics of his career . . ."

"That was already a problem for him when I knew him.

He rather expected editors and publishers to come to him."

"He learned all he could safely bear to know. Then broke it off."

"He needs a Jungian."

"Do you really believe people like Benjamin can be analyzed? I don't any more. They need treatment from time to time, medication, even to be hospitalized when things get out of hand. But analysis? For one thing, they break the rules and get away with it. Analysts, no matter how hard they try not to be, are impressed with them, seduced by their brilliance. . . ."

"Or so they imagine."

". . . More important, they don't want to change. They're terrified of doing anything that will tamper with their creativity."

Phoebe looked thoughtful. "You counted on treatment to help. And you're disappointed."

It was true. Rosy had hoped for too much. She had naïvely hoped for a cure.

"Yet you're willing to go on? You've been happy enough to make it worthwhile?"

Phoebe hoped for a denial: this was why she had come. There was a plea buried in her questions. It was important for her to believe that Benjamin was unfitted to make any woman a husband. That she still loved him or, as she might have put it, that she was still fixated on him was clear. Her analysis had not helped her there. She had come today hoping to hear something that *would* cure her. Some admission of Rosy's failure?

A wish to help Phoebe tempted Rosy to tell her her decision. But whether out of loyalty to Benjamin, whom she should tell first, or out of fear of hearing herself say it aloud, she said only, "Happy? I have been happy."

If Benjamin was disappointed in Rosy's bland account

of her visit with Phoebe, he hid it well. He fell in readily with Rosy's plan for going home. Yes, he would go as soon as he could book passage on a ship, taking the luggage with him. If she could really bear to stay alone—she could?—it was the most sensible arrangement. Thank God they had had their return tickets. Money was beginning to be a worry now that he had to pay for his room. He might have to borrow from Andrew to pay the doctor. She was sure her hospital insurance would cover the London bill? Well, that was a break. Yes, to tell the truth, the more he thought about it the more impatient he was to go home.

The scuffling and giggling outside her door told Rosy that Benjamin had not come alone for his final visit. "Darling, if we're late it's Andrew's fault. We couldn't get him out of the pub. But I've brought you a lovely surprise. Rodney."

Rosy was sitting up in a chair. Rodney bent over to kiss her. "It's a crime that this has happened. We were crushed at the news," he said. "Margaret isn't here yet. She told me to tell you that she'd be in to see you the instant she arrives. She'll look after arrangements for you."

Andrew, who'd been looking at Rosy in sideways squints, hiccuped.

"Step up here, Andrew," Rodney said. "I was shocked to hear this wretch hadn't been in to see you, Roxana."

"Sorry, Roxana." Andrew kissed Rosy's cheek gingerly. "I've been madly busy at the BBC."

They all laughed. Since the arrival of the Bennington girl, Andrew had hardly been to the office.

"More flowers from Addis?" Benjamin asked. "He's been as attentive as a lover," he said to the others. "If he were here I'd take it up with him. Since he's safely in Canada . . ."

Rosy blushed. "They're from Will Hendy."

"Hendy. You hear that?" Benjamin appealed to his

friends. "What's he doing sending flowers? Has he been in?"

"He came yesterday."

"The bastard," Andrew said. "We waited hours for him in the pub and he never showed up."

"Wasn't he unbelievable?" Benjamin appealed to the men again. "Darling, it was killing. At the luncheon at Lady Bartlett's—she's an English version of the Duchessa—"

"Nothing of the kind," said Rodney. "She's not at all like Flossie, except that she's generous to writers. Hendy hit it off with Flossie very well, but Lady Bartlett, or maybe it was Linton House, seems to have overwhelmed him."

"Lady B. is a monumental snob," said Andrew to no one in particular.

"She asked him"—Benjamin kept up the continuity— "where he was from. He said, 'Wichita.' " Benjamin half sneezed, half gagged the word out.

"She turned to him"—Andrew took up the story—"and said, '*Do* tell me, Mr. Hendy, what is it they make in Wichita?' "

"As if scalp-making might have been the leading industry." Benjamin danced a step or two to help him get it out. "Will slapped her on the back . . ." Benjamin broke down and tried again. ". . . on the back, like this"—he hit Andrew between the shoulder blades—"and said, 'Money, Madame, money.' "

When the laughter subsided, Andrew said, "The only one besides Lady B. who didn't think it funny was Ann Hendy. I was sitting next to her, so I saw. She made jabs at her raspberry bombe as if the spoon were a knife and she were jabbing into Will's big belly."

"That marriage isn't going to last," Rodney predicted. "I flew up from Rome with them, and saw signs. Those adoring students—"

"Oh, come, they've only just married," said Andrew, who felt Rodney's words as an attack on his romance.

Sometime after the luncheon, while the others were waiting for him at the pub, Will had come to the hospital. He had buried his head in the side of Rosy's bed and had burst into tears. He'd been so nervous about Lady Bartlett (who affected him much as the Duchessa had affected Benjamin) that he'd had five shots of Scotch before the luncheon. "I don't see why Ann got so mad with me," he had said, blowing his nose and pulling himself together. "Why should she give a damn if I slugged Her Ladyship? You know, Canary, I'm wild about that girl, but I warned her before we got married that I wasn't housebroken. She wouldn't listen."

This morning, with the flowers, Will had sent a note:

Forgive my drunken drivel. All is well. Alleluia.

"I don't know what it is about you poets." Rodney shook his head, half serious, half joking. "Alcohol, break-downs, divorce . . . It seems to me the older generation managed better somehow. And without psychiatry."

"Changing fashions," hiccuped Andrew. "It used to be tuberculosis and syphilis."

"This is the age of . . . the age of . . ." Benjamin looked around the air myopically and pinched his fingers together, as if the word were eluding him like a butterfly. "The age of a . . ."

"Anxiety?" Rodney offered.

"That's it! Anxiety! I will have none about you, Roxana, now that Rodney is here," Benjamin said, coming to kiss her goodbye.

"We'll take good care of her," said Rodney. "Although I can't see why you want to leave just as I've arrived."

"I must go. I must go." With predeparture euphoria, Benjamin stretched out his arms. "I'm sailing home to the New World. To a new era."

eighteen

Two weeks later Rosy was well enough to follow Benjamin. The bus for her flight was being announced as she waved goodbye to the Munsons and hurried after her porter to the check-in counter. She felt a bubble of pleasure, the first in weeks—light, clear, and evanescent like the bubbles children blow—at being almost late. Afflicted ordinarily with *Reisefieber,* which made her arrive prematurely for planes and trains, she admired extravagantly those more cavalier about timetables. The bubble burst: her lateness marked no progress in their direction; it was simply that she dreaded going home.

The waiting room was as noisy and crowded as a cocktail party. Rosy took a seat a little apart. Her eyes toured the room slowly, like a searchlight making a routine turn in its arc, not looking for anything in particular but lighting whatever is in its path. They were women mostly— not surprisingly on the chartered flight for schoolteachers Margaret had found for her—and excessively animated.

Rosy took out her book—a shield, she hoped, against casual conversation. Her natural shyness about talking to strangers was magnified today by a feeling of alienation from these cheerful, buzzing women, who were exchanging anecdotes about their vacation and going home, reluctantly perhaps but not painfully, to lives they had left for a summer hiatus.

There was a rush to the door when the flight bus was announced again. Rosy remained seated. She pressed her back, or rather the steel cage which encased it, against the wall. She told herself she did not have to go. No one, not even he, knew. Of course, it was not true. She might delay, but she could no more go back on her decision than a skin once peeled from a fruit could clothe its flesh again. She was the last to board the bus.

It twisted and turned out of London, past row after row of semidetached villas. Men in shirt sleeves worked in narrow, identical gardens before their evening meal. Hollyhocks stood stiffly against the fences. London through glass: that had been her view of the city. When the bus stopped she joined the ragged, windblown single file and boarded the waiting aircraft. There was one seat left, on the aisle. She fastened her seat belt and took out her book.

Some time after takeoff (another nervous moment she uncharacteristically missed today), Rosy became aware that she had less and less room. A woman was leaning well over her, to listen to a story her neighbor was telling. The woman's jacket brushed against Rosy's hair.

"Would you like to change seats?" Rosy closed her book and prepared to leave.

"Is it *that* good?" her seatmate asked. "You haven't had your nose out of that book since the waiting room."

The standing woman, somewhat embarrassed, said to Rosy, "Don't get up. I was just going back to my seat." To her friend she said, "See you, Judy." And then, bracketing Judy and Rosy with a wink, she called, "Here come the marinis, girls."

Rosy fixed her eyes on her novel with little confidence that she would be permitted to continue reading. (A book was clearly a conversation piece to Judy.) The steward rolled up a cart of drinks. While he was reciting what he had to offer, Judy reached across Rosy and deftly removed two martinis. She put one on her tray, and drank the other in a single swallow. It happened so fast one could not be certain. The English steward gave no sign. "And you, Madame?" he asked Rosy.

Judy moved the second martini toward her on her tray, slowly, as if it were a chess piece for which she had elaborate plans. "You're not a schoolteacher," she said, not taking her eyes off the glass.

Reluctantly, and only half giving up her pretense of reading, Rosy admitted that she was not.

"You don't look the type." Judy lifted the glass and downed its contents. "You don't look as though you spent your life with women, the way the others on this plane do. Even the men. I noticed you in the waiting room. You were looking at my dress. How do you like it?" Judy turned toward Rosy. She had a small, deeply suntanned face. It was difficult to tell whether she was a young woman aged by the tan, or a middle-aged woman made more youthful by it.

Rosy, who did not remember having seen either Judy or her dress before, made an inane appropriate reply.

"It's from Paris. It cost a fortune." Judy threw back her elbow-length cape. "That's a sleeve *à l'américaine*." She fished out of her pocketbook a pack of Gauloises and lit a cigarette. "I want to knock my husband's eye out when he comes to meet me." She blew thick, well-formed rings of smoke. "Married?" she pounced.

Never good at fending off inquisitive questions, Rosy knew she would answer; how she wasn't sure. "Separated," she heard herself say.

"At least you had a man. How did you like traveling alone?"

"I wasn't alone."

The steward stopped beside them with another tray

"It's not a very sexy group we're with," Judy observed, not lowering her voice, "but where else can you get first-class treatment at bargain fares?" She watched the steward pour champagne. "I'm not like the others," she said, taking the glass he offered. "In the first place, I'm married. To a very handsome guy. He's in TV. No civil service sinecure, as you probably know. It's a tough racket. That's where I come in. Old Judy brings in the steady, if less flavorful, bacon." She held her glass up to show the steward that, the bubbles having subsided, it was only half full. "The other teachers in the art department at Julia Richman are heavy on teaching, light on art. Maître d'," she interrupted herself to call after the steward, "Would you be good enough to sell me a bottle of that Piper Heidsieck?"

"I'll be back in just a minute, Madame, to refill—"

"I don't want another glass. I want a bottle. It depresses me to have a *glass* of champagne with a meal," she said to Rosy.

A barely perceptible tightening around the lips was the only sign of the steward's displeasure. "Just a minute," he said, and walked to the pantry.

". . . . while I'm the reverse," continued Judy, with hardly a breath for this aside. "I'm a painter. Art Students League. A year at the Beaux Arts in Paris." Judy seemed suddenly dispirited. Her spirits rose as she caught sight of the approaching steward. "How much is that?" she asked, putting her hand out for the bottle.

Not immediately releasing it, the steward said primly, "We'll give this to you, Madame, if you promise not to be—"

"Sick?" Judy's laugh was like the sound seals make at feeding time. "That's the only condition under which I promise *not* to be sick." She took the reluctantly released bottle, and expertly poured a glass for Rosy and one for herself. "You like champagne?" She slipped the bottle into the elasticized pouch attached to the seat in front.

"It's my favorite drink." Or rather it was, thought Rosy, for whom champagne was inescapably associated with festive occasions.

"Thought so. When I saw you in the waiting room I said to myself, That one wouldn't be half bad if she just defrosted a little, and took the ramrod out of her back. I like you, you know? You've got to come to see us in New York. We have one of the brownstones in Chelsea, across from the Seminary. Know where it is? We have champagne breakfasts every Sunday. They last all day. Will you come?' She turned to face Rosy, wanting an immediate reply, like an unpopular child extending an invitation to her birthday party.

It had not occurred to Rosy before, but of course she would have to go alone. It was part of what was called making a new life. "I'd love to, but I live in—"

Judy cut her off: "You're nice, but too polite." She poured herself some more champagne. Remembering Rosy she aimed for her glass and missed it. "Were you in Venice this summer?"

Rosy mopped up the spilled champagne with a Kleenex and admitted she had been there.

"Where'd you stay?"

"In a little place near the Fenice." It was Theo who had given her the name of the hotel. Theo would have had her letter by now.

"Don't worry. You don't have to be vague with me. I won't put it in the school bulletin. And I may even tell you *my* secret place. You like Venice?"

Rosy had noticed that it wasn't always necessary to answer Judy.

"I stay in a beautiful run-down palazzo on the Giudecca. We've been going there for years. From my room I could look across to San Marco. There's a little garden in the back where I paint. Ever read *The Aspern Papers*? It was written there."

Rosy and Benjamin had heard of two other candidates when they were in Venice. "What's its name?" Rosy asked with interest.

"Not so fast. I'll tell you later. If you come to one of my breakfasts. I said we always go there, but we hadn't been in three years. Broke. Never, never, never try to fix up a brownstone." Judy poured herself another glass. "Reggie decided that this summer I needed a change, was overtired, run down. He swore he didn't mind staying alone." She gave her hungry-seal laugh again. "I'm sure he didn't spend *all* his time alone."

The steward came to remove the trays. Seeing Judy's food untouched, he asked, with a combination of solicitude and reproachfulness, if she would like something else.

"No." Judy held on to her champagne glass, as he took her tray. "It was great. I just wasn't hungry. And don't bother with the dessert and all that jazz. Just black coffee and cognac."

"I'll be back with coffee in a few minutes." The steward didn't like to have his routine abbreviated or hurried.

Judy took the champagne bottle from its pouch and held it up to the light to see how much was left. She poured a little where Rosy's glass had been. "What a waste," she said in an aside as if Rosy had been careless. "Want a little more?"

Rosy mopped up with the same Kleenex. "No, thanks."

"You know, I like you. You're a good conversationalist. And what a relief it is to speak English! My Italian is O.K., but I feel as though I have lockjaw if I have to speak it through a meal. At the pensione I sat at a table alone." The corners of Judy's mouth turned down like commas. "To tell you the truth, I was too damn much alone. And Reggie's letters didn't come all that damn frequently, either. I suppose he was busy," she added hastily, as if she'd opened a door better left closed.

The steward had poured their coffee and was offering brandy and liqueurs. Judy leaned across to study the selection. Her elbow slipped and hit the edge of Rosy's coffee cup. The steward, as if anticipating disaster, was ready with a napkin to clean it up.

"Courvoisier," Judy said, pointing to the bottle. "Best sedative in the world. Never need a pill. Makes me sleep like a baby. Not so great at getting up. What's there to get up for? There are days better spent in bed. When I first got to Venice I was so excited, I walked around from morning till night. Then I tried to settle down to some painting. It wouldn't come. I was too tired. *And* goddamn lonely. Wanna know how I spent my birthday?" Judy looked at Rosy belligerently. "In bed. Alone except for a couple of bottles of Asti Spumante. After a while I stopped going down for meals. The Signora had her eye on me. Was worried that I wasn't eating." Judy interrupted herself to beckon to the stewardess who was going past preparing passengers for the night. "May I have just a drop?" she coaxed, holding out her empty glass.

"You didn't get any?" the stewardess asked apologetically. When she returned, she too looked prim. She gave Judy the brandy and said, "Here's a nightcap. Let's put the light out soon, shall we, so we can all get a little sleep?"

Judy smiled vacantly, promising nothing. "I'm not so sure it was for me to have a rest," she continued to Rosy. "I suspect he wanted to get rid of me. After the first two letters he didn't write." Judy drained what remained in her glass and stood up abruptly. " 'Cuse me." She went to the front of the plane holding her empty glass. When she returned some time later, she looked sallow beneath her tan. There was a large coffee stain on the cape which covered the sleeve *à l'américaine*. "Let's put out the lights, shall we, so we can get a little sleep?" she mimicked, snapping off her overhead reading light.

Tired, but not sleepy, Rosy was thrown back on her book. It no longer held her attention. As a woman who nurses her husband through a terminal illness begins to long for the inevitable, although she knows that when it comes she will be grief-stricken and inconsolable, Rosy had become impatient during the month at University College for the moment when she would tell Benjamin her decision. Now, with that moment only a few hours away, she was filled with fresh dread.

Should she tell Benjamin at the airport? Or in the taxi? She must not delay, that much she knew. She would be the one to stay in Cambridge, because of her job. Benjamin, with nothing to hold him there, would move to New York. To give him time to pack, she would have to go away for a few days. Somewhere where she knew no one, where she wouldn't be tempted to talk. To a beach. What was the name of the inn on the way to the Thornton estate? A funny name that Benjamin had wanted to change. With the first warm days, long before it was time to swim, they had packed wicker baskets of lunch and had driven off with the Happy Extroverts (one of them had been at Harvard with young Thornton) for a day on the beach. The first view of the sea through a break in the dunes made them as excited as children. "The sea! Isn't it beautiful?" they shouted to one another. "And no one, not a soul, for miles!" It seemed, now, so long ago that it might have been part of her childhood she was remembering.

Sometime after four o'clock, she must have dozed off. She was awakened by the aroma of coffee. Weak, American coffee. The taste reminded her how close she was to home.

"We land in an hour," the stewardess said, forcing a customs declaration on Judy, who had refused breakfast.

"Nothing to declare but a hangover," Judy said, turning her face to the wall.

Rosy looked out at the monotonous landscape of

clouds. How little it would matter to her, she thought, if the motor began to sputter, the wings to spin.

Judy was still sleeping when the plane taxied down the runway. Rosy didn't see her again until she had gone through customs. When Benjamin and Iphigene caught Rosy in a simultaneous embrace, her head fell between theirs. Judy stood not ten feet away. Her dress, a mass of wrinkles, wore the stains of the night's activities. Her empty portfolio rested against her legs. Reggie was nowhere in sight. She looked at Rosy with naked envy.

nineteen

Why had the name always seemed so comical to them? Over the front porch, repainted for the current season in bold black letters, and already blistering and peeling like the overzealous sunbathers with only two weeks' vacation, the sign, LOW TIDE INN, was an advertisement for the modest American middle-class needs one could expect to have gratified here: plain but ample food; healthy but noisy children; people of a like kind, without elegance or pretension, as predictable and as homely as the low tide itself, which daily exposed broken shells, clumps of seaweed, pails and other toys stolen from the children by the waves, as well as the deep valleys between the sandbars which made crosscurrents in the tide—the sole reminder that even here complacency was dangerous, for each summer they were the cause of at least one death by drowning.

The town, like the others along the coast, once the vacation spot of large comfortable families from Boston, had been taken over, with the disappearance of servants and the advent of birth control, by the hotelkeepers who alone could afford to staff the big houses. The lawns between the houses had been sold to developers who had stuck bungalows, higgledy-piggledy, between the hotels, and filled in what space remained (with the horror vacui indigenous to seaside places) with gas stations, hotdog stands, and shops which sold ceramic gnomes and ducks for decorating the pocket-sized lawns where grass had snobbishly refused to grow for the new owners.

The Bolds had come to know the Inn when postwar traffic through the seaside towns had forced them back on the old beach road on which it was situated. Although filled with potholes, it did not have the traffic lights of the highway (set for the convenience of the bathers rather than for the traffic bisecting their crossings) which came at a moment in their outing when, so close to the Thornton estate, they were impatient of any delay.

A hotel called High Tide Inn would have been more to their taste, as Benjamin had once remarked. Better still was not to vacation in such a place at all. Unlike the families that stayed at Low Tide, they did not look for homey comfort when they went on vacation, but the *dépaysement* of Europe, or the remoteness of the woods and ponds of Maine and the narrow end of the Cape. But before and after vacation, from May to October, they stretched the summer out at either end on the neighboring though vastly different Thornton beach.

"Mrs. Bold?" the man leaning against the porch door asked as Rosy came up the path. "This is your lucky day. Someone was just here begging for your room. Only one left in town. I said I'd give you another half hour, and if you weren't here by then he could have it. I'm Mannes, the manager."

"I missed the bus," Rosy said, by way of explaining her lateness.

"New York train late again?" Mr. Mannes opened the door and followed Rosy in.

"No. I was telephoning and didn't hear the bus being called."

"They don't call it." The manager turned the registry

pad around for Rosy to sign. "Got to keep sharp," he added, not unkindly, as though he knew keeping sharp was not easy. "You look bushed. Must have been a scorcher in town."

Rosy nodded. "It's been a long day."

"Guess you'd like to go to your room." He brought his hand down heavily on the bell and shouted, "Jumbo, Jumbo —desk," as if the bell were out of order.

A door swung open behind him and Jumbo, a genial giant, flushed from the kitchen heat, his sun-bleached hair standing up in a cowlick, appeared drying his hands on the large white apron which encircled his waist.

"Take the lady to Room Thirty-eight," the manager said. "Hope you'll be happy with us, Mrs. Bold. Never had any complaints yet," he added quickly, apparently not wanting to encourage contrary emotions. The manager of a seaside hotel, invariably blamed when the weather turns bad, learns to stand like a fencer, on guard, his foil ready at all times. "Not expecting supper, I hope," he said as if to parry a possible thrust. "They're just finishing cleaning up. Breakfast is from eight to nine-thirty—some folks like to sleep late on vacation; dinner from twelve thirty to one thirty. We have supper early, six o'clock, to get you to the movies on time. We've got two, so you can go every night. If you're real hungry you can get a burger and shake down the highway."

Rosy had expected supper. The line to the dining car on the New York–to–Boston train had been so long she had not been able to face it. Her hunger was killed by the thought of having to walk another step. "I'll just go to my room, if I may."

"Right, right." Jumbo sprang into action. "Where's the rest of your luggage?"

On the floor by Rosy's feet was the hatbox Margaret had lent her for the flight home. "That's all I have. I'm only staying a week."

"That's not much for a week," Jumbo said, and then, afraid he might have sounded critical, added quickly, "Ever been to Low Tide before?"

"First time," Rosy said, climbing the stairs behind him.

"You don't look familiar, and I've been here three summers now. I'm at the Ag. College. I'm gonna be a farmer."

They had had time for these and other fragments of Jumbo's autobiography because the route to Room 38 was long and devious. "You're in the annex," Jumbo explained, aware that Rosy found the trip long. They had started up a narrow stairway. "It's newer and you get a view."

He put the key in the lock. The door resisted. He applied his shoulder and fell into the room. An overpowering odor of fresh paint came out to greet Rosy. "Most of the rooms are bigger," Jumbo said apologetically, as if, had it been up to him, the proportions would have been more generous. "But they're doubles. We don't get many singles." His sand-colored head drooped like an unwatered sunflower. He was afraid he had been tactless again. "There's no shower in this room, but there's one next to the john, and another one outside, so you can get the sand off before coming in."

"I thought there was a view of the ocean." Rosy looked through the slats of the venetian blind.

"There's supposed to be." Jumbo pulled up the blind. "Gee, I don't see it." He looked bewildered, as if the view had somehow been misplaced. "Oh, yeah." His large, freckled face broke into a grin. "Here. Let me show you." He dropped to his knees and looked out the left-hand corner of the window. "There it is! Standing up you don't get it." He laughed like a child playing hide-and-seek. When Rosy didn't join him, he stood up, pawed the floor with his feet like a timid bull, and sidestepped out of the room.

Rosy sat down on the straight-backed chair, the only one in the room. With its narrow bed, bare pinewood floor, curtainless window, and undecorated walls, the room had clearly been arranged for occupants who would be in it only long enough to change from a wet bathing suit into something dry, or fall into a dead sleep after a day on the beach. No provision had been made for inclement weather or low-keyed moods.

The odor of paint forced her to her feet. She tried to open the window. When she had more energy she would kneel down to see the view, she promised herself. Tonight she would settle for a breath of salt air. The window, like the door, resisted. She made a fist and banged at the corners as she used to as a child on Long Island, to loosen a frame swollen by the sea air. The window was sealed not by the air but by paint. Dr. Birdbyle's interdictions came back to her: "No standing; no swimming—the season is almost over anyway; no lifting; no pulling"—the list had been endless. She gave up trying and looked around for some way to ring the desk. There was neither bell nor telephone. Jumbo and the manager were miles away.

She sat down on the edge of the bed. Her jaw locked in frustration and fatigue, she asked herself what she was doing in a convent cell of a room, in this absurd hotel, alone. Remembering, she gave out a choking cry and fell down on the bed. The weeks of unshed tears came spurting, bubbling, gushing from her eyes.

Her heart felt as if it had folded back on itself, its raw pink interior exposed like the flesh of a split fig. Her hands pulled at the bedspread. They made slow tears in it which sounded like adhesive tape being ripped off the fine hairs of the skin. She clutched her pillow to her, tightly, as if it had a waist, and pressed one corner of it into her mouth, to muffle the noise she made. Images of being cut off from the rest of the world—trapped in an elevator in an empty building, cornered in a mine cave-in, waking up in a sealed coffin—crowded her mind. She threw the pillow on the floor and gasped for air.

She had been so calm, telling Benjamin, she had begun

to think she had outgrown tears, the way a child outgrows a lisp. There had been the welcoming dinner to be got through. Iphigene, high and sentimental on martinis, toasted Benjamin's book, his wife's beauty, their future. "When I see you two together I wonder if there is a couple anywhere more to be envied."

Benjamin tried, good-humoredly and without success, to restrain her. "It's almost as bad as the old days when she tipped the orchestra leader to play Happy Birthday, and had a cake with lighted candles brought to my place," he whispered.

The instant Benjamin closed the door on their room Rosy had told him. She had outlined her plan. (How easy it is to undo a marriage where there are neither children nor money!) The whole thing hadn't taken five minutes.

"I see" was all Benjamin had said. And, "I'll do, of course, whatever you ask." His face was a mask, but she had felt his emotional temperature drop, as if, after months of illness, his fever had broken.

The next morning there had been Iphigene to tell. Even that went without a tear on either side. "I trust your judgment," sober Iphigene had said. "If you feel there is danger to Benjamin's stability. . . ."

Anything for Benjamin. The only hitch had come when Rosy had pressed on to say this would mean that Iphigene and she could not see each other, or correspond either. (Benjamin, never wholly pleased with their friendship, would feel bound by invisible threads of steel if they did; or worse, feel that he was being spied upon.) After an initial protest, Iphigene, feeling the strength of Rosy's resolve, acquiesced. Their embrace, in parting, had come close to making Rosy feel something. Then there had been the long trip, full of misadventures, to Room Number 38 at Low Tide Inn.

The sun burned aggressively through the uncovered window, heralding another day of the heat wave. Rosy looked cautiously through slits of eyes. Was she coming out of surgery? There was the bright light, and the feeling that if she moved she might start up some terrible pain, or exacerbate an open wound. The odor of paint, making its way slowly up her blocked nostrils, reminded her eyes of their tears.

There is a moment of euphoria when one comes out of an anesthetic, before the pain begins, when one thinks: Thank God, I'm alive! Rosy knew, for the first time, what it was to wish she were not. Was this how Benjamin felt when he said he wanted to die? With a feeling of panic, she realized that she couldn't remember what Benjamin looked like—his private face, the face she used to see in the morning before he put on his glasses. She could put it together except for the eyes. Where they should have been, she could see no farther than thick, blank lenses. Their color? Was it possible she couldn't remember? She was already at as great a distance from him as everyone else. Even the photograph which she had taken for the jacket of his book, with the haughty, truculent look having his picture taken always gave him, would not come into clear focus.

The room was a furnace. Sitting up to breathe, she saw that she had fallen asleep in her clothes. Like someone who awakens under the weight of a hangover (like Benjamin again), she wondered what else she'd done that she ought not to have done, and saw the torn bedspread. A door, slamming in her ear, made her jump up, guiltily. A voice close to her ear said,

"Just drink your juice and sit quietly until I come down. Do you hear? Debbie? Are you listening? And don't slam the—"

Debbie put the door between herself and her mother, and thudded down the hall. Debbie's father, in the shower, pounded his fists against his chest and gave the cry Tarzan gave as he went swinging through the trees.

Low Tide Inn, where privacy was a relative term, came

to life with a convulsion. The rooms hid the body more efficiently than the bathhouses, open top and bottom, that lined the beaches; but there were no secrets to the ear. The gargling, throat-clearing, flushing, snoring, quarreling, love-making of the neighbors, the slamming of doors and thumping of bare feet, told more than one cared to know about the other guests. Children shouted at each other, their mothers shouted at them not to shout, venetian blinds clanged up and down. It was best to be well and busy. Not to be, made excessive demands on the Inn's flimsy structure.

Had her noises of grief been overheard? Rosy wondered as she stood at the sink to bathe her eyes. The plumbing, too fragile for the briny water which gushed spasmodically through the pipes, was chronically as much on as it was off, which accounted for the rust stains in the basin. A stale, dank odor worked its way up, dyspeptically, through the pipes.

Rosy caught a glimpse of a mongoloid image in the mirror: puffy, almond-shaped eyes; swollen nose; mottled skin. Vanity alone should have cured her of tears long ago. It would take more than tepid water to camouflage the damage. Even makeup . . . Where was her makeup? She could find nothing—no compact, or lipstick, not even a comb. She had left her cosmetic case in the hotel room in New York. In the state her eyes were in, anything, no matter how trivial, could start the flow of tears again. She began to cry out of simple vexation. Then, remembering what she had to cry about, she fell back on the bed again, overcome with grief.

Some time later, when her tears had stopped, she lay arguing with herself about getting up. There was no place she wanted to go, no one she wanted to see, nothing she looked forward to. In Paris, she had read a newspaper article about a French Jew who, during the war, having missed the freighter which would have taken him to freedom, hid out in an attic room of a Marseille hotel and was fed leftovers by a kindly servant until the Liberation. Couldn't she stay in this room until her period of mourning was over? Jumbo, although kind enough to feed her, would tell Mr. Mannes. Mannes would call a psychiatrist. It was the odor of paint which finally forced her out of the room.

On the way down the back stairs, she thought that if only she could find a side door and slip out to the drugstore to buy some makeup before anyone saw her, she might feel another bubble of pleasure, like the one she had felt in the London air terminal. There *was* a door. She pushed it open and hit a solid mass. Mr. Mannes. He was coiling the hose with which he had watered the lawn.

"Hey! Oh, it's you, Mrs. Bold. How come you didn't use the front stairs?" Mr. Mannes's sharp New England eyes looked into Rosy's puffy ones. "You missed breakfast."

"I wasn't hungry. I was just going to the drugstore."

"Can't get breakfast there."

"I was going to get something. . . ."

"Oh. I see," said the embarrassed manager, misunderstanding. "To get to Oglethorpe's, go out the front, turn right, and walk two blocks. Too bad not to have had breakfast. Something warm inside . . ."

Nothing for it. She would have to walk past the guests, sitting on the front porch while they digested breakfast, eager for a new arrival to concentrate on. "Will you have someone open my window? I couldn't budge it," Rosy said as she started for the reviewing stand.

"You slept with the window closed? Too bad you didn't get the benefit of the sea air. That's what most folks come for. You should have come down and asked me. Room hasn't been used all season. We don't get many . . ."

The only single at the Inn walked past the line of occupied rockers, her face buried in a handkerchief as if she were about to sneeze.

twenty

Summer is a season for the young, the healthy, the happy, Rosy thought. As the August sun beat down malevolently on the Inn's small beach, narrowed by the crowds that had fled the city's heat and had overflowed the public beaches on its either side, Rosy saw that a dark, anonymous, air-conditioned hotel room, which gave on a courtyard never visited by the sun, would have better suited her need. Mr. Mannes, Jumbo, the women in the rockers, Debbie and her parents could not help but be interested in her because of her freakishness: she didn't swim, she ate little, she was polite but distant, and most curious of all, she was a single.

It was not that she cared what they thought (as she had done at the pensione in Rome, when she had still had something to lose), but their thinking about her at all made her feel as if she were going about in their midst without a skin, her nerve ends exposed and morbidly sensitive to their strident voices, their intrusive friendliness.

The Inn had no public rooms, except for the porch—which left her her cell, the beach, and the movies.

One evening, hurrying out of the brightly lighted dining room to the protective darkness of the movie house, she arrived so early that the doors were not yet open. She found herself surrounded by a group of young people, high school boys and girls, who had obviously grown up together through the summers. They were at that stage before dating when their crushes changed as frequently as the movie. Bursting with health from the enriched American foods which nourished their shining hair and strong white teeth, and dressed identically in shirts and Bermuda shorts which gave off a fragrance of Ivory soap and sun-dried laundry, they were an unconscious insult to the older and less healthy.

At their ages she too had belonged to such a group at a not dissimilar seaside resort. The misty warm night air had made her hair curl in springy ringlets, just as theirs did. She had felt, in those days, that she was approaching, after the dreary apprenticeship of childhood, the stage when life was beginning. And now it was over. Or, at least, an important part of it was.

A warning gong, deep, chilling and as troubling as had been the sight of her first gray hairs to Emma Bovary, gave Rosy a premonition of what it would be like to grow old. With it came a newly formed, but already unshakable, awareness of the shortness of life. As the years went by would she become envious of the young, like a spinster who had missed her chance?

Doris had already shown her how little sympathy she could expect for her new and unattractive role. When she had called her from the Boston bus terminal to tell her her news (in the hope that Doris would spread the word around Cambridge before she got back, to spare her the pain), Doris had greeted her with her own exciting concerns:

"It worked, Ro! I could *hug* you. Your advice. You've forgotten? About not writing Richard. That did it! It tipped his hand." The wedding would take place Labor Day weekend. Doris was already planning little dinner parties for the fall season. It was an awkward time to tell of the undoing of a marriage.

"I don't believe it," Doris said, and repeated, "I *don't*

believe it. Ro? Wouldn't it be better not to say anything? Maybe that time in the hospital made you lose your perspective. Why not think it over a little longer? At least while you're at the beach."

That there was nothing further to think over, that she had already told Benjamin, that he was now at the apartment packing, made Doris wail, "Oh, Ro! Just now when Benjamin is going to be so *famous*. And I was planning such cozy dinner parties." A thought occurred to her. "Sweetie, is there someone else? You're sure? Couples who break up always deny it at first. The funny thing is that I had lunch with Jane Talmadge—that cat!—yesterday. She tried to tell me that you'd gone off to a remote island off the coast of Italy with an Italian writer. Killing, isn't it? She must have been reading movie magazines under the dryer. Can you *see* Tullio Fancelli on Ponza?"

Rosy could, clearly: dressed all in white, with a blonde on his arm.

"I quashed that. I said *I* had been your roommate." Doris stopped laughing abruptly. "Ro? Does Benjamin have someone else? Then I know you're crazy. Besides, you can't. You're a *Catholic*." Doris gave the word the weight of Unitarian severity. Nor did she want to be reminded that Catholics could separate, but not remarry. "Wait a minute. You're not going to tell me you'll *never* remarry."

Rosy had been as little prepared for this discussion as a widow at the funeral lunch is prepared to listen to hints that she must (not right away of course, but one day) get over the husband she has just lowered into the ground, and look for another one. "I can only hope I won't be tempted" was all she said to Doris.

"God knows you're not likely to be in Cambridge. With so few extra men." (The dinner-party problem again.) "And most of them latent. There's Hector, of course. He's not very exciting, but he is an escort." The seating, at least, looked as if it might be worked out.

The movies turned out to be no more satisfactory a pastime than being close to the ocean without being able to swim. Something trivial, subliminal, in each of them reminded Rosy painfully of the past. She often left before the end, to avoid being seen with swollen eyes. This particular evening it was an eroticism (which only she heard, saw, and was deviled by, as a paranoid is tormented by insinuating voices only he hears) which drove her out on the street earlier than usual.

What kind of life would be possible for her? she asked herself as she walked like a derelict along the deserted beach. She would become a nun. As with all convent-bred girls that had been her ambition as a child, but by the time she was the age of the boys and girls outside the theater, she had left the idea behind with her dolls. Occasionally, even when she was older, inflamed by a novel in which the heroine, usually unrequited in love, took the veil, she had entertained the idea anew. Uncle Jim had been quick to remind her that the convent was not a romantic trash can. The first question a priest would ask her now was why she thought she had a vocation. If she admitted that she had none, he would undoubtedly reply that cowardice was not sufficient motivation. No convent would have her.

What *was* there for her, then? Bitterness and rage temporarily checked her tears. Why had she taken all the blame for the failure of her marriage? What about the others? Iphigene. Gone was the charitable view Rosy had expressed to Phoebe. Surely it was Iphigene's adoration that had wrecked Benjamin for any other woman. Hadn't her possessiveness (the price he'd had to pay for this adoration) made even the loosest tie with another woman insupportable?

And Benjamin's psychiatrist. With greater skill couldn't he have held on to Benjamin, brought him closer to a cure?

The thought of Benjamin made her anger and resentment suffocating. She threw her arms up over her head to get air, like a lunatic choking on imaginary poison. She had lived a marriage based on hollow promises, so that after twelve years she was as emotionally bankrupt as a woman who has squandered those years in a hopeless love affair with a man she knows will never marry her. A woman whose house has burned to the ground refuses, in fresh despair, to comb the ruin for what she can retrieve—books, charred but still readable; photographs; love letters, safe in a metal box; perhaps even enough pieces of furniture to make a new beginning. Rosy had no interest in remembering what she owed Benjamin. She had to have it as she felt it, blackened and burned beyond recognition.

The day the horseflies drove all the sunbathers from the beach into the water, where they remained submerged to the lips like large, overheated dogs, Rosy walked to the souvenir shop. It was air-conditioned. With excessive care she examined the earrings and bracelets made of seashells, the pine soap, bathing caps, suntan oils, paperback mysteries, hard-cover children's books, balls and jacks, Parcheesi sets, playing cards, bayberry candles, water wings, beach balls, cork ashtrays, dolls that drank and wet, combs and bobby pins and hair clips, writing paper and envelopes. She examined them again. When the owner began to look at her as if she might be a shoplifter biding her time, she bought a small hopsacking pillow filled with pine needles with the legend SMELL ME AND REMEMBER SEASIDE HAPPINESS, and left.

The heat mounted a fresh assault as she closed the door behind her. The wind sock on a nearby pole was flat and stuck to itself like last year's bathing cap. Tar bubbled and burst on the highway, filling the air with its odor. There was little traffic. The sidewalks were empty. Wandering along a blistering back street, she came to a frame church covered with gray shingles. The sign read, OUR LADY, STAR OF THE SEA, R.C.

To escape the lunatic sun, she went inside. It was dark

and, almost, cool. The wiggling lines of children waiting to go to confession (they seemed not to feel the heat) told her it must be Saturday. The girls whispered among themselves discreetly. The boys nudged, pinched, and pushed one another. What confessional problems could they have at that age?

Father F. X. O'Brien, who looked fresh from the seminary and more like a lifeguard than a priest, came out of the sacristy. He threw a few light cuffs at the troublemakers, and entered the box with his name above it.

There was no name over the other box. The priest, who had already been hearing confessions, came out of the box for a breath of air. He paced up and down reading his breviary, fanning himself with a holy picture. An elderly, white-haired man, he might have been visiting his maiden sisters in town and have offered a hand with the Saturday-afternoon work of the parish. Rosy had been taught to believe that a priest was merely a vessel through which Grace flowed, and that one confessor was as good as another (only converts and intellectuals had spiritual advisers). Nevertheless, it occurred to her that the visitor, being older and more experienced, might be a better choice—unless, of course, he was deaf—than F. X. O'Brien.

The visiting priest followed her into the confessional, turned out the light and turned his profile toward her.

"Yes, my child?" he prompted, when she remained silent.

She had not been to confession for so long she couldn't think where to begin. At University College Hospital a priest had come to visit her. He had been at Oxford, and was a convert. He joked about how little work there was for a Roman priest in an English hospital. At the moment she was the only patient who was an R.C. She had talked with him about the new encyclical, searching for a tactful way to tell him that she did not want to go to confession: she hadn't felt ready. "I don't know where to begin," she said to the white head on the other side of the screen.

"How long has it been since your last confession?"

"Six months."

"Remember that it doesn't matter where you begin. Just tell me in your own words, as simply and as honestly as you can. As a child would."

She told him about Theo, as simply as she could.

"What about your marriage?" he asked when she paused. He put his ear closer to the screen, trying to sift the liquid from the solid. "There, there. Try to speak calmly, so I can hear what you're saying."

She wondered if she was making sense. Did he understand her?

When she finished, the priest made a gothic structure with his fingers. (She could see him clearly; he could not see her.) He studied them for some time, thinking. Of the many things he could have said, he said only, "Poor Benjamin! Do you pray for him?"

The priest's words burned through the caul of self-pity she had been enveloped in since the beginning of her stay at Low Tide Inn, as the sun burns the early-morning haze off the shore. "I haven't been able to pray," she said.

"Pity Benjamin, not yourself," he said. "Pray for him, and I will pray for you. Go to the sacraments frequently. They will give you the grace you stand in need of. And now for your penance read the Twenty-first Psalm. You know where to find it in your missal? It's a beautiful prayer. Benjamin might even call it a great poem. Meditate on each word. And now, say a fervent act of contrition."

They prayed: he in Latin, absolving her; she in English, asking to be absolved.

"God bless you, my child," he said before he drew the shutter over the screen.

Instead of going to the beach after mass on Sunday, Rosy wrote letters: one to Uncle Jim, telling him the necessary minimum; the others to those she couldn't count on Doris and the grapevine to reach. She telephoned Erika (who hadn't been back from Europe when she'd tried to call her from the bus terminal). Erika would be happy to come pick her up, to drive her back to Cambridge.

Jumbo paused at her table that night at supper. After he'd cleared her place he said, "Can I tell you something, Mrs. Bold? You look lots better than when you arrived. I can always tell a sick horse or a sick cow, and the first night I saw you . . . I don't mean to make any comparison . . ." Jumbo's perceptiveness, unmatched by savoir faire, kept him dancing a two-step, putting a foot in, taking it out again. "Animals are my specialty, but when there aren't any of them around I can't help noticing people. The other folks here thought you had hay fever—on account of your eyes being so swollen and all—but I was sure it was your back. The way you walked. A disk. Right?"

"Right." Rosy smiled at Jumbo's freckles and cowlick.

"A guy in my dorm had one. He had to wear a brace for months too. That's how I guessed . . . I mean . . ." Jumbo did his two-step again.

"I'm having a guest for lunch tomorrow," Rosy said, to put him out of his agony. "Should I tell Mr. Mannes?"

"I'll take care of it," said Jumbo, glad of the busywork. "You're leaving tomorrow evening?"

"Right after lunch."

"Too bad you can't stay another week."

Rosy didn't think so. Low Tide Inn had served its purpose. It was one place she would leave without regret.

It wasn't until she and Erika were in the car, on the way home, that Rosy said, "I gather you haven't seen Doris since you got back, or you would have heard my news."

"No, but I heard hers. So Richard at last gets a divorce. And what about that wife who wouldn't let him go?"

"She came around quickly enough when Richard made up his mind."

"And Doris is in a big excitement?"

"You can imagine. A round of parties, and then a big wedding."

"And what are your news? Another prize for Benjamin?"

"Benjamin and I are separating."

"What? What's this?"

"In the hospital I saw that Benjamin had left me no other choice but to leave him."

"Ah no, Rozan. This is a tragedy. I think you make a big mistake. You are too impulsive."

"I had weeks to think it over."

"You were already thinking about it in Ponza?"

"That was the reason I went. I left Benjamin a letter. I asked him to think about our future, to decide what he wanted."

"And he said he wanted to leave?"

"Nothing so simple. He acted, at first, as if he hadn't read it. Later, as if he hadn't understood it."

"Maybe he hadn't. Why must you be so American, so . . . so . . ."

"Decisive?"

"With someone like Benjamin it's a mistake to be definite, to close doors. You must wait, check your decision."

"I checked it, over and over again. And I knew I was right by his reaction when I told him."

"Which was?"

"Relief. Gratitude."

"So it's done. You didn't wait to see how things would work out this fall."

"If I'd waited I would have been drawn into the Cambridge life again and wouldn't have had the courage."

242

"Ach! Courage. It's not courage you need but wisdom."

They drove in silence for some time. Erika shook her head.

Would no one approve? Hector perhaps. Paul would be baffled. He had seen Benjamin only at his most uxorious. The Happy Extroverts would lose a celebrity. (Even before he was one Benjamin had played the part with authority.) Those with shaky marriages would feel threatened. The women unsure of their husbands would feel apprehensive about having an unattached woman around. How long would it take to reassure them?

"In Vienna couples who couldn't remarry didn't separate," Erika said. "To the European mentality *ce n'est pas commode*, especially for the woman. You have to live with a man, so why not with your husband? You have your room, your work, your flirts. He has his."

"That life is based on shared property. It's not practical here. There's not room enough for such a luxury—in a one-bedroom apartment?"

"Of course, Benjamin would have to be more sensible. He would have to get a job, earn more money, so that you could have a bigger place."

"But you see, he doesn't want something *commode*. He wants to be free."

"What for?"

"Who knows? For itself, I suppose. There are people who can live together without intimacy"—Rosy was still thinking of what Erika had suggested as a solution—"barely speaking to each other. Ours was never that kind of marriage, even at its most difficult."

"That means it was a good marriage."

"While it was good."

"All right. Suppose he does want freedom. Let him wait for it a little. Until it's more convenient for you. You look around, find another man . . ."

"I found one."

"You? I can hardly believe it." Erika sounded not only surprised but as close as she could come to being shocked. She was silent, trying to think who it could have been, when it could have happened. "And what happened?"

"Nothing. He was a diversion, an infinitely appealing and seriously tempting diversion. I was so desperately trying not to see what was right before my eyes that I tried to complicate things. I wanted to fall in love with him. It would have been so easy! But I couldn't."

"You make me very, very sad. You're still in love with Benjamin. What kind of life do you think you can make for yourself?"

"I don't know. I don't see it at all."

"First, of course, you must get well. I'll find out immediately whom you should see at Mass. General. I'm not convinced of this no swimming and wearing a brace. That English doctor sounds very old-fashioned. And what about money?"

"I have my job."

"What will you do with your energy? Your job won't be enough. You'll have to find something to fill your life."

"In the beginning I'll have to learn who I am, what I am." Rosy said, Theo's words ringing in her ears. "And then . . . Last night I dreamed I was in a large lecture hall."

"A student again? How depressing!"

"Paul, Meyer Shapiro, and André Chastel were on the platform."

Erika laughed. "Zo, if you're to study art history you'll have the best, even if it means stealing from Columbia and the Sorbonne. And what about Theo Addis? He wasn't there?"

Rosy was silent a moment. "He was there too." She remembered how vivid he'd been in the dream.

"Graduate school. Maybe that's not a bad idea," Erika said hurriedly, as if she were afraid her question had been indiscreet. "You must talk to Paul about it."

On Prescott Street, outside Rosy's apartment building, Erika stopped the car. Rosy looked over at her ground-floor windows. They looked blank, as Benjamin's eyeglasses sometimes did, as if there were no life behind them.

"You must move," said Erika. "To get away from memories."

"I haven't the energy. Not now, at least."

Erika took Rosy's hand. "Rozan, Rozan, what can I say to comfort you? This year will be an agony. There is no way out of that. We are here—you know how fond we both are of you—to give you what sympathy you can bear. Sometime, near the end of the year, when you've made a new beginning, Benjamin will come to ask you to go back to him. You don't know that? For sure he will. That will be the most difficult moment of all. Then you must decide what *you* want."

Rosy started to get out of the car. Erika put her hand on her arm, "Why wouldn't you come home with me now, stay for dinner tonight? I will improvise something."

Rosy shook her head. "I'm not looking forward to going in, but to delay won't make it easier."

twenty-one

Turning the key in the lock, Rosy put her shoulder to the door, to give it the nudge she knew it needed to open. From the table a sheet of paper, fanned by the draft, leapt up like a white flame. With unthinking joy she ran to pick up the note—as if nothing had happened, as if it might say that Benjamin had gone out to buy a package of cigarettes, or to check a reference in Widener. She put it down, unread. What did it matter what it said? Had he had anything to say which could have changed her mind, he would have said it when she got back from Ponza, or at the latest, the night in the New York hotel.

She walked into the bedroom and dropped her jacket on the bed. She ran her finger over the dust on Benjamin's dresser. Laundry cardboards stuck out of the empty drawers. She closed the door of his closet on a moth-eaten sweater that hung half off a wire hanger.

The living room was smaller than she had remembered. It was badly in need of paint. How little the room reflected her taste! She must move one day. Even before that, she must set about making the apartment look like hers. "Bricks and boards, and bits and pieces of other people's furniture," as Doris had said. Her easy chair had been willed them by a neighbor going to teach at Berkeley. There was Benjamin's desk, bought at the Morgan Memorial, and the folding gate-leg dining table and chairs Iphigene had given them. A grass rug, which served in all seasons, was scarred with cigarette burns around Benjamin's chair. On the table next to his chair were a half-empty coffee cup (still warm?), a stack of unopened bills, and a metal ashtray full to overflowing. The room smelled of stale summer heat, cigarette butts, and mildew from the books in Benjamin's library. She ran her hand along the books, regretting those she hadn't read. Sometime they would go too. There were two copies of *War and Peace*—Benjamin's, full of annotations, and her old Modern Library edition. They kept ten dollars between pages 500 and 501 of her edition for household emergencies. The bill was where it should be. Had Benjamin just replaced it? She put the book down on the coffee table. When she was able to read again, she would begin with it. An enormous panoramic work would remind her of the vastness of life, and how little, in the scheme of things, what she was experiencing mattered.

The telephone rang shrilly. Rosy walked to the entrance-hall table. She paused before picking up the phone. Someone was probably calling about a party for Doris and Richard. She wished she didn't have to go. She must remember to say 'I'' and not "we" when she accepted. She lifted the receiver, nervous about her new role.

"Where have you been? I've been calling you for hours."

Benjamin sounded as if he were within touching distance.

"How could you have stayed away a week without letting me know where you were?"

"What did it matter?"

"Suppose there had been an emergency? Suppose I had wanted to reach you?"

"Why would you have?"

"For any number of reasons. Theo, for one. He called

from Canada. It was awkward not being able to say where you were."

Silence.

"Did you find my note?"

"Yes."

"Have you read it?"

"No."

"Well, hurry and read it. I'll write a real letter soon. I just called to tell you where you can reach me. I'm at the Chelsea."

"I'll forward the mail."

"I closed the account at the Cambridge Bank and Trust." Benjamin laughed. "I could have sworn I heard them sigh with relief to see the last of me. I'll send you a check for half. Damn little, but it should tide you over until your first paycheck. Roxana? Are you listening?"

"Yes."

"Don't go so long without letting me hear from you again. And ring me if there's anything special. Hear? 'Bye darling."

Rosy's legs were trembling as they had been that first day she tried to walk at the hospital. She went to her chair and sat down. Had Benjamin not taken in what she'd said? What *had* he understood? She picked up his note.

Darling,

The night you told me you were leaving me—it seems a hundred years ago—I left the hotel feeling as if the top of my head had been blown off. I walked and walked, and then sat up the rest of the night in Childs 42nd Street. I decided that you (as always) were right. For the moment I do need to be free. For a reason that is not completely clear to me, I want to be alone when my book comes out. Then . . . we'll see.

In Childs I outlined what I'll do. I'll probably go to a hotel (Uh-uh. I have no intention of staying with

248

Iphigene) until I can find a room. I plan to pound on my publisher's door for an advance on any one of a number of irresistible, to them, projects.

What is this nonsense about not seeing Iphigene? You cannot, must not, keep to it. It would wound her deeply.

There's my taxi. I fly.

I count on you to take care of yourself. And *write me.*

With grateful and most love,
B.

P.S. I put $10 in its place in *W&P*.

Rosy threw the note down angrily. Benjamin had taken in, of what she had said, only what suited him. Fear crept into the place where anger had been. Somewhere in the note there was a threat buried. She picked it up and reread it. When she came to "Then . . . we'll see," she knew that she had oversimplified Benjamin again. She had not thought (as had Erika) that he would continue to play his bright light over her life, the way the lights of a speeding car are cast at unpredictable intervals on the façade of an ill-placed house. His car would careen around the curves, tires screaming, brakes screeching, horn honking, floodlights flashing through her window. There might well be a crash, an accident. She would be called (hers was the closest house) for help. The dead-of-night terrors were far from over.

The room was almost dark when the phone rang again. Rosy stood up. She walked to the window, opened it, and leaned out. A sprinkler lapped at the lawn. The grass had been cut that day. Its odor filled the air. Close by, someone was pounding a typewriter. In the apartment across the court, a family of mathematicians were playing the Mozart trio they'd been working on before she left for Europe. She listened to the beginning of the allegretto. It no longer gave them difficulty. They played it now with ease. By the time they'd reached the end of the movement, the telephone had stopped ringing.

Soon the new academic year would begin. She would live through it, and the next one, and the one that followed the way women who live on the edge of a battlefield live through a war—women whose husbands are away fighting, or have been killed, are prisoners, or are merely missing. She would get up in the morning, straighten her house, go to work, eat her meals, go to bed—grateful for a day without an alarm or test of endurance, grateful for a day that was merely dull and gray and empty. Then one morning she would notice that it was the beginning of a pretty day. The sky would be clear. The rumbling would have stopped. The war would have come to an end.

ABOUT THE AUTHOR

Eileen Simpson was born and educated in New York. During her eleven-year marriage to John Berryman, she made a study of creative energy in poets, a study that became her thesis for a graduate degree in psychology at New York University. After her divorce, she established a private practice in psychotherapy in Princeton, New Jersey. She remarried in 1960 and moved her offices to New York City.

Although Mrs. Simpson has written many articles for professional journals, it wasn't until she lived in Paris, where her husband's work took her in 1962, that she began to write fiction. She returned to New York in 1966 and has since divided her time between the practice of her profession and writing. Her short stories have appeared in *Transatlantic Review, The Southern Review,* and *Denver Quarterly,* and her articles have been published in *The New York Times Book Review, Saturday Review,* and *Vogue* and *Glamour* magazines. Mrs. Simpson at present is working on a new book.